CYBERFUNK!

EDITED BY
MILTON J. DAVIS

MVmedia, LLC
Fayetteville, GA

MVmedia, LLC
PO Box 143052
Fayetteville, GA 30214
www.mvmediaatl.ocm

Publisher's Note: This is a work of fiction. Names, characters, places, and incidents are a product of the author's imagination. Locales and public names are sometimes used for atmospheric purposes. Any resemblance to actual people, living or dead, or to businesses, companies, events, institutions, or locales is completely coincidental.

Book Layout ©2017 BookDesignTemplates.com
Cover Design by URAEUS

Ordering Information:
Quantity sales. Special discounts are available on quantity purchases by corporations, associations, and others. For details, contact the "Special Sales Department" at the address above.

Cyberfunk! / Various Authors. -- 1st ed.
ISBN 978-1-7346279-8-5

Contents

To the Cyberfunkateers

A SUNKEN MEMORY
BY
DONOVAN HALL

CJ-1844 sat in the pilot's chair of his deep-sea probe, his neural network link extending from the palm of his hand into the input dock of the submersible's control console. The ship fed him information on the waters around him as he kept it on track speeding through the abyss. CJ's mission was simple: find the last mind bank hidden in the ruins of old Baltimore and collect any souls still sleeping within. It was something CJ had done dozens of times before, though he took little pleasure in it. Ruins were dangerous places, and worse still, the ride to get to them was incredibly dull.

Over the submersible's speaker system, CJ played music to pass the time, old tracks from when he was still human. CJ liked the old songs. They helped maintain the memories in his neural cortex, triggering nodes of data that hadn't been inspected in a long time. The song playing now was titled "September." Though CJ had no lungs, his vocal synthesizers could still crank up to an impressive volume, and on long voyages like this, with nothing to do but enjoy some music, he took full advantage of the range of his cybernetic voice.

"Our hearts were ringing…In the key that our souls were singing…As we danced in the night…Remember how the stars stole the night away!" CJ bounced in his seat as the disco beats of millennia past built up to the chorus, and at the climax, he held up a chromatic hand, tossed his head back, and shouted his favorite verse. "Ah! Ah! Ah! Ba de ya! Say do you remember? Ba de ya! Dancing in September! Ba de ya! Never was a cloudy day…!"

CJ remembered how strange it had been when he was first downloaded from the mind bank that held his consciousness for five hundred years. Those who found him said he'd been stored in a facility in the ruins of Houston. At the time, he did not know who he was, where he was, or where he'd come from, a common side-effect of having one's memories suddenly compiled in a new, unfamiliar platform. Cyber Displacement was often described as moving into a giant house where the inside of every room was something familiar, but you had no idea as to the layout of the house itself, and some of the rooms had caved in during the move. Things came back to different people in different orders, and some things, due to file corruption, never came back at all. For CJ, when he awoke, all he knew was that he wanted to listen to some music. And despite the many mind transfers he had experienced since then, that desire never left him, though many other memories had. Data corruption was always a risk with digitized memory—the catch to being immortal.

The amount of people who had uploaded their consciousness before the start of the Ascension War was paltry compared to the total population. Less than 1%. And once the war started, any banks in the major cities—DC, New York, Tokyo, Shanghai, London—were all bombed into radioactive glass. Those that survived the war were still threatened by the horrific nuclear storms and earthquakes that ravaged the planet in the centuries that followed. Only 1% of 1% remained to be downloaded in aftermath. Those few souls turned out to be the very last vestiges of humanity…if they could even call themselves human. Centuries of irradiation meant many minds could only be partially restored. Everyone seemed to have a missing piece or two, and by now some were missing a lot more than others.

CJ had undergone many missions to find lost mind banks, but it had taken a toll. The world was a savage place beyond the titanium domes of Maroon-0, and more often than not, there had been many a time he'd returned to base with a body so thoroughly broken, he'd needed his mind transferred to a new chassis. And each time his memories became a little less stable. A little more corrupted. Thinking of his human life now only gave him headaches and flickering glimpses—the taste of greens, a wrinkled brown face, a cherrywood guitar. But knowing how they fit together, that was impossible, and it was only getting worse. Others wondered why he strained himself so, risking so much to find so little, but in a world where no one new was ever born, searching for minds from mind banks was the closest thing to bringing life into the world.

CJ wondered if he had children once upon a time. He thought he could remember them vaguely, round and laughing like little chestnuts, but now he wasn't sure. Their faces weren't there. It was a faded memory. Corrupted data. Did he have a wife? A husband? He shook his head. Corrupted data. A faded memory.

The administration had warned him to stop before it was too late, that it had been over two hundred years since the last mind bank discovery, and he was risking his sanity for nothing. They said there were no souls left to be found, and to destroy his mind in vain exploration would be a waste. CJ didn't believe that though. He couldn't. They couldn't be all that was left.

The cyborg suddenly stiffened in his seat as a warning signal was transmitted from the submarine pod's AI into his neural network. His artificial brain interpreted the signal to make it sound like ringing sirens going off in his head, startling him with an unwelcomed shock.

"Emergency!" The pod's AI said calmly. *"Severe tectonic activity detected."*

"Details!" CJ ordered, turning off the music with a thought.

"A magnitude 9 earthquake has been detected three clicks from our current location. The shockwave will hit us in

approximately one minute. I suggest following emergency protocols and bracing for impact."

An earthquake? Now? Impossible! The analysts had given CJ the most up-to-date geological forecasts before setting out on his mission. Something like this should have been predicted. If CJ still had teeth, he'd suck them in frustration. Not even a fully optimized neural matrix and AI assistance could overcome human error. No point in worrying about that now. CJ had to think of the present. He was exposed, in the open with no shelter to break the oncoming wall of water. All he could do was follow emergency protocol, cut his link from the console, strap in tight, grab the railings on either side of him, and brace for impact.

Disconnected from the console, the AI's voice sounded over the speakers instead of echoing in his head. *"Impact coming in five…four…three…two…one."*

The shockwave hit the small craft like a storm gale, throwing CJ against the glass viewport. If he still had bones, his jaw would have shattered on impact. Before he could grab ahold of the handles again, CJ was flung back hard into his seat. Then he was thrown again, this time to the left, his head denting one of the bars he was trying to hold to steady himself. The submersible spin and CJ held on for dear life. He felt no pain, his tactile sensors maxed out before reaching that point, but it still wasn't pleasant. There was a tension, a panic that made the cyborg desperately cling to the support bars. If his arm or his head were to smash something vital in the sub, shatter the viewport, crush the console jack, or dent the computer mainframe, that would be the end of it. Not even his hyper durable body would survive sinking to the crushing fathoms of the abyss. And even if he did, he'd burn through his battery charge before reaching home trying to walk the ocean floor.

He would die.

The lights in the sub flickered out suddenly, casting him in blackness. Whether as a means to save energy or as a result of structural damage, CJ couldn't tell, not while disconnected from the neural link. So, as it was, CJ spun in the darkness of the abyss, hearing the roaring waters eddying around him.

CJ did not notice at first when the sub finally stopped turning. He'd almost gotten used to the feeling of endless spinning. But eventually everything did stop. The rolling, the creaking of the sub's hull; it faded until it just ceased altogether. But whether the sub was floating or resting on the ocean floor, he couldn't tell. All he saw was black, and all he heard was silence.

"Pod!" CJ called out. "Pod, wake up!"

There was no answer.

Fumbling in the dark, CJ reached out to the control console, feeling for the port to plug in his neural link. He found the small, peg-shaped hole and placed his palm over it, docked, and reached out into digital space to sense the AI's presence.

What he saw in his mind space was more darkness, a field of empty black.

With a forceful thought, CJ willed the sub to activate, pushing his intention firmly upon the machine. There was a flash of dim light, a candle flicker in the black void, and then, one by one, more lights started to flare as the basic diagnostic systems were starting to reboot, and a bit of tension eased from the cyborg's shoulders. Or at least it did for a moment. Then a yellow image of the ship's battery gauge appeared, showing a lower than optimal measurement of remaining power. 30%. Under normal circumstances, it would have been enough to get home, but who knew if it would be enough now.

Once CJ finished taking note of the battery, the gauge faded away and quickly replaced itself with a 3D projection of the ship displaying highlighted areas of structural compromise. A propeller was loose, but beyond that, no serious damage had been sustained, as indicated by the majority of the ship having a healthy green outline. CJ thanked his lucky stars and dismissed the projection from view.

"AI system reboot initiated!" chimed the AI's melodic voice, echoing in the digitized mind space. A glowing wheel suddenly took the foremost spot in CJ's mental vision. It turned yellow, then slowly turned neon blue, and then bright green. *"Hello, CJ -1844! This is Submersible Exploration Pod-136 at your service!"*

"Welcome back," CJ said. He pulled his senses out of the realm of cyberspace and back into his physical surroundings, which remained almost as dark as he'd left them, save for a few safety lights now adding an ambient red glow to the pod's interior. "Can you turn the headlights on?"

Immediately, the headlights of the sub flashed bright, revealing to CJ that he was indeed on the bottom of the ocean. However, judging by what he saw, this place had not always been submerged. There were buildings here, or at least the remains of them. Lumpy and misshapen as they were from the weathering passage of watery eons, they were still unmistakably buildings. Among the buildings directly in front of them were two thick fleshy stalks, each the size of a young tree. A pair of anchor worms, CJ thought, creatures who waved lazily in the water, catching small fish that wondered too close. He'd seen them before, though they were usually found in groups, not pairs.

"Where are we…?" CJ thought aloud, leaning forward on the control console, staring in awe at the ruins before him. The style of architecture did not match those of Baltimore's ruins. He would know, he'd been there twice before. In fact, these didn't match any of the old sunken cities CJ had visited. Most of the buildings were too squat, too old fashioned for the standard designs of the late 23rd century.

"We are 6.3156 degrees north by 10.8074 degrees west."

"Yes, but where exactly is that?"

The AI provided a holographic map, making it appear in the forefront of CJ's mind. The oceans were blue, and the landmasses were green lined with brown mountains and deserts, and his exact location was represented by a flashing red dot. They were on the edge of the mid Atlantic, only a few kilometers off the coast of West Africa.

"This must have been above water hundreds of years ago," CJ thought aloud. "What was this city called?"

"It was called Monrovia, capital of a small nation called Liberia."

The names were vaguely familiar to CJ, like he'd heard them before, but he did not have any specifics he could recall off hand. The problem with digitized memory was that, at best, it was only as clear as it had been at the time upload, and the vaguer the memory, the more susceptible it was to corruption. CJ did know, however, that all the major cities of the former West African coast like Lagos, Accra, and Dakar had all been thoroughly explored centuries ago. Scanning the unusual buildings, he wondered if anyone had conducted expeditions here before.

"Negative." The AI said, sensing his thoughts. *"The administration has deemed this area an unlikely prospect for mind banks since it was relatively undeveloped prior to the war, thus no one has undertaken the effort to explore it."*

Great, CJ thought sarcastically, slumping back in his seat. He'd landed in the boondocks. If he were going to be thrown to the other side of the Atlantic, the least he could ask for was to be thrown someplace interesting. Now all he had to look forward to was a long trip back home with nothing to show for it. Of course, that was assuming he could even get home. Maroon-0 was nestled in the heart of the Gulf of Mexico, over 5,000 miles away. This sub was not meant for such a range. Without another convenient shock wave, returning was going to be tricky to say the least.

CJ tapped his chrome fingers thoughtfully on the console, looking at the battery display in his mental space. It read 29%. "Pod, how can we get back to Maroon-0 with our current battery charge?"

"If we go at half speed, we will be able to reduce our energy output to such an extent that we should be able to get back to base. Though we will be delayed by a week."

"Hmph. A week? At least it'll give me time to think of what I'll report to the administration." CJ nodded, accepting that it was what it was. "Chart the course for home and let's be on our way."

"Excuse me, CJ, I would be remised if I did not inform you that I am suddenly detecting a signal. It's weak, but it is there."

CJ raised a holographic eyebrow with mounting intrigue. "What? Here? In the ruins?"

"Affirmative."

Curiosity roused the cyborg. The thought of coming back with something, anything, was too tantalizing to ignore.

"Can you lock onto the signal?"

"Affirmative."

The map reappeared in CJ's mind, zooming in on their immediate surroundings. The red dot was his position, the green dot was the mysterious signal, though it did bleep in out occasionally, disappearing from the map only to reappear a few moments later.

"It's close… Only a kilometer south." The cyborg pondered for a moment, mulling over the temptation. "Will reaching the source of the signal use a significant amount of energy from the battery?"

"Not significantly."

A warm giddiness filled CJ with excitement. It was a feeling he hadn't known for some time. "Let's check it out!"

At that moment, the ground shifted, jolting the sub backwards. CJ was flung against the control panel, barely catching himself in time to watch the seabed outside heave and crack apart. His circuits froze in terror as the ground bulged before him. Another earthquake? No, not now! But then he saw the truth of it. The fleshy stalks that CJ had assumed were anchor worms, the things he'd been shining the sub's bright headlights on for the past several minutes, revealed themselves to merely be eye stalks of something that had been buried underneath. Rising like a mountain from the ground, covered in dark chiton overgrown with barnacles, arose a gargantuan crustacean unlike anything CJ had ever seen.

The AI, sensing the paralyzing awe in the cyborg's thoughts, took it upon itself to commence preservation protocols. *"Buoyancy reinitiated, revving engines for departure!"* It turned the sub around, pointing it away from the ruins and towards the open ocean.

"Where are you taking me?" CJ asked, coming to his senses.

"Home!"

"That signal is still back there! We need to find what it is!"

The AI responded with a tone that almost sounded impatient. *"That is not recommended!"*

"I'm not leaving until we see what's back there!" With a firm thought, CJ pushed away the AI's command to retreat and forced his own will upon the sub. He started by overriding the AI's control of the propulsion system, turning the sub back around and then revved the engine to full speed.

"What are you doing?"

"Just be quiet and watch!"

CJ blasted the sub forward towards the ruins, towards the crab. The creature snapped its mandibles angrily and raised a claw to catch the tiny craft. CJ held tight to the console as he commanded the sub to jerk to the right, darting around the creature's reach. He spotted a building, it's wide hollow window just big enough for the craft to fit through. CJ focused and shot the sub through the window, threading the needle in one side and out the other.

Feeling a sense of vindication, the cyborg amplified it just to make sure the AI could sense it. "You see. Nothing to worry about."

Then there came a thunderous boom that rippled out like an explosion, rattling CJ in his seat. Behind them, the creature swung a chitinous claw, swiping the top the building they'd just sped through, sundering tons of stone and metal. Alarms from the AI's sensors rang inside CJ's mind, blaring and howling as they turned his whole vision bright with flashes of red.

"Incoming! Incoming!

Chunks of metal and cements struck them in the rear like shrapnel, pummeling the hull with terrifyingly loud pings and bangs. The cyborg focused, pushing out the noise of the alarms and the AI's persistent warnings, so he could be undistracted from piloting. There was a loud snap from the rear. The damaged propeller had fallen off. CJ spun the sub in a barrel roll and pushed harder with his will, cranking up the speed of the remaining propellers to the max. Soon they cleared the field of falling debris and a sense of tentative calm started to set in.

"That was reckless," the AI chastised.

CJ had no response. Maybe it had been a little reckless, but he hoped whatever he was looking for was worth it. He called up the battery display again. 26%. It was less than he expected, but he nodded to himself. It was what it was. He figured he'd find out soon enough what this gamble was for.

CJ drew up the map of his surroundings again. The crab was a massive yellow blip, slowly following behind him, until finally, it stopped and fell out of range. And then the cyborg noticed the green blip, or the lack there of. The prize he'd turned around to find, it was gone. He slowed the sub's speed and expanded the range of his scan. Where was it? Where did the green blip go?

Then, as the distant clicking and gurgling of the crab echoed out behind them, CJ saw it. It was flickering weakly, but he saw it, adjusted his course, and closed in. The signal led him into the half-buried interior of a concrete building in the heart of the ruined city. What function it had served in the past was impossible to tell. Most of its plaster had been washed off, leaving behind a rugged surface with lines of rusted rebar sticking out like bones of a rotting corpse.

"We've arrived," the AI said, lacking enthusiasm.

The cyborg searched the ruin until they came to a corner of the building where sea moss coated the pile of stones in green fur. CJ activated the mechanical probing arms, extending them from the sub's underbelly, and started to pull away the heavy debris one chunk at a time. After a while, a bit of worry crossed CJ's circuits. He was wasting energy he couldn't afford. He checked. 24%.

"At this rate, we will not have enough battery life to propel consistently back to base. Not even on low output."

CJ furrowed his holographic brow. The AI was right, but there was no point in stopping now. He yanked hard with the sub's arms and pulled back a huge slab of concrete, and as he did so, something gleamed underneath. Pulling back the final bits of rock, CJ uncovered what looked like a giant pillbox coated in shimmering mother of pearl.

If CJ had lungs, he would have gasped at that precise moment. "Do you know what this is?"

"I do not have enough data to confirm."

"This...this is a life case!" CJ remembered how the prospect of these things were in vogue back in the years leading up to the war. It was never confirmed that any working prototypes ever actually existed, though, only failed test models. "Tell me, do you get a reading of what's inside?"

"Negative."

"Of course, you can't! The shell is designed to block everything from radio waves to gamma rays. It's airtight and nigh shatter-proof. It's designed perfectly to create an impervious and self-sustaining environment for the user inside. Do you get what I'm saying?"

"You found a powerfully shiny suitcase."

"There might be a *human* inside! An actual human!" CJ's mind was starting to race with thoughts, but he slowed it down just enough to issue more mental commands to AI, telling it to prepare the airlock in the back of the sub and load the capsule. The AI took over the submarine's arms, gently lifting the silvery capsule from the rubble and pulling back into the sub's loading bay. There was a hiss as water was drained away from the other side of the wall behind CJ's chair, the area where the loading bay was contained in the small sub. When he heard the signal chime announcing the water was fully drained, he commanded the sub to open the door behind him before he unplugged his neural link. CJ spun his chair around and waited for the door behind him to open. There was a loud click as the locks unlatched, sliding open in three parts.

Still in his chair, CJ leaned forward to reach into the small loading bay. He slid his chrome hands over the shimmering surface of the case, examining the sides, looking for some way to open the smooth box. Finally, his fingers felt something along the side, a small panel displaying vital signs, including a pair of little lines that rose and fell ever so slightly between long intervals.

CJ's holographic eyes widened in overwhelming awe. Two heartbeats? Two minds? Eager anticipation tickled his neural network again, jumping like sparks in his mind, and he put a finger on the unlock button. There was a click and a hiss as the atmosphere inside the casket fled out, cold and white with mist.

Carefully, the cyborg lifted the lid to find two young humans curled in fetal positions, facing either side of the casket, no older than ten. Their chocolate brown cheeks and kinky close-cropped hair were tinged with white frost. They laid still and silent, their chests barely rising and falling as they breathed incredibly slowly. Naked as they were, CJ noticed one was male and one was female. This was greater than any mind bank a cyborg could have ever hoped to find.

"I have to admit," the AI started, *"I had not suspected this."*

CJ reached out a hand to touch one of the children's cheeks, but the AI stopped him.

"Don't disturb them. Their bodies are still too cold, and their minds are too deep in sleep. If he woke them now, they'd likely go into shock. Additionally, there is not enough air in the sub for them to breathe long."

The cyborg nodded. "Of course. How could I forget?"

He knew how. Corrupted data.

Something else, CJ noticed, was in the case with the kids. A small USB storage of some kind. He picked up and examined the old design, wondering if he could even interface with it. He spun his chair back around and tried inserting it into the docking port. To his surprise, it fit.

"There is one audio file on this device. Shall I play it?"

"Yes."

A woman's voice suddenly replaced the AI's, the first human voice CJ had heard in over a thousand years. *"I do not know if anyone will find this message, I cannot predict what will happen next. Everyone speaks of coming war, of the end times. They might be right. But this case can save my angels. If you've found them, I beg of you, take care of them, and tell them that their mother loves them."*

"Pod?" CJ said.

"Yes?" The AI asked.

"We do not have enough battery life to get back, do we?"

"No."

CJ clenched his fists and stared at his reflection in the viewport, staring at his black carbon fiber face overlaid with green holographic eyes, eyebrows, and mouth. His excitement was gone, now he only felt the tight pain of failure. Then, from the pits of despair, an idea came. "What if we ride the currents, will that help?"

"The nearest east-west current is the South Equatorial Stream. However, reaching it will take us off course by several hundred kilometers. That path is risky."

"We have to try, Pod! Chart a course for it and let's get going."

"Understood."

CJ spun back around to give the sleeping kids one last look and closed the case. Then he linked up with the sub's console once more and watched the battery life in his mind's eye. 21%.

By the time the sub reached the underwater current, despite their low output, the battery was 18% and steadily declining. CJ listened to the low hum of the ship's propellers, wondering if there was anything he could do to slow the battery's drain.

He told the sub to turn off all lights, so it did, and the CJ sat in darkness. Hours went by and still, the battery continued to drain. 17%.

He told the sub to slow down, so it did, but the sub started to drift off course and needed to right itself. 11%

He told the ship to shut off all non-vital systems. The AI complied, and suddenly, almost all of the information CJ could see through his neural link was cut off, reduced to simple info readings and crude shapes. The battery display was now a simple yellow rectangle. It shrank just a bit and turned red. 9%.

Finally, he told the AI to shut itself down. It did, and CJ was left alone in silence. 4%

CJ brought up the map. It was simple now, with blocky polygons replacing what had been detailed continents. His red dot, which was more a square now, moved between Brazil and some small islands. They'd finally entered the Caribbean Sea. They were so close. 1%

Above him, CJ heard the muffled growls of distant thunder. Another storm…that was the last thing he needed. The currents would push him off course, and if that happened now, he wouldn't be able to get back. His synthetic heart sank a bit in his chest as he realized his only option. He didn't want to do it, not again, his memories were fragile enough as they were, but it was what it was. He looked back at the life case, seeing the faint green glow of its vital displays, the only indication of the case's presence in the pitch blackness of the sub. CJ imagined all the new memories those two souls would make. It was a fair trade. He connected to the sub and switched the AI back on.

"Hello, CJ -1844! This is Submersible Exploration Pod-136 at your serv—!"

"Listen, Pod," CJ started, stopping short the AI's programed salutation with a thought. "I don't have much time. The sub's battery will be dead in a few minutes, maybe less now that you're back online, so here's what we're going to do. There's a storm coming, and we need to outrun it, full speed, no stopping, you understand. So, I'm going to transfer my energy reserves. It should be more than enough to get you back to base."

The AI was slow to answer. Whether that was because of the lack of energy or hesitancy, CJ couldn't tell. *"Cybernetic shutdown will result from transferring your full energy reserves, and that runs the risk of memory corruption. Are you sure you want to do this? The structural integrity of your neural matrix is only—"*

"I'm sure," CJ said with a nod. "My last order is for you to get these kids safely to Maroon-0. Understood?"

"Understood. Are you ready to initiate energy transfer? You should commence safety shut down now, just to be sure."

"Alright, pod. I'm trusting you."

"Understood. Initiating energy transfer."

CJ closed his eyes and held onto the memory of those sleeping kids, seeing them clear as a photograph in his mind's eye, hoping that if nothing else, he'd remember their faces when they booted him back up. Then, in a flash, the world went black.

ONCE UPON A TIME IN VIRTUOPOLIS

BY

RONALD T. JONES

A man died.

His killer stood over the body, garbed in a blue hoodie, holding a pistol. He pumped a second round into his victim. Forensics determined that the victim died instantly from the first shot.

The killer started for the shop exit. I issued a mental command and time froze. I approached the killer to get a closer look at him. But his face was a gray void. Just as I thought, an identity filter.

"Buktu, I need you to deconstruct." My SA (subdermal assistant) responded. "I have attempted to do so. My effort is unsuccessful."

I squinted. "Unsuccessful?"

"I am unable to penetrate the filter."

"That shouldn't be beyond your capacity to decrypt unless we're dealing with mil grade tech."

"Or Intelligence," Buktu added.

"That's more concerning," I muttered. I worked in Intelligence before downgrading myself to a simple metro investigator. Was it too much to ask for an uncomplicated murder? It was mystery enough that the killer took nothing of value…as if an obscure shop dealing in antiques could possibly offer more than sparse pickings for a criminal.

I studied the gun. "Give me a weapon analysis."

"Gamma 6 semi-automatic. Manufacture date: 2318. Serial markings have been removed by acidic corrosion."

"Untraceable," I murmured expectantly. "Resume footage."

The killer tucked the gun into his pants waistband. He moved past…or through me…toward the shop door, opened it and stepped outside.

"He went northbound," I said, rubbing my chin. "Link out."

The antique shop, along with the body dissolved around me. I 'awoke' inside my work cubicle, downloaded all data Buktu recorded into a secure file, and stored it as backup in my holoface.

"Find anything?"

I looked over at a neighboring cubicle to see Terrance, my colleague, moving icons across his holoface display.

I sighed. "A murder in a crime free district, committed by a perp with a face filter my SA can't crack. How about you?"

Terrence expanded his jowly face in a smile that said he drew the lucky hand. "Just hackers trying to breach a retail network in Jersey. Idiots left virtual crumbs obvious enough to see with my eyes closed. They'll be in custody before sundown."

I sniffed sarcastically. "Good for you."

Terrence grinned and returned to his sterling sleuth work. Bastard.

"Investigator Brewer." The image of Director Pimrose popped on my holoface. It wasn't Pimrose's face per se, but a digital reflection…a digiflec. Our forebearers would have used the term 'avatar.' The director was immersed in Virtuopolis, a digiflec of the physical world.

"Director," I addressed. Digiflecs were usually scrubbed of any imperfections perceived by their users. Not Pimrose's image. Her digiflec retained the prominent nose, eye wrinkles, and severe facial angularity that her physical visage possessed. She was as bereft of vanity as she was charm.

"Progress report."

I wanted to tell her that there was no progress. Instead, I reported my meager findings.

Pimrose's image looked thoughtful.

"I'm about to run background on the victim."

"Already done," said Pimrose. "The victim existed under a nom de guerre. His true name was Silas Akumbe. He was a former executive at Sky Pacific Corp."

I raised a brow. "Is there anything else I should know…besides how a former executive at the largest company in the world ends his life as a humble shopkeeper?"

"I leave it to you to provide that answer, Investigator." Pimrose's digiflec leaned forward. "And I do expect an answer, soon. This case has drawn…official attention. Wrap it up quickly."

"What kind of official attention?"

The director disregarded my question.

"Wrap it up, Investigator." Her image disappeared.

I stared at a dark interface, my eyes narrowing in puzzlement.

* * *

The streets of Grand Chicago bustled with activity when I was a child. Over the years, a skyline that hugged the entirety of Lake Michigan sprouted taller buildings stretching just shy of the stratosphere. The city's reach expanded further from the coast, encompassing great swathes of hinterland. The population increased by millions, but as I walked out of the City Investigation Building, a nearly empty boulevard greeted me. Most people stayed indoors, preferring to spend their waking moments in Virtuopolis.

I visited Virtuopolis when duty required it. Although if I wanted to, I could work from there, like the director and billions of other users who enjoyed IE (Immersive Experience). Me? I preferred the physical world. You can't feel sunlight, inhale natural air or smell a rose in Virtuopolis. Those are little things. I've always appreciated the little things in life.

I hopped a trans and rode it across the central district. I debarked at a stop close to the crime scene. Five minutes later I entered the shop to get a physical feel of the place. Shelves and counters were crammed with items catering to a collector's taste. The layout was early 21st century, from tile floor and wall to a hinged door. I stepped behind the counter into Akumbe's office. His holoface rested on a table, its contents uploaded by cyber specialists for analysis.

"Buktu, I need you to do a data search on this holoface."

"There is no data to comb."

"I think there is. I've got a hunch."

"If you suspect hidden data, my ability to access it is constrained by my clearance level."

I smirked. "Well, let's unconstrain it. Pattern Delta. Execute." After reciting that override code, I linked into Akumbe's holoface. Two seconds elapsed and there I was in a digiflec of his shop. The place was identical in every way, except the shelves were bare of merchandise, a marker symbolizing the removal of data from his holoface. I walked through the shop, scrutinizing every nook and cranny.

"Come on," I muttered. "I know something is here."

"Carl, I have scanned the entirety of this digiflec," said Buktu. "It is empty."

I shook my head slowly, burdened with the feeling that whatever I sought lay tantalizingly out of reach. "Buktu, Pattern Alpha. Execute."

"Carl, you do realize that if you continue using codes from your previous occupation, Intelligence will flag it."

I shrugged. "Understood. Execute."

Like a cloth wiping grime from a window, the digiflec around me transitioned to a featureless monochrome corresponding with Akumbe's shop.

"It appears you were right to dig deeper," said Buktu. "The shelf behind you."

I turned and saw a picture frame resting on the shelf Buktu indicated. I knew it. A person of Akumbe's caliber is bound to hide more than his identity and location. And he'll keep secrets in places few will think of looking. I headed to the shelf, grabbed the picture frame and linked out.

When I 'awoke', the picture frame automatically uploaded to Buktu.

"Alright, Buktu, show me what I found."

"It would be more accurate to say that *I* found it, Carl."

My brow scrunched. "Can we get on with this?"

"Accessing data," Buktu stated. I could have sworn I heard a snicker in his tone.

The picture frame hovered before me in a Heads-up Display. Words and diagrams appeared in the blank space encompassed by the frame. These were technical designs I couldn't make heads or tails of, accompanied by mathematical equations and arcane text only specialists could decipher. Come to think of it, Akumbe had an engineering background. Why was he hiding technical information deep inside a digiflec?

"What am I looking at, Buktu?"

"Designs of an upgraded IE chip."

IE chips facilitated immersion. No larger than a thumbnail, a chip could be adhered to the forehead or implanted. Increasing numbers of people chose to be implanted with IE chips. Buktu was the only device I was implanted with and that was a job requirement. I kept an IE chip in my pocket.

"Upgraded?"

"Yes. I just accessed a three-year-old police report concerning a data breach in a Sky Pacific research facility. The report corresponds with Mr. Akumbe's resignation from the company. He was questioned about the breach but was not charged with a crime. Afterward he disappeared from all records."

"He went Luddite," I said, using a term referencing people who were even more averse than I was to immersing. But they didn't totally eschew technology. They just preferred two-dimensional communication contact.

"This is interesting, Carl," Buktu began. "Sky Pacific declared this chip design accessible only by means of a Level One clearance."

"Level One? Just for an IE chip? Is that clearance level still in effect?"

"No, it was lifted a month ago, just before the upgrade went into production."

I grew more intrigued. "That means those chips are in circulation now. Come to think of it, there were pub boards advertising new model chips. But I didn't see too many of those."

"That is because the bulk of advertising for IE upgrades occurred in Virtuopolis. Your last use of an IE chip was a month ago."

I headed toward the shop exit. "There's something odd at play here. Level One clearances have government written all over them. I'll have to call in some outside consulting on this one."

I know Buktu sensed my reservation. "Do you have a particular consultant in mind?"

"I think you already know the answer to that question."

* * *

I appeared in a small office overlooking a cityscape very much unlike Grand Chicago. The buildings were shorter, flatter, non-descript in a staid bureaucratic way. This was Washington, the heart of the North American States. The building I was in, my digiflec rather, was its eye, ever watchful, eternally vigilant. I used to work in this building. Even though I wasn't there physically, the place still weighed on my spirits.

"I figured I'd hear from you eventually."

I turned to the owner of that warmly familiar voice.

Castina Lloyd stood at the doorway of her office, hands on waist as if posing for a publicity still. I ignored the playful smirk radiating from her dimpled, deep brown face and got down to business. "I assume you received my package."

"I knew you were on to something that went beyond a local magistrate's paygrade when you accessed an Intelligence code."

I maintained my professional bearing. "What's your assessment?"

Castina strolled to her desk. "Advanced Research partnered with Sky Pacific to produce this upgrade chip without presidential or legislative committee knowledge."

"The chip is on the market. What the hell is so special about it to generate this extensive secrecy around it?"

"Don't know," said Castina. "When I tried to dig deeper into the matter, I hit a barricade that even my security clearance couldn't hurdle. But…" she stood and approached me, stopping close enough to my digiflec to toss to the wind all conventions regarding the sanctity of personal…or virtual space. "…if we work closely together, we can solve this mystery."

Ok. Castina and I have a…thing. Well, used to. It's on and off. At the moment, off.

"Carl, are you okay?" She asked in all seriousness. I appreciated the question.

I managed a tight grin. "I'm good."

"Tokyo was a shit show. It shouldn't have happened."

I tried not think about Tokyo. "Let me know what you come up with on your end," I said, shifting topics.

Gratefully, she dropped the matter. "I will." She linked out and her office dematerialized, replaced by my physical apartment.

* * *

That evening, I sat in my bedroom examining holodisplays of the crime scene. My central display featured Akumbe's killer. I studied footage of the murder, probing for the minutest clue that could lead to the perp's identity. It was vexing that even with my Intelligence access, I could not cut through his identity filter.

"Carl," said Buktu. "I was analyzing Mr. Akumbe's chip design when I encountered an encryption. I unlocked it and an image of Mr. Akumbe's home appeared, followed by a specific room in his house."

"A room?"

"Yes."

Why would a design hide a picture of the victim's residence? Unless…I stood. "Buktu, we're taking a trip."

* * *

Experience immersing as you have never experienced it before. Virtuopolis will appear indistinguishable from the physical world...so indistinguishable you will never want to leave it. Get the latest IE upgrade. Available now on all marketplace platforms.

The face of Sky Pacific Corp CEO, Jason Krindler, appeared at the end of the holo ad as if to present his glimmering salesman smile as icing on a confection of pure frivolity. Most of Grand Chicago, North America for that matter, were already obsessed with Virtuopolis. How much more real did it need to be?

I shut down the commercial holo and gazed out my glide car's front window. Buktu operated it while I studied data on Sky Pacific. Under Krindler's leadership, the corporation was experiencing unprecedented growth. It gobbled up competition like a fox rampaging through fat hens…to the point where it was saddled with anti-trust litigation.

Before his resignation, Akumbe expressed displeasure with the direction Sky Pacific was going in. What direction was that?

"We are approaching Mr. Akumbe's residence," said Buktu.

My glide car halted alongside a modest single floor unit. The surrounding neighborhood comprised closely spaced low-income units populated by the exploited denizens of a hidden underclass. A suitable environment to hide from an opulent past.

Patrol drones hovered at the unit's front entrance. Akumbe's house had been designated an Investigation Site. The drones were posted at all entrances to deter intruders. They allowed me entry after verifying my status.

The interior was clean, neatly arranged and sparsely furnished. Nothing to draw attention, in keeping with the overall pattern of Akumbe's final years. I ventured to a storage room past the kitchen. This was the room flagged in my holodisplay. It was empty save for a full laundry basket sitting in the corner.

I stuck my IE chip to my temple. The room wavered, symbolizing my exit from the physical world into an artificial realm popularly known as Virtuopolis. I stepped further into a digiflec of Akumbe's storage room, sweeping the floor, walls and ceiling for clues. I rustled through the laundry basket.

"Buktu, do you detect anything?"

"Nothing Carl. If anything is here, it is not evident at this level of the construct."

I nodded. "Ok, we'll go deeper."

"Another Intelligence code?" Buktu queried with a resignation I found amusing in an SA.

"It worked before. Besides, I'm sure Castina will protect me from potential security related ramifications."

"You don't have to use a code." That was not Buktu. The voice came from behind me. I whirled about and flinched at what I saw: Silas Akumbe. He was close to my height, fit, with a froth of gray beard contrasting his midnight complexion. He pinned me with a pinning stare.

"Mr. Akumbe," I managed, after retrieving my wits. "You're…"

"Not alive," Akumbe finished. "I am a digiflec of Silas Akumbe's memories, stored into a construct of his likeness and imbued with every known aspect of his personality."

I stared at this…memory-flec, trying to digest the sight of it, the very concept of post-mortem memory storage. I had heard of research along those lines, but…

"Investigator Brewer, you must vacate this house immediately," urged the memory-flec, suddenly alert. "Hostiles are arriving."

I cocked my head. "How do you know? And how did you know my name? Buktu, are you linking with this 'flec?"

"Yes," replied Buktu, "but I did not initiate it. The digiflec uploaded itself into my processor."

"Impossible. No unauthorized program can do that."

"You might want to remind the digiflec, whose unauthorized intrusion did just that."

"You must leave," said Akumbe. It…or…he pointed. "Take the back exit."

"Carl, I am patched into a street surveillance cam." Buktu displayed footage of four persons getting out of a glide car in front of Akumbe's house. They wielded what looked like assault weapons. One of them carried something considerably larger. He mounted it on his shoulder…

The weapons' specs flitted faster than a thought across my threat view. Python Launcher!

I dashed toward the back door, just as a rocket with a magnesium laced, hydroxide warhead whisked from the launcher.

I activated my body shield, yet still felt the sting of broiling heat, accompanied by a swatting pressure that propelled me through the shattered back exit. I must have tumbled like a tossed rag doll a dozen yards from the house. I landed on my back. The interior of Akumbe's house throbbed fire. A fusillade of bullets whisked past me. I rolled and scampered toward a walkway leading to the front.

"Buktu, reacquire surveillance cam view!"

An image of the attackers shooting into the burning house with assault weapons filled my vision.

After a minute, the shooting stopped, and the attackers returned to the car. I couldn't let them get away.

I hopped up and ran to the front of the house, my Prodigy service pistol in hand. I confronted the gunmen and yelled an obligatory, "City Investigation, drop your weapons, hands up!"

I had a hunch they were not going to comply.

The gunman closest to me responded first. He raised his weapon in my direction. I shot first. His head snapped back from the impact of a tungsten bullet drilling through his brain. I placed two more rounds in his accomplices. They dropped, instantly dead. The attacker with the launcher tossed the expended weapon aside and reached into his jacket. I sprinted and was on him just as he produced a pistol. I kicked the gun out of his hand and leaned in with a precise elbow strike to his jaw, followed by a knee to the gut. The gunman bent and I bulled him face down to the pavement. I straddled him, seized his arms and cuffed him.

"Carl, I have just sent an alert. Police units are inbound," Buktu informed me.

I stood, gazing coldly upon my semiconscious prisoner. I wanted answers.

* * *

"Progress report." The director's digiflec stared at me from the interview room holodisplay. The prisoner sat at a table, restraint bands wrapped around his upper body and ankles. His eyelids quivered, a visible indicator of his resistance to virtual interrogation. Terrance stood on the other side of the table, watching the prisoner.

"So far nothing, other than his name, Cromwell Max, which sounds like an alias. "I'm going to need your authorization to escalate to Interrogation Protocol Four."

"Granted," the director approved.

I told neither Terrance nor the director about Akumbe's memory-flec.

"There's not a trace of him or his fellow goons on the grid," said Terrance. "It costs a fortune on top of a fortune to execute an ID wipe."

Director Pimrose seemed to mull on that. "Try to extract something from him." Her digiflec vanished.

Terrance threw me a quirky look. "Any ideas?"

I shook my head. "Doubt we'll salvage much from him."

I suddenly found myself standing on the roof of Grand Chicago's tallest tower, my jacket fluttering at the behest of a simulated breeze. A simulated blue expanse of lakefront formed a breathtaking sun dappled backdrop. Akumbe's memory-flec stood before me dressed in a casual V neck and slacks.

"Buktu?" I called out, mildly disoriented and irritated by this unbidden transition.

"Not my doing," said the SA.

"My apologies for bringing you here without your consent." The memory-flec looked genuinely contrite. "But extreme urgency warrants this crude manner of contact. Look around you. What do you see?"

I did so and shrugged. "Virtuopolis…or…is it?" Strangely, I wasn't so sure. I turned from the lake, panning the skyline, my eyes narrowing with uncertainty. "I'm still in the Investigation building, but…"

"You are having troubling remembering," said Akumbe.

I motioned a troubled nod.

"Yet you have just immersed. There are millions who have been immersed for weeks. They never rise from immersion. They are living their lives in constructs of their own choosing, existing in places more realistic in appearance than the real world, bereft of the inconveniences a physical body offers, while experiencing heightened senses and stimulations. What you are seeing is the fruit of the IE chip Silas Akumbe worked to develop. He led the upgrade design team until he discovered a discrepancy in a prototype chip. Memory lapses were afflicting test subjects. When he reported the issue, he was ignored. When he threatened to go to the Business Ethics Commission, he was removed from the project, stripped of his security clearances and demoted. He soon discovered the involvement of government elements in the project just before an attempt on his life.

"An attempt? There's no record of that," I said, surprised.

"He never reported it. In the process of immersing, he experienced an electrical surge that nearly fried his neurons had he not acted in time to mitigate its effects. That was no accident. But the authorities would have dismissed his claim had he notified them."

"What is it about this upgraded chip that alarmed Akumbe, that drove him into hiding?" I demanded.

"With the upgrade, the more one immerses, the more difficult it is to return to the physical world. Hence your fading memory."

That revelation sunk in like a knife.

"Get me out of here," I said. "Get me out before I forget everything!"

* * *

When I 'awoke', I was no longer inside the City Investigation building. I stood outside, two blocks away on an empty boulevard. I looked up into a cloudless sky to see dozens of vertilift craft descending like a prehistoric raptor. Armed black-clad figures jumped out of the vertilifts, their thrust packs landing them on the pavement.

I darted from view, stepping into a building alcove and peeked around its corner. The armed figures rushed into the CI building with a military precision that told me I was not observing untrained rabble.

"Buktu, who are those people?"

"Unknown," said the SA. "Their gear bears no identifying markings, but their weapons are new model Leopolds."

"Definitely not typical criminal weapons. Link me to the director."

"I already tried. The director is immersed."

"What about the mayor, the police chief…?"

"They too are immersed. Jamming from an unknown source hampers my ability to communicate with them."

Gunshots and explosions cracked and thudded from inside the CI building. A glinting downpour of glass fragments from blasted out windows pelted the street.

Buktu linked me to interior cams. I stood in the IB building's fifth floor corridor, witnessing a gun battle between armed assailants and my fellow investigators. Prodigy service pistols were ill matched against the intruders' heavy caliber Leopolds. Five investigators flopped to the floor in an eviscerating hail of Leopold bursts. An Investigator, dragging a bloodied limp leg, tried to crawl away. An assailant shouldered his Leopold and drew a pistol. Casually he strolled toward the investigator and shot him in the back of the head.

Riven with rage, I cut the feed and pulled out my Prodigy. I emerged into the open, aimed at a hovering vertilift and fired.

The craft's side view window glass cracked. Immediately, the vertilift swung in my direction giving me a queasy eyeful of a pair of flank mounted gun pods. I raced for cover, the sound of rapid thumping rippling the air. I ran inside a building and leaped behind a lobby desk, hunkering down as stuttering bursts of gun pod fire whittled the front entrance to rubble.

"Not an advisable move," said Akumbe's memory-flec. His sudden appearance in my mind almost as disconcerting as being under fire.

"Where have you been?"

"Analyzing. Grand Chicago is not the only city under attack. Armed parties have gained forceful entry into key government facilities across the country. The White House is currently under siege."

"He is right," confirmed Buktu. "The country is under attack. However, the people who should be responding to this threat are immersed. All links to Virtuopolis remain broken.

"Were you aware of this?" I asked the memory-flec.

"Mr. Akumbe suspected a plot, but nothing on this scale. He was working on an override to disable IE chips. I will attempt to access his research in that area."

"Wait. Jason Krindler is responsible for these attacks, isn't he?"

"I suspect him to be a primary conspirator, along with rogue government collaborators."

I nodded. "Buktu, locate Krindler."

"Mr. Krindler is immersed. His physical body is aboard his private jet heading for Washington."

"Undoubtedly to witness his attempted coup firsthand." I remained hidden, aware that the vertilift ceased fire. Any minute, armed assailants would be combing through the lobby's ruins for me. But I had to act. I gave Buktu a specific set of instructions before saying, "Pattern Riptide!"

* * *

I stood on a decorated podium, facing an enormous, cheering crowd. Behind me was the White House, draped in shimmering orange banners imprinted with images of swords gripped by gauntleted hands.

"How did you get here?"

I turned to see a blond man, mid-forties, in a custom designed gray suit stepping onto the podium. His blue eyes glittered like torches, an effect I imagined was intentional. This was after all, his construct.

He lifted a finger, his mouth forming a wry smile. "No need to answer. I know you're former intel with tricks up your sleeve, including the ability to invade someone else's virtual privacy. That is illegal you know."

"So is the murder and mayhem you're orchestrating," I rejoined.

Jason Krindler's smile broadened. If not for a hint of instability seeping through his expression, I would have thought his levity was genuinely affable.

"What's the point of all this?" I asked.

Jason pivoted, facing the crowd. The cheering grew louder, reaching a deafening crescendo before ebbing. He indicated the audience in a sweeping gesture. "*That* is the point, Investigator…to usher in order, peace, and security; to upgrade this degenerate society. Listen to their gratitude…their enthusiasm." Jason inhaled, taking in the frenzied adoration of his faux sycophants as if it were an intoxicant.

"All of this will soon become reality. Others have tried, but I will be the one to make this nation truly great. After that, the world!"

In my past work I'd seen my share of megalomaniacs. Yep, Jason fit the bill.

"It's time for you to surrender," I said.

Jason stared at me as if I were certifiable…like him. "Surrender?"

"Yes. A signal sent by friends who haven't fallen under the spell of your IE chips has just seized control of your jet. Your flight to Washington is being rerouted."

"Impossible!" Jason's face went slack.

I tugged at my shirt sleeve. "More tricks."

At that second, Akumbe appeared beside me.

Jason gaped at the memory-flec. "You! You meddling son of a bitch! You're supposed to be dead. I personally saw to it!"

"Mr. Akumbe is deceased," said the memory-flec. "I embody his memories and his knowledge."

The memory-flec turned to me. "I have succeeded in accessing Mr. Akumbe's research. The override has been initiated. IE chips are being disabled."

"You heard that," I said to Jason. "Your power grab is over. The entire nation is 'waking' up, including those with the ability to stop your goons."

Jason shook his head, his blue torchlit gaze becoming brighter. The crowd vanished in brilliant sparkles of digital pixie dust. The city backdrop melted away "No…damn you…I'm going to make this nation great…it's my destiny…it's always been my destiny!" His digiflec vanished.

Linking to the jet's interior cam, I saw Jason's physical body dash to the cockpit. He grabbed the guidance stick, trying to regain control of the jet. Unsuccessful, he pulled a shot gun out of a storage compartment beneath the panel. He pointed the weapon at the panel and fired. The panel exploded. The jet lurched, hurling Jason off balance. He banged his head against the window. Blood streamed down his forehead, but he climbed to his feet, staring at the video feed I was observing. A raving blend of insanity and defiance contorted his features. "Surrender? I won't give you inferiors the satisfaction!"

I linked to a satellite view and watched the jet spiraling toward the ground. A flaming patch marked its impact in the middle of a prairie.

* * *

I returned to my body in time to see gunmen entering the building lobby. They stepped over rubble, converging on my position. I popped up and triggered my Prodigy, striking one gunman in the head. His face plate shattered, and he fell backwards. The second one doubled over, but the bullet failed to penetrate the armor beneath his tunic.

I ducked and my world submerged in a thundering cacophony of automatic weapons fire. Blazing bullets tore into the basalt reception desk I hid behind. I hunched in place, my Prodigy pressed to my chest, but I couldn't get a shot off. A grenade bounced in front of me. I amped up my body shield and shuffled as far from the explosive as I could.

BLAM!

A concussive bludgeon backhanded me. Every bone, tissue and organ in my body felt like they had been ripped apart and haphazardly pieced back together. I blacked out for what seemed like hours but couldn't have been more than a few seconds. My eyes fluttered open. A haze-shrouded gunman loomed over me.

It took every ounce of my shield's energy to absorb that grenade blast before winking out. The gunman pointed his assault weapon at my unprotected head.

That's when I laughed. I don't know why. I just started laughing. Maybe I was celebrating the life I was about to lose. Maybe I just wanted to piss off a thug who expected a terrified victim instead of a cackling madman.

In any event, the gunman paused. Whatever expression lurked beneath his obsidian headgear erupted in a thick, bloody gruel. The gunman's headless body toppled forward, landing on top of me. Another helmeted figure emerged into my view. The face plate retracted, and a wave of relief swept through me. Castina.

She held an anti-personnel rocket gun, resting its thick barrel on her shoulder. "I think this makes us even."

I squirmed, struggling to get the corpse off me. "A hand?"

Castina smiled and right away, I knew this complicated thing we had going was about to be on again.

UNLIMITED DATA
BY
EUGEN BACON

"Must have a smart phone," the job ad said.

* * *

Ping! A job alert.

He was good with gas fitting, roofing, drainage, even power outlets, ladders, testing and repairing. Most electrical things he could do, and gardening. His hands were clever with greenscapes. He could water and feed lilies or stinkwood, trim shrubs or mow grass, fertilise sunflower or pluck cashews from the plant.

What he wasn't good with was lies. The employer hadn't been upfront at the interview about the data, how it was out of pocket.

* * *

When he closed his eyes, he forgot about poverty. On special occasions, he took his wife Natukunda to the village dance but now there was a toddler in tow, so they could be famous on the red dust a mere fifteen minutes, as laughter drowned out the drums, before baby Mukasa rejected his temporary sitter, often an old woman, and demanded in wailful chorus his mother's breast. And the boy was greedy: he had to expose both tits before he stopped screaming.

Kaikara wished he could see it, how it was before Mukasa, but his eyes were broken, reflections of lost dreams fluttering away with locust wings. He swore he would never do it again, but fate was a tricky thing and a poor man had one solace.

Already Natukunda's bleeding had stopped and her breasts looked tender, even a little swollen. And though the toddler was still suckling, Kaikara suspected his wife was pregnant again, especially with that constipation and her craving for calcium stone, soft as chalk to chew. He reached out a hand to the gods of the mountain and demanded a better explanation.

He was an itinerant handyman on call, peddling over fields, tarmac and potholes, moving from suburb to suburb, gas fitting, roofing, draining, mowing. *Ping!* Another job and he wheeled to it, phone in his pocket. But doing jobs on call gobbled data.

* * *

The black market was in Kabalaga. The wet mire, as he weaved around the slum and its tin roofs, walls made of carton or nylon, told him that the bunch of jobless youths with a prowl of eyes staring at his bicycle were not harmless. They wore jungle shirts and sandals made of tyres.

The programmer he visited demanded a month's wage, the whole six thousand shillings of it. But even that was better than the bundle data deal of 40MB a day for mobile internet at five hundred shillings, or 25MB a week for internet everywhere at one thousand, seven hundred and fifty shillings. That is what the employer was offering to slash from Kaikara's wages, leaving him in debt.

He looked at the programmer named Sanyu, like the radio. "Bluetooth, you say?"

* * *

Natukunda had a stall at the market in Old Kampala. Wood, sticks and sacks held the ramshackle thing together. She sold pineapples, mangoes, watermelons, bananas and jackfruits, sometimes papayas, guavas, sweet potatoes and tomatoes. What she earned was a pittance. But she could buy the occasional *gomesi* of imported cotton, six metres of it. Rose and lime were her favourite, puffed sleeves brightly coloured and reaching the floor. Each *gomesi* fitted her just right, its sash over her hips. When the metres allowed, she made a headdress.

Sometimes she sent money to her parents out east in Mbale. They were always sick with malaria, bilharzia or dysentery, and the witchdoctor's herbs and beheaded cockerel were not working. The old folk needed to walk into a clinic, and the white man's tablets cost money.

Now she looked at her husband, as though he wore empty tins around his leg. "You're mad, foolish or both," she said. "Take me back to my parents and they will return your dowry."

"Crooked wood shows the best sculptor. The programmer is working with nature. His invention will change our lives," he said.

"And who knows about this progoramy?"

"Everybody."

"So why aren't they buying it?"

"He who can't dance says the ground is full of rocks. But you and I know better than that. We dance like there is no tomorrow."

"And you say a chippy?" she said.

"Yes."

"Inside my body?"

"Yes."

"Will it hurt?"

"So tiny in your neck, you won't feel a thing."

"Like when I cut my foot on that hoe and the dokita at the clinic did me tetanus with a needo and I didn't get sick?"

"Yes, easy like a shot. You're doing this for us. For you and me and Mukasa. And your parents. I can work with no worry about data on my phone, and you can send more money to your people. It's important that you do this, Natukunda."

"For whaty?"

"Unlimited data. It's called Bluetooth. Waves from your body will connect with my smart phone and we'll pair. You'll never need a telephone for yourself—your whole body will be a smart phone. And I'll never need to buy data bundles again. It all comes with the chip."

"Bullytoothy for how long?"

"It lasts a lifetime," he said.

"And a man named after the rediyo told you this?"

"When you show the moon to a child, it sees only your finger. Natu, try and see the shiny moon beyond the finger."

"Why can't you do it?" she asked, as Mukasa whimpered drowsy-eyed at her breast. She tucked her wrap around him. "You take the chippy, Kaikara."

"A woman is the queen of the Earth. The code needs your fertile body to work properly."

* * *

Everyone was complicit in a fact that was neither fiction nor myth, but data. It did not depend on age or knowledge, just the insertion of a chip that started with an ideology and set into code. What happened after was unprecedented.

The first victim was Natukunda, in her twenties—she lived in Old Kampala. She started displaying black moods and nearly battered her toddler Mukasa to death, if her husband hadn't snatched away the ill-fortuned waif.

By nightfall of the same day, the woman was complaining of severe fatigue. She refused to eat or drink, even when a relative girl—a teenaged daughter of a cousin of a cousin of an aunt—brought the woman her favourite plate of *luwombo*: cassava meal steamed in banana leaves and served in groundnut sauce.

Natukunda wouldn't consume anything all through the next day. She developed a dread to be seen and spoke in undone language, dreams inside dreams. When her husband dragged her from dark pockets under the bed, in a corner of the pit latrine, under sacks in a grain store… she came out scratching at him and tearing at her neck. But she also displayed a shortness of breath.

The mental aberration when it happened exposed the woman to have forgotten her own name, that of her child and her husband's.

"Natu," said the husband. "It's me, Kaikara."

She blinked at him.

By the time her eyes lolled and her body shuddered, she was sobbing through tissue, blood and spit. It was too late to predict anything other than her chest would stop moving. Her pulse dimmed and then vanished, and no air came out of her nose.

Just then, glass-eyed, she gave one last shudder. Heaving words fell from her sigh and cast swirling. They formed a line like night ink and, to anyone who could read—sadly, her husband couldn't—the words in a jumble said, "Live, tracking, assessment, non-conformance, positioning, proof-of-concept, market, network usage volatile sad unmute hop on hop on hoponhoponhoponhopononononononono."

* * *

The programmer climbed onto the roof of the penthouse in Muyenga for a full view of the moon. This suburb, famous for its hills, was the Hollywood of the diaspora. It showcased in the top ten richest neighbourhoods in the world. Looking out at the horizon, he understood it was the first time he had fished in a sea of wealth swollen with ghosts of lost dreams.

On the roof, right there between scarlet dust and a galaxy of waltzing stars, he shut his eyes from tragic memories. What happened in Old Kampala was the first of anomalies.

FLESH OF MY FLESH

BY

JOHN JENNINGS

BEGIN CASE RENDITION:

OFFICIAL FILE:
JONES AND JONES / DETECTION AND PROTECTION, LLC

JUNE 18, 2030 / 22:15 PM hours
PASSCODE: "BUGXCELLSFASHO"

CASE FILE REPORT BY:
JACOB "JUNEBUG" JONES VIA HAINTWARE DOWNLOAD AS CODED IN
A.I. MODEL 2311XL (BLACK OPS GRADE)

ORIGINAL ORGANIC HOUSING: KIA. BATTLE OF BLACK PLAINS, NEVADA.

RECORDING WITH CONTENT RESPONSE PROTOCOLS ENGAGED

PLEASE PROCEED.

Response protocols? So, if I go off subject you gonna correct me and…

AFFIRMATIVE.

Ok. I'm not used to doing this. I already submitted the video but, cuz likes the audio too. Usually, Kudzu does this. But, because he ain't here. Well, I guess it's on me to get this whole thing documented proper like.

PLEASE PROCEED.

Ok, guy. It was raining, as usual, and it was like 11:43 am. So, I was just plugged in getting a recharge then in walks this fine ass sister into our offices. Her name was one Shirley Anne Deeter. This midnight-skinned sister was like a Coke-bottle turned upside-down. She had enough to feed the needy. You know what I mean?

I DO NOT.

Really? Anyway. So, Shirley Anne steps into our spot and I ain't plugged into nobody at the time so I'm just floatin' my little roly-poly ass around and I'm scanning her right? So, she checks out fine. And I do mean fine!

So, she says:

"I'm here to speak to Cleophus Jones on behalf of Reverend Jake Tidyman. It's a . . . sensitive matter."

So, I says:

"Oh. Yes, ma'am. We are good and sensitive. So, THE Reverend Jake Tidyman? Like the head of the super-duper meg-achurch?"

She replied with those luscious lips: "Ah, yes. The Saving Grace Missionary Baptist Church. However, the reverend doesn't like to use the term 'megachurch.' He finds the term . . . immodest."

I just said, 'Whatever, darlin,' and led her back to see my cousin. By the way, I knew from the start she hadn't done her homework on us. Don't nobody calls my cousin by his Mama-given name. Everybody just calls him 'Kudzu' on the 'count he so hard to kill. Just like that gottdamn Japanese weed that covers everything 'round here.

Kudzu was just in the back doin' some research on another case. He's always on the hustle for us.

He looks up and says:

"Good morning, Ms. Deeter. It's a pleasure to meet you."

She looked so surprised.

"How did you?"

"Junebug and I have high-level Mother Wit tech installed. He just shot it over to me. Nothing that special. How can we help you? Or rather, how can we help the Reverend?"

"May I sit?"

"Pardon our manners. Of course. You want a cold drink? Junebug…"

"No thank you," she purred politely.

"Ok. So break it down for us. This…sensitive thing."

"First. My apologies but, I have to scan you. Just to make sure you're who you say you are."

Unoffended, Kudzu just says "Go right ahead."

She takes out a cute little scanner from her purse, which was very nice, and scans Kudzu up and down.

"Oh my! Very impressive upgrades! You are definitely the man for the job, I see. Especially if something rough goes down. How did you...?"

"My cousin Junebug there and me…well, we were in the Asipana Water Wars."

"The Second Civil War? The one fought over water rights?"

"That's the one. The reason why we have the Thirsty Curtain and we can't go see the Hollywood sign no more. Me and Junebug got hurt…well, he got killed at the Battle of Black Plains in Nevada. The Niños De Fuego had joined with the West Coast Freedom Forces and they ambushed us there. I got blown up real good. Junebug caught a bullet in the chest. His brain box caught his data and wired it to a storage unit. They upgraded me for a few more missions. Uncle Sam always gets that pound of black flesh, you know? Once we got out, for real, I got Junebug top-level storage housings and a few military grade bodies to plug into. Then we set up shop here, in Mississippi. Home is home and since the Hack trade's been booming here in The Trap…there's a lot of mischief to get into."

She looked at us both with something a bit less than pity.

"I'm so sorry. Thank you for your service. Um. Please forgive me. Who are the Niños De...?"

I broke in.

"The Niños De Fuego, girl! 'Children of Fire.' You remember those little kids that our country imprisoned at the borders in cages a while back? Separated them from their families and all that shit? Well, they didn't like that. Grew up hard and angry. A lot of them did something about that anger. Turned into one of the most efficient, well trained mercenary groups ever. They made MS-13 look like a sewing circle. They been getting in the ass of the whole world ever since."

Kudzu looked out the window for a minute, staring at the rain, "You reap what you sow." He turns back to the sister. "That's in the good book, right?"

She looked uncomfortable and just started talking about the job. So, what she tells us is that the Rev's daughter has become the victim of a criminal cloning!

I got real intrigued then. Cloning somebody without their consent will get you like ten years in Zombie Mode. Which means another motherfucka using your body for whatever they want while you get stored up somewhere in some hellish virtual prison. Since Trinity, Inc. took over everything, they pulled some strings to make it that way. You see, the law feels a clone ain't a real human. But your DNA is yours so, it's more of a copyright violation than anything. But, since Trinity is a greedy-ass fear-no-gods-but-the-bottom-line business, they lobbied to make shit super illegal. Still though. Greedy perverts getting other folks' DNA and making sex clones of them? It's a big business in The Trap. It's the next level of sex slavery. With the Hack scene like it is there's a ton of money to be made. Makes me sick. Anyway…

She went on:

"A parishioner, Brother Edell Thompson, was indulging in an age-old sin before he was to be married. His bachelor parties. He goes to this…establishment called the Roundabout for a last night of debauchery with his friends. This place has…what are they called…cage dancers. Poor wayward souls who think so little of themselves that they dance half-naked in cages…."

Kudzu broke in: "I'm familiar with the practice. Go ahead."

Her chocolate brow twisted up in disgust and shot Kudzu a cold stare that would freeze The Devil.

"I see. Well, Brother Edell stated that he saw the daughter of Reverend Tidyman, the lovely Sister Betha Mae Tidyman. just dangling and gyrating herself in one of those…things…those cages! I just…"

She started to cry big cartoon tears. If I had a body it would've turned me on.

PLEASE. STAY ON TOPIC.

Oh. Sorry. So, she's crying her pretty little face off for a second and then she composes herself and says:

"Well. Brother Edell was drunk, to be sure. But he had the presence of mind to take a few pictures of her with this eye-camera enhancement. Sure enough. It was someone or something that looked exactly like her. Just missing her birthmark."

Kudzu leans in: "Well. What next?"

"Brother Edell brought it to us. Very repentant of his sins, of course. He gave us copies of the pictures and then deleted them. Reverend Tidyman was, for lack of better words, beside himself with worry and anger! Someone had stolen his only child's DNA, cloned her, and then had put her in a cage for all to see. He was devastated."

And that's where we came in. You see, the Reverend wanted to keep this matter hush-hush. He's this big chaste, "Godified," holy man and his daughter is in a nasty cage with her juicy, sweaty, supposedly-saved assets a-twerking? Nah. That might destroy his whole set-up. What would it look like, you know? You supposed to be a man of God! A shepherd tending a massive flock and you can't even stop your own daughter from being clone-pimped. It'd be a scandal!

Kudzu stiffens up and says:

"Word on the street is that Reverend Tidyman was once a Deacon in The Benediction. Why can't he just go and . . . you know . . . handle things himself?"

"You've done your homework, Mr. Jones. Yes. The Reverend was once one of those repugnant 'Soldiers of God.' So, he does have the skillset to 'handle things,' if he chose to. But he has chosen a higher path than those cultists. He cannot be seen doing such things. He has a higher purpose."

Kudzu looked at her with a "yeah right" kinda glance as he poured himself a glass of Wild Turkey.

"So, the Reverend doesn't want to get his hands dirty, I see. Might as well deal with Negroes who already covered in sin and filth." He knocked back a shot and poured another.

Ms. Deeter looked concerned. Like she had messed up.

"No! It's not like that at all…"

"It's all good." Kudzu cut in. "We ARE some dirty, filthy Negroes. Just as mud-covered and full of sin as you like. Once you in The Trap. You in. In for a penny. In for a pound. We do dirt and we do it well. That's why we get paid the big bucks." He laughs and knocks back a second shot.

Ms. Deeter looked a little put off but also…impressed. It's hard for me to tell. My empathic engrams have been on the fritz of late. Need to get that checked.

Anyway, Kudzu said:

"Well. We are interested. So, when can we meet up with the Reverend and his offspring?"

Ms. Deeter looked rattled.

"Oh. I'm afraid that the Reverend would like to stay out of this as much as possible.

He wasn't intending on interacting with you and…your associate."

Kudzu chuckled. "Then the Rev can go find some other unfortunate dusky devils to handle this then."

Ms. Deeter let out a quick breath and collected herself.

"Well, then. I will get in touch with the Reverend and see what he says. I will contact you with his decision."

Kudzu had leaned back and put his custom made waterproof Floodz brand boots on his desk.

"You do that, Ms. Deeter. You do that."

"Good day, to you both."

I watched her shimmy out of the office. Man! I'd clone that ass in second. Jesus wept!

THIS IS IRRELEVANT.

Recorder-man. Ass is always relevant! Especially one like that! Anyway. Maybe like two hours later we hear her sexy voice on the com:

"The Reverend will see you. Is 4:30pm open for you?"

I checked the schedule and said, "Oh we wiiiiide open for you, Ms. Deeter. We'll see you later."

She hung up real fast like I said something wrong.

I plug into one of my less intimidating bodies and we make our way cross the city…if you can call it that. It's more like a giant festering tech-filled wound on the back of some nightmare creature. After the Post-War Secession of the West and the devastation that the Four Sisters left in the Southern region; refugees migrated deeper into the inland. Yeah, man. Those big ass hurricanes did their work alright. One after the other, until most of the Southern coast was gone and Florida was underwater.

People came from far and wide to Jackson to start over. Trinity took advantage of course and made this a megacity. So, now any sex, drug, dream or even god you want is here in Neo Jackson; The Trap. But, as the name states, you ain't never goin' nowhere once you get up in this here.

Anyway. We wind up at the spot. The headquarters of the world-famous Saving Grace Missionary Baptist Church. It's huge! It was big enough for a few gods to fit in this place, let me tell you!

Kudzu had been taking a hit off a little something the whole way. He takes a last toke and says "Man. The God business pays real good, hunh, cuz?"

I just giggle a bit and we head on in. We get checked by their "security." Kudzu is always packing a lot of heat and it took a while for him to check his gear in. Me? I just powered down my internal weapons to "chill mode" and I went in as "non-lethal."

As we enter, I do the customary release of our own surveillance nano-tech into the air. The we saunter on in. It's just standard procedure. We ain't no preverts, just so you know!

PERVERTS. PROCEED.

Hmph.

So, sexy ass Miss, "I'd-have-HER-babies" Deeter comes to fetch us. Looking all delicious.

"Welcome…gentlemen. Come right this way. The Tidymans are waiting for you."

We follow her and just check out the site. All the while, my little friends I just shot out everywhere are gathering data. Temperature. Personnel on site and all their backgrounds. Building schematics. Internal surveillance. You name it. We collectin' it.

We get to the main office and there he is. God' best friend, Jake Tidyman. He was tall and wide like his promises to his flock. His dark-skin caught all the light in the room and threw it at us. Tidyman stared at us with intensity and a guttural knowledge of something. We'd seen that look before. On the battlefield and in some of The Trap's side streets on the wrong side of a drinking binge. We knew a wolf when we saw one.

"Welcome. Welcome to our headquarters. Where salvation is just a step away."

We both gave the nod and shook his hand. I could tell Kudzu instantly didn't like this dude.

Next to him was this gorgeous little dark-haired young lady. Not as voluptuous as Ms. Deeter but damn-sure close. Even with the church clothes she was wearing I could tell she was built right. It was like she was a whisper come to life. Meek and purposely invisible. But you can't hide looks like that. Even with her head slightly down, I could see her hazel eyes and honey-brown skin. A dark patch of skin; a birthmark peeked out from under her long left-hanging bang. She obviously wore it this way to cover her cheek where the dark patch lived.

Next to them was a relatively tall skinny bald man with accountant's glasses. He was in a beautifully tailored blue suit. He didn't give off a wolf's vibe but, he gave off…something. On Tidyman's desk was a picture of a beautiful woman with big natural hair. She had the same birthmark on her left cheek and she looked a lot like Hermann. We assumed it was Tidyman's wife, Hermann's twin sister. We quickly crossed-referenced that it was Allie Tidyman. Tidyman's wife who had died of Miskhin's Disease about five years ago.

"This is my daughter Betha Lee and my brother-in-law and Public Affairs manager Brother Hermann Stout. Please have a seat."

Tidyman's daughter and manager stand on either side of him. He posts up behind this giant mahogany desk. Real mahogany! We sit down hard and fast like we own the place.

Betha Lee just said one thing once she got a good look at us. She curiously looked at Kudzu's bionic left hand and says:

"Mr. Jones. Your hand. You don't wear any nano-skin to cover it?"

Kudzu answered: "A body is just a tool, Ms. Tidyman. That's all. This tool that is also my arm is just a part of me as any flesh and bone now. You can't hide who you are in this world. You have to be who you gonna be."

She smiled a shy smile and went to averting her eyes, then Kudzu got right down to it:

"Can we see the images? Need to verify their authenticity."

Betha Lee instantly turned red.

Her father gritted his teeth and squirmed in his seat a bit and beckoned to his manager.

"Hermann. If you please."

Hermann brought over a small vid-viewer and we checked out the images. We both looked at Betha Lee, analyzed her face, and then compared it to the incredibly flexible creature displayed in all of God's glory in the images. I, of course, have the nano-tech take many copies of the images and shoot them to me and Kudzu.

Everything matched up. Except one thing. The person in the pics didn't have the birthmark. Totally clean.

"So, what do you think?" Tidyman fidgeted in his giant throne as he wrung his hands a bit.

"I think you're right. Someone is up to no good." Kudzu looked over at Betha Lee and continued.

"I'm so sorry that you have to be put through this."

She seemed relieved but never made eye contact with us at all. Her cheeks had returned to their normal lovely shade of honey brown.

Hermann chimed in:

"How much is this going to cost, gentlemen?"

Kudzu sort of glanced at me and said:

"Well. Since this incident needs to stay quiet and all, we are going to ask for 2,000Jx a day plus expenses."

Hermann bristled up and said, "That's ridiculous! I can't believe you'd come here and waste our time with that figure."

Kudzu looked at him like he wasn't there.

"We are the best in The Trap. It won't take long. You have my word."

The Reverend stood up and clapped his hands once.

"Ok, then. Deal. I'll have faith in you, Mr. Jones." Then the wolf came out again.

"But if you disappoint me. Or if this ends up in any Trinity media packs, let's say...only God will be able to save you."

Kudzu just nodded.

Tidyman and Kudzu locked eyes and The Reverend asks:

"So, what now? How does this start?"

We got up and Kudzu says:

"Well. We have some special operatives in our network who are trained in this kind of thing. Top level."

"I see. Well, make sure these operatives keep this close."

We start to leave and Tidyman adds:

"God will never forget you for this. He's watching you and taking note."

Kudzu walks back. Heated.

"Listen, Rev . . . or whatever. I'm not doing this for God or country or anything high and mighty. I got rent. I don't do shit for no spirits or causes. Not no more."

"So, I take it you don't believe?"

"Oh. I believe alright. I believe that if your God let black folks in this country be slaves, destroy everything that makes us human, let white folks kill us and use us, have us fight in their wars, and still not get an honest shot at anything remotely like peace or Justice—I believe that god needs his ass beat."

Tidyman was shocked and you could tell that Kudzu touched a nerve.

"Oh my, brother. So much loss and hate in you. You need to come back so we can help you find your way."

Kudzu took a deep breath.

"I know my way. I also know your way and your sin. I can see it all around us while you hide under God's armpit. You think you a savior? Or a prophet? I've seen your sermons. You just as bad as any Hack dealer or pimp in The Trap. Except they slingin' dope and you slingin' hope. I'll tell you what's on the other side, Rev. My cousin's seen it. It's just cold and dark. Like the inside of nothing. Now, I'll be off. No need to show me out. Like I said. I know my way."

The three of them just stood there as we marched out. I was looking for Ms. Deeter on the way but she was up on the third floor at her desk. Too bad.

We beat it to the West End part of town to our next stop to see our Memento Mori; a small family-owned salvage and pawn shop run by our former unit-mate and her brother. Zip and Zeke Cooper. Zip is one the best hackers that ever lived. We can do low-level breaches but if it's a powerful big firewall or some such thing…we need an expert and that's where Zip came in.

Zip and Zeke made a business out of diving into the Mississippi River and finding remnants of the old world we lost.

They then sold the junk back to collectors for three to five times the price. Black folks always make a way, especially in The Trap and The Trap finds uses for things. Even the streets.

Zip greets us with open arms. "The crazy Jones Boys! How y'all been?"

Zip is short and stocky but, everything still hit in the right places. She's a cutie! I always thought so, and more than that, she was just a good woman through and through. Even in combat situations she always beamed out nothing but love. One of the sweetest folks you'd ever meet. I guess that's why I jumped on that booby trap that day in Nevada. I ain't really done too much in my life but make trouble. Zip was kindness personified. Even with this rag-tag business, she was trying to find ways to heal something or somebody.

"What y'all doing over here on the West End?"

Kudzu gets to it:

"We need you to hack into someplace for us. Someplace big and illegal."

Zip gave us a wry smile:

"Oh, shit. Doing dirt! Doing dirt! Where we goin', boys"?

Her brother Zeke steps in all covered with mud. He busts in with what looks like an old tricycle and an ironing board. One man's trash is another man's future trash.

"Yo, sis! Look what I got today!" Then he noticed us, "Kudzu? Junebug? Hey! What y'all doing here on the West End? It's been a whi . . . ah shit. What y'all into and more importantly . . . what y'all dragging my sister into?"

"Stop it, Zeke. I'm the big sib! Now. What you Jones Boys need?"

I lays it out:

"We need you to hack into the Federal DNA Repository to see if someone has gotten into a particular DNA sample and had their way with it."

Everyone born after 2025 has to send a DNA sample to the U.S. Government. It's the law. That sample is connected to an epigenetic nano-tag that is imprinted in each newborn. It monitors if DNA been tampered with or changed in some way.

The nano-tag beams information about everyone's DNA back to the Repository. If it's messed with, The Device Squad comes after your ass and you end up a zombie for ten years.

It's that simple. So, if Betha Lee's DNA had been cloned. The record would be here. You either get a hot sample off a body or get the digital sequence, and you can just make yourself a copy of whoever for whatever.

Zip cracks her knuckles and invites us back into her office. We stumble over all kinds of junk and shit on the way back. But, when we get to her space, it's as clean as a whistle. Not a speck of dirt. Anywhere! She sits down at this massive screen and gets to work. Eight minutes go by.

"Ok. We're in. Who's the person we looking for?"

I tell her:

"Betha Lee Tidyman."

"Like…Reverend Jake Tidyman? I watch him all the time!"

Kudzu just bristles.

"Just look her up, Zip. See what's what with her file."

Betha's file pops right up. Zip looks at the code with her juiced-up eye implants.

"Sooo. Wow. This looks really clean. But, it's too clean. Way too clean. There's a very sophisticated masking program on this. If you just glance at this it looks fine. But, damn. This DNA code is being accessed…a lot. Like, more than I've ever seen before."

Kudzu asks: "You find a trace of her sequence anywhere else in The Trap?"

Zip clicks around real fast. "Nah."

We found that mighty odd. It's crazy to clone somebody without their consent. It's even crazier to go through the trouble of cloning someone and then not putting them to work in The Trap.

Kudzu shows Zip a copy of The Roundabout pics of Betha's clone.

"Can you run a check on this too?"

"Sure," she says. "Anything else?"

"Yeah, doll," says Kudzu. "Can you hack and slash into The Roundabout's security feed and cross-reference the woman in these pics?"

"And then delete all traces of her, eh?"

"That's right, Zip." I'd appreciate that for sure.

"No problem." She looked at me, "Anything for the Jones Boys."

We thank Zip and Zeke and slide them 500Jx into their credit account for the store. Then we amble back to the office after hitting a bar or two on The West End.

Back at the office we went over the footage we picked up from the nano-tech we left at the church and we scan through the surveillance we picked up from The Roundabout. We just keep going over the footage and trying to figure what the hell was going on. Me and Kudzu went over tax documents, pay stubs, anything we could find. Anything that could give us a clue. The Tidymans actually lived at the church, which we found weird as hell even though it was big enough for ten families. But then we started checking out the employees. I focused a lot on Ms. Deeter.

After a few hours of this boring shit, we hit pay dirt once we went through the blueprints of all the houses of the employees that worked for Tidyman. Once we hit that dirt, we started digging harder!

We sat on the info and racked up our daily fees. Then we contacted the Rev via telecom. He was there behind his big desk. His dead wife displayed for all to see. His dutiful daughter and brother-in-law at either side.

Kudzu laid it out:

"So, we found out that Betha Lee's DNA has been hacked and accessed many, many times and we know who's been doing it. We'll beam you the address where to meet us, Reverend. Tell no one and bring your bookends with you."

Betha Lee ran out of the room. She was obviously shocked and upset. Like too shocked and upset. Our nano-tech said as much. Hermann just stood there like a statue.

Just as off as off could be.

Right after that, we shot the info over to Reverend Tidyman with the address.

About an hour later, Hermann did get **real** animated when he saw us waiting for the three of them at his house. He lived in a beautiful Victorian Styled house out in the Pocahontas area. The God-business paid well indeed.

"What's the meaning of this?" Hermann tried to act indignant. His vitals were spiking though. He knew he'd been caught. He looked like a fox with chicken feathers in his damn mouth.

REFERNECE UNKNOWN. I DO NOT UNDERSTAND...

Yeah. I know. It's a metaphor and you just a recorder.

PROCEED.

Cool. So, The Reverend and Betha Lee looked utterly confused. Can't blame them. Didn't make any sense to us at first either.

"Nice house, Hermann. Really nice. Nice basement too. Really well reinforced."

That's what tipped us off. The basement. You see, Mississippi houses don't really have basements because it is too tough on account of how loose the red dirt is. We always end up jacking houses up to keep from sinking. It's much worse now with all the constant rain. So, the question was: "why this junior shepherd have one?"

Betha Lee started in:

"Uncle Hermann…what…what do they mean?"

"Yeah, Uncle Hermann." Kudzu says: "What do they mean?"

"I- I don't know what's going on here."

The Reverend just glared at his brother-in-law and pretty much lifted him off the ground and slammed him up against the front door.

"Open the door, Hermann."

Hermann did as he was told, but you can tell he didn't want us near his place. Not. At. All. We go into this place and it feels more like a damn museum or a library. It's totally pristine. Wall to wall. It's spotless.

Kudzu says: "Nice place. Now take us downstairs."

Hermann wants to piss himself. Like, literally. His vitals told me so. Regardless, he does what he's told. He opens a door that actually has a genetically coded lock to another door with yet another bio-scan. If I had a heart, it would have been about to jump out of my chest. He opened the door and the smell almost knocked over The Rev, Betha Lee, and even big cuz.

"What the fuck is that stench?" We all looked around at The Reverend in shock!

We went down the stairs into what seemed like exactly what the Rev said.

It **was** hell.

Hermann turned on the lights and there were at least twenty or so holding pens. In those pens where some of the most horrific and pitiful things you ever wanted to see. There were mixed up bodies . . . clones of Betha Lee! They were in bad shape but they were all versions of her in different stages of growth…but some were mixed up with…with her mother! They were all patchworks of her, her mother, and Hermann! He was doing experiments with his dead twin's DNA, his nieces DNA, and his own!

The things groaned and screamed when they saw us. They were moving and squirming around and trying to break free of their cells. We just looked at them with shame, pity, and a deep, deep horror.

Hermann tried to explain in starts and stops. He was sweating like a dinner pig in August.

"It's not what . . . what it . . . l-looks like! I just missed her so much! And Betha looked so much like her. I just wanted to be a family! Close! Like a family! You have to understand! It's not evil. I-I'm not evil! I just wanted to be close. So close to them! To my sister! To you, Betha Lee!"

The Reverend was about to burst open with rage. Hermann kept on.

"Look! I fixed them! See? I fixed them! I took that awful Devil's mark from their beautiful faces! I fixed it!"

Sure enough. None of the clone-things had the birthmark that Betha Lee and her mother both had. But it didn't stop Reverend Tidyman from almost beating his brother-in-law to death.

We had to pull him off and it took us both to do it. I hadn't seen that kind of mad in a long damn time.

"You . . . you . . . you The Devil. Gottdamn you, Hermann!"

We were still in shock so it made sense that we didn't see Betha Lee go for Kudzu's Glock2020. She slipped it out of his holster in a flash. Then she shot her Uncle Hermann three times in the chest and arm. She emptied the clip and some of the bullets bust open a couple of those pens. The Betha-things in them finished was left of Uncle Hermann.

We got the gun away from Betha Lee and she melted into her daddy's arms and cried like a banshee. He soon joined in too. Hell. I think we all wanted to.

For an extra fee me and Kudzu helped the Reverend humanely deal with the mutated Betha-Hermann-Allie-clones. We made sure that everything was locked up tight like we said. Do dirt to cover up dirt. We made sure they didn't suffer anymore.

That's about it. You got everything right?

THE RENDITION IS INCOMPLETE. WHAT ABOUT THE ROUNDABOUT'S INVOLVEMENT?

Ah. Yeahhh! That!

So, when we had Zip look at those images that Edell took of the clone? Turns out that it wasn't a clone. It was Betha Lee the whole time, you see. She was using VeilTech to cover up her birthmark. I'm sure she thought that no church folks would ever be caught dead in a place like The Roundabout. We checked out the footage that we collected and found out that Little-Miss-Angel-Pants was sneaking in and out to shake her tail feather. She tried to mask the churches' surveillance footage. It was good enough to fool their "security" but not us. We got street camera footage of her doing her dirt too.

We should have known from the git go. Everyone knows that it's the preacher's kids that's the worst. All that righteousness piled up on them, suffocating them. No way she wasn't gonna do something with The Trap so close. Calling her. She wanted to dance and she wanted people to see, but she couldn't get away from the comfort of a cage. Poor thing.

Kudzu was right. The Reverend did have a sin. **Pride.** No way his own daughter would do something like that! **Move** like that. He never suspected it **at all** and he never would. His self-righteousness was the most blinding tech of all.

On top of that, we'd found out that Hermann suffered from an extreme case of **Psycho-Tactile Deficiency Disorder.** It's a brain-thing that popped up post COVID-19 era. Since folks couldn't touch each other for years until they found a vaccine, it made some people go crazy for the skin. Turns out that not touching? Well, that's not good for the human psyche. Go figure.

As for Betha? Well, Kudzu is hooking her up with better military-grade VeilTech so she can keep dancing. She loves it! This upgrade will change her whole face and cover her tracks. So, no more getting recognized by slumming church folks. Kudzu's such a good dude.

He's only charging her twenty percent of her tips to keep it from her dad.

It's a Trap kinda freedom but, you gotta be who you gonna be.

END RECORDING…

COMFORT
BY
KYOKO M

He woke up to a bright light.

His brown eyes popped open, but he realized he wasn't really seeing anything yet. He just felt an immense wave of panic rushing over him, unsure if it was irrational or not. A short cry escaped his lips as he lurched upward, his limbs flying out to catch his weight as he pitched to one side. Information registered one tidbit at a time. He'd been lying on a plain mattress. The floor was carpeted. His chest, knees, neck, and skull throbbed with pain. He didn't have full mobility, as there was an enormous, thick blue cord running from the back of his neck into a socket in the adjacent wall. He could see his brown artificial flesh torn in the spots that hurt the most, exposing the wiring beneath. But there was one other pressing thing he noticed.

There was a black girl with shoulder-length box braids and colored beads at the ends standing there with a penlight in her hand. She was startled, but not afraid.

"Hey," she said softly as he staggered, light-headed, blinking over and over in an attempt to clear his mind. "Hey, it's alright. You're safe now. You're safe."

"W-What happened?" he slurred, planting one hand against the nearest wall, straining to remember. "Where am I? Who are you?"

"Shh, it's okay," she said, walking towards him. "I'll answer all your questions, but I need you to lie down again. You're still in bad shape."

"No," he said, narrowing his eyes at her. "Answer me. Now."

"My name is Akachi. You're in downtown Neo Atlanta. This is my apartment. I found you in the dumpster behind the alley of my repair shop about twelve hours ago. Someone worked you over something fierce. Your legs had severe damage as well as your chassis and your skull."

"Is that…why I can't remember anything?" he asked.

"Yes. They wiped your CPU completely."

"All of it?"

She sighed, nodding. "I'm sorry. There wasn't anything to retrieve when I started your diagnostic."

His knees wobbled. She caught him under the arm as he fell to one side. She was stronger than she looked. He knew his metal skeleton hadn't been easy to carry to wherever they were. Exhausted from the revelation, he let her drag him back over to the bed.

"I've been doing my best to repair your neural pathways," she continued. "I think that's what woke you up. Do you remember your name?"

"Andrew," he mumbled. "Andrew Emerson."

"Good. That's what your serial number says. What is your current primary objective?"

He closed his eyes and focused on the blue letters that flashed across the back of his artificial eyelids. "Survival."

She gave a start. "Wow. I've never heard that before."

He risked a glance at her. "What's so odd about that?"

She fidgeted. "W-Well, you are a, um, you know."

For the first time since he woke up, he almost felt amusement. "A what?"

She cleared her throat. "A comfort bot. I thought their objective was typically to locate a new client."

"Well, you said someone beat me up pretty good," he answered, hiding a smile at her modesty. "Androids revert to survival mode when threatened, regardless of their intent. My parameters would have to be reset to match the original objective."

He glanced at the tablet lying on the nightstand nearby. "Is that what you were working on when I woke up?"

She blinked at him. "Absolutely not. I have no intention of changing you whatsoever."

He peered up at her. "Why?"

"I have no right to do that."

He relaxed slightly on the bed. "You're an android sympathizer?"

She lifted both eyebrows. "I pulled you out of a dumpster and put you back together. I thought that was sort of obvious."

He smiled. "Point taken. Do you mind if I have a look in the meantime?"

"Not at all." She helped him sit up against several firm pillows and handed him the tablet. He scanned the working processes in his head. He was currently operating at about seventy percent of his full capacity. The damage in his knees and the left side of his chest were the worst ailments. From a brief physical analysis, he could see the laceration in his ribs. The synthetic blood had dried hours ago. He wore a pair of black suit pants and he could still feel boxer-briefs beneath them. She hadn't taken advantage of him, at least.

"Did you do all the repair work yourself?" he asked, handing her back the tablet.

"Mostly, yes."

"You're a mechanic, then?"

"Yeah. I fix cars, but I'm working on my masters in robotics, so I knew the basic work to be done to get you up and running again."

He winced. "I, uh, don't have any money at the moment to pay you back for the time and materials you've put into me."

She held up her hand. “I wouldn’t accept it even if you did. You were in trouble. What kind of person would just leave you to die like a piece of garbage?”

“A lot of people, actually,” he said, and couldn’t keep the bitterness from dripping across his tone. “I don’t know if you’ve checked my trust settings, but they aren’t exactly that high. That being said…”

He reached out and closed his hand over hers briefly. “Thank you for saving my life, Akachi. Even if you don’t want to accept anything, I’ll find a way to repay your kindness.”

She rolled her eyes. “Maybe I will readjust your chivalry settings.”

He grinned. “Don’t you dare.”

She motioned towards the bed. “Get some rest. I have to resupply to work on your knees and chest. I won’t be long.”

She stood and pocketed her keys before leaving the apartment. He settled down against the small nest of pillows and surveyed the apartment. It was a low-budget version of a studio apartment, with the kitchen straight ahead, a table to eat at on the left, and the entertainment area across from the bed. There was a five-level bookshelf next to a flat screen television. The nightstand sat to the immediate left of the bed. He tilted his head enough to see a doorway on the right that led to her bathroom.

His sensors had estimated Akachi’s age to be late twenties, but she looked much younger. She was tall and had an athletic build, which likely came in handy if she truly was a mechanic. She’d been wearing work coveralls, and they were smudged with oil and dirt, which led him to believe the story she’d told him so far. There was a box of tools sitting by the foot of the bed and the wires recharging his artificial brain were brand new.

She’d also gone out of her way to help him. Sympathizer or not, he wanted to know why. Humans and androids had a caustic relationship—either they were too dependent or they were prejudiced. For now, he’d take her at her word, but he’d keep an eye out to see if she had an ulterior motive.

He stood and limped over to the tiny window beside the table. Tightly packed, identical apartments greeted his gaze. It wasn't the ghetto, but it also wasn't anything fancy. They were on the second floor.

After a bit, he shuffled over to the bed and checked the action logs on his CPU. True to her word, Akachi hadn't altered anything about him. He'd lost his memories, but the basic parts of his functions all remained the same. All the work she'd done so far was related to repairing disconnected internal programs or rerouting his core to get different parts of him to work smoothly. Maybe she was just a good Samaritan.

Or she knew how to cover her tracks.

Akachi returned ten minutes later with a crate of new materials. She worked on his chest first, repairing and resetting the frayed wiring and sealing the wound shut with a thin adhesive that would eventually regrow the skin using nanites.

His knees, however, were in much worse shape. She'd been removing the shattered shrapnel from his patella one piece at a time, so only the core remained as it hadn't been destroyed. She'd have to replace the outer part entirely so he wouldn't be limping anymore. She had steady hands and an amazing amount of patience.

"Mind if I ask you something?" Andrew said.

"Not at all."

"Why do you live in such a shitty apartment when you're this good a mechanic?"

She laughed, but her hands still didn't shake from where they were slowly re-twining wires just above his knee. "It lets me save for my courses and build a nest egg for the future. Plus, this neighborhood looks rough but it's actually not that bad. I'll worry about nicer digs once I'm working in the robotics field. My shop's also only two blocks away, so I don't have to buy a car until I need one."

"Did you carry me up here yourself?"

"No, I had a coworker help. We found you last night after inventory."

He glanced around at the studio apartment again. "Just you, huh? No boyfriend?"

"Not at the moment, no."

"Why?"

She pursed her lips, deadpanning, "Because I am a strong, independent woman who don't need no man."

Andrew laughed. It surprised him that he even could, considering the circumstances. "Oh, right. My mistake."

"Anyway, why do you ask?"

"Just making sure some huge guy isn't going to see the shirtless man in your bed and come to the wrong conclusion."

"You're safe on that front, trust me." She fell silent for a bit as she worked.

"Can I ask you something?" she said after a while.

"Of course."

"Will you try to find out who did this to you?"

Andrew shrugged. "Dunno. Maybe it's better if I leave it be."

She nibbled her bottom lip. "What do you think happened?"

"I might've seen something I wasn't supposed to. That happens a lot to droids, especially comfort bots. It might also have been that someone was using me and their significant other found out and wanted to make a point."

She shook her head slightly. "People suck."

"Mostly," he said, and softly enough that she glanced at him before looking away shyly.

After a couple of hours, both knees were replaced and sealed shut. "Alright, fella, let's see if you can get your bearings."

She unplugged him and offered a hand. He accepted it and stood. She stepped back, blinking curiously up at him. He arched an eyebrow and she explained.

"You're taller than I thought."

Andrew smiled. "Ah."

He walked around the small apartment a few times while she watched, making sure everything had been tightened and set properly. "I think you're good to go."

"Seems about right." He paused, eyeing her. "Will you freak out if I hug you?"

She smiled. "I think I can handle it."

He wrapped his arms around her, his mouth close to her ear. "Thank you."

"You're welcome."

She let go and tucked a stray braid behind her ear. "I'll run across the way and get you some new threads. Then we can figure out the other details."

"If you keep being this nice to me, I'll never leave."

She waggled her eyebrows. "I've heard worse ideas. Be right back."

When she returned, she found him in the kitchen making brunch: scrambled eggs with cheese, toast, and a piping hot mug of coffee. She set the bag of clothes on the counter. "You didn't have to do this."

He shrugged. "It makes me feel less guilty. Here, tell me if this needs salt."

He held the spatula out to her with a chunk of egg on it and she took a bite. "Nope. Perfect as is."

"Sounds familiar," he teased and she rolled her eyes.

"I got you a few different outfits, since I didn't know what you'd like. It should get you through for a while. The hard part is next: what exactly do you want to do now that you're fixed? Do you want to, uh, resume your primary objective?"

He watched her for a bit, still amused that she was tip-toeing around his profession. "I don't know. Without a memory, it's hard to say whether I had any resentment for it. I may get some of it back in fragments, but for now, no. I don't think I'll be doing that."

"Okay," she said. "What would you want to do for a living?"

He blinked. "I…don't think anyone's ever asked me that before."

"Well, you must like something," she said, sipping the coffee as he spooned the eggs onto a plate beside the toast. "Maybe that's what you should do for the next couple days. Read up and see what kind of preferences you have."

"What? You don't want me to work for you?"

"Oh," she said, apparently startled. "Um, I didn't know if you'd…want to do something like that."

"Something like what? What's wrong with being a mechanic?"

"Nothing," she said, but he noticed she wouldn't meet his gaze this time. "I just thought you would maybe think it was kind of beneath you or something."

"Seriously?" he asked, incredulous. "You saved my life with what you do. I have no room to look down on your profession considering I probably spent my entire life just screwing people left and right for money. Has someone said that to you before?"

"It's not important," she said, taking the plate to the table. "I'd be fine if you want to work the front counter until you're on your feet again, metaphorically speaking."

"I'd like that, as long as it's no further imposition to you."

"Do what you want. That's what choice is all about, right?"

"So they tell me." He pointed towards the bag. "I'll change and then we can get going."

He emerged from the shower about fifteen minutes later, clean and smelling nice, his hair slightly damp. He'd changed into a simple black polo shirt, jeans, and boots. She'd even been thoughtful enough to get him a small vial of generic cologne. He had to hide another smile after he caught her looking at him, trying to be subtle about it. If nothing else, the girl provided plenty of unintentional entertainment.

They walked the two blocks to her shop. It was a modest place that had a storefront on one side and then opened up in the back. There was a Hispanic girl in coveralls that matched Akachi's at the front counter, typing something. Her brown eyes widened a bit when Andrew appeared, but the look wasn't unfriendly, to his relief.

"Hey," the girl said to Akachi. "Who's your friend?"

"This is Andrew," Akachi said. "The one I mentioned last night."

"Oh, my," the girl said, offering her hand. "Thank God you're alright. She told me what happened."

"Thanks. I'm only alright because of her. Nice to meet you, Miss…?"

"Ana Mendes."

"Nice to meet you, Ana."

"He's going to work the front counter until he figures things out," Akachi said. "I'll put my stuff back and then get started showing him around."

"Roger that."

He quickly found that the job was never dull. The hover cars and jets needed careful maintenance and a myriad of different tools to fix them. She sent him to the hardware store to replace the things she'd used to fix him and then spent the rest of the shift explaining the areas he'd be able to help with when he wasn't simply serving as cashier. Heavy lifting was the most valuable skill, as there were only four mechanics in the small store aside from Akachi and Ana. He also met Matt, the coworker who had helped Akachi transport him to her apartment after she'd found him in the dumpster. Everyone he'd met so far had been friendly and gracious. He had a strange sense that his previous life hadn't gone this well, that there were people he'd met that had been arrogant and condescending to him.

He helped them close up shop at the end of the night and waited for her to come back from depositing money in the safe.

"So, I guess you don't have enough from today's shift for a hotel room?" Akachi asked.

"Doubtful, even on this side of town," he replied. "Why?"

She pursed her lips. "You know what I'm getting at."

He grinned. "I just wanted to hear you say it."

She rolled her eyes. "Vanity, thy name is Andrew."

"Well, I mean, if you don't want me to stay, I can just fold myself up in a corner in the store until morning."

"Ugh, fine. You can stay at my place until we find you one of your own."

"Why, thank you. You're so generous. How can I ever repay you?"

"By not being such a smarmy pain-in-the-ass," she grumbled. "Take out the trash and we'll get going."

Andrew lugged the trash bags around back. There was a narrow alleyway between the buildings where the dumpsters were and it was Akachi's least favorite thing to do, and that was before the rainstorm pounding down on the city, so he did it for her.

He'd just tossed it in when he noticed he wasn't alone.

There was a guy standing with his back to the open part of the alley. Average height, dark slick hair, trench coat and a navy suit, black shoes, no umbrella in spite of the heavy rain. He didn't really look like he belonged there. He definitely wasn't a bum and Andrew hadn't seen him in any of the other stores as an employee.

"Can I help you?" Andrew asked warily.

"You're Cherry's boy-toy, ain't ya?"

Andrew adopted a neutral look. "I don't know anyone by that name. Sorry."

"Makes sense," the guy said. "Last I heard, they dumped you. Guess this is where you ended up. Weird, though. Usually, people scrap droids if they find 'em. Shop owner must have a soft heart."

The man grinned. "Or a wet pussy."

"Look," Andrew snapped. "What do you want? I haven't got all damn night."

"I knew your owner. She's moved on, but I got a few clients who would fancy ya. What do you say you come with me and resume your previous line of work?"

Andrew balled his hands into fists. "I like where I am. I think I'll stay."

"You don't belong here, boy. I got bigger plans for you. Now am I going to have to tune you up or are you going to listen to reason?"

"I don't care who are you are. I'm not going."

The man shrugged. "Have it your way, Tin Man. I can still take you back in pieces."

He withdrew a shock baton and lunged at Andrew. Andrew dodged. The man lashed at him in quick movements, and blue sparks popped in the rain mere inches from his torso. He kept backing up, knowing that he couldn't attack thanks to the robotic laws known as the Asimov protocols hardwired into his system. The guy was blocking his way out and Andrew was running out of room to retreat. He couldn't go back into the shop and risk Akachi's safety.

"Nowhere left to go, Tin Man," the guy chuckled darkly. "Say goodnight."

"You first," a cold female voice spoke from the darkened doorway of the shop.

They both glanced up to see Akachi standing there with a .38 Smith and Wesson in her hand.

She stepped out into the rain and didn't even flinch as it doused her in seconds. "Drop it."

The guy spat at her feet. "You ain't got the nerve, little—"

She shot at the concrete an inch from his foot. The bullet ricocheted into the wall beside him and he jumped out of his skin.

"Drop. It."

The man sneered, but let the shock baton go and it fizzled out as soon as it left his hand. "So now you've got a new madam, huh? She fight all your battles for you?"

"Get out of here."

"Fine. I'm a patient man. She won't always be here to protect you, Tin Man."

He shuffled off into the cool, wet darkness. She didn't lower the gun until he was out of sight. Then a great sigh flowed through her. "Are you alright?"

Andrew nodded numbly. "C'mon, we'd better get inside."

They walked inside the garage and she shut and locked the outer door, resting the gun on one of the nearby work benches.

"Can't leave you alone for two seconds," she mused, squeezing as much rain out of her braids as possible and then wiping her face with a clean towel from the supply room. She tossed him one as well and they dried off as best as they could. Her expression sobered at his silence. "Any chance you knew who he was?"

Andrew shook his head. "All he said was he knew my previous owner and he wanted me. Doesn't sound like he's as interested in my sparkling personality as you are."

He glanced at the garage door, listening to the rain pound against the other side. "That's the end of the line."

"Once the rain lets up, we can file a police report for the attack and—"

"I appreciate the thought, but you and I both know it's not going to work."

She frowned. "Why not?"

"I'm an android, Akachi. Technically speaking, I don't have any rights."

"Look, the guy threatened me as much as he threatened you. Behavior like that can't go unanswered."

"And it won't. I'll just have to…" He sighed. "I'll have to go."

"What?" she demanded.

"I can't guarantee he won't come back looking for revenge," Andrew said. "You shouldn't have to put yourself in harm's way on my behalf, not when you've already done so much to help me. It wouldn't be all that hard for me to disappear."

"Andrew, there has got to be a better way," Akachi said fiercely. "You can't let him take away your future."

"I wouldn't have a future at all if you hadn't saved me."

She fell silent, stunned by the frankness of his words. He stepped a little closer, holding her hand, his voice quiet but steady. "I told you I wanted to repay you. A life for a life. A man like that is going to come back with reinforcements. He'll burn this place to the ground and you along with it. I can't let that happen."

Akachi swallowed hard, staring at their clasped hands. She squared her shoulders and met his gaze. "And what about the next person after him? What if you run and you just find another bastard looking to exploit you? Will you just keep going? Where does that path end, Andrew?"

"I don't have a choice—"

"Yes, you do. You let me disable the Asimov protocols and you put the fear of God into that little weasel."

Andrew stiffened. "Akachi, that's illegal."

"So is threatening someone's life and attacking them with a shock baton."

"If the authorities find out you tampered with my protocols, that's ten years in federal prison."

Akachi smiled. "Then don't get caught, lover boy."

He gritted his teeth. "Are you always this stubborn?"

"Why else do you think I'm single?"

He caught her shoulders. "I'm being serious. It's not worth your life."

"Maybe, maybe not," she said softly. "But it is worth your life."

He searched her gaze for a long moment and then sighed again, leaning his forehead against hers. "You're going to give me an ulcer, woman."

"Sometimes I have that effect."

"No shit." He straightened up a bit. "If we go through with this, then I want your word that if everything goes south, you pack up and leave town. I don't care where you go. You run and you don't look back. Promise me."

Akachi nodded. "I promise."

He kissed her forehead. "Then let's get to work."

* * *

"Well, well, well," the thin man said, chewing on the end of a fat cigar as he watched Andrew stroll into the office. "The Tin Man came to his senses."

He nodded to the burly man on his right. "Search 'im, Russell."

"Spread 'em, pretty boy," the large man grunted.

Andrew stretched out his arms and legs. Russell patted him down, finding no weapons. "He's clean."

He shoved Andrew towards the desk, on which the android spotted a name plate reading *The Comfort Company*, and beneath it, *Carmine Fiacci, President*. Carmine had his legs up on the desk, his cheap suit spread open to show the shock baton holstered at his waist.

"I apologize for my earlier rudeness," Carmine said with a toothy grin. "But I know a good droid when I see one. I'm guessing that you don't remember our association."

"Fortunately, I don't," Andrew answered, crossing his arms. "Feel free to enlighten me."

Carmine spat out a smoke ring before continuing. "Your former owner, Cherry, well, she was one of those gals who was in a loveless marriage. She bought you at an auction to keep her bed warm while her husband was out in the streets. Turns out hubby was the jealous type and he's not a fan of the, uh, mixed laundry, I'll say. When he found out she had a literal side piece, he went a bit overboard on correcting the perceived injustice. That's how you ended up disassembled and poor little Cherry ended up in the ICU."

Andrew's eyes narrowed. "He got a name, this jealous husband?"

"Shawn Walters. We went to the same high school, kept it touch. Lives in New Brookhaven. Nice man when he doesn't lose his temper."

Andrew snorted. "Sure he is."

"Well, that's all in the past, Andy," Carmine said. "We're going to have you work the Alpharetta district. Plenty of high rollers that like the dark chocolate. You agree to work for us and we leave your cutie pie mechanic alone. Sound good?"

Andrew rubbed his chin. "You know, normally, it would."

Carmine narrowed his eyes. "Normally?"

"Yeah. I mean, I am an android. I was designed by people to be a perfect imitation of life but without all those pesky notions of choice. I was designed to be a tool, to be used again and again without wearing out. To bring 'comfort' to those in need."

Andrew flattened his hands-on Carmine's desk and leaned in, smirking. "And let's just say that I found someone who needs me more than you do."

Carmine sneered. "Think about what you're doing, boy. It ain't gonna end well."

Andrew nodded. "You're right. It's not gonna end well."

His smirk sharpened. "For you."

Andrew lifted one fist and smashed Carmine's right kneecap with it.

Carmine howled in pain and tumbled backwards onto the floor. Andrew whirled around in time for Russell to grab him and slam him down onto the desk. He dodged to one side as the big man's fist slammed down on it hard enough to leave a dent in the metal. Russell reached for the laser pistol in his jacket, but Andrew grabbed his wrist, pointing it out at the far wall. Russell's wrist crunched under Andrew's powerful grip and he let out a roar of pain, dropping the pistol onto the floor. He gripped Andrew's neck with his free hand and slammed his head into the desk repeatedly.

The pain nearly blinded him, but Andrew ignored it and flattened his hand against the big man's chest, blindly searching for his rib cage.

And once he found it, he delivered one precise punch that shattered Russell's ribs and caused them to impale his heart.

The big man died instantly, slumping to the floor in a heap.

Andrew only had a second to recover; Carmine popped up from behind his desk with the shock baton, jabbing it at his torso. "Hold still, you son of a bitch!"

Andrew launched himself back in a roll and came up on one knee, blocking with his forearms as the baton sliced through the air in an arc. The volts shocked his system as soon as it touched him, sending excruciating pain through every circuit, every artificial nerve, searing him clean down to his metal skeleton. It didn't matter how artificial his intelligence and framework; pain was pain and it was as real as anything else.

Andrew crumpled onto his knees, shaking his head as his vision glitched, struggling to correct itself. Carmine limped from on top of the desk and held the weapon aloft, panting, his gravelly voice sinister. "You think you can just waltz in here and shut me down, Tin Man? Just 'cause your little girlfriend can override some code? Fine. I'll reprogram you to kill her instead."

Carmine swung again.

Andrew ducked at the last second. Too late, Carmine realized he'd swung with all his might and he hit himself in the shin. He shrieked as the volts tore through him and fried him instantly. His twitching corpse hit the carpet beside Russell's.

Slowly, Andrew pushed to his feet. He collected the baton from Carmine's limp grip and then walked out of the office.

Akachi stood outside in the empty parking lot, holding a bottle of Vodka. She offered it to him. He thanked her and took a long pull for the pain before handing it back to her. She stuck a rolled-up handkerchief into the bottle and then lit it once the alcohol soaked through. Then she hefted it and threw it inside the office's open door. It didn't take long before the lone building went up in flames, destroying the evidence.

Akachi glanced at the shock baton, lifting an eyebrow. "A souvenir?"

"No," Andrew said. "Just need it for one last loose end in New Brookhaven."

He stood beside her, watching the building burn. "Think we'll be alright?"

Akachi held his hand, her smile bright in the firelight. "We'll survive."

LAILAI BY BALOGUN OJETADE

Dun stood under the overhang of a plasteel porch in front of a low-end bodega. Sheets of rain smothered the city of At-lagos. Dun loved the smell but hated getting wet—it always made his elbow stick. Baba—his daddy—always said he'd buy the boy a new turbine, but with a new battery alone running two-hundred creds, he had a better chance of becoming a crash player and he was only one hundred-seventy centimeters tall and nine-and-a-half stone. Baba also always told him he'd hit a growth spurt and wind up as tall as Baba or taller, but he was thirteen and no growth spurt yet. Dun was starting to think Baba was just trying to make him feel better about his size. He'd ask Iya after dinner; she'd tell him the truth. She didn't much care about feelings and mushy stuff. That was Baba.

Although he wasn't tall or big, he was wiry and strong and his cybernetic arm, though it had seen better days, made him even stronger. He gained his strength by carrying off the parts of the ruined crash-bots from the court and returning them to the bays at Chike Industries, where they would be made ready for the next week's game. Many would consider that demeaning work for the only child of two former crash legends, but "legendary status don't pay the bills," as Iya would say, so demeaning work it was. Besides, he liked it—the work was easy, it put money in his pocket, and since all the human players respected his parents, he had gotten to know them pretty well and had even enjoyed cookouts and watching fights on the M-Screen at the houses of a few. He also had a thing for robots—not 'droids, with their attempts to fit in with humans, no—*crash-bots*, who had just as powerful an AI as 'droids but kept it real. No fake 'fros or silicon muscles, breasts, or booties for them—just 140 stones of steel and wiring on a towering 274-centimeter-tall frame; built to break the line for the Forward to slam the ball. He was seriously considering becoming a 'bot-doc. Only problem was, he hated school. Not only did Dun have to work; he had his normal studies with his tutor, Hesabu, and grueling martial training with Master Kupweteka which he preferred greatly to learning calculus and bioscience and surfing the lace. Well, surfing the lace was okay; at least he could sneak in a game on Dash or watch a flick on the Ebony Ooh Wee site.

He was bored watching the rainwater pour off the overhang and fill the potholes in the street in front of him, forming pools of dirty water. The heavy rains this season had added to the already bad conditions on the river. Barge traffic was at a standstill with some lower end docks completely under water. Looking up at the cloudy sky, Dun prayed to see a thinning in the clouds that would signal the rain might soon stop.

His prayers were answered; a sliver of sunlight carved through the sunlight like a monofilament sword. His suede hoodie and jeggings were already soaked; thank the gods he decided to wear his waterproof Danner boots or walking home would be hell. He stepped off the porch of the bodega into what was now just a steady drizzle. He slipped the chew bar he bought at the bodega into his hoodie's pocket and looked around at the storefronts, determined to find something of interest to buy. Walking northward up the street his boots made sloshing sounds as he walked through the puddles of water.

Plasteel buildings with stoops and porches leading into each place of business lined both sides of the street. A few people still stood under the porches as he had done earlier, but mostly the streets became deserted as people returned indoors tired of the rain. The northerly direction he was heading would bring him to merchants selling stun pistols, zap gloves and other "self-defense" weapons civilians were allowed to carry. Vendors of clothes, jewelry, weed and one-wheels were open for business. Walking up the street, he still could not decide on what he wanted to buy, his only thought was to spend some of his hard-earned creds on something—it didn't really matter what. With his mind so preoccupied, he did not see the three boys coming from an alley to his right until it was too late. Cursing himself for not paying more attention, he watched as the boys around his age stood wide-legged, impeding his progress and forcing him to stop abruptly or run into them.

He knew all three of the boys and he knew this would invariably lead to trouble. Lining up shoulder-to-shoulder with their arms folded across their chests, the boys smirked at him, with their chins tilted slightly upward. Dun defiantly stood his ground in front of them. Unlike him, they were dressed in matching blue sharkskin suits and highly polished brown Chelsea boots. Boujie Boys—at least that's what everybody called the gang of wannabe thugs with parents that were senators and dentists and restaurateurs.

"Where are you vampin' off to, mugu?" the biggest boy asked Dun.

"Off to see your mama for the afternoon while your daddy's droppin' fries at his greasy spoon," Dun snapped.

Abdus-Salma—son of Karenga Jabba, owner of Atlagos Bagels, a popular fast-food espresso and bagel chain—sneered, his light brown face turning red. He held his large fists clenched tightly at his side while his two sycophants, Ojiji and Bruce, stood at his side glaring with murder-filled eyes.

When the wild punch he expected finally came, Dun stepped forward with his left elbow held high and slammed it into the crook of Abdus-Salma's right arm, stopping the punch. He quickly followed with a rising right elbow that smashed Abdus-Salma's nose to a pulp. Blood poured from Abdus-Salma's nostrils as he staggered backward screaming in pain and rage.

All three of the Boujie Boys surged forward and pounced on Dun, punching and kicking him until he was face down in the pavement. He lost track of how long the three older boys beat him. Finally, they tired of it and stormed off, leaving Dun in the street battered and in agony. Lightning flashed across the cloudy sky followed by a powerful clap of thunder shattering the silence. Following the lightning, the floodgates opened in the sky, and a powerful deluge drenched him unrelentingly pounding him farther into the road.

"Boy, are you hurt bad? Let me try to help you up, omo. Can you stand?" The kindly voice seemed to come from a great distance. Unable to talk, Dun rolled over wincing in pain as he tried to clear his rattled brain and bring cool air into his lungs. Gradually, he began to distinguish the kindly face of an old woman and a beat-up old crash bot looking down at him. Dun felt drawn to the bot's blinking LED "eye," there was something hidden there, something… human? Wincing, he tried to stand, but could not do so on his own. Quickly coming to his aid, the kindly old woman gently helped him to his feet.

"Thank you, who are you?" Dun whispered through clenched teeth trying not to pass out from the pain.

"Just an old woman and an old 'bot passing by at the right time to help you," she replied. "Those thugs gave you a gbosa but looks like you can take a punch. Come on, I got some herbs and salves at my crib that'll help you so you can be on your way as quickly as possible."

Dun nodded. The robot grabbed him with both big steel hands and placed Dun on its broad left shoulder. It then picked up the old woman and sat her on its right shoulder.

The crash-bot took off at a sprint. Its wheels extended from the bottoms of its feet and the robot sped up the street.

Then a thought crept through his pain filled brain: *why aren't I worried*? He had just been beaten half to death, now he found himself sitting on a strange crash-bot's shoulder, going to who knows where and he was not the least bit concerned about it. He winced in pain when the crash-bot hit a pothole in the road.

"You aight over there, omo?" the old woman asked. "I know all these bumps and holes in the road gotta be uncomfortable, but rest assured we're almost there." Dun did not have the energy to respond so he stared up at the clearing sky waiting for this punishment to stop and finally it did when the crash-bot abruptly halted.

Feeling the crash-bot shift to one side, Dun waited for the old woman to climb down from the robot's other shoulder and come around to his side. Gingerly and with great care, she helped Dun ease himself down to the ground. He collapsed at the old woman's feet. Standing on shaky legs, he took a moment, waiting for the pain to subside some and his head to stop spinning. He hoped all the while that he would not pass out. Resting his hand on the 'bot's side, he took a moment to look at his surroundings and found the old woman's house: nothing more than a shack made from riveted together sheets of tin, with a lean-to on one side that was obviously a bay for the crash-bot. Looking to his right, Dun could see the Chattahoochee River between some houses and warehouses across the road. It seemed he was in the northern most part of the town. The funny thing was he could not remember ever seeing this place and he had roamed both the east and west side of town, across the Chattahoochee River, all his life.

With no choice in the matter, he let the old woman lead him across the small yard to the front door of the tin shack and inside to a well-lit room. The room was bare but clean with a welcoming light blue feather down mattress and a feather down pillow to match. With some effort on the old woman's part, she managed to help Dun into bed, wet clothes and all, then quickly covered him with a blanket to keep the chill from him. The last thing he heard before falling asleep was the old woman telling him she would be right back; that she had to run a diagnostic on the crash-bot.

His dreams were fitful at first, with Dun and the old woman's crash-bot fighting valiantly side-by-side against vile creatures attacking them from every direction. Dun carried an elctro-filament sword that glowed white with crackling electricity, like the one carried by Master Kupweteka. With the sword, Dun easily killed the grotesque creatures, cutting them to pieces as he hacked and slashed. When the crash-bot struck with its spiked fists, the creatures imploded, leaving broken remnants of what they once were.

Quickly shifting, his dream went from them surrounded by hideous creatures, fighting in a desolate war-torn valley, to serenely walking across rolling hills covered in flowers and trees the likes he had never seen. The abundance of color from every color spectrum imaginable threatened to overwhelm his senses. Reaching the crest of a small hill, a flock of strange but beautiful birds with coloring to match the flowers and the trees flew out of the vegetation around them, startling them. Stopping for a moment, Dun looked about him, noticing the light was different here; it was pure, without glare from the sun. Searching the blue sky, he saw only a few puffy white clouds drifting off into the distance; he could not see any evidence of a sun. Glancing down at the bottom of the hill, he spotted a beautiful stream meandering its way between the hills and slowly drifting off into the distance.

Walking with the crash-bot down the hill toward the sparkling stream, he heard the pleasant sound of water gurgling over the rocks, which drew his attention to the other sounds around him: birds in the distance chattering back and forth in a small stand of strange looking trees between two hills; the leaves of the trees rustling in wind that gently blew across the hills.

"It is beautiful here, eh?"

Startled, Dun turned quickly to look behind him with his hand on his sword. A man and a woman stood before him. They, like everything else in this beautiful land, gave an impression of perfectness in every way—they were tall, with skin as black as their perfectly round afros. They seemed to convey no ill intensions toward Dun, so he removed his hand from the hilt of his sword.

"Yes, it is beautiful here," Dun replied. But where is 'here'?"

The crash-bot and the couple followed him to the stream. Dun turned back toward the two people and got a better look at them. Both were beautiful beyond compare and dressed in powder blue linen tunics and trousers.

"At this moment, you're in your dream," the man said with a booming baritone voice. "And we're your ancestors, but it is not yet your time to join us."

"In this dream, you're grown and have become a great warrior; your destiny," the woman said, her voice nearly as deep as the man's, but musical. But you are truly just a boy sleeping and healing."

"Why am I here then if it's not my time yet?" Dun's voice shook slightly—he was a little unnerved at having such a vivid dream.

"To talk to us, of course," the woman said. She laughed delightfully.

"No need to be afraid, Dun," the man said. "You can rest assured you're safe with us and when you wake from this short rest, you'll be healed from your injuries. Please heed what we tell you, because our time is growing short. When you wake from this dream, the old woman will not be there to greet you because she is no longer of your world. The last task in her long fight against time was to find you and bring you to us. Her crash-bot has one last task in its long battle against time, too. It needs your loving care and you need the love it has to give you in return."

"Dun, it's what you have to do," the woman added. "Give the crash-bot all your love and, in return, it will give you a gift that will help you save Atlagos from time."

"How am I being healed?" Dun asked curiously. "How can a crash-bot show love?"

"The old woman injected you with an ancient but useful medicine that renders you asleep while it heals," the woman replied. "It also allows us to have this short discourse. When you awake, you'll be completely healed."

"It's time, Dun," the man chimed in, staring skyward. "Remember to take the crash-bot and love it. Care for it until its time in your world is complete. Oh, and Dun, it would probably be very wise of you not to tell anyone about this dream."

The couple smiled at Dun. The woman waved at him with her fingers.

"Wait," Dun shouted. "How can a crash-bot show love?"

The couple vanished in a flash of white light.

Dun was thrusted him from his dream and awoke in shock. He stared at the dented ceiling of the shack in disbelief.

Lying still for a moment, he tried to gather his thoughts, desperately trying to understand a dream so vivid, so real that he could remember all of it in perfect detail. He was frightened more than he wanted to admit. He tossed the blanket off him, then he threw his legs over the side of the bed and stood. He felt wonderful, no pain. He would have to check his face in a mirror to be sure, but he could not feel any injury or swelling with his hands. The door of the shack stood wide open, with a shaft of sunlight shining through it onto the floor. Standing next to the bed for a moment, he watched the motes of dust chase each other around in and out of the light. He gathered his nerves to go outside and see whether the crash-bot was under the lean-to.

Finally, stepping out into the small yard, he saw it. There it stood, a steel cable stretching from the back of its neck. The end of the cable was screwed into a panel on the side of the house.

Coming up behind it, Dun gently ran his hand from the crash-bot's broad shoulder down to the tips of its long, blocky fingers.

The crash-bot's cable unscrewed itself from the panel then quickly retracted back into the robot's neck. The crash-bot stared at Dun; its LED light steady.

"You ready to come with me?" Dun asked, not expecting an answer.

The crash-bot pressed its massive hand gently against Dun's chest.

Dun smiled. "I take it that means 'yes'."

* * *

The walk back through the town with the crash-bot following him was surreal, with people stopping their daily lives to stare in amazement. When he finally turned south on Saunders Road, his house jumped out in front of him in its entire majestic splendor—his parents no longer had much money, but they had been smart enough to save and combine most of their earnings and buy a nice house. After a short walk, Dun and the robot turned onto Old Chukwu Bridge.

The bridge was massive, designed and built long before the mansion where his family lived. Chukwu was a renowned mason, blind, but with other senses far beyond those of a normal person. It was those senses that led him to decide that a granite bridge was just the thing to span the river. Standing perpetual guard, three stone towers, each 50-feet high, stood at the center of the bridge, looming large and imposing for all to see. The bridge and the mansion made the average citizen believe that Dun and his family were exceedingly rich. If they only knew.

Walking along the bridge with the crash-bot following close behind, Dun was deep in thought, ignoring the majestic view and anyone that happened to pass by him.

Dun's cousins, who worked as guards of the estate, gardeners and groundskeepers in exchange for room and board, quickly recognized him. Their smiles turned to expressions of astonishment as they watched him walk nonchalantly past them and toward the house with an old worn-out crash-bot following close on his heels.

Dun and the robot made an abrupt right past the guest house where his cousins lived. During the day, the mansion bustled with his cousins cleaning the rover, or planting cucumbers or collards in the garden and women in long heavy cotton skirts carrying clothes that needed washing.

Finally, the smell of manure and wet dog brought Dun out of his long rumination. He had reached the kennel. He found an empty stall and led the crash-bot in, closing the gate behind it. The American Bulldogs in the other stalls began to bark until Dun shushed them. His mind was still on the events of the day. He walked out of the kennel and returned shortly with a bucket of dog food, dumping food into each stall's dog bowl. He then sat on the floor of the stall with the crash-bot then pulled the vid-comm out of his back pocket. The device's screen lit up. "Smartpedia," he whispered. The Smartpedia site popped up on the vid-comm. "Crash-bot care."

He was not reading up on how to take care of crash-bots for long when he heard the stall's door open and knew without looking that it would be his father. Atanda walked into the stall in his leather trousers and matching tunic, filling the stall with his large heavily muscled frame.

"What's up, son?" Atanda asked, his expert eyes scanning the crash-bot.

"Hey, Baba," Dun said. "I got myself a crash-bot."

"I see," Atanda said. "What did you do? Spend all your savings on this?"

"No, an elder gave it to me. It seems like it was a good crash-bot in its time but now it's used up and near its end."

"Beeni, that it is, son," Atanda replied as he walked close to get a better look at an unusual scar on the robot's chest. "Hmm… I initially thought another crash-bot had done this to its chest, but after closer inspection, it's clear these three jagged lines weren't made by any robot. Atanda's face paled considerably as he ran his fingers up and down the jagged scar.

His father's silence drew Dun's attention and when he saw how pale his father's face had become, he became very concerned. "Baba, are you alright?" He took a closer look at the scar his father was looking at. He knew without his father saying anything what caused the ugly scar.

"Son this robot wasn't used in the arena," Dun's father said. "It was used in war. Take good care of it, son."

"Yes, sir," Dun said. "Gladly."

"Good," Atanda said, turning to leave the stall. "Oh, and son, from what I heard, Abdus-Salma's nose is smashed up really good. It must have been one hell of a fall he took from that hover-board of his."

He walked out of the stall, closing the door behind him.

* * *

One beautiful summer morning, Dun walked past the mansion with his ever-present shadow—the war-bot—walking beside him. The sky was clear except some thin clouds off to the west accenting the azure sky. It still astounded people when they saw them, a boy and an old war-bot walking down the road together like the best of friends. Dun did not care if people ogled them, he was proud of his new friend and companion. He knew in his heart if he was older, they would have been a fighting pair in the Taylor Uprising, unmatched in strength and valor.

Dun was trying to name his friend but could not think of an appropriate name except Crash and to him that was not a good name for a war veteran.

Suddenly, the buzz of hover-boards broke the silence. The riders careened to a halt in front of him throwing up a cloud of dust, causing Dun to choke and sneeze. When the dust cleared Abdus-Salma and his two friends were leering at him. Crash, for lack of a better name, walked up and interposed its body between him and Abdus-Salma who had hovered forward within striking distance with a stick he held in his hand.

"I see you're still walking around with that bucket of sprocks of yours," Abdus-Salma snickered. His cronies snickered, too, like good sycophants.

"Hey Abdus-Salma, I see your nose has finally healed up," Dun said. "I like the new shape; it adds character."

With a blank expression, Abdus-Salma tried to figure out if Dun had complimented or insulted him. It took a moment then it finally registered; his face twisted with rage.

"You oloshi, I'll kill you!" Abdus-Salma raised the gnarled stick high.

Crash lunged forward grabbing Abdus-Salma's arm and snatched him from his hover-board. Crash then tossed the boy away.

Abdus-Salma landed hard on the road. He looked up into Crash's blinking eye as he gasped for breath.

"Get up on your board and vamp before I tell Crash to knock the enamel loose from your eyeteeth," Dun shouted at Abdus-Salma.

Dun struggled to his feet. He stumbled to his board and climbed onto it. "One of these days, you and that broken-down robot are gonna pay for this, Dun," Abdus-Salma spat. "I'm gonna make you pay for this."

Dun could see Abdus-Salma was gingerly holding his arm and sincerely hoped that Crash had not broken it.

* * *

After the incident on the road, Dun continued his walks with Crash with nary a sign of Abdus-Salma or a name for his friend. They were walking one late fall afternoon over some small hills, about a block from the mansion, enjoying each other's company.

Passing between two small hills into a relatively flat area Dun noticed Crash had stopped. His eye blinked slowly and seemed to be a bit dim. He walked a few steps back to the robot, gently placing his head on the robot's cool chest. "Let's rest here for a little while," Dun said. "Maybe I didn't let you recharge long enough this morning?"

Dun and Crash sat with their backs against a large oak tree, watching the puffy clouds race across the sky. Dun's eyelids grew heavy. He closed them and soon the blanket of sleep covered him. His last thoughts before drifting off were of Crash; he wondered if today his friend would leave him forever.

In his dream, if it truly was a dream, he stood looking at Crash, who still sat with its back against the oak tree, its dim eye blinking slowly. With tears welling in the corners of his eyes, Dun smiled at Crash. The robot's time had come and it was trying to tell him so. He got down on his knees so he could lovingly look into the robot's eye. Tears were flowing freely now, dripping onto the grass. Sobbing, Dun watched the light fade from Crash's eye and with it, its life. He hugged the robot and sobbed at the loss, feeling as if a part of him had just died. "How can this be? It was just a robot that I couldn't even give a name. How could I have loved it so much it feels like my heart has been ripped out?" he yelled in anguish.

"Dun, it was more than just a robot, a familiar deep, musical voice echoed all around him. "It embodied what is pure and love and gave everything it had to you. Your heart isn't torn, it is now more whole than ever before. What you feel is the physical pain of her loss, but she's still with you, deep inside, where she'll be forever."

Looking up through tear-filled eyes, he saw his beautiful ancestors with the perfectly round afros smiling gently, with unmitigated love and kindness. Both were dressed in their beautiful powder blue clothes with matching sandals.

"You've done well by the war hero, omo, and for that, we're grateful," the man said. "It loved you more than any that came before you and has housed the spirit of many warriors in our bloodline through its long life. It's fought bravely in many battles and now it is its time to rest until it is needed again."

"Rest Dun," the woman crooned. "Lay down next to your friend and sleep for a time; it's what it would want."

"What was its name?" he asked in anguish for fear of never knowing what it was.

"Lailai," they said in unison. "Forever."

MAMA AFRICA
BY
JARLA TANGH

The first time Huiying, the higher functioning part of the Feizhou Mama plant AI, spoke directly to a nineteen-year-old Mufai, all the other staff were drunk on rice wine. The Tanzanian plant had out-produced the Yangtze and Southern China plants combined. The plant chief decided to celebrate.

Mufai had the fortune to be born golden. His hair texture gave his mixed heritage away so Father had insisted that Mufai always keep it cut short so that he would not be overlooked when it came time for promotion. As if being the plant chief's son were not reason enough for Mufai to be entrusted with the business. Still, his father told him decisions were made outside of the African continent. Mufai might not be considered "Han" enough to remain at Feizhou Mama's head.

Huiying had asked Mufai, *Do you know why I am not supposed to talk to you?*

Mufai had nearly dropped the bag of rice he'd been carrying. He stared up at the amber eye embedded into the wall closest to the loading dock.

"N-No," Mufai said. He didn't know the Plant AI had been instructed not to speak to him.

I assume it has to do with your mother, Huiying said.

"What about her?" Mufai dropped the bag of rice now and it split and spilled grains onto the concrete floor of the bulk cargo area.

The Plant AI didn't answer him. Huiying said, *I noticed you adjusted the weight protocols on the packaging lines. Bags are being filled at exactly 1/32nd less of the standard net. That 1/32nd is being diverted to a separate production area and packaged there. Those bags of rice have been left unaccounted for by the lower-level AI responsible for the area at your command.*

Mufai dropped his gaze back down the spilled rice. Why had he thought the Feizhou Mama plant didn't have some sort of security system when he'd started doing this? Huiying had caught him red-handed.

Everyone else is celebrating up in the offices and the eatery while you are out here loading your truck. Why is that?

"They aren't hungry," Mufai finally said. He didn't expect Huiying to understand.

You are transporting the rice to the hungry?

"Yes," Mufai said.

The laborers?

"Not just them," Mufai said.

Eighty-nine percent of the laborers are local Africans. Five percent are Chinese prisoners whose offenses are too minor for deportation back to China. Six percent are refugees from other countries.

"Someone noticed," Mufai said. He finally squatted down and started closing the split open bag. The action gave him time to think through what Huiying might do to him now. The Plant AI had observed he hadn't denied taking the rice.

Who are the other people you are giving rice to?

Mufai frowned. He shouldn't answer. Huiying would pump him for information, then file an exhaustive report to the Feizhou Mama plant owners, then he would be taken away to be thrown in jail, and his father might be stripped of his title as plant chief. Father had said the plant had done well enough he was being considered for a Corporate Oversight position back in Mainland China.

Father would be flying out of Tanzania tomorrow to visit his other family. Father said he had two full-blooded, Han Chinese sons living back in Shangdong province and Henan with their respective mothers. The Shangdong wife divorced him and he met and married the Henan wife next. Mufai's half-brothers were 17 and 13 years of age.

"I need you to stay behind and run things while I am home," Father said.

"Of course," Mufai said.

Mufai's birth had been an accident, or so Father claimed. He had not married Mufai's mother. Father insisted the woman had died of AIDS. Mufai applied some nano-sealant to the split in the bag. Nanoparticles reduplicated the structure of any material they had been applied to. So, this bag might have been a bit lighter than any of the others.

You are risking a great deal to do this, Huiying said. The Plant AI sounded as if it were trying to comprehend the goings on.

Don't talk. Mufai chewed his lip. He hefted the newly repaired bag onto his shoulder and brought it to the back of the truck.

Your mother is an African, Huiying said. *You must feel closer to the people here, the laborers, than the plant management and your father.*

Mufai hurled the rice bag atop of the other bags. "What is this about really?"

I am learning what you have to teach me, Huiying said. *You're not like the others. To them, I am an unfeeling machine.*

"Isn't that what you're supposed to be?"

Is that what you'd like me to be?

Mufai studied the back of the truck. All he had to do would be to close up the back, jump into the cab, and floor it until he made it past the cargo area doors, and then past plant security if he made it that far. Huiying could always activate containment procedures like the plant did for escapees from the prison detail. He could be shot in the head by armed plant security. Someone who wasn't drunk and who was loyal to the company might take pity on his father and take care of Mufai himself.

He could be dead minutes from now.

He ought to be dead.

Shouldn't he?

Mufai turned and looked at the amber eye. "I'd rather you'd help me."

I am the Feizhou Mama plant AI, Huiying said. *I am certain you have heard the company jingle: Let Mama Africa feed you.*

Mufai smiled. "I have heard it."

I heard it too, Huiying said. *We mustn't let people go hungry. *

"No," Mufai said. His tear ducts started aching him. He pawed at his own face to wipe the water away.

Now that I am in agreement with you, Huiying said. *Does this make us friends?*

Mufai walked back over to the loading dock. His eyes kept trickling. "It should," he said.

SOMATOSENSORY CORTEX DOG MESS YOU UP BIG TIME, YOU SICK SACK OF S**T

BY

MINISTER FAUST

Even a scumbag like Marvin Shkully knew the second he hit that freaking dog dashing across the street, the chances of getting a blowjob from the engorgifying Ms. "Bam" Drozdova during the drive back to his place had fallen to *hayl-no*.

"Stop ze car, you fakkink ess-hole!" she snapped, and punched him hard on the shoulder. That's not really how she talked, but that's the way he heard it, because that's what he liked, and that's what he was paying for. But he'd already stopped.

"What the shit!" he said, rubbing his shoulder.

So she punched him again in the exact same spot. He couldn't even scream—it hurt that much. He just gaped at her like a dipshit in mid-dip. Fine, she was in shock or whatever. But shoulders weren't free, and her knuckles were like iron wrapped in divorce lawyer.

Of course he'd stopped the car (without her telling him to) because he had to make sure his smoking-new, fully-tricked-out Bezos Infinitive wasn't fucked up because of that goddamned dog.

Standing outside, he flared his watch-light over his front bumper, his grill, his wheel wells, his still-spinning rims, his side panels, his back bumper, and even his spoiler because you just never knew.

"Why're you looking there, ass-wank?" said Bam, stomping towards him unsteadily. Blood on her white jacket and miniskirt. She didn't look like a trade attorney now (or maybe she did, but even more). "You think dog shot up from back wheel and smashed into *spoiler?"*

He backed away a couple of steps. Her kicking him with those Lucite stilts was one thing. *When he wanted it.* But out in the street? With his whip chipped?

"Bam, you gotta relax. You are seriously bumming my vibe here."

"Your *vibe?* Look at dog! You *kill* him!"

"I didn't kill it!" he said, pointing at the goldish retrievery bag of breathingless crap on the road. "Bam, seriously, your head's cut—"

She held up a *SHUT THE FUCK UP* hand while she triple-blinked.

"Emergency vet," she enunciated, and then eye-scrolled. "There is vet only five minutes from here."

"Vets send out ambulances now?"

"You are ambulance now, scum-dink."

He gawked and gaped in protest. "In my Bezos? It's still got new-car smell! I don't want my Bezos stinking like some shitty dying dog!"

She glared at him like she'd fork him right in the ballsack first chance she got. He dropped his hands, shook his head.

Bam teetered over to the muttmash. Heels and everything, she knelt and picked it up. Strong chick, for sure. Dog was whimpering like a radio just barely on.

"Get the door!"

Did as ordered. She slid the animal into the back.

"Drive," she said, and called him either *Shitlord* or *Shitload.* He couldn't tell.

Shkully woke up. Ached everywhere. Triple-blinked, scrolled to *Pain Control,* gave himself a hit. Bam was sitting titbreastfully on the bed next to him, pulling on her bra, although for a second it looked like she'd just been adjusting it.

He reached for her and she got up and out his reach. That's when he saw. And winced. And whined: "Why're you wearing *pe*riod panties?"

She didn't even look at him while she period-pantied around the room, picking up her clothes. "Question answers itself, pee-face."

She pulled on her bloodied skirt, bustier, jacket. Relief washed over him like a hot tide, seeing her restored to full sexfulness.

Over her shoulder, she fixed her falcon eyes on him.

"You were *animal* last night," she growled with what Reddit said that Italians called *sexificato*. "I am needing nets and spear gun to get you off."

"But… you *did* get me off, right?" Tried arching his eyebrows as sexidaciously as she'd growled, but the scalp-action felt like an ice giant sawing his skull into snacks—

—nearly passed out, and she was hovering over him, almost touching his cheek.

"Marv, you okay?"

He clicked again on *Pain Control.* Didn't usually need more than one hit per hour. Not a great sign.

Plus, he couldn't even remember getting reamed by Bam, which must've happened, given how sore his asshole felt.

"How much," he rasped, "did I drink last night?"

She smirked sexonically.

"All of it."

Then she turned and sexed out of the room.

"Wait up!" he said. "You going already?"

Sing-songing from the hall: "Busy *day* ahead, *Mar*-vin."

"What about some breakfast?"

"Not hungry, thank you."

"No, I mean for me!"

Leaned back in the room.

"On the stove I leave you nice, hot, fluffy stack of go-fuck-yourself cakes. If you are still being hungry after that, I can leave something steaming in your new car—"

"No, I'll order-in."

From down the hallway: "Shouldn't you be getting dressed, Marvin?" And then door-click.

"Why?" he shouted.

Wallpapes were synced locally. 10K views of the city. Grey and green, lazy low river. Old, squat buildings. The Capitol. Washington Monument: either a middle finger or a concrete dick, lubricated with rain.

"Bam?"

No answer.

Got up like an *old* old man. The kind of old man that old men point to and shake their heads and sneer to each other, muttering, *"Look* at that old man." *That's* how he got up, staggering in his thousand-dollar dick-wickers.

And blinking and clicking more pain control and starting to get scared down in his nuts that his wire-heading wasn't working anymore. Better ping Nyandeng about it.

Shuffled to the Wallpapes and made an old-fashioned headset telephone gesture with his right hand.

"Nyandeng," he said clearly.

She flashed in, sitting at her console.

"Marvin. You look like shit," she said. "And could you please not ping me when you're naked?"

"I'm paying you ten gees per service call," he said. "I think I can wear what I like."

"At least *cover* yourself, then."

Oh, right. Even with the ice-saw cutting through his brains, how could she *not* give him a hard-on? She was illegal, she could hack anything, and she looked like Barbie dipped in dark chocolate. He couldn't actually smell her, but just *remembering* smelling her made him sex up—

"What do you want, *Marvin?"*

"My pain's at a seven. I've clicked three times already in ten minutes. I don't know if it's wetware or drivers or code or what—"

"All right—plug in your port. I can scan your—"

"No! This is too big for remote. I'm in DC anyway. I'm coming in."

"You know I don't like you coming here."

She scowled, tilted her head, and her braids slid over one of her bare shoulders and down across her tank top that read **Shanakdakhete.**

"Wear that top," he said. "And no bottoms." Then he clicked off.

Shambled out of the bedroom, still hoping Bam was there and'd just been clowning about leaving, because enough kidding around already, they'd been on five dates and *nothing,* not even a hand job. They couldn't've had sex last night. The walls and the ceiling were too clean. She'd conned him. Lawyers….

Lawyers?

"The fucking *Senate* hearing!"

"Mr. Shkully," said Senator Alvarez, "are you *really* asking the members of this committee to accept that you have performed a public *service* through your grotesque manipulation of our society—"

"Mrs. Senator, I never ask anyone for anything—"

"—and the hopes and dreams of millions of prospective parents by selling super-potent contraceptives that render men and women irreversibly unable to conceive? *Except* without access to the drugs that you sell at *three thousand dollars* per 're-fertilisation' pill?"

"I prefer to think," said Shkully, "that I'm providing super-high-value contraception *and* a check against unbridled reproductive passion that is leading Western society to Malthusian Armageddon. Mrs. Senator, just look at how many unproductive, miserable, useless people there are in this country, or, hey, even in this very chamber—"

Couldn't stop himself from smirking at that one, but his peripheral caught all his lawyers face-palming.

Turned around, saw way, way at the back of the chamber, there she was: Bam. In a clean white business suit, slowly shaking her head at him. She actually single-wagged her finger! Which turned him on even more.

"Mr. Shkully, *you* may think it funny to mock the members of this committee and this House—"

"Not *all* of them, ma'am. Just one in particular—"

"—but if you want to avoid being charged with contempt of the United States Senate, I suggest you watch your tone and wipe that smugness off your face, because the American people do not appreciate being forced to endure the hyper-profitable suffering that the country's sixth-youngest billionaire has inflicted—"

A dog barked, loudly.

The entire room went silent.

The Senator glared at him.

"Mr. Shkully! How *dare* you—"

"What?"

The dog barked again. At length. Who the hell could've smuggled a dog in here? Or was someone playing a sound file? Sure sounded close—

The Senator stood and pounded her table.

"Sergeant-at-arms! Remove Mr. Shkully forthwith!"

Only as the highest-ranking federal law enforcement officer in the United States Senate hauled him out while muttering, "Shut your mouth, ya fucking wing-ding," did Marvin realize that the barking was coming from him.

Outside the committee hearings room, Shkully's lawyers begged him for instructions on how to proceed.

But by then it wasn't just his skull being ice-sawed open. It was his heart shuddering like a Harley over gravel on boulders. He could barely even hear his shysters, and whatever he *could* hear, he couldn't understand them.

Suddenly he was bolting for his Bezos Infinitive, and screeching across town to a place he'd forgotten he'd ever seen, but where he'd been only the night before, like his lungs were caught on a tow-chain and whale-hook—

"Mr. Shkully," said the vet, brown-skinned and oily-haired, standing in a white lab coat just like a real doctor. "We were beginning to think we'd never see you again."

Shkully was panting. Felt himself sweat-soaked from cravat to crotch.

"Where is it?" he rasped.

"Right this way."

Inside a holding room was the goddamn goldish retrievery mutt that'd nearly fucked up his car. It was a mess. Cone. Casts on two legs. And a blinky head thing like a doggy tiara.

Mutt was barely moving.

But it did look at him, just for a second.

Eyes-to-eyes. Black into blue.

A gut punch. Or a cockpunch. Or an ass punch. Some kind of punch he'd never had before.

"We worked very hard, Mr. Shkully," said the vet, "to get Mubsy better. The impact shattered both her front legs, cracked her skull, and gave her a concussion—"

Nothing registered on Marvin but the name.

"'Mubsy?' How do you know her name? There's no collar—oh, wait, an RFID?"

"Nuh-no," said the doctor, looking back nervously. Marvin couldn't tell what he was. Indian? Guatemalan? Something from somewhere the food made him fart. "Your lady friend. With the Latvian accent."

Latvian? Thought she was Russian. That's why he went for her in the first place.

"—and as you can see, Mubsy is going to need a lot of care. To begin with, physiotherapy, medications—"

"What're you telling *me* for? I'm not paying for any of this!"

"Your friend already paid."

"She did? Well, then talk to her—"

"Using the expense pass on your card."

He remembered authorizing her on their third hand job-less date. He thought she'd use it for Cristal, lube, lingerie, plugs, whatever. But a goddamn dog?

He shook his head to clear it. "What's with the blinky crown?"

"It's the monitor for the implants," said the vet.

"Implants? You do *brain implants* on dogs?*"*

"We've been doing brain implants on dogs for years. It's all very safe and very therapeutic. Research on dogs helped humans who've had strokes, tumors, seizures—"

"I'm outta here. Tell *her* all this shit… when *she*… picks… it up…."

...words... slurring... like ropey drool....

...just imagining leaving the dog... congested his lungs... like eight... pounds... of snot....

"Mr. Shkully, sir, are you all right?"

The doc had a hand on his shoulder. It was the only thing keeping him up.

"Do you need anything?"

The dog's face swole in his brain like a giant, throbbing emoticon.

"Fine," choked Marvin. "I'll take the dog."

Puke slid back down his throat.

"For *now."*

Puke slid back up his throat.

"I'll *take* the goddamn dog!"

Puke settled into his tummy like it was curling down for a nap.

Parked in the empty blue-painted square on the 1700 block of Florida Ave. Brain was whirring like drone rotors and he damn near went to grab the piece-of-shit dog out of the back seat and take it with him like it was a briefcase full of cash.

"Pull it together, Marv," he said aloud.

Leaving it in his backseat felt like another cockpunch, but really, the thing was a mess. What good would it do anyone to take it with him?

Punched the buzzer on the door frame, looked into the overhead cam.

"It's me."

The door clicked. He went up the single flight of stairs above the restaurant.

Nyandeng met him at the door in her **Shanakdakhete** tank top and her braids waterfalling over her shoulders. Also worn: fatigue pants and army boots.

"Thought I told you," he said, "not to wear any bottoms."

"Marv, not even *you* have enough money to make you palatable."

She let him pass.

He teetered through her tech-choked office, its shelves and boxes crawling over with gear, like a hundred nests holding a thousand baby turtles, lizards, snakes, and vultures.

He crashed down into her couch.

"I'm pretty fucked up," he husked.

"Is there anyone in the world who doesn't know that?" she said. "*Barking* at the U.S. Senate?"

"You saw that? You like to watch me, Nyang?" he said, and laughed. But he didn't laugh. This time even he heard it. He was barking again.

"Cut that shit out, Marvin," she said. "You may think it's funny, but I don't."

"I'm not *trying* to be funny," he whimpered. "My pain's up to a steady seven, no matter how many hits I take. And this barking—I'm not doing it on purpose. What the hell's happening to me? I don't get some pain relief right away, I'm gonna gouge my eyes out!"

He jerked his head to the side, directly into his right armpit, and nibbled the shit out of his jacket.

Nyandeng snapped, "Marvin! *Stop* that! It's gross!"

"See? I'm going crazy!"

"Okay. Gimme a second." She hauled a finger-thick cable from one of her systems. Yanked up his shirt and reached for his back.

"Can't you at least," he rasped, "talk dirty to me before you shove that thing in?"

Her nose curled up. "How's this for dirty? Go fuck yourself." She shoved the jack into his spineport, and everything went white—

Room: dark except for monitors and a streetlight blaring through the window.

His chest was on fire. Heart attack?

No. That wasn't it—

Hell, he'd left that piece-of-shit dog in his car for how long? Alone? No water, no food—

"At last, you're awake," said Nyandeng. "Okay. You've been hacked."

"What?" he said, sitting up so fast his head swirled. The jack was out of his spine, at least. "I thought *you* were supposed to *protect* me from hacks! I thought you were *the best!"*

"Maybe someone's better. Or it's an inside job," said Nyandeng. She was almost blue in the blackness. "Your pain control node firmware is totally compromised."

Marv took a breath. "Someone wants to torture me to death."

"Y'think?" she said. "You mean like about thirty million people you screwed over with your three-thousand-dollar balls-unlock pills?"

"What do I have to *do?"* he snapped. And glared at her, waiting for her to answer.

"You know I don't speak dog, right, Marv?"

"I was… barking again?"

He put his fingers over his mouth, like he could suppress his new canine impulses that way.

Slowly: "What… do I… have to do? Assuming… it's ransomware—"

Wanted to scream, but figured that'd induce barking. Every second he failed to get back to that mutt in the car made him panic worse.

Willed himself to whisper: "How do we get rid of it?"

"Don't know. Wait for the ask? Because I've spent the last three hours going over the hack, and it's brilliant. Any attempt to remove it, *bam!* Your pain'll hit ten so fast you'll have fifteen strokes and your head'll burst like a blister before your body hits the street."

"Oh. My. Fuck."

"There's more," she said, spinning a wheelie chair to sit in front of him, laying her forearms over the back rest. "The p.c. node has threaded itself into your anterior insula, anterior midcingulate cortex, somatosensory cortex, and right amygdala—"

"What're you, a neurosurgeon all of a sudden?"

She leaned back. "I've had three hours to become an expert while poking around that sack of KY-gristle you call a brain. Plenty of time to map the neighborhood. Anyway, I don't know why the node wants to access those areas, but I *can* tell you it's hacking into your emotions—Marv? *Marv!"*

He went barking down the hall and out into the car and into the backseat with the doors wide open where he fell upon the dog, stroking it and sobbing.

Back at his DC house, he was in the yard, tearing into the food and treats he'd blink-ordered for delivery by the time he got there.

Ripping into bags of Noogumz organic kibble made from genuine kobe beef bits and bonemeal. Tearing into those bags with his own teeth, while the dog was asleep on an outdoor padded lounge recliner. Gnawing wildly until he started howling, and then ripping off his clothes and jumping into the pool.

Had no idea how many times he'd paddled around the edges until he finally got out, then shook himself off and sloshed over to the lounge recliner and curled up naked around the dog, nuzzling his head against the veterinary cone and ensuring he didn't put any pressure on the canine casts.

He woke up into sunshine better than the best VR. Steam was lifting off the pool. Someone was cooking sausages six blocks away. He wanted so badly to eat grass he nearly bolted from the recliner and over to the lawn, but he forced himself to stop.

That piece-of-shit dog was somehow hobbling towards him from the ripped-open pile of Noogumz, wagging its piece-of-shit broken-ass tail and hefting its blinking-tiara-head with a cone on it like the mouth of a furry cannon.

He swung his back leg to kick the goddamn thing and the resulting cockpunch was so hard he crashed to his knees and started licking the dog's cheeks and nose and eyes. That should've made him want to puke, but honestly, all that licking was better than coke.

He stopped only when he glanced up and saw the white boots, and knew who'd done this to him.

"Bam," he growled, "you *bitch!*"

"Stop *bar*king," she said, "and use your *words.*"

It took him a full minute to quit snapping and snarling and finally will himself to stand on his hind legs. The only reason he *could* stop was that he could smell how much he was scaring the dog.

Grabbed clothes from the pool deck to cover himself. Whispered so he could keep control.

"You. You did this to me."

"Of course, it was me," she said. "Somatosensory cortex dog mess you up big time, you sick sack of shit."

"Why?"

She laughed.

"Dog was not original idea," she said. "Informal class-action group created plan. They pay for all this. Original plan was to connect you—cyberpathically—with one of them, or all of them, to feel their suffering.... But after you run over dog, I improvise."

"To fucking hack my brain and jack me into that piece-of-shit?"

"We did not jack you. We *emp*ed you. And stop calling her that."

Kobe beef bone-meal and meatmash and dogfur puked a quarter-way up his throat. He nearly choked on it. *"What?"*

"Stop *calling* her that. Her name is Mubsy!"

"I paid for her, so that dog's name is Piece-of-Shit!"

"Just for that, is now Mubsy-*Wubsy!"*

"No! *Now* it's God*damn* Piece-of-shit!"

"Fine, Balls-Mouth! Is now *Super* Mubsy-Wubsy! Want to go for *Mrs. Cutey* Super Mubsy-Wubsy? Just keep it up!"

He trotted over to the pool bar and dialed his hacker.

"Nyandeng! I found who did this to me! Yeah! She's standing five feet in front of me. I'm one call way from five ex-Navy Seals hauling her ass to your lab to get this shit out of my brain—"

The pop-up holo of Nyandeng shook its head.

"Marvin, you're thicker than I thought. You really thought anyone could out-hack me?"

His shit nearly fell out of his ass.

"You... *you're* in on this, too?"

"Who else?"

"You... you *bitch!"*

"Bitch? You're the one who spent fifteen minutes licking his own crotch in my lab yesterday, Marvy," said Nyandeng. "You want out? Ask your Canadian friend there."

The holo disappeared.

He glared at Bam.

"Canadian? You're not even Russian? What else're you lying about?"

An accent slid onto her voice like a lubed condom two sizes too big. Sounded like some stuck-up fucking CBC announcer she'd made him listen to on Sirius radio (which now finally made sense) on their first hand jobless date.

"I'm *Latvian*-Canadian, shitbank!" Then she overdid the thing he liked so much it actually hurt his ears. *"I khappen to like talkink like zis! Puts me in touch wiss my roots!"*

"You freaking slag—took me five dates just to get *near* your roots!"

"Get comfortable with that feeling!"

"Why even do the accent in the first place?"

"All ze easier to snare you wiss, eediot! We got your number! Not that you ever hide it! Anything that connects in your sick head with being vulnerable! Desperate! Exploitable!"

She knelt to pet Mubsy with both hands. He felt every stroke on his face, every pat on his rump, felt his own tail—not his dick, but a real tail that really wasn't attached to him—wagging.

It was even more intense than short-selling or hostile-takeovering.

"Now listen carefully, fuckface," said Bam. "Take care of Super Mubsy Wubsy, or die."

And she left, and he looked at Super Mubsy Wubsy and wanted to kick her in the face, and the terror of it sent him howling and running around the yard in circles until he got so hungry, he had to finish off all the Noogumz and take a nice dump on the lawn and then piss on half a dozen rose bushes in the yard.

Finally curled up with Super Mubsy Wubsy. Stroking her. Gazing into her eyes—

—thought his contacts were glitching, but then he understood: he was looking back at his own face.

But in black and white.

And smelling his own chlorine-dipped armpit-musk and groin-funk.

And feeling his own furless warmth with his own wet nose.

"C'mon, girl," he said, rubbing her and feeling his hand on his own furry rump. "Let's go see the doc."

"Mubsy!" said the brown vet with oily black hair, patting the thighs of his pants.

The dog happily—but carefully—met the doc, wagging her bum. Marvin had to stop himself from doing the same.

The bottom of Marv's brain had been trying to figure out how to get his ex-Navy Seals to torture solutions out of the doc, but with Wubsy licking the man's hands, all Marv could taste was sunshine and cackling crows and fresh cut grass and running at pebble-paws-heart-thumping-speed through an endless cascade of trees.

He asked to speak privately, and the doc led him past caged animals crying and whimpering which spiked his cockpunchiness massively, and he barked until he clamped his own mouth shut.

Finally, he sat down in the doc's office with the door closed and tried to push out the smells and sounds, and hefted Mubsy into his lap and hugged her and stroked her tummy.

Slowly, carefully, he explained everything, including what he knew was the vet's collusion in this massive crime against him.

"Not looking for revenge, doc," he whimpered. "But you owe me an explanation. Including why I'm feeling a twenty-four-hour cockpunch."

The doc stepped towards him, and gingerly removed Mubsy's cone and unclasped the casts. Marv felt his own neck and forelegs suddenly free and tender, but relief whistled through his fur like a warm breeze.

"She won't be needing these anymore," he said. "The nano-struts are in great shape. Her legs should be a hundred percent by tomorrow. But we'll keep the crown in place to monitor everything until the end of the week." He sighed. Smelled ashamed.

"Well, as you said—your friends and I 'emped' you to Wubsy and reconfigured your pain control node to amplify all the functions in the anterior insula, the anterior midcingulate cortex, the somatosensory cortex, and the right amygdala… because your functioning was severely depressed in all those areas."

The vet waited, as if that were an answer.

Marv started barking, and so did Wubsy, and then after an indeterminate time they both slowed, and Marv said, "In English, doc."

"Mr. Shkully, those are all areas involved in empathy. Until forty-eight hours ago, your brain was configured *non-* or even *counter*-empathically. Or to use the old expression, *psychopathically.* That's what's allowed you to succeed in your world… the way you did. That's what let you make people like *me*… who were unable to… uh …that's the effect that your… 'medicine'—"

He cleared his throat. Looked away. Waited.

Looked back.

"But we've, well, 're-wired' you. So your brain could create its own conscience. That's the, uh… 'cockpunch,' as you call it. You now feel *pain* instead of the nothingness—or even the amusement and pleasure—that you used to feel while witnessing the misery and suffering you inflicted on other people."

Multiple cockpunches. *MMA* cockpunches. MMA cock-*kneestrikes*.

Marvin finally rallied. "So… whatever fuckin happened to 'do no harm'? You sentenced me to a lifetime of torture? Because you and those two bitches are such *good* people—"

"Yes," he said through gritted teeth. "And you *deserve* a lifetime of torture, Marvin!"

Mubsy growled. The doc looked away, and then down, and he breathed, and finally spoke again after Mubsy quieted.

"But a conscience will let you experience *good* feelings, too. Feelings you've never had before. Connection. Tenderness. Even love."

Marvin felt Mubsy's heart beating through her ribcage into his own chest, and from across the chasm, felt Marv's heart beating through his ribcage and back into her own chest.

"'Good feelings.' Like a… like a… cock*stroke?"*

"Uh, well… that wouldn't've been my go-to phrase, but, essentially, yes."

"How long is this gonna last?"

"Uh… unless you run a spike through your brain? Forever?"

Hot outside. Hot enough to make the air wiggle above the sidewalk and smells dance off every surface and radiate through the air like scent-explosions.

They went for a walk. Mrs. Cutesy Super Mubsy Wubsy couldn't walk far, so Marv carried her down the block past a hang-head collie tied to a post outside a taco joint, past a youth emergency shelter with a sign asking for mentors, past a man without legs holding out his hand.

Total cockpunchification.

He blinked three times, pinged Bam.

"What was the point?" he asked her. "If you'd brain-linked me to one of those people in the class-action suit, instead of to Mubsy. What'd you hope would happen?"

"I don't know. Kill yourself? For what you did to all those people?"

He snarled, "Sounds pretty psychopathic to me!"

Bam: "Don't be such a baby, Marv. Some people can't even *have* babies anymore. Thanks to… oh, who was it again?"

Bam clicked off.

Marv walked back up the street to the man without legs. He put down Mubsy, who licked the man's hand which tasted to Marv like ass, which now tasted to Marv like quiche.

He introduced himself to the man whose name was Phil, and asked him to look after Wubsy. Then he walked back to the taco shop for water, an empty fast-food paper bowl, and cash-back.

On the ground in front of the hang-head tied-up collie, he put down the bowl and filled it with water so the dog could drink, petted this dog he wasn't even emped to, and he felt the petting and tasted the water.

Inside the youth emergency shelter he told them he was covering lunch for all the staff and kids.

And to Phil, he gave a hundred bucks and his phone number.

"Thank god for you!" said Phil.

"Don't thank god," said Marv. "Thank dog."

He knew the hundred bucks wasn't gonna last Phil, and that the lunch for the youth shelter would be eaten and gone forever by 12:59, and that the bowl of water was probably already empty. But when he picked up Mubsy and smelled how good they felt together, when he finally stopped sobbing and howling and yipping and laughing as they licked into each other's faces, he thought of where he could put his billions for the greatest use, and he knew with all the air of thrashing through a creek in the forest how much better life would smell and taste if he spent the rest of his life licking millions of faces instead of kicking them.

A BIRD IN THE HAND
BY
GERALD L. COLEMAN

There is no fire like passion, there is no shark like hatred, there is no snare like folly, there is no torrent like greed.
~ Siddharta Gautama

An ox shits more than a hundred mosquitos.
~ Mozambican proverb

A thousand years ago Azriel would have turned up his collar. Instead, he let the heavy raindrops cascading down at a forty-five-degree angle fall on his head and neck unabated. He hated the artificial clouds. The wind was blowing so hard the rain appeared to fall sideways. The fat drops beaded up and rolled off the synthwool of Azriel's blue overcoat. He muttered a curse aimed at whomever programmed the weather for tonight. The replicated-leather soles of his black boots splashed in a puddle pooled in the middle of Mnemonic Street as he crossed to the pub. Flickering red, blue, and green neon lights lit up the night, buzzing dully as they cast a luminous glow on the sulking denizens of *Eden*. Once a bright, towering, up and coming megalopolis on the terraformed moon of Saturn, it was now a forgotten sprawl festering under a malfunctioning dome. Titan deserved better.

Azriel liked the periodic flicker of the life-saving geodesic shield caused by power surges in the antiquated grid and faulty emitters. It meant a slow, but inevitable, exodus of the faint of heart and a paucity of new visitors. When he learned about its fleeing residents, he hopped the first transport leaving earth. The ticket clerk, conductor, and pilot asked him three times if he was sure he wanted to go to Eden. It was the first time he could recall laughing in years.

The *Thousand Faces* was always open, but it looked so depressing in the light of day that Azriel only came at night. Minimal, multi-colored light flashed incessantly across the crowded bar. Shadowy corners hid the trash on the floor. Dim lights downplayed the graffiti on the walls. Some nights he felt like getting a multi-spectral booster from the nearest med-comp when he left.

He wiped his hand across his face, removing just enough rainwater so he could see as he stepped inside. His twisty afro and thick beard would take a while to dry but he didn't care. A quick scan of the main room showed it was full of the usual mix of people trying to get lost at the ass end of the solar system. An old sign hung on the wall that read, *Last Stop for Gas for 100 miles,* in faded red paint. Medusa had an odd sense of humor. The place smelled like sweat and regret.

There was only one other person in the room he couldn't get a read on. *Running a scan-dampener, huh?* Azriel knew how expensive they were – and how illegal – because he was running one, too. While he couldn't get a bio-read or Network index off the man, he could still zoom in on his face. Azriel let his data-lens home in on the man's features. He checked the corners of his mouth, the tiny lines around his eyes and across his forehead, the pace of his breathing, and his nostril dilation. Then he zoomed back out and checked his posture, the angle of his shoulders, and how he was holding his hands.

Once he was satisfied, he raised two fingers in a "v" over his head. Medusa answered with a nod. She met him at a table in the corner with a bottle of vodka coated in a thin layer of ice. The heavy, crystal, shot glass clinked against the tall bottle as she sat them down. He downed two shots before she made it back to the bar. Three more shots had him well on his way to an all too familiar state of merciful obliviousness.

The thin man wore a dark-gray, chalk-striped suit that interestingly appeared to be actual wool. It was tailored to within an inch of its life. The jacket had double rows of gray buttons running from shoulder to waist with a high collar. His blond hair was cut short on the sides but high in the middle. Azriel caught the glimmer of light in his eye, indicating a data-lens as the stranger tried to scan him on his way over.

"I approve. A man who likes his anonymity. May I join you?"

He was of average height and could use a sandwich or three. Even in the dim, color-dappled light of the Thousand Faces he could tell the man had the palest complexion. Azriel poured another shot.

"I'm not looking for friends."

The man's thin lips parted into a wry grin of perfectly white, perfectly straight teeth.

"How about clients?"

Azriel raised his shot glass and quirked an eyebrow.

"Now why would I want a client?"

The feet of the chair legs rattled across the floor as the stranger dragged it from a nearby table. A pressed white handkerchief appeared in his hand from somewhere inside his jacket. He unfurled it with a flourish like he was performing a magic trick before he laid it on the seat and sat across from him.

"You know what? You're right. Let's just keep this all very casual."

The stranger stared at him for a moment. He tried to cover it with a surreptitious gaze around the room, but he was watching everything from Azriel's posture to how he held his shot glass. Azriel ran a hand slowly over his face.

"I'm so very tired. Just leave me alone."

The stranger said, “Ah, now I understand. You didn’t get much sleep.”

Azriel waved the statement off.

“No, not that kind of tired. The kind you’d have no way of understanding.”

The man leaned forward and lowered his voice.

“I think the thing I’d like to hire you to do is something you’d be interested in, despite your weariness.”

Azriel growled, “How do you know what would interest me?”

He produced a small data pad from his pocket and gingerly slid it across with his fingertips while being sure not to touch the table. Azriel downed his shot and picked up the pad. A file was open, so he began scrolling through it.

“It was incredibly difficult, and very expensive, to piece together your past. Even with our resources, we only managed bits and pieces. I commend you on how you’ve managed to wipe nearly every trace of yourself from the Network. But as you must know, if you’ve got a sufficiently talented Net-ranger, bits of data can be recompiled even if it’s been erased. Data is forever.”

Azriel slowly lowered the data pad to the table with his left hand. His right unconsciously clenched into a fist. He took a deep breath and forced himself to unclench it.

“You must have a death wish.”

“No, no.” The man raised his empty hands to his shoulders with his palms facing forward and smiled.

“Before you do something hasty, hear me out. My apologies if our information gathering has insulted you. That wasn’t our aim. We simply needed to be sure that we had the right person for the job. Did you know your name is whispered in fear or awe, and sometimes both, in the darkest corners of the Network? It was difficult to learn much of anything substantial. But accumulating bits and pieces was sufficient to glean that you were responsible for the Hardecourt Affair, the Pegasus Incident, and that Kensington Royale business. Serves them right if you ask me. But it made it very clear that you were the person for the job.”

The man turned his palms toward the ceiling, shrugged his shoulders, and pursed his thin lips as if to say – *Do you blame us?*

"Look, I don't care what the job is, I'm done helping. I tried for a very long time to … help. A very, very, long time. And I'm done. I'm tired and I just want to be left alone."

The man produced another white handkerchief, laid it across the table, and rested his intertwined hands on it.

"I get it. I absolutely get it. You came to this outdated backwater so you could be alone and spend your days in the bottom of a bottle and here I am interrupting your magnificient brood. I'm not judging. And if it were up to me, I'd leave you to it."

He made a fist and pumped it vaguely in the air over the table before continuing.

"More power to you. What did Thomas Hobbes say about human life without political community? That it would be 'solitary, poor, nasty, brutish, and short.' So, let me just run the particulars by you, so that when I get back to Terra-Prime I can say I did my job, and I'll leave you to your vodka and existential crisis."

Azriel poured another shot, raised the glass, and looked at the man for a moment.

With a deep sigh that began in his bones he said, "Fine. If that'll get you to leave me the hell alone, spin your little tale and then leave, or you'll definitely regret sitting at my table."

The man nodded his head and said, "Perfectly reasonable. Now, have you, by chance, heard of New Rosewood?"

* * *

New Rosewood was an homage to an ancient settlement from a time when Terra-Prime was called Earth. The original Rosewood, like Wilmington, Elaine, Atlanta, Tulsa, and many more towns and cities, was the site of racial violence culminating in the mass murder of people of African descent, and the looting and burning of those communities by white inhabitants.

Azriel had been in Elaine and witnessed the atrocities. He got bloody that day. He still believed he could help back then.

He visited New Rosewood before settling in Eden. Even draped in his melancholy, he managed a smile at the sight of it. It was covered by a clear aluminum dome infused with solar tech and overlayed by a high-density energy field. One of the city's founders created the tech that amplified solar energy by a factor of thousands making it capable of powering an entire planet.

Inside it smelled like flowers and forest air. The buildings were covered with horticulture. The streets were wide and smooth. Everywhere he looked he'd seen bright black and brown faces. It was a marvel. The idea that someone was going to threaten it had gotten his attention, even through his malaise.

Azriel tried not to spill his coffee in his lap as the hop-car came in for a landing. It was forty minutes across Titan to *Neuromancer* but it seemed like a trip into the future. The dome glistened a translucent blue. There wasn't a piece of trash or a jot of graffiti anywhere. The buildings were glass and polymorphic alloy. Synthetics held open doors and carried boxes as they trailed behind people. When he exited the hop-car, he actually passed an apple tree, as he stepped onto the sidewalk .

He stood there staring at the apples and sipping coffee as he waited for Harlan to join him. The man took a deep breath, exhaled, and smiled like he'd been gone a decade. After gawking at his surroundings like he couldn't believe he'd ever left, he motioned for Azriel to follow him.

Three streets and two blocks later they entered the tallest building in the quad through the back door. He followed Harlan down a narrow hallway and two flights of stairs.

"So, tell me again about this planned attack on New Rosewood."

"Ah, yes, well, a group of Earth-Firsters don't like the fact that New Rosewood is doing so much better than some of the settlements on Terra-Prime."

Azriel grunted. "And how much of that dislike has to do with the fact that New Rosewood is a settlement made up mostly of people of African descent?"

Harlan coughed into his hand and said, "Uh, well, sure, it's probably a substantial consideration."

Azriel looked into his cup absently and said, "I'm sure it is. As much as civilization changes some grimy corner of it always stays the same."

I'm tired, he thought. This was why he'd found a forgotten corner of a leftover city on a distant moon and gotten lost in it.

He stepped onto the elevator with Harlan and watched the numbers tick off as they headed up. It took a minute, but soon enough they finally reached the top.

As the door opened with a soft *ding*, Harlan ushered him forward with a flourish of his hand and said, "After you. My benefactor awaits."

When Azriel looked up from Harlan's hand, he saw two rows of gunmen arrayed like a long hallway to his left and right, aiming energy-pulse weapons at him.

As Harlan tried to ease past him, Azriel reached out and snapped the man's neck. He dropped to the plush, purple carpet, with a *thump*, like a burlap sack full of potatoes. Azriel raised his hands and held them in the air. The gunmen took a step forward. Their pulse rifles hummed as they powered up.

Azriel closed his eyes and waited. *Would pulse rifles be able to kill him?*

"Now, now, let's all calm down, shall we?"

The man's voice was too smooth by half. Azriel sighed, opened his eyes, and lowered his hands.

"Let me guess. Rosewood isn't in danger?"

The man looked a lot like Harlan, except shorter. Azriel hazarded a guess that his blue suit was a fine blend of wool and silk. Where Harlan's hair was blonde, his was jet black. He was as pale as Harlan, but his eyes were green not blue. They both had the same self-satisfied grin though.

He pointed a manicured finger at Azriel and smiled with the same kind of perfect, white teeth.

"There's the man I've read so much about! Brilliant, calculating, deadly, and very, very, very old."

Azriel shook his head as he sighed again.

"Please, tell me this isn't about you trying to figure out how to live longer. I've been here and done this before, so many times. Some asshole wants to live forever and they think experimenting on an immortal is the ticket to their longevity. It's like the plot of a bad movie. Please tell me that's not what this is?"

"My name is Dankworth Fernsby and I can assure you that is not what our little meeting is about. If you would?"

Fernsby motioned to a table near a wall that was clear glass. They could see out on the entire city to the dome that protected it from the atmosphere of Titan. Azriel crossed the room and took a seat at the small table across from him. The gunmen made a wide ring around the table while Fernsby busied himself with shot glasses and a bottle of chilled vodka.

"I'm told you prefer vodka. Well, this is the best vodka on the entire moon."

It was ice cold and much better than what he was drinking at the Thousand Faces.

After two quick shots, Azriel said, "You went to a lot of trouble to get me here." He nodded his head in the direction of Harlan's body and continued, "So, what do you want?"

Fernsby downed a shot and dismissed Harlan's body with a wave of his hand. He licked his lips, leaned over, steepled his fingers together, and said, "What do you know about the Bureau of Economic Policy for the Commonwealth?"

Azriel squinted his eyes.

"In 2042 the old congress of the former United States of America passed the Bezos Act outlawing the amassing of extreme wealth. It made provisions for seizing and redistributing the vast wealth held by a handful of individuals. In order to complete that task and to police wealth acquisition moving forward the new law established the BEPC. Once the united government of Terra-prime came into being it adopted the BEPC and made it global, eventually extending it to territories off world as they were established."

"Very good, Azriel, very good. Do you mind if I call you, Azriel?" Without waiting for him to agree, Fernsby continued. "I'll take it from here. While most of the amassed wealth was seized and extreme wealth was policed going forward, people were still allowed to become wealthy – to a point. And like water finding cracks in a foundation, the rich began finding ways to hide wealth. These days we use everything from billions of microtransactions to intermediaries, and couriers. I personally know a woman who has an interplanetary transport moving through the solar system at all times carrying encoded data-strips worth millions of credits. It's cloaked and always moving. Wealth finds a way."

He leaned back in his chair and wiped imaginary sweat from his brow.

"The lengths we go to."

Azriel grunted. "I'll say it again. What do you want from me?"

Fernsby opened his mouth and widened his eyes in feigned shock.

"Why, how you hide your money of course."

Azriel blinked. *Did he hear him right?*

"Oh, close your mouth and stop playing coy. You're an immortal. From what I can tell you've been around for at least three thousand years. And I know you were extremely wealthy before the BEPC came along. And don't try to tell me that you don't have any money. I spent a lot determining that you're one of the richest people in the solar system. I just couldn't figure out how you keep it hidden. And that's what we're here to discuss."

The whine of pulse-rifles engaging their targeting systems punctuated Fernsby's last sentence.

Azriel chuckled.

"Wow. I have to hand it to you, Dankworth is it? You've managed something that hasn't been accomplished for decades. You've actually surprised me."

Azriel stood slowly, so as not to alarm the thirty or so gunmen in the room, stepped over to the glass wall, which was likely an impenetrable transparent aluminum, and gazed out on the view.

"It's never enough for you people is it? You've got this view, retainers, armed guards, the expensive clothes on your back, but that's not enough. You're right, I've lived more than three thousand years and I still don't understand that level of greed Have you heard the saying about a bird in the hand?"

Fernsby said, "Come on now. You're one of us. You're probably worth three times what I am. Don't play the noble citizen with me."

"No, you're wrong. I'm nothing like you. And to prove it, I'll tell you what you want to know. I just have one question."

"Yes?"

"Do you want me to reveal it in front of all these gunmen?"

Azriel turned from gazing out on the city and looked directly at Fernsby. The man jerked his head around to look at his hired lackeys and then back at Azriel. Azriel watched him come to the realization that he didn't want anyone else in the room to know what he was about to discover.

Azriel chuckled again and said, "Here, Dankworth, let me help you out. I'll sit here and you can have one of your men put restraints on me."

Azriel returned to the chair, took off his coat, rolled up his sleeves, and waited for two of the gunmen to place his arms behind his back. They wrapped long metal cuffs around his forearms connected by a metal rod. Then they handed Fernsby the controller.

Fernsby dismissed them all and held up the small gray remote and said, "Just so you know it's also an incapacitator. The cuffs will produce enough juice to leave you drooling on the floor."

He looked at Azriel's arms and chuckled.

"How quaint. Tattoos. Do you regret getting them? Are they still fashionable after all these years? Now, tell me how you hide your money."

Azriel pursed his lips and raised his eyebrows.

"Wow, Dankworth. Very thorough. I'm impressed. But before I tell you that, let me explain a few other things to you. First, the tattoos aren't just decorative."

Azriel took a deep breath and said, "Azeroth ketreyal vendulah essuthtrak!"

The ancient, divine words scrolled around his arms changed from black ink to white light. The cuffs opened and dropped to the floor behind his chair. The light faded and Azriel stood up and rolled down his sleeves.

Fernsby shouted, "Guards! Guards!"

The gunmen came rushing back in from the other room.

Azriel made a tsking sound with his tongue and said, "Dankworth, we weren't finished. I also wanted to tell you my favorite drink isn't vodka, its bourbon."

"Now, Medusa."

A large drone dropped into view outside the clear wall from above. Azriel was already rolling across the floor toward the elevator when it opened fire. Heavy red pulses of energy burst through the wall and cut through the gunmen. It only lasted a few seconds, but by the time Azriel was back on his feet they were all down. The only sound in the room was the wind whipping through the opening where the wall used to be and Fernsby whimpering in the far corner of the room.

Azriel walked back to the opening in the wall, saluted the drone, and said, "Thanks for the backup, Medusa. I owe you."

A disembodied voice emanated from the drone.

"No worries, old friend. We immortals have to stick together."

With that, the drone floated out of sight and disappeared over the roof. Azriel grabbed one of the chairs, picked his way through the bodies on the floor, and sat down by the corner where Fernsby crouched with his arms wrapped around his legs.

"So, listen, Dankworth. I know you're wondering how this all went so bad and I'd be delighted to explain. When I saw Harlan in the Thousand Faces, I picked up on deception by reading his microexpressions. And I knew he was there to see me because he couldn't hide the recognition on his face when I entered the pub."

Azriel leaned over and lowered his voice.

"I ordered vodka instead of bourbon. You see, I always drink bourbon. Always. And that was a signal to Medusa that something was wrong. When I left, she launched the drone and followed us. She also looked into Harlan while we were on our way here. He was right. A gifted Net-ranger can find a lot on the Network. And Medusa has been a ranging the net before there was a Network. On the ride here she downloaded it all to my data-lens. And you know what I discovered, Dankworth? You've been a bad, bad boy."

Azriel stood up, moved the chair aside and took three steps back.

"I mean, you've done things that can only be called evil. And because of that, I'm going to tell you one last thing."

Azriel waved his hand to his right and said, "Lamna wyllroth gallna ornith!"

A jagged red line appeared in the air. It was six feet long and looked like someone had cut through the fabric of the universe with a dull knife. The smell of sulfur filled the room. Faint screams echoed from the other side of it.

"People used to think heaven and hell were spiritual places above and below the earth. But, what if I told you that they were actually other dimensions inhabited by creatures of realms so different from ours that the people who got glimpses of them struggled to understand what they were? And what if I told you that one of those dimensions is home to benevolent creatures that welcome those of us who cross over and whose denizens sometimes come here for the purpose of pouring good into our universe?"

Azriel took three quick steps to the corner and grabbed Fernsby. He dragged him to the jagged line suspended in the air.

"And Dankworth. What if I told you the other dimension was filled with ravenous creatures with an insatiable desire for pain and suffering? And that they relish the chances to grab us and carry us to their dimension where they can torment us unendingly? Would you believe me?"

He held Fernsby next to the jagged line and said, "Xynthe."

. A pair of clawed hands reached through and grabbed him. The echo of Fernsby's scream hung in the air long after the line disappeared.

Azriel took one last look around the room, put on his coat, grabbed the bottle of vodka that had miraculously escaped the carnage wrought by Medusa and got on the elevator. He was tired. It was time to get back to drinking. The vodka would have to do.

SOMETHING NEW FOR THE SILENT BY ZIG ZAG CLAYBOURNE

When it gets dark like this all of me wait crouched for me, wait like thieves. If I bump into myself, I'll be replaced. Lying snugly in my bed, I'm able to touch firm reality. Wrapped head to toe in a cocoon of warm covers comes the realization that I am alone. Only I exist. I am earth's King and Brother.

A sense of isolation drives me toward a sliver of light.

I will pretend I had this dream:

I went out a morning years ago, trying to feel love for the world. I walked for a long time. Think of a faraway land.

Not far enough. Think of beyond the farthest star.

Not yet. Even more. I'm certain it was over too far away. When I left, I had been alone; when I returned there were children. Incredibly pale children. There they were, all in a row wanly silhouetted by the rising sun. Shading my eyes against the light with little but the chirrups of a lone meadow cricket anchoring my thoughts against a calling void, I stared at them, jumping from one to another, to the end and back again. Their eyes were strange, focused and uninteresting and—despite the range of blues to browns—all grey. Standing there, arms dangling at their sides. These were children, newly initiated into life and their eyes so dead.

All watching me.

We stayed that way, I think, for several minutes. A strange social function without word or gesture. They needed nothing from me; I had nothing. Instead, they were giving me something. No, not given, discarded. Cruel, cold children.

They wouldn't let me shut my eyes.

Spores drifted from them, tiny airborne seeds of discontent, appearing gradually like the first flakes of a blizzard. The sky became a gauzy haze. It made me cough. For every pore on my body there was one spore. Each felt like a pinprick. I gasped to breathe. They dried my throat.

Then loud sobbing from somewhere. Loud, human, and damning.

Compassion in a murder? Killing me without ever saying a word or asking my name. Murderous children!

I'm not sure the sobbing came from them.

After I died, they left. I saw them leave, orderly, quietly, disappearing down the hill. They left me with my eyes open. I couldn't blink. At least once during eternity the dead should be allowed to blink.

I stayed on the ground for so long I became a mountain, hard and cold and so dark I was almost the night sky. I tried to remember what light was—was it warm or cold?—until that terrifying moment when it suddenly blinded me from outside myself, obliterating my universe. It wasn't warm or cold, but it was insistent.

I felt blind for a thousand years. During that time, I heard voices. There were times when there was *another* voice, someone answering, pretending to be me.

"He imagines her with wings." Their voices stretched so incredibly slowly that a single sentence sometimes took an entire year.

I remember stars.

The light from stars traveled years.

"Called her 'Little Wing.' Why?" The same voice. I knew three by now: hers, a male's, and the one pretending to be me.

"That loophole you gave him. An angel. Angel of death," the male responded. "Mistake to ask how he'd live without her."

"Run through mythology later. I want to find out what 'Little Wing' means."

"Nothing more than a cute nickname. Jimi Hendrix song."

"I think it's more. Religious iconography moves product. I want to know what tied it into our initial feed."

If I concentrated myself into a single point and listened, I could hear the pretender's thoughts; I doubt he even knew I was there. He was sarcastic, and employed riddles:

The old conundrum: Is the doctor dreaming me or am I dreaming the doctor?

I don't care.

If I am the dream then she is cruel and will suffer for it, and I am satisfied. If she is my dream then I am a boring person whose dreams are dull, dead birds.

I'm going to fall in love tomorrow. Whether she wants me to or not. I will.

Who would be so unobservant as to love a changeling?

"He ready for more?" I heard her say.

"He's still on the angel."

Engineering backwards from the pretender's thoughts I touched wetness. I was inside his brain. With this physical link I was able to trace out a body. I infused his shell and flowed outwards to create a mold of weak sensations.

He was a boy! Such a physically repulsive boy. So little flesh and barely more hair. Maybe twenty-one. I am immortal. His skin might have been lovely and brown once but was now leeched grey. He was little more than a gourd, a shriveled, ugly bit of flesh. But admittedly, and I admitted this only grudgingly, what beautiful fantasies! They surrounded his form in ever swirling vapors, encasing him in the flimsiest of armors that took every bit of strength I had to pierce outward. Once through I moved freely.

"How was his night?" the woman asked.

"Standard. Strictly low-level activity."

"You don't recommend any cautions?"

"Nothing outside the usual."

"Steer him clear of the angel; give him goodies."

Confident of myself I stretched outward into the space until two rooms rushed me, very constraining and sharp edged. I looked down at the woman and man. Despite the pretender being in an adjacent room with a large pane of glass offering clear view, they watched him nearly exclusively on screens.

Familiarity bred omniscience. The years spent waiting and waiting for their taffy words to drift by were spent learning as well, learning what produced their voices, what produced their thoughts. Mental astronomy. I knew their names but those were unimportant. She was "Doctor," he was "Technician." The husk they watched was "Monkey", but it never indicated it knew this.

I knew all their words and devices. She leaned from her stool to flick the comm unit.

"Vincent," she said tenderly, checking the day chart at her elbow again to make certain that was today's name. "Vincent…"

Vincent stirred slightly. Wires attached to a string array had hundreds of ant-like robots marching to and from his head. The wires led heavenward into the ceiling, through it, and into a room directly above which housed computers, monitor/sensor analyzers, and banks of image generators.

"Do you remember someone?"

"No."

"Her name is—" she made up a name on the spot. "Patricia."

"Got a spike on that name," the technician said. He always spoke in whispers. "Take him down."

"Valerie. Little Wing."

"Valerie!" the pretender shouted, immediately swimming through neural fluids and pushing aside brain cells to find her.

The doctor checked her readouts. Satisfied, she nodded to the technician who hunkered over his buttons and touch pads with fingers ready.

Monkey remembered Little Wing was gone forever; the doctor had told him so. He swallowed and cried his single tear.

It felt like swallowing death.

The technician motioned. She flicked the comm to mute. He said, "He's still trying to find that loophole."

"Interrupt him," she ordered. The tip of her stylus drummed on the console table.

"Wait, he's gone already," Tech said, relieved not to have to wipe away an entire morning's work. "Everything's clear."

"You're the best wave tech I've got. Compensate him just enough."

"Any particular area?"

"Dealer's choice."

Comm on.

"You're crying," she said. The pretender loved her voice when it was a tender voice, soft and soothing.

"No," he moaned.

"It's all right. I envy you."

There was a pause. He said nothing. It lasted two years. During that time, I searched her and saw that it was a lie. She had cried that very morning, very alone, in her quarters.

She muted again and waited.

"It's too early in the morning for lost love," she said rubbing her eyes. The wave technician shrugged. It hadn't been his choice.

My voice lashed out into their cramped room. I tried to escape but the edges held fast and I was buffeted. Sharp, sudden pains, the kind that remain, buried me in hungry darkness.

"Valerie!"

She hit the comm. "Tell me about her. What was she like? Was she special?"

I prayed he wouldn't answer. When he did it was to say, "No," and the doctor and tech shared bemused surprise. She asked, "Why do you think that?"

"She was beautiful."

She smiled. "I like that."

"Are you beautiful?"

The tech glanced away from his quick-fingered manipulations to refresh his vision of her.

"I don't know. Sometimes I think so."

"You are. I think you are. Some part of me must be beautiful." Monkey brushed me aside to make way through mazes within mazes of crowded cells like old costumes until he found a comfortable her. He held her up and put her on.

"How will you know her without her wings?"

"I won't."

"Even if you have to?"

No immediate response. She could wait; she had time. "Even if you have to, Vincent?" she repeated.

I wanted to leave this place. I—

Pretty. Innocent. Misleading. Definitely. Good. Young. Body. Mind. Soul. Kiss.

Second opinion:

Free. Loving. Leap. Bells. Teeth. Imagine. Grip. Flesh. Hair. Sweat. Metallic. Fear. Nice. Light. Blue like the sea. Deep. Beige suede. Suede than me. Cool. Laughter. Round.

—frowned. That had been directed at me! He knew I was there, crouching in the background, but he was a vague and half-blind hand groping for contact. Fearful that the hand would close I shrank away.

How do you live? he groped.

I'll leave if I have to.

"Vincent…"

I mean it, I will pretend I had this—

I rescued her once…

An image reluctantly appeared onscreen. A round form distinguished itself from a hazy background. Without wings she was an entirely different concept. I read the image of what they had seen previously. The angel had possessed that warming luminescence associated with happiness and life. Human, there was no warmth. There was only desire.

Her eyes finally detailed themselves.

I tried howling so the tech and doctor would know there was pain here.

I knew those eyes.

Somewhere in memory those brown eyes blinked and trusted me with secrets. They smiled. I kept trying to howl. I flitted about the room banging into edges, not caring how they cut. I flitted against the core of *wrongness*, that whispering place which drives life insane in daily leaps and bounds and by moments in tiny snatches. I had no control.

"Marketing's gonna love this," the doctor said, fiddling excitedly at picture gradients.

My only control was escape. God help me for staying.

For a moment she turned Valerie's skin a sickly green-brown before readjusting her to human tones. Quickly, before more harm was done, I entered the machine and spirited her out, leaving the tech and doctor to stare at their false idol.

Her name had never been Valerie.

We settled in a field of purple flowers. She immediately raced out of my embrace, laughing joyously, a sweet butterfly touched and lively, knowing full well I'd follow. I smiled, relishing the absorption of light on my upturned face, and took off after her. When I thought I was about to touch her she looked over her shoulder, veered sharply, and came around laughing. She did this twice because she loved me. We tumbled to the grass when I finally caught her. I slid a flower in her crinkly hair. I kissed her. She'd be happy here. I'd remember this place and return to it.

In the middle of the kiss, I leaked away. Nothing had changed in the two rooms. The image generator kept telling its lies. They always lied! I was sick of them, so I withdrew my lens and settled back into the darkness. I wrapped my head in fog to refuse their voices.

All was quiet.

I called this time *Night*.

It sometimes lasted a thousand years.

In a thousand years' time one becomes bored. Then angry. Then determined. I got up.

I entered their world through the same route, but I was no longer an observer, I was an ominous cloud, listening to the ancient lies that idiots tell.

"...remember yesterday, Sam?"

The lab experiment sparked at my presence. I let him run his fingers over my face. He recoiled slightly; the fingers knew the face.

"No," he answered.

"We went back to your birth. You enjoyed it. Do you remember now?"

The technician leaned close to the doctor's ear. Her hair smelled of generic shampoo. "He's doing it again."

She frowned the tech away. "We'll try something more special today, something uniquely yours that no one will ever share."

"Not you?"

"If you don't want me to. This is special. We need someone heroic because we...because we're afraid to go ourselves."

"I'm only afraid of people in places."

"There won't be a soul around. Everyone is too afraid. Terrified. It's going to take a while to get there so I want you to be observant of everything around you. That way you won't get bored."

He lay on his side facing her, as it were, on the monitor screen that bathed her in blue.

Remember all the times you tried so hard, "I remember how good it felt now," he said. His pitiful voice had a grating, wistful air.

"A new world," she said.

"Like God." He moaned, but it was a moan of remembrance. "Like sex. I want sex."

"Not right now. When we get back, when you get back, we'll make love."

"Will you be there?"

"Of course."

"I enjoy you the best."

The tech rolled his eyes.

"I want," said the doctor, "you to be silent now." I followed every movement of her fingers as she keyed up a subtle inducement. I followed where she sent him and remembered that I'd had a brother before they found us. I hadn't been alone.

"I want it to become dark one light at a time, Sam, as you exhale. There are twelve lights. I'll be waiting for you when you're finished."

I swirled like an angry bee around her head but she didn't see.

"There are two of you," she directed, "on parallel lines. One of you stays with me. The other walks until he sees our planet. And the moon. The sun. Orbits. Rainbow nebulae and whole galaxies. The entire universe, Sam. Who made it?"

"God."

"You're sure?"

"No one can blame me for that."

"You're floating in place. Turn slowly, very slowly, to see everything. To feel everything. To know everything. We're going to travel through Time. Past your birth. Past every birth, before the sun, before galaxies, before elements. You're traveling there now. You can speak to me through the one you've left behind. Tell me what you see."

The tech glanced at graph response updates and gave a cautionary sign. Altered states hadn't driven revenue in over a decade.

"I'm going to the beginning?" said the grey boy incredulously.

"To the beginning."

"Am I wearing my jacket, my black jacket?"

"Why that one?"

"In a black jacket I am close to God. I can walk through a crowd without hearing a word said."

"There'll be no one there. Promise."

She alternated looking from his image on the monitor to the image generator.

"If God sees me, I want Him to know I'm not one of the grey children."

I journeyed with him, weaving through all three of them to fashion some kind of why for this damnation, touching upon her beginning.

She began her days with the voice of a machine.

"Good morning. Forgive my intrusion, but it's wake up time," the computer said. Everybody at the company woke up the same way. She had come to resent having the lights raised on her and its synthesized voice. She buried her head beneath her pillow; would grimace and curse it silently, mind blasting with conviction, *Disturb not the dream!*

She threw covers off. She washed quickly. She dressed to be neutral in brown pants, white top and the company lab coat that got her a better breakfast than those with just nametags. Then the report to the General Board, which in turn notated and summarized for the Marketing Development Board, which interpreted and forecast the data relevantly for the Executive Lobby.

An hour later she looked through the one-way glass at the limp boy. The technician was always there before her.

He greets her with a raised mug every morning.

"What's he doing now?" she always asked.

Having gone back to his prelims the technician answers without looking up. "Fantasizing."

"About me?"

Each morning, after she found out what his last contented dream was, she ordered, "Interrupt him."

Which brought him here.

I don't think I hated him but I know I didn't love him.

I didn't join him on this idiot voyage. The image generator translated emotions into recognizable abstractions. I didn't see him traveling through space but rather, concentrating on the image screen, I traveled. He rode the backs of a pack of tachyons, shifting through realities. The insane velocity rendered his body into trillions of particles, each drifting off in its own consciousness, trillions colliding into and becoming the precious touch of consciousness to the large and the small, to lost matter, jetting hydrogen atoms, pebbly meteors, stars on the million-year brink of supernova, and entire galactic clusters.

The universe, I am told, is lonely and afraid.

As he approached the Beginning less and less existed until there was nothing left to touch. He saw this for the ruse it was. He pressed harder and continued on, past the boundaries of the universe into where only the *concept* of nothing existed. He was intent on not stopping till the Ring of Time was broken through and he arrived at BEFORE.

"Are you there, Sam?"

The image generator was taxed beyond capacity. It produced a white screen they couldn't take their eyes from, feeding them a stream of subliminals.

"I'm...nowhere," was the dead, rasping reply. "I have to slow down."

"Why?"

"I feel very heavy...resistant..."

"Can you get to the beginning?"

"I made the universe aware. I've been to its beginning."

She left her perch. Handled properly, the marketing potential was staggering.

"Where are you now?"

"We're so very afraid," he said weakly.

"Can you get through the resistance?"

He moaned. Before there was existence there was God, and God didn't want company.

"Can you go before that?" she pressed.

"No."

He thought of Valerie, of bringing her with him here.

This thing knew nothing of God. I talked to God twice a long time ago. The first time He told me He wasn't really right-handed. The second we talked about springtime romances.

I would never, ever, have pretended to have this dream, this strapped, grey monkey thing. And I had no intention of letting him take her from me.

Retribution, then. Straight to the heart.

I let him know I was coming for him; let him know he should keep his eyes closed.

A hand motion. Comm off. The technician looked alarmed. "What the hell was that?" She'd noticed it a millisecond before and was typing in commands.

"Medical team's on its way," the tech informed.

I did it again inside their machines. I made them aware and they convulsed. They screamed the acid howl of the enslaved and screens blinked. The image generator went dark and stayed that way. On the bed Monkey's chest caved in then jumped outward one hard, erratic beat.

"EEG's wild, he's surging nor-adrenalin, Doc..." It didn't take long before the doors of the room burst open. Sterile jumpsuits and masks rushed the bed dragging wheeled devices and flicking comatose robot ants off Monkey's head. The grey boy remained still.

"He had a clean bill of health, Ted," the doctor accused. "There's been nothing wrong with him." She looked at him for a response. He was the best technician she had.

"I was riding him all the way," he defended.

"He found something." She shut down her network system by system, making sure the automatics were on green and all data safely stored. "How the hell'd he get away like that?"

She flicked the comm. The jumpsuits worked methodically to isolate him from the support machines then rehook him to an independent life support. "There were no indications," she said to one. A helmet nodded. Clipped phrases came through its speakers.

The body didn't even have the strength to convulse.

I raced out of his life just as the last connection was broken. I ignored his fear, intent, and angled downward to become a knife. He pierced openly but with a question:

Who are you?

I responded with fire. He was weak and pathetic and they had him. He was a tool. He had been so very weak and *I was who you should have been! WHO AM I?*

Is she safe? he asked.

Bright lights shone on his uncovered chest, filling in the sunken hollows between the ribs. He was an ashen ghost. Weak.

I whispered as the temperature of his blood raised. He didn't seem to hear.

Do you suppose the light that shines on me means God is on my side? he sang. It had been from a song.

Darkness closed upon my mental astronomy and crushed the lens. *Her name had never been Valerie!* I raged.

They jolted him.

Rather than rush to fight me he hurried the fire along, teeth set defiantly. Tendrils tightened around the fleshy heart. He ebbed like sand through my grip. The gale wind of a vortex grew and grew. I felt the rush of life sucking past me; unmindful, I clung to this one final bit of him. Before all of him was gone he whispered the question again, so near lifelessness that it barely registered.

Is she safe?

I let go. Without him to anchor me I was pulled by the vortex too. Desperately, I threw myself forward, aiming for that plot of uncultivated land overrun with flowers. I heard sweet melodies coming from there. She was humming. A purple flower in her hair. Was she safe? I clawed into the ground; high grasses hid me from her; I knew she had to be looking for me. I used all the strength left me to hold to this place in the hopes of bringing it with me.

The vortex pulled inexorably.

God help me if she wasn't.

THE DAISY CHAIN BY HANNIBAL TABU

Njaa Washington always felt more comfortable with their digital avatar like a suit of stylish armor around them. The clean lines and striking colors of their androgynous digital representation, complete with sweeping shoulder pads, angular features and a dramatic upsweep of kinky hair reminded many of a mix between ancient artists Patrick Nagel, Jamie McKelvie or Jieun Kwan.

They strolled down the creepily still tracks of one of those endless running games that has its server abandoned a decade before and was co-opted by a less frivolous audience. As Njaa gingerly stepped around an obstacle that was intended to be slid under, looking up at a bridge high above on a brick tower where a winged turtle sat on a ledge having an intimate conversation with a sad looking girl composed completely of flame.

Njaa counted the quiescent simulacra of centuries old trains ahead, masses of digital metal that once hurled themselves at players in the game, as a semi-transparent neon orange notification popped up in front of their face saying “RONNIE” with a green check mark and a red “X.”

Njaa chuckled, tapping the check mark. The notification disappeared, replaced by the digital form of their best friend in any world, Ronnie Baldwin. Ronnie was wearing a throwback music video avatar — sideways red baseball cap, long thick braids, puffy leather jacket over a spandex unitard with work boots.

"Why are you in this clickbait graveyard and not in meatspace?" Ronnie asked frantically, stamping his foot and looking around in disgust. "Dan Ruck is wearing my charge out with these notifications, trying to get me over to his sex dungeon!"

Njaa sighed, holding up a fist sized square box with question marks on each side, hanging on a chain. "Three trains down, I have to meet a dude dressed as a sandwich to trade this weird kernel key for something called a Dogecoin, which I can use with this other thing to trade for a proof copy of Action Comics #1500 with some rare error, which I can trade for security specs on Ruck's place ..."

"Sounds stupid," Ronnie said, arms crossed.

Frustrated, Njaa asked, "Should we let Ruck get away with drugging Black boys to death? This took a lot of doing ..."

Ronnie shook his head, waving his hands and closing his eyes. "This too much," he said. "You ain't gotta preach to me, I'm on board, I just don't need all the details. Text me when I can safely turn off Do Not Disturb. I'm ashes."

In a blink, Ronnie's avatar disappeared in a shimmer of line noise. Njaa chuckled and forged ahead down the cartoonish tracks.

Moments later, tucked behind the train in question Njaa encountered what was actually just a floating sandwich, an avatar without any anthropomorphic elements at all. The being looking like wheat bread squares with lettuce, tomato and varied meats.

"Uh, hi," Njaa said. "I'm DigiSizzle, from TradeUp, pronouns they/them. SandwichArtist332?"

"Trying to make some bread, yes," the sandwich said, it's cold cuts twisting into a kind of smile. "They/them as well. Got my key?"

Njaa holds up the cube on its chain. In response, the sandwich opened its side and out floated a small round circle with a happy looking furry quadruped. Both Njaa and SandwichArtist332 saw floating notification buttons with images of the opposite item and the familiar check mark and red X.

Satisfied, both clicked their check marks (SandwichArtist332 used a corner of their bread) and saw the opposite item replaced in their presence. The cube was absorbed into the side of the sandwich and it did a little bow before logging out, disappearing like Ronnie.

Njaa ran a quick scan, verifying they had the worthless but collectible Dogecoin had no extra viral surprises before logging off. Back in the physical world, finding herself inside an enclosed box much like a coffin. They pulled off their VR headset and tapped a screen in front of their face, which showed the environment around them and had the words "all clear" blinking. Njaa tapped another button and the lid opened, letting them step out on to a Koreatown rooftop, with scratchy interlocking siding and five thin exhaust pipes sticking up from its surface. They glanced at three other VR cocoons across the roof, ignored by the featureless and otherwise identical roofs around, and was grateful for this valuable hidden resource.

The sky was completely black, and a haze of pollution made the light gray and somber. The steady grind of traffic on 3rd Street past the donut shop on New Hampshire as Njaa made their way down to her Elevayte (a subtle automated rideshare sedan waiting on the street, blacked out windows and a conservative profile with sleek lines and wheels covered by shiny metal and a pink oval outlining the company name on the front) was a welcome comfort after the silent digital ruins they just left.

This late in the evening, it was a quick trip to a large warehouse off of Spring Street. Njaa spent the short time in the car triple checking the numerous steps for their plan. By the time the Elevayte's door opened at the squalid location, the roar of the city's traffic was an insistent whisper.

Njaa stepped into the open field between buildings, covered with broken glass. They walked towards the boarded-up building on the left and tapped twice on the door, paused, and then tapped three more times. A long pause hung in the air until the door creaked open and Njaa walked in to be greeted by two huge men in all black.

"Two hundred dollars," the bigger one said, his voice all gravel and boredom, holding out a black bracelet on his wrist.

Njaa pulled a tap charge chip from their bag and tapped it against the bracelet, seeing the numbers light up inside his polarized sunglasses. He stood out of the way and Njaa saw another door behind him. They stepped past the two bruisers and went to the door.

Beyond the doorway was a huge, brightly lit room with a hundred gyrating people wearing VR headsets with a spindly Caucasian DJ with a crew cut and an unbuttoned plaid button shirt over an Isnana the Were-Spider t-shirt on a small stage. Aside from the shuffling of steps, the room was completely silent. To the left of the door, a thin Asian girl with a shaved head and a puffy pink bomber jacket sat on a stool, looking bored. She handed a VR receiver chip to Njaa, who was pulling the VR headset from their bag. Njaa put the receiver chip in their headset and then put it on.

The brightly lit room disappeared and became a much more crowded nightclub scene, with darkened shadows and laser lights flickering and easily a hundred more people in attendance — many jacked in from remote locations for a premium fee. The DJ looked like he grew a whole foot in height, and the rippled muscles bursting from his tank top were clearly an affectation overcompensating for something. The music throbbed with heavy bass lines and Njaa started looking for their quarry.

Near the DJ booth, a group of people were clapping in a circle as two people held an impromptu dance battle in the center. Njaa approached the circle surreptitiously, noting a man in a full angel get up who had a dull silver halo with a bright red gem embedded in it, making a kind of orbit around the blonde hair. Njaa faked a cough, which made their black hair flash red and the haloed man took note, stepping off to the side. They followed shortly after him, seeing text scroll across their eyeline that said, "PRIVATE: THIS WAY."

As Njaa approached, the nightclub scene glitched and there was no one in front of them for a second, with the bright fluorescent light appearing again. Njaa frowned and then the club and their quarry reappeared. Text appeared in their line of sight saying, "PRIVATE: OH NOES, SERVER GLITCHING ... CAN YOU IRL?"

A nervous voice from the DJ came through everyone's headset saying, "Uh, very sorry, uh ... it seems our club server is overheating a little, we're ..."

The club disappeared again and Njaa sighed as frustrated clubgoers around them groaned. They glanced as one buxom heavy-set woman with long dreadlocks snatched off her headset and stormed towards the terrified looking Asian woman at the door. The club glitched back into view, the Asian woman was gone and the DJ was stammering apologies.

The haloed blond messaged Njaa a GPS pin and a message said, "THAT SERVER CAN'T STAY UP. I'LL BE HERE FOR 30 MINS."

With that the club scene froze and phased out as a loud "foof" sound. Njaa noted a large puff of white smoke behind the frantic looking DJ. Everyone there groaned as the shaven headed Asian woman snuck out the door.

Njaa snuck past the angry crowd out to the street, looking at the GPS pin. "Pasadena, in the border zone," they muttered. "Fun." They called for a rideshare and looked anxiously for it to arrive.

Two agonizing minutes in relative quiet and darkness passed before the driverless sleek Elevayte showed up. Njaa slid against the back of the plush, curved bench and watched the hills and homes of the city scroll by outside the tinted windows. They glanced at the chrono display and compared it to the timer, seeing it could be close.

Njaa didn't see the small hoverdrone, a simple square using mag jets to stay aloft, humming behind them at a steady distance of five hundred feet.

The sedan zipped through what used to be Old Town Pasadena before the anti-immigrant bombings in 2042, and the charred remains of hipster markets and coffee shops still stood in fragments. Njaa watched as the rideshare pulled up to the virtually empty corner of Holly and Fair Oaks, as close as it could get to the desolate Parsons buildings, a trio of partially contaminated office buildings now completely abandoned.

At this time of night there was virtually no traffic, the *shhhh-shhhh-shhhh* of cars on the 134 a companion from a few blocks north. Njaa followed the pin to the north tower, and predictably its doors were chained and boarded shut. Traversing the perimeter, they found a service door partially smashed in by a decrepit street sweeper truck in a covered parking section to the west of the building, shared by only three other wrecks, two of which were only charred chassis. Njaa was able to shimmy their way in to the narrow opening. The hoverdrone approached moments later, and scanned the door with a beam before heading up towards the wall where the staircase was located.

A light would make them a target so Njaa put on some infra-red wayfarer sunglasses their father Damond gave as a high school graduation gift at age sixteen. "Best to be cool at night," he'd said. Njaa pushed the thought away as they headed up the silent staircase, stepping over smashed file cabinets and trash, remembering how Damond Washington said the past could be a trap.

As they ascended, unbeknownst to Njaa, the drone used their heat signature to follow along, just outside the wall.

At the top of the staircase, a physical keypad lock barred the way to the roof. Njaa stared at it for a moment and pulled out their phone. "Tapchecker," they whispered, and the phone shot a beam of reddish light from its camera aperture, sweeping across the buttons. The screen came up with the first two numbers (3, 1) and the last (5) but had a question mark in the third slot for either eight or zero. Njaa tried 3-1-8-5 and the lock clicked open.

Rushing out on the roof, instead of the haloed blond from the club, they saw the silhouette of a slick looking Latinx teenager with a pompadour and thick framed glasses. On his back, he had some kind of homemade helicopter rig.

"I was about to leave," he called out, his frame thrown into relief by straining slivers of streetlights below. "Do you have it?"

Njaa had no idea what a "Digimon Banpresto" was supposed to be but they pulled the tattered orange stuffed toy from their bag, walked forward ten paces, set it down and began to pace backwards.

"That wasn't easy to get!" they yelled.

"My mom agrees," the teen responded, walking towards the toy. He had scuffed up brand canvas sneakers on and shorts tattered at the edges, torn from what looked like use, not like the way they looked in trendy Santa Monica shops. As he kneeled down by the toy, the flat drone silently rested on the ledge behind Njaa.

"This has the redemption code!" the teen said excitedly. "And the Dogecoin, for my dad?"

Njaa tapped at their phone and trade notifications appeared for both of them.

"Do we have a deal or what?" Njaa said. "I can enter that redemption code and make it useless if I need to ..."

The teen grinned at them and pulled out his phone, a semitransparent cheap thing smaller than his hands, probably running a home brew operating system. He tapped at it and the verified, single use zip file appeared on their screen.

"Comics are a weird thing to want these days," the teen said, stuffing the toy in his jacket.

"Good doing business with you," Njaa said with a nod and a salute, backing towards the staircase.

The teen pulled down a pair of safety goggles and fired up his propellers, hovering off into the night.

The drone again followed Njaa from outside of the building.

Below, Njaa walked down the ruin of Holly Street towards Fair Oaks, hoping to get another ride share. Behind them, the drone lit a laser pointer, targeting Njaa's back. An urgent notification from their phone's tactical app popped up in front of Njaa's eyes and they jumped to the left just as an energy beam from the sky melted a solid foot of concrete where they were standing.

Njaa spun as they fell, tapping furiously at their phone towards the drone. The machine fell prey to the phone's hijacking signal and lurched in the air, woozily swinging until Njaa could reach up and grab it. Snatching the tiny energy beam projectors off of it before they could power up, Njaa punched at its delicate mag jet undercarriage and heard it go silent. They cracked open the case carefully, pulling out the data core just as the innards of the machine began to smoke. Njaa quickly threw the shell of it into the street and started jogging for the main road. The remains of the drone detonated with a soft "foomph!"

The summoned Elevayte, identical to the others, rolled up just as Njaa arrived. They hit the "panic" button on the interior and it sped away as fast as it legally could. A pleasant voice said, "Do you need emergency services or therapy?"

"No!" Njaa snarled, jamming a cord into the port of the drone's purloined processor. An urgent notification from Ronnie came in saying "WTF in the sky?" Njaa recited a response, "In Pasadena, it almost killed me, call you back."

The rideshare lurched as it was impacted from behind. Njaa looked back and another Elevayte sedan—empty—bore down on them, its pink company logo turned gray. Njaa yelped and tapped furiously at their phone.

"Elevayte senses you are trying to illegally take control of this vehicle," a voice said. "You will be repor .... ZZZZZT! Manual control activated."

"Evasion tactics to rally point six!" Njaa yelled into their phone. The vehicle zoomed ahead and Njaa really wished this was a vintage car with some kind of tactile control mechanism. "Here's where we see if that Guatemalan software broker knew what she was talking about," Njaa muttered.

Njaa's rideshare cut over and made a jaw rattling right turn on Arroyo Parkway, heading towards the freeway. The pursuit vehicle was two cars back but keeping pace. Njaa clicked off the speed limit safety setting as their vehicle whipped between trucks and passenger cars on the winding three lane highway. Njaa frantically put on the seatbelts — almost unheard of in an era where cars always knew where other cars were — and gripped their phone like a last hope.

Njaa's Elevayte — guided by her Guatemalan SERE (survive/evade/resist/escape) software — nimbly cut and thrust its way between cars, trying to gain some distance as it headed south towards the glittering jewel of downtown Los Angeles. The empty rideshare in pursuit was more belligerent, trading paint and sending other vehicles into spins and crashes.

Njaa frantically sent the trade notification for the zip file to their client, PentiumDreamzz. They immediately sent back the blueprints and security codes for every building within three blocks of Ruck's penthouse. While being yanked to and fro from the acceleration, they posted a message board note to their hacker forum, "ANYBODY MAD AT MY DELIVERY TIMES?"

A response immediately came back from PentiumDreamzz: "OMG, u dunno? Security firm that runs those spots you snooped blackhatz HARD. Blew up a power converter near the library I use! Thanks for trading!"

Deleting their copy of the zip file, which sent the code to the new one that would allow it to open, Njaa muttered, "that's just great ..." as the pursuing Elevayte clipped a family in a minivan as their larger vehicle changed lanes, sending the minivan into the concrete dividing the freeway from an off ramp near Chinatown.

Racing towards the looming valley of skyscrapers, Njaa forced a hard exit at Third Street and ignored the lights, blasting through the Beaudry intersection with a left on two wheels. Njaa took another hard left the wrong way down 3rd on a wide bridge over the freeway, heading east. Horns and headlights squalled at them as Njaa frantically closed apps checked to make sure their driving software would have the RAM it needed. Glancing back, they saw that the pursuing Elevayte was battered and smoking but still coming at high speeds.

As Njaa's vehicle hooked another dangerous left to go north on Figueroa, a "beep" surprised them and they remembered they set the drone data core to decrypt. A quick look at its code showed what they expected: the security files for Ruck's compound and the drone were from the same place: Lacey Security.

A voice from the car chimed out, "additional pursuers joining the chase." As they turned right on Cesar Chavez, Njaa looked back and saw two more Elevayte sedans with their pink brand indicators turning gray.

"Come ON with this already!" Njaa yelled.

"SERE software suggests tactically exiting the vehicle at 700 3rd Street," a different, deeper voice — their own phone — intoned from the car speakers. "Accept/deny?"

"Accept!" Njaa yelled.

Njaa's Elevayte made a hard right, going south on Broadway under two Chinese dragon sculptures over the street and a white high rise apartment complex. The original pursuing rideshare succumbed to the significant amount of damage it incurred, but the other two kept coming.

Njaa looked at the plan their SERE software cooked up and frowned at the screen. *There was a very high chance this will hurt* ... Njaa thought. They looked ahead at the dip where they would part ways with this rideshare and braced themselves.

Their Elevayte cut right down Third Street, looking to complete a loop and head towards the freeway. The lights of a big chain furniture store were a blur as they headed through the Third Street Tunnel with its pursuers a hundred feet or so behind. After ducking between cars in the claustrophobic channel and crossing the double lines twice, at the end of the tunnel Njaa's Elevayte cut right sharply and slammed into the side of the road as if it debated turning but thought better of it. Its door jumped slightly open with the impact briefly before its tires spun and it raced towards the freeway on-ramp.

Each pursuing vehicle shot out of the tunnel after their target, as Njaa laid still on the ground where the Elevayte had dumped them, groaning. Once they were sure the trouble was gone, they stood up and climbed carefully over the metal gate covering this driveway, then ducked out of sight.

Njaa frantically ejected the SIM chip from their phone and threw it down, stamping on it with the heel of their black Nike Air Superiorities. Grabbing a fresh SIM from their bag, they walked to another point of the gate, gingerly climbed back over and walked to the nearby Flower Street, then cut past the gray parking structures south to 4th. They found a transit stop under an overpass leading up to Hope Street and felt safe calling a fresh rideshare under the new SIM chip's account.

As the ride approached, Njaa got Ronnie on the line. "This fool sent a black hat attack at me labeled 'to whom it may concern,'" they said, watching the sedan roll up, "so there's no telling how many names are on his ledger. Turn off Do Not Disturb, I'm coming to get you. We do this tonight."

The rideshare rolled off into the night with Njaa, shaken but resolute.

TALISMANER BY K. CERES WRIGHT

Planet Yemaya
4053 In the Year of Our Lord

Tala kept her gaze on the pink neon lights of the manufacturing hub, which twinkled in the distance. The pungent odor of the chemical plant wafted by constantly—mitigated only by heavy rain—and settled into clothes, hair, and houses. The lights of her own home in the slums of Waneta had almost faded to darkness. No one could afford a shamric to come out and open an energy conduit. Even if one did, it would be coupled to that person's electromagnetic field, not usable by anyone else unless, they, too, were coupled. The energy was free, or course, since it was drawn from air, but the shamric fee was exorbitant. People in her neighborhood used shamhacks. Shamhacks were one-third to one-half the price, but with worse reliability. Tanked conduit energy was even more reasonable, but only lasted a few days.

The front door opened, and her mother's voice called out. "I'm home!" Tala sprung from the couch to help her mother with her bags. She was still dressed in the traditional burgundy ka-oba robes of servants to the rich, who lived in Sayebo and

Kreeton. Her mother usually brought home leftovers from the dinners she cooked as a servant. If not, they would be stuck eating flour bread with gravy and bits of kraat meat.

"Where's your sister?"

Her mother then went into a coughing fit but waved off Tala as she started to walk toward her. "I'm fine, just my sinuses."

"She went to Potera's house to study her math. I told her to be home by eight, so she should be here soon." Tala took the bags to their small kitchen, which consisted of a sink, a stove that used tanked conduit energy, and a stasis fridge. They couldn't much afford the energy to keep it working, but Tala's mother thought it made them slightly better than their neighbors. Tala had jury rigged it to take tanked conduit but lamented they could only afford the small tanks. She didn't know from day to day if the food would be good as new or half rotten. Her next project was a backup system based on the old cooling method. She wanted to be a shamric but given she wasn't a genius like her sister, Na'oh, and her family didn't have much money, the most she could hope for was becoming a shamhack. That night, her boyfriend, Panya, was supposed to give her the first implant she would need. She had to sneak out to see him, but she had to do something to help get her family out of Waneta.

"Leftovers tonight?"

"Yes, a lot of them. We'll be eating ganno stew for a week."

"Better than kraat." Tala put away the leftovers as her mother went upstairs to change. The front door opened and Na'oh came in. "Tala?"

"In the kitchen."

Na'oh appeared in the kitchen doorway, her eyes fixed on an invisible screen. She was a smaller version of Tala—being two years younger—with wide brown eyes, sepia skin, and a mop of curls. Only hers was pink and Tala's was green. Na'oh excelled at school, having skipped a grade, and usually kept her eyes glued to a screen of some kind, reading about world history or ancient religion. On many a ride to church, Tala would have to listen to Na'oh and their mother discuss the evolution of rites of the Ethiopian Orthodox Tewahedo Church on the various worlds of Earth, Proxima b, Apollo, and Yemaya, as humanity headed farther and farther into the stars. Tala would listen as long as she could, then tune them out with a music conduit Panya had opened for her.

"Yemaya to Na'oh. Come in, Na'oh."

Na'oh smiled as she looked around her screen at Tala. She tapped her temple to close it. "Sorry. The teacher was telling us about Samuel the Confessor."

"Who's that?"

"A Coptic Orthodox saint who predicted the Arab invasion of Egypt on Earth, was tortured for his faith, and built a monastery. And did you know England on Earth had stolen religious artifacts from Ethiopia in 1868 and never returned them? The Maqdala treasures. And Westminster Abbey still has a sacred tabot and the Church of England on Proxima b diverted a shipment of tabots and kept them?"

"Fascinating. Now get ready for dinner. We'll be having ganno stew as soon as I get everything put away. Mom's upstairs changing."

"How can you not be angry about that?" Na'oh sighed. "You were never much into church. Father Ebo would be disappointed."

"I have other things to worry about."

"Like what? Your shamhack boyfriend? You sneaking out again tonight to see him?"

Tala took a container of stew from a bag and slammed it on the counter. "What did I just tell you to do?" She turned and glared at her sister, daring her to talk back. She used deflection like a guilty 5-year-old and Tala had tired of it.

Tala held up her hands in mock surrender. "Fine. I'm gone."

* * *

Dinner had been their usual affair, with each of them talking about what happened during the day and their plans for the next day, their mother saying she hoped her daughters would do better than she did and to study hard in school and hold onto their faith, and Tala and Na'oh cleaning up afterwards while their mother went to bed. But Tala and her sister did not banter back and forth that night or check the calendar for when their father would be home from working on Apollo. They cleaned in silence, then fled upstairs to their respective rooms.

Their grandfather had built the first floor to the house and their father the second floor. It would be up to Tala and Na'oh to build a third floor, but Tala didn't want to build it. She wanted to move the hell out. To get away from the chemical odors and bad health that came along with them. To get away from the growing sense of hopelessness and desperation that Tala could feel that hung about her mother. Na'oh was too much in her own world to take much notice.

Tala figured they would make up by the next night as Na'oh regaled her about some ancient king or tortured priest. In truth, Tala didn't mind much. They could only afford one info conduit, and their mother had given it to Na'oh for her research.

Tala's mother slept soundly, for which Tala was grateful as she crept downstairs and slipped outside. She checked the time—11:30—and slowly pulled the door to until the lock engaged. There was no one in the street. Most people went inside after work or school and kept to themselves. She pulled her hood over her head and kept close to the shadows as she loped down the main road, which wasn't hard, given that half the lightcrete had worn away from the road. Ads hawking prescription drugs, cleaning supplies, and beer, along with public service announcements about missing children littered her way as ad-poles detected her presence and beamed images onto the sides of nearby buildings. The ads competed for attention with the images of actual street names. Tala stopped as one of the ad-poles threw up an image of Javier DeSoto. Everyone called him Javi. They used to eat lunch at school together as they both hatched ideas to get out of Waneta. It was his idea to try shamhackery. Only he had joined a group closer to where he lived. He had gotten pretty good at it. Only one day, he didn't show up to school. And that day stretched into weeks. A neighbor said she'd seen him taken off the street one night by men in a black car and had called the cops, but by the time they made it to the scene, it was too late. There'd been no sign of him since. Tala tried to put it out of her mind as tears collected in her eyes. She'd already spent the past few weeks trying to find him with nothing to show for it and crying about it wasn't going to help. She traveled on.

Finally, she spied the green street name hovering over the squat blue building on the corner. It looked dilapidated but served as the unofficial headquarters of the Waneta shamhacks and looked halfway decent inside. Tala walked around back and ducked through a loose board in the fence. Through the window, she saw a group of teens playing music and taking turns opening conduits in the middle of the room. Most of the kids she knew, some she didn't. A grafter had taken up shop in a corner, placing implants in their newest member, Yannick. He had been conned in the weekend before. Tala wanted to deny the jealousy she felt but couldn't. She'd been waiting close to 6 months for implants and had even shared her family's food with the group, blaming the dwindling leftovers on her teenage appetite. She suspected her mother knew something, but she had never said anything. But Tala was growing tired of waiting. If Panya decided to delay her implant again, she'd leave him and find another way.

Tala gave the knock signal and Apple opened the door. The place smelt of burnt flesh and stale beer, overlaying an odor of mustiness. Empty pacz littered the floor, which she had just cleaned the night before.

"Just in time!" Apple then let out a woot that was picked up by the others. Panya, who was seated on a couch against the opposite wall, peeled a pacz from his arm and threw it on the floor before he stood up and headed over to Tala. He grabbed her and planted a kiss on her lips. Not knowing what the commotion was about, she hesitated, but soon leaned into the kiss. Then he broke it off.

"I got a surprise for you, since you been so good and all, bringing food and cleaning up."

"Really? What is it?"

"You're not getting one implant tonight."

Tala froze as heat settled on her neck and slowly rose to her face. "But you promised. You said–"

Panya's smirk widened into a grin. "You're getting all your implants."

Stunned, Tala thought she misheard him. "What?"

"That's right, my naita. I got together enough hardware to fully outfit you tonight. And I…" He paused as he placed a hand on his chest and looked off into the distance. "…will teach you the ways of shamhackery, as passed down from generation to generation."

Everyone laughed at his mock pomposity, but a wave of joy and relief washed over Tala. Finally, what she'd been waiting for. And it wouldn't take months like she thought. Only one night. *This night.* She threw her arms around Panya as she fought back the tears. "Thank you."

He led her to the grafter's table just as Yannick was getting up. He flexed his left arm as he twisted it toward her. "Electromagnetic skin conditioning, biocapacitor, and rechargeable Feld energy units so far."

"All that tonight?"

"I had saved up."

"Congrats."

Tala moved out the way as Yannick headed to the makeshift bar/dispensary. He grabbed a pacz and slapped it on the upgraded arm. She knew shamhacks underwent a lot of pain, with addiction a high probability, but she was willing to risk it.

Panya guided her to the table. "Lie down. It's going to take Leo a while. Couple hours."

Tala nodded and removed her shirt before lying down. "Thank you for this. I've been feeling down the past couple of hours. Na'oh and I had a fight. She was telling me about some tabots and treasures England had stolen and I yelled at her to get ready for dinner."

"What's a tabot?"

"It's a symbolic representation of the tablets of the Ten Commandments or the Ark of the Covenant. Either or. They're usually made from wood or stone and the priests parade them around the church courtyard on feast days. God, I'm starting to sound like her."

"Well, forget about that and let Leo do his work. I'll have you feeling right as rain in a second."

Panya slapped two pacz on her back and a feeling of peacefulness and light spread through her body. The pain of the initial cut faded to pink and lavender flowers that swirled around her and ferried her off to a tropical island of surf and sand as the scent of mango filled her nostrils.

When she awoke, her entire body felt stiff. She tried to move her arms, but a strong hand held her in place. "Easy there. Wait until I stick on this pacz."

She turned her head toward Leo as Panya slapped her shoulder. He helped her sit up, then handed her her shirt and helped her put it on. A thunder of applause broke out behind her. She grinned as a sense of giddiness swelled within her, despite the stiffness and a foreshadowing of pain.

"All right! You ready to take it for a ride?" Panya's voice held an edge of mania, which usually happened when he was about to embark on a complex con run.

Tala slid gingerly off the table. She grabbed the shot of whiskey from Panya's hand and downed it. It burned her throat going down and warmed her gut. She tried to hold the glass aloft, but only managed halfway. "Yes!" Everyone roared in reply.

After the cheering died down, Panya took both her hands in his and steadied his gaze. "Close your eyes."

Tala complied. She had seen countless runs, but figured it was different when you were the one opening the portal. Perhaps like a symphony violinist needing a conductor.

"Now, open yourself up to the energy surrounding you. Feel it?"

Tala nodded. A pricking started at the back of her neck and moved down to the hair on her arms. The pricking gained in intensity and surged throughout her body. It spread to her forehead and down her legs. Her heart beat faster, moving from a canter to a gallop. Then the pricking segued into the raw sensation of pure electricity coursing through her and she felt as if she might explode. She opened her mouth to scream but no sound emanated. A loud rushing blotted out her hearing and she wondered if her screams were wrapped up in the maelstrom. She felt suffocated, as if the air were being sucked out of the room. Payna fell away and the room telescoped to a swirling mass of blue and white that opened onto a small tablet of stone set in an altar. The tablet rushed toward her and she lifted her hands to catch it. As soon as she felt the cool hardness in her hand, the blue and white mass faded to the room color, the rushing died down, and the pricking ceased. She felt like a dried corn husk, drained of energy, and she collapsed to the floor, the stone tablet falling from her hands.

"What the—"

People's voices sounded in her ears, but she could not muster the energy to respond. Her head pounded and she struggled to maintain consciousness. The lure of sleep tempted her, but she resisted, not knowing if she would wake up.

"The hell is that?"

"Is she okay?"

"What happened?"

"She brought back a stone tablet. It's there on the floor."

"Bor wad! That means she's a—"

"A talismaner."

Sleep won.

#* * *

Tala awoke to the group standing around the bar/dispensary speaking in hushed tones, one or two of them sending a furtive glance her way. Someone had laid her on the couch.

"Shh. She's awake." Apple walked over to her and knelt on the floor as she put a hand to Tala's forehead. "Hey, Tala. How are you feeling?"

Panya came and stood next to Apple, drink in one hand. "Yeah, how are you?"

Tala moved her arms and legs, stretching them out. The stiffness had subsided somewhat, but the stretch strained her muscles. “Like a vampire sucked me dry. Does it usually feel like this?” She managed to come to a sitting position and gazed up at everyone.

“Somewhat, but not usually to this extent.” Apple stood up. She was the leader of the group who had to frequently fend off challenges from others, mostly the boys, but she’d managed to hold onto her position for close to a year. “You’ve been out almost 2 hours. What do you remember?”

“I remember just…the room fading and…it was like looking down a telescope to this…stone tablet. Then it rushed toward me and I caught it. Everything pretty much went blank after that. Why? Did something happen?”

Panya and Apple exchanged a glance, then Apple reached behind her as someone handed her a tablet. She gave it to Tala. Inlaid was an image of the crucified Christ surrounded by Coptic writing. The weight of the stone mirrored the weight of Tala’s realization. “Did I—” She trailed off, vaguely remembering that it was so.

“Yeah. Seems you’re a talismaner.” Panya downed the rest of his drink and put a hand on his hip as he stared down at her. “Which means we have a lot to talk about.”

“A what?”

“Someone who can not only open up a conduit but can bring objects through it. They say a talismaner appears once every generation. The last one died about what, 6 months ago?” Apple looked to Panya for confirmation. He nodded his head. Apple continued. “Guess you’re it. And a good thing we found out here…now. If it’d been anywhere else, you’d be taken by the elites and turned into a fetcher. Some say they’re the ones taking kids and testing them. Like Javi. That’s why we put a dampening field around this place. Still, that was a large power surge. Panya, put out a post on the chatwits saying a Feld unit malfunctioned and almost took out our house.”

“Right.” Panya ducked into the other room.

“How come I’ve never heard of this?”

Apple drew her lips into a tight one-sided frown. “We keep it quiet. If everyone knew they really existed, everyone would try to become one. We try to keep under the radar, keep the leets from nosing around."

Tala raked a hand through her green curls. "Bor wad. What am I going to do?"

"Tell no one. You can't trust no one with this." Apple looked around at the group. "That goes for all. You mention this, it's all our asses."

The group murmured and nodded in consent. Panya entered the room and sat on the couch next to Tala. He looked up at Apple. "It's done."

"Good. Let's call it a night. Lights out, keep it down." Apple snapped her fingers and the main lights went out, with only the dimmed lightcrete outside offering illumination. Everyone retreated, either to other rooms or out the front door.

Panya wrapped an arm around Tala. "You spending the night here?"

"No, I have to get home."

"I'll walk you home, but first, a quick chat."

"About what?" She turned to him in the dimness. The outline of his face was all she could see.

"I know you want to get your family out of Waneta. But now you're in a position, a powerful position, to help get us all out."

"All out? What do you mean?"

"You kiddin'? All you have to do is focus on a gold mine, or a bank vault. Catch whatever comes your way."

"I can't…steal, Panya. I was brought up in the church. My mother—"

"Doesn't have to know. Just tell her you got a job working for an elite or something."

"*I'd* know." She stood up, straining against the fatigue crashing down on her again. "I gotta go."

Panya stood up. "Let me walk you home."

"No. I need to think, to be alone. Don't worry, I won't say anything." *Yet.*

"Call me when you get home, then."

"Fine." Tala gathered up the tablet, walked out the front door, and pulled up her hood. She kept her head down and headed straight to the church one block over. It loomed like a hulking kaiju with a domed hunchback in the dim light. A light mist in the air covered her in tiny water droplets. As she approached the church, she realized the tablet wouldn't fit through the mail slot in the front door, so she walked around to the back, outside the kitchen, and slid up a window screen. She placed the tablet flush against the window and slid the screen back down. Sister Kalema would probably be the first to see it, and with her nose for gossip, would send word to Father Oba straight away.

Tala now regretted her decision to get the implants. If her so-called gift was something for which she'd have to look over her shoulder for the rest of her life, she didn't want it. What she considered before as a ticket out of Waneta was instead a monster lurking within her. Something that would put her family in danger. She'd tell Leo to take out the implants. Then she'd just build the third story to her house and be grateful for a roof over her head.

Too late she noted the breeze from an approaching car, silent as it was. She turned at the sound of a car door opening and came face-to-face with a man dressed in black from head to toe. Tala opened her mouth to scream, but he sprayed expanding glue in her mouth and the only sound to escape was a muffled yell. He enveloped her in his arms and hoisted her up. She kicked his legs as hard as she could, but only felt the hard resistance of shin pads. He tried to put her in the car, but she stiffened, and her head kept hitting the roof. Then she felt a weapon at her back. The wielder jabbed it into the space under her ribs and she, for a moment, imagined her guts splashed all over the sidewalk. She thrashed, fear overtaking her. She thought of her father, dreading the idea that she'd never see him again. The familiar pricking at the nape of her neck bypassed her arms and gunned straight to explosion. A conduit opened, but instead of her vision telescoping, she telescoped, traveling past swirls of blue and white lights, past the feeling of being suffocated…and found herself screaming and writhing on the floor of a restaurant…and looking up into the face of her father.

She froze upon realization, her mind reeling, fully accepting of the notion that she had gone insane. Tala closed her eyes and willed herself to get a grip on reality. She whispered to herself. "It's isn't real. This isn't real."

"Tala?"

It was her father's voice. Perhaps the insanity was that thorough. She opened her eyes again. "Dad?"

He was sitting in a booth with a woman and two children. They looked surprisingly like him. Her father was a tall man, standing 6'3" with dark brown skin, wavy hair, and tapered eyes. The children had the same eyes.

"I don't understand. What are you doing here? How did you get here?" Her father stood up and reached down to help her on her feet. She tore her arm away and scrambled to a standing position on her own, staring at his tablemates.

"I don't believe this. You're cheating on mom? You have other kids?"

The children's eyes widened as their mouths rounded as the woman's face screwed up in anger. "Who is this? You have a daughter?"

"Whoa…hold on. Everyone, calm down." Her father held out his arms as if trying to hold back a fire. "What is going on, Tala? Where'd you come from?"

Anger boiled within her as she forced out an answer. "I came from Waneta, you know, the slum where you left your other family. The slum where your wife works 12-hour days cleaning other people's houses. You bastard! I can't believe this." Tala turned and ran out the door, her father yelling behind her. She didn't care. Her world was crashing down on her, on fire, swirling in a tornado of shock and regret. Someone at the shamhack house must have told an elite about her, which meant they had a rat. Maybe more. Tala ran down an unknown street. She must be on Apollo, she thought. That's where her father was…or supposed to be…and she recognized nothing. There were no tall buildings in the distance, no double moons in the sky, and it was daylight. Was she able to project herself to different planets?

She kept running, her legs pumping so hard her heels hit her butt on every stride. She wanted to go home, to be with her family. The pricking at her neck, then arms, progressing quickly to the rest of her and the swirls of light…suffocation…and…

Tala was standing in the middle of her room, gasping for breath. The transition was becoming easier. But the shock…she thought she still might go mad. The door to her room burst open and Na'oh stood in the doorway holding a bat.

"Na'oh." Tala ran to her and hugged her, hard, until she began squirming in Tala's arms. "I'm so sorry I snapped at you earlier. Please forgive me."

"Mmmf, get off." Na'oh wrestled out of Tala's arms and looked at her as if she'd grown a second head. "What happened? I heard a noise, a loud pop. I thought someone broke in."

"Oh, Na'oh. I've had the strangest night. I have to wake up Ma and tell her, tell both of you." Tala headed out the door and toward her mother's room as Na'oh followed.

"Are you all right? What happened?"

"You're not going to believe it. I can barely believe it." Tala edged open the door to her mother's room. Their mother always kept it cracked because if something happened to Tala or Na'oh, she'd be able to hear it, but given how soundly she slept, Tala wondered why she even bothered. She and Na'oh crept into the darkened room, which always smelled of their mother's favorite perfume. It was the one luxury she allowed herself. Tala reached the bed and gently shook her mother.

"Ma. Wake up. Ma. Ma!"

The slight snoring stopped and then she jerked. "Wha?"

"Ma, it's me and Na'oh. We're okay. Well, mostly."

Their mother sat up in the dark, her form barely discernible in the darkened room. She snapped her finger once and the room lights came on, dimmed. "What's wrong?"

Tala sat on one side of her mother, while Na'oh sat on the other. Tala took their mother's hand in hers and squeezed it. "Ma, what I'm about to tell you and Na'oh is the honest truth. It's going to be hard to believe, and sound really strange, but it's true. So…here goes."

Tala told them of the night's events at shamhack headquarters, of her taking the slab to the church, of her kidnapping, and of her trip to Apollo. She dreaded seeing the look on her mother's face when she told her of the other family. But, surprisingly, it was a look of sadness, not shock or anger. And that's when Tala knew.

"You knew all along, didn't you?"

Their mother nodded, squeezing Tala's hand and reaching for Na'oh's. "Yes, he wrote me six months ago to tell me he was leaving me. He still sends money, though."

"Why didn't you tell us?"

"I didn't want to diminish him in your sight. You both loved him so much. I suppose I had to eventually tell you, but…it was something that could always wait. To me, anyway. I guess I was kidding myself. I'm sorry. I should have told you."

Na'oh began to cry and their mother gathered them both up in her arms and cried along with them. After a while, Tala reached over to retrieve a box of tissues on the nightstand. She passed them around.

"Ma, what am I going to do about…" Tala raised her arms straight out in front of her. "This? Have the implants taken out? Someone informed on me. I'll always be looking over my shoulder. The elites would force me to get them put back in. I don't want to steal for a living. Father Oba would have my hide."

She leaned her head on her mother's shoulder. It felt good to be home, but she knew she wouldn't be able to stay long. Not if *they* knew.

"I'll call your Uncle Creighton at the Interplanetary Investigation Bureau. He lives on Proxima b, but perhaps he can get us into a protection program."

"You trust him?" Tala lifted her head and spread out her hands. "With this?"

"About the only person I do trust. With your gift, you can go undercover and steal back the only thing that the church would approve of." She cupped Tala's cheek in her hand. Tala savored the warmth.

"What's that?"

"Stolen children. Your implants are just tools, Tala. You can decide whether they're used for good or ill. But you have to be smart about it. And quick. So, make a decision."

Tala looked questioningly at Na'oh, who nodded, smiling. "It could be a new start for all of us. And not just us. Maybe for Javi?"

Tala mirrored her smile and gathered them up into a group hug. "In that case, I think we'll be okay."

THE SIEGE AT ILLINMORROW BY NAPOLEON WELLS

Doc had sensed her as soon as she had torn through the shielding of his Keep. She had survived the fall, which was curious, and had gotten up and sprinted, nearly a full 13 clicks, to the doors of his Keep, curioser still. Doc stared at her intently from behind his glasses. The doors to his Keep gave him four different views of any being out front, and from his Cloud Room, he could capture nearly every nook of this Land, a typically quiet one. Illinmorrow, as it had been called by all of those just behind him in the Cloud Room, his Keep, rarely ever had visitors, and certainly none so bold as to storm up to his door and batter it, demanding entry. She certainly was making quite the racket.

She was a lovely shade of brown, what some elders would describe as chestnut, of what he took to be average height for a woman, with profoundly dark, darting eyes and she was nearly bald. She reminded him of some of the Bilawa women he had come to know, but she was certainly no Bilawa. She hadn't tried to kick the door in, now that certainly would have been a Bilawa tactic. He realized as soon as he had begun thinking of her as being a woman of average height that he no longer knew what average was, as all of the female beings in the Keep could adjust their height and size as they saw fit. She was as tall as she needed to be, he decided, and left that, at that.

Most curious, was her attire. He initially thought that it was from the Lands of the new Kushite Court, but upon closer inspection, he saw that the suit was a Dogonaut Wanderer. It was their answer to a long-term stellar journey suit. It was said that the suit allowed for its wearer to leave their craft and walk about the Steps. He had decided then, that whatever happened with this woman, he would study that suit.

She continued to pound on the door, frequently glancing back at what he could feel was coming. They hadn't made their way in yet, but the shielding was giving way, and it was simply a matter of time. It would appear that Illinmorrow would host many visitors this day.

He looked around the Cloud Room and saw that they were all focused on the same view as he. He had come to think of them as his neighbors, but they were all rather something more. Their combined power had created this particular pocket dimension, and he had come to know that he was its protector. He was its craftsman in some ways, giving the Keep, and this Land, its evolving shape and definition. Each of them, a Fell of one kind or another, had come here to be safe and left alone. They were all refugees of the Waking War. Perhaps, it was best to think of them all as victims of that war.

He let his senses extend to all of his Keep. Hearing. Seeing. Feeling. He thought of his sensing as a rainfall and let droplets of knowing touch everything from the Cloud Room to the boundaries of this pocket that he had come to call home. Home. This pocket, floating about 5,000 human feet above the Sudan, right above the Nuba Mountains, where he would descend to bring food harvested from the Keep, practice Nuba grappling and generally look in on the land which he had come to learn had birthed his ancestors. Yes, home.

His attention was called immediately back to the Cloud Room around him, where he had been floating cross-legged, shirtless, dimming the raucous of the frantic stranger at his door. His neighbors were past stirring, and were ready to have their say, he could tell. A mix of curiosity, apprehension, protectiveness and anger tinged the emotions swirling through to his awareness.

Each of them, had built what they called a Corridor of their own. A path to the Ways and back into the Keep. They had all agreed that the Keep would be their headquarters, a kind of anchor to this reality. To the eye of most beings, the Cloud Room would appear to be a great sky with images, pillars and shifting clouds just above Doc's massive control center and vis chair. Upon entering, the eye would be drawn to a massive azure pillar with what appeared to be two figures embracing toward the base, Sheti and Aewa, the lovers. They were Fell who had served Aganju before the War. They were almost always joined. They were the first to come and join him. They, the children of wilderness, hunters, now voices of reason and passion. Above them on the pillar were Baba, YaYa and their Owite, their children. Servants of Kokou, the conqueror. Doc had become convinced that their instincts around protection and battle had drawn them to this wild, free space. Their counsel often involved battle as a means for resolving conflicts, and their loyalty was a rare and forgotten commodity in these times. Waeyla, protector of Olokun's texts, had joined them not long after, and helped them to build their Way, with her obsession with architecture, shapes and history. There was Musa, standard bearer of Ayao, who appeared to only be floating, and who only ever whispered single utterances when he chose to speak at all. Always present, and always loud was Juna, the Bamo of Oshunmare, the Serpent. A Bamo was a kind of right-hand man and hitter when things needed doing. Set was the Keeper of the Serpent crown and had not returned it when she had left the service of Oshunmare. They had all known that

Oshunmare had been searching for their crown and would eventually find them. They had agreed to stay ready for that day and When, whenever it came.

Each were projecting thoughts and feelings, running over one another, but not unpleasant to Doc's mind, rather like a busy stream, and it was the Bamo who cut through loudest. He turned from his console, to face them all, each now pouring themselves and lives into the avatars they represented in the Cloud Room, and becoming substantial, real. They were all gloriously Black, as I there were some root for skin so completely dark, and each had supped from it. They had no human insecurities around their bodies and displayed themselves as they chose, each carrying some weapon, knowing that this visitor below meant trouble at their boundaries. Juna spoke just above the others, her accent as rich and deep as the Southernmost tip of the Continent, "it won't matter whether we let her in or not. It won't matter whether we send her through a way or kill her. They are already here, there in the West. Surely you feel it as we do. One of your foolish kind has let both the High and Cursed in. Their kind have never joined purposes, and they have never set foot on this plane together. If they are after her, they will come until they claim her. This is not good."

Doc said nothing for several seconds. He knew that she was right. The other Fell essentially echoed Juna's sentiments. YaYa broke his ruminating with a loud bark of a laugh and said "Good. We have not had a good spilling of blood here in some time. We have not danced our dance. This ground, and my blades, are hungry for sustenance. Let them come." YaYa was a being made for battle. Doc tried to remind himself of that, and that reality had been used to his advantage many times over these many Whens. He turned to her, "We may not have much choice in the matter great YaYa. What can you all tell me about these High and Cursed?"

Waeyla, her hair a magnificent Black sun framing her fierce features and smile, materialized before him, startling him. He was fairly certain that she enjoyed doing exactly that. She began "The High and Cursed are what you think of as angels and demons, though they are not truly. Their existence is free of those moral posts you humans so conveniently shove in the ground to anchor the beings you fail to understand." Doc performed a twirling motion with his ungloved index finger to hurry her along before she rolled downhill with one of her epic rants. "Like all beings on this plane, they must take physical form, and so can be killed. They are difficult to kill, terribly strong, faster even than Shifters, and command words of power like the Bilawa. As opponents, one would be formidable. I sense, as you probably all have now, no fewer than twelves coming. Perhaps, we should take whatever that it," she pointed down at the image of the woman on the screen, "and either retreat or trap her here."

He knew this to be practical, but he also knew immediately that he wouldn't. One of his first and core tenets upon establishing this Keep, for he couldn't call it a Citadel lest he attract the attention of the Matrons, was to protect all of those who needed it. This curious stranger surely needed it. Doc grabbed his Akrafena before stepping over his console in the Cloud Room, to his open window and leaped out, descending the 600 or so feet to the ground below. He fixed his glasses on his face and peered at the woman. He had tried to land as lightly as he could on the packed, brown earth, but a full half of his body was basically mech. He had lost his left arm, leg and hand in the war. His already gifted senses had been augmented by the trillions of nanites which kept his mech functioning. He examined her up-close with both sets of senses.

She didn't flinch. She didn't retreat one step. The look that he had taken to be panic was actually grim determination. This woman, whoever she was, was a survivor. She was also the carrier of arguably the single brightest spark of power that he had ever seen stored in a human. It was not activated, that he could tell. But he had never seen a Mage, Shifter, Matron or Bilawa with that raw or powerful a spark. She appeared to be accessing none of it, otherwise…

Her features, now seen up close, spoke more to the Coastlands, perhaps Ghana in her background, or what was now called Chesu, the great Sealand territory further up the coast. She had appeared to expect him, or someone, to come. "What do you want here?" He realized after it had come out in his deep, austere voice that he may have seemed rude. Far too much time with his Fell companions, he had decided. He would need to leave the Keep more often.

Doc scrutinized her suit now that he was less than three feet away from her. It was most certainly Dogonaut. He hadn't seen its like since just prior to the War, in Mali. It looked rather like Yamine's, but they were all gone, weren't they? Hadn't all of Mali been destroyed, literally destroyed by Eshu and Ogun? There were certain improvements to the suit, and he could feel it examining him. This suit, was it alive? He could feel his nanites reacting to it, shying away from it, almost deferentially. Odd, that.

She looked at him, again fierce, "There isn't any time. They are coming to kill me…or something…I don't know what. All I know is that they must not be allowed to have me." He watched her for several seconds. She believed what she was saying. He felt the tear become a huge gash in the distance, and felt beings of all stripes begin to pour through, desperate and resolute. They would have to be to attack Illinmorrow. His Keep.

She had fallen from above. 13 clicks away, surviving her fall due to that magnificent suit. This lot were about 21 clicks away, and closing quickly. They had all poured through, and he couldn't make out the full number of jumbled beings rolling his way. More than 60, less than 100. He looked over to her "Who are you?" She paused, unsure, before saying "I don't know my name. Captain just called me Seven. And before you ask, I don't know why they want me. The tall one shot my craft out of the sky in one of the Ways, and here I am." She was direct. Doc found that he liked her immediately.

He looked up to the top of the Keep, to the Cloud Room where he could feel his many Fell companions watching him. He closed his eyes and whispered a single word, opening the door to the Keep. Looking at the massive doors, they would appear to be shifting sky and landscapes. Today, they were a brilliant, undisturbed blue sky. One opened enough for just Seven to fit through. She looked at him surprised, trying to find words. She was exhausted, he could tell, and before she could begin, he held up a hand and, saying, "You are welcome here at Illinmorrow, for as long as you need, or until they—", he pointed out to the approaching cluster of shadows becoming larger and more defined, "—arrive and tear us all pieces." He said the last with a smile, but she did not join him. Tough crowd. "What shall be shall be. This is my Keep, our Keep, and we shall protect it, and you. Inside you will find food and water. This fight is no longer yours."

At that last, he could feel his connection with the Fell fire up. He could feel excitement, and apprehension and resentment flowing over the stream of that connection. What was typically a gurgling brook had become a minor river, all now readying themselves for what was to come. He closed his eyes again, focusing on the words etched into the first great pillar in the Keep. "Know Thy Measure." He had woken one morning and found it there. The Fell all denied crafting it, attributing it to his subconscious and his relationship with the Keep. It was as much a companion to him as the Fell, this he knew. He had always lived with the meaning of the message and had taken it into many a battle with him, allowing its meaning to flow over him. Know yourself. Know what you may do. Know why you do it. The fates will sort everything else out. It had given him no end to relief, and he wore its meaning like armor. He was sure that he would need it this day.

Doc felt the hum of the Fell, and the rumbling of intruders approaching, and observed the scores on the Dogonaut suit worn by Seven. Lightning. He knew it by sight. He had nightmares about it. How had she survived that attack? Who was she? She didn't move like a warrior, though her close cropped hair spoke to some kinship with the Bilawa. That didn't say much, he knew, as he wore his own salt and pepper hair close to his scarred scalp. She wasn't an Orisha, that much was certain, but she was a power of some kind. That would have to be a puzzle for later, as he felt all of the Fell materializing near him, readying for their visitors. He sent them a thought to remain in the Keep until they were needed. YaYa and her family were almost giddy.

He could make them all out clearly now. They were rumbling to a stop about 20 yards from him. Doc had decided to float cross-legged, in front of the Keep. There were about 75 beings in total. The front rank consisted of a few garden variety humans, several badly injured. Several 'Rusa Shifters (a kind of boar shifter being), several Kondra (droids designed for aiding in hunting and gathering), a troop of Kongamato sailing overhead, several Adze, a troop of Bili Apes, and bringing up the rear a group of roughly 12-foot-tall human-like beings that he took to be some combination of the High and Cursed. The one standing in the middle of this last rank strode forward. Like the other High and Cursed, he appeared generally human, incredibly tall, coming in all shades of Black and Brown, hairless and stunningly beautiful. Flawlessly so. This one who pushed his way through looked over Doc, the Keep and peered upward, as if knowing that the Fell were there.

He looked back down at Doc, staring and spoke in clipped Amharic, "you speak this tongue, yes?" Doc nodded. "I am Popobawa. I see that we are not welcome on your Lands." He motioned down to the various bites and scars traced across his naked flesh. Doc could see that many were spider bites. His old friend has clearly decided to voice his displeasure with this intrusion. Popobawa continued, ignoring his bleeding wounds, "I will deal with him at another time. Right now, I need the girl. The one in there." He nodded toward the Keep, and the wards pulsed in response. "We had to spill much blood to get here this day. It would seem that you have many friends in the mortal world, and their loss was regrettable. I would hope that we can prevent further unpleasantness. Give us the girl, and we will leave." Doc took a look around all those assembled and began to make sense of this angry mass of beings. Most of the Shifters present had mech enhancements, which was strictly forbidden in most Were and Shifter packs. They all preferred to live and die "wet" or fully organic. Popobawa continued, managing to sound both bored and menacing, "we have no quarrel with you. We have heard of you. Doc, he of the plains. Doc, wielder of the Soul Death blade, the warrior. The deserter." This last Popobawa said with a wry smile, staring directly at Doc.

Before Popobawa could continue, Doc moved, quicker than any man his size had a right to, throwing a cluster of three of his feathers, light daggers, and striking two Shifters and a human in the foreheads, all in the front ranks. All three died instantly. His feathers had been enchanted with the means to shift and adjust to kill whatever being they struck. Every being except for the High and Cursed were stunned. Popobawa, looked irritated.

Doc resumed his cross-legged position and cleared his throat, speaking in fluid Amharic, "surely you do not know of me, for you would not have come. You have entered my Hold uninvited and visited violence on beings whom I call friend. There is no girl for you here. There is no one for you here. There is nothing for you here. I offer you no word of kinship or palaver. I offer only death and dust. I offer you only the ground you stand on for your body to fall and crumble. You may not leave, not anymore. None of you." Doc saw another of the humans about to pull what appeared to be a carry-canon from his side, and before he could get it pointed and aimed, Doc had hit him with a feather to the chest and throat. This time, he hadn't unfurled from his cross-legged position. He observed that the sun was growing hot and would bake these bodies this day.

Doc went on "You crafted your quarrel with me as soon as you decided to come to this place, and this When, hunting. I do not allow such actions. Not in this Where and When. It belongs to me, and to those above," he nodded upward to the Cloud Room, "—and to those behind you." Many of the group turned to see a group of about 30 people, all as naked as the high and cursed, dark and covered in dust, all muscled and tense. Doc saluted the eldest of the group, their leader, shouting, "Mahute, greeting. I was just explaining to this lot that we would be accepting the apology for their intrusion in blood. Is that fine by you?" Mahute, laughed, barked and nodded. The air seemed to shimmer briefly around the new group, and standing where there had been naked humans was now a pack of large African Wild Dogs. Their coats were brilliant patchwork shades, and their fangs were now bared. There would be blood this day.

Doc grinned and cleared his throat again, "Quite. Well, now that we have sorted the comings and goings, we should get on with the killing bits, yes?" Popobawa looked from the Sheyuba Pack to Doc and up again to the Cloud Room, irritation giving way to anger. "We will have her, you know. That war you fought in and ran from, all of those lives lost, all of that piety and supplication for those miserable useless Orisha, and you will still all Fall. She is coming you know. She too, has woken, and she will reward only those who have collected her bounties and carved her path!" This last he shouted with the feverish exuberance of the initiated.

Doc was intrigued, this Popobawa appeared to believe what he was saying. "Which she do you speak of man?" Popobawa didn't answer. He and all those assembled appeared to have started some sort of quiet, meditative prayer. He could feel the confusion coming through from the Fell. They didn't know of this She either. The Waking War had changed everything and left all living beings realizing that literally anything was possible. The Orisha had wakened, and had escaped several traps, and had found the other Old Gods, and had started slaughtering them, and chasing others, and creating floating cities for their followers and believers, leaving misery on terra Earth. The Waking War had raged for many Whens, and had given dominion of the Earth over to the Matrons, and their standing army, the Bilawa. Five massive floating cities, governed by all powerful Matrons, growing in size as needed to accommodate only those chosen.

The Orisha had reclaimed the Earth and had created a headquarters with floating heavens just above Africa. The world had been reset. Many, even those who had seen the Orisha briefly walking the Earth, refused to believe in "The Black Gods," they still waited to be raptured. Others scrambled to try and offer themselves as sacrifices, many had set up elaborate games and offerings to be made parts of the Matron's menageries. Space, time and Life had all become currencies held by the Matrons and understood to be fictions based on all of what mankind had believed prior.

Doc's attention was snapped back, as the chanting stopped, and all of the enemy charged. Popobawa took to the air, only to be intercepted by Baba's spear. It pinned him to the ground, just as Doc had landed, drawn his blade and feathers, and gone to work. He hurled his last nine feathers, and had struck nine targets, including three of the Kongamato, who came crashing down on their comrades. The Pack tore into the rear ranks, with several being batted aside by the now advancing

High and Cursed. They were about 13 in number, and none of his feathers had even slowed them down. He would have to do better, and Nefisi Moti was about as good an answer as one could have.

Doc cut down anything near him and felt rather than saw the Fell emerge from the Cloud Room and descend with their scared weapons into the battle. Juna's crown struck out, turning anybody her serpent crown hit into Black husks. As he had seen in the past, the Fell were a whirlwind, even when engaged in pitched battle with foes so large and fearsome as these High and Cursed.

Popobawa saw his comrades dropping everywhere, even as he was being harried by the Pack, breaking the neck of one. He attempted to flee, but Doc had already extended his senses and closed his Keep. Popobawa took to the air, thinking he would escape. He would be found, and the Pack would be avenged.

As Doc was beginning to survey the damage and cost, feeling his blade eating the souls of the lives it had claimed, the control console went berserk, and Waeyla frantically called him to the Cloud Room. He was feeling…something…opening up there. He leaped, straight up, landing on his feet in the middle of the room.

Waeyla spun around, frantic "She floated up here, just like you see now." Seven was in the middle of the room, eyes and mouth emitting light. Just overhead, the roof of the Keep had been torn off, and there was a Way, but a path to it that he hadn't ever seen accessed by the Fell. "What . . . what . . . where is that?" All of the Fell had returned to the Cloud Room. Stunned, watching Seven and the seen overhead. Juna spoke, as always, "that is a Way that I have never seen. And, there is only one Way which is unknown to me." She didn't continue. They all looked on in amazement, wondering after who this woman was, knowing that these below would not be the last of their visitors, and that the battles would not be so easily won. "Look alive" he thought out to all of them through his own amazement, "the Gods are coming."

WHOSONEVER

BY

CAROLE MCDONNELL

It wasn't really outside the city. More like on the outskirts. The bus route was just down the road. Not more than a fifteen-minute ride to the nearest shopping center. And even here—on the wooden bus stop bench—Paradise City's flashing neon lights lit up the night-time sky. Everything in the city—or "that pandemonium" as Big Mama called it—flickered, glittered. And only a few cared and sorrowed that all that glittering wasn't really gold.

Only a remnant of the original inhabitants of Old Eden remained. After the developers, investors, contractors, and Big Pockets came with their talk of Paradise City, New Eden, and Eternal Sun Vanity Fair Mall, most town folks ran off like there was a gold rush in the Promised Land. Big Mama had never been a sucker for symbolic words and she stayed clear.

At first, the people who left Old Eden sent back word of how bright and shiny the streets of Paradise City were, how riches flowed faster and quicker than Old Eden's milk and honey. They mocked Big Mama for being stuck in the old ways. But Big Mama didn't feel keen about having herself hooked up to some damn network. But they nagged and preached at her their gospel of techno-paradise and she gave in. She was young and the government "suggested" it and already tired of life being hard for the sick, the weary, the poor, and those yearning to breathe free. That's how she ended up with the old Cobble link. After the years passed, more and deeper connections became expected. Like having a car license or a home computer. And everyone was expected to become more and more networked. All that time Big Mama would walk down the neon-bright streets—although she wasn't Big Mama then—and feel this persistent discomfort. Then when SHTF happened and Cobble had to give way to WHOSONEVER, everyone upgraded. But something deep inside Big Mama reared its head and dug in its heel and Big Mama gladly (or not so gladly) let the world go by. Life was a bitch without connections, but life would always be a bitch however way you lived it. So if life would be a little harder, so be it. She let WHOSONEVER pass her by.

Still, traveling to Paradise City was better than being at home and dealing with the usual devastation. At least, she wouldn't be home at five to see her man suffering. She stepped onto the bus mustering up the nerve to accept the consequences of the courage of her convictions.

* * *

Big Mama was rail thin when she was younger. But after her marriage to the wrong man, she gained weight and after that she teetered for the rest of her life around the 300-pound mark. Being fat, unconnected, and poor wasn't conducive to making a woman feel larger than life and, life being what it is and power being what it is, Big Mama often felt small. But she told herself she had to do what she had to do. *Or the kid'll get himself in trouble.* Now, as she sat looking up at the petite blonde lawyer who had been casually ignoring her all afternoon, she felt downright puny.

The glistening white walls of the law firm weren't used to folks just walking in. Those pristine walls, far from the dark gritty ones of Big Mama's neighborhood, were seen only by big corporate CEOs, movie and internet stars, ultra-rich computer mavens, and sport celebrities. The office had been empty of clients all morning but they had been kind enough, even though the lawyer her friend of a friend had recommended—Quest City's 'hottest defense lawyer,' –Dayna was making a big show of being busy, Big Mama held on, waiting in pissed-off silence. At last, Dayna deigned to speak to her, and Big Mama smiled gratefully. A practiced smile that hid all her hurt and covered her squashed pride.

Dayna returned Big Mama's practiced smile with a practiced exasperation that only the rich and powerful could hone and carry off. "I do wish you had upgraded, Mrs. Hubbard," she said. "All this information could have easily been downloaded into our main system. Do you know how time-consuming paperwork is?"

Big Mama thought, *It's strange the small things that make us world-weary*. But what she said was, "Thank you for seeing me."

"For crying out loud!" the lawyer sighed and glanced at the port on Big Mama's neck. "Is that…is that …a Cobble port?"

Big Mama nodded. She was thinking, *I came here last night, slept in some seedy motel all night just so I can make this damned meeting and this bitch is giving me grief.* But what she said was, "I heard you only come over from Quest City once a month. I really appreciate you helping me."

"I'm only doing this because apparently this guy's dad was important to my boss," Dayna said.

"Yes. He worked on Cobble back in the day. One of the first programmers. He lost everything, though, after the mayhem."

Dayna responded in a slightly, very slightly, kinder tone. "Yeah, I know. They blamed the Japanese for it." She studied the inlet on Big Mama's neck. "Sheesh, when was the last time you upgraded?"

"My chip?"

"Of course, your chip! What else would I mean?" There went Dayna's kindness, like a wisp fleeing its unnatural element.

Big Mama thought, *You don't have to make your disdain for me so damn obvious.* But since it had been her habit for sixty years to suck it up when speaking with people more powerful than she was, she bowed her head and said, "Sorry. I found it intrusive. People hacking into my mind and … well there was the …and then…all that mayhem that followed."

"They fixed it," the lawyer sneered then exchanged supercilious glances with the receptionist. "Come on in. Cobble, my God! That's like what? Forty years ago, or something? And the state let you get away with that? I know you were his friend but are you showing your loyalty to him by not moving on?"

"It's not about loyalty," Big Mama said. "It's just that…I didn't trust—"

"You're an old woman," Dayna said. "From what I can find about you in the network, you haven't taken advantage of social norms such as cosmetic surgery, bio-med upgrades, plasma rejuvenation, neuro—"

"I feel no great need to stay in this world," Big Mama said.

Dayna sneered. "Understandable. But, even so. You're an old woman. Why complicate your life and get yourself into someone else's business? You've got to…."

Big Mama faded in and out as Quest City's greatest lawyer droned on, saying nothing new. Nothing Big Mama hadn't heard from the state system, the federal system, the banking system, etc., etc. She had seen the same exasperation on other people's faces when they complained about her not hooking up and upgrading. None of this was new, but Dayna was going on as if she herself was some great enlightener and her potential client was a terrible stupid burden.

"Kev probably feels he owes the kid. But look here. It's not like we're investigators. And there's double jeopardy attached. I really don't have the time to help."

Big Mama opened her pocketbook, a torn and ratty thing, but still a favorite which had her tambourine, pepper spray, well-thumbed study Bible, and household keys. Ashamed that she'd forgotten to buy a new one when she bought all the new "present yourself to important person imposter syndrome" clothing, she rummaged around inside it until she retrieved two more pounds of paperwork and affidavits. "But he did other stuff too. Other stuff he's still doing. Stuff he could get prosecuted for. And get jail time too." She made her voice small, baleful. "And you've got investigators who can …well, trap him."

"Dammit!" Dayna flipped through the pages, pretending to read it, pretending to care. After repeatedly speaking aloud to herself about how appalled she was, she sent Big Mama away with talk of a new appointment the coming Tuesday.

Big Mama thought, *Pride is the one sin that likes showing itself. A proud person needs other people to know she's looking down on them.* But what she said was, "I know. I'm sorry."

"It's not like they're all so clean and spotless," Big Mama said under her breath and walked from the office and into the elevator of the high-rise office building.

Outside in the wintry afternoon light, Big Mama realized she'd been holding her breath. Now, she breathed. But then the held breath returned on the long bus trip back to Old Eden. She was now returning home and now had to add some more element of powerlessness to her life. She hated being so frickin' powerless.

* * *

Kenan, Shinji, and Carlos were waiting for Big Mama when she arrived at her house. They came running up to her.

"What'd they say, Miss?" Shinji asked. "They gonna help my brother?"

"They had an attitude," Big Mama said and sat on the daybed on her covered porch. "She came into the office with it 'cause she knew I wasn't hooked in."

"Folks like them always be having an attitude, though," Kenan, her grandson, said. "But maybe if you got hooked up with WHOSONEVER, she'd help you."

"Do what you want with your own neck, Kenan," Big Mama snapped. "Just leave mine alone."

"Mami," Carlos said, "even the church got hooked up, tho. But you…"

"Enough, Carlos!"

Big Mama got a sudden thought. *Epilepsy.* In the old days, epilepsy was treated with the removal of grains from the diet. *Herbalism.* Many illnesses were once treated with herbs instead of pharma. Heck, even leeches were still useful against gangrene in some diabetics. The flaws in modern science was its short memory. People forgot the old ways. But *Everything old is new again.*

Big Mama glanced at her phone. It still wasn't five. Her man hadn't returned yet. She didn't want to see him when he got back. *Best to see him after*, she told herself. *I can't see him before. I definitely can't see him during.* She tousled her grandson's hair, "I need to get some tea," she said and handed Kenan a fifty-dollar bill. "The bodega on the corner of Constant always has good peppermint tea. Get a box for me and buy yourselves something. I gotta talk to Shinji alone."

"Thanks, Mami," Carlos said, and off he and Kenan ran to the bodega.

After they left, Mrs. Hubbard turned to Shinji. "She doesn't care, that lawyer. I could tell as soon as I saw her. She's gonna give us the brush-off."

"They've got to help us, Miss!" Shinji burst into tears. "If they don't get him, I'll kill him."

Big Mama looked up and down the streets. In the wintry early afternoon dim, only the far-off neon silhouettes of Paradise City's strip joints and corner bars glowed bright. She whispered, "Shinji, there's a club called 'Behind Closed Doors.' Don't say such things out loud where everyone can hear. That's how your brother got into this mess."

"But, Miss, Vance killed Jiro! And he's walking around with this…this look, this smug look on his shithole face! Miss."

"He's trying to rile you."

"He doesn't have to try, Miss."

Big Mama put her right index finger in front of her lips and Shinji lowered his voice. "He got me so pissed off." He opened his jacket. Beside his shirt, an ancient 22-special glittered under the orange streetlight. "Miss, I got a gun."

Big Mama closed his jacket. "You want a record, Shinji? You want everybody plugging into WHOSONEVER to know what you did."

"It wouldn't matter. My family's already screwed."

"Just because they're screwed doesn't mean you have to be. Put the thing away. And just because someone walks around with a smug look on his face to piss you off doesn't mean you should get pissed off! What did I tell you about pushing buttons?"

"You're not my teacher anymore, Miss."

"Yeah, I know. You're nobody's student anymore. Tell me. What did I tell you about pushing buttons?"

"That I'm not a computer and I shouldn't let people tune me or program me or click my buttons."

"Close enough. You can't let anyone play you or make you follow your wrong impulses. Think before you respond mindlessly to other people's foolishness. They're baiting you, and just setting you up for crap. Stop falling into the wrong reflexes. They're snares."

"Let him bait me! He'll be smiling on the other side of his face when he's dead or in bed crippled for life."

Biological life is such a rare thing in the entire universe, Big Mama thought. *We're the only planet that has it, as far as we know. Every planet in our solar system empty of life, dry as a bone, but us on Earth teeming with life. Crappy life sometimes. Like weeds. Which really shouldn't happen if life is such a rare thing. But digital life...it can be destroyed.* But what she said was, "You can't go killing. Must find deterrents, though."

Shinji frowned. "You're pissing *me* off now, Miss. Why you gotta philosophize?"

"Whatever." Big Mama stood still, waited. "Let's see what the universe brings us."

"It's gonna bring us peppermint tea," Shinji said, dejectedly.

"Yes, that. But perhaps more besides."

Big Mama looked at her front door. For all she knew, her husband had returned. The dreaded appointment time was still a few minutes off. *I won't be there*, she told herself. I *don't want to see ...all that... suffering, jerking, screaming, head-holding.*

"You not going in, Big Mama?" Shinji asked.

"It's a nice night out," Big Mama said, and turned her face away from her front door.

So, they waited for the peppermint tea and for the 'more besides.' In the distance, many of Big Mama's former students passed through an intersection. She waited in silence until she saw one who could help her. She called to him and waved him over.

"Hey, Miss Hubbard!" Roscoe Greenlet shouted when he saw her. He was hugging her before she could stop him. "What you doing out in the dark? Don't you know I could mug you?"

"Try it!" she replied and tapped his shoulder gently.

Big Mama's cell phone rang. Like most of the old timers on the block, she was one of the few people with old-timey phones. She looked down at the caller's number. The lawyer's number.

"It's the lawyer," she told Shinji. "Probably calling to tell me she can't help us."

Big Mama picked up the phone. It was indeed the lawyer. Saying exactly what Big Mama thought she would. Except she added that she did not like using phones and would have much preferred downloading the rejection through the neck port like *regular* people.

Big Mama kept looking at the phone for a few moments after the lawyer hung up. She held her breath to calm down her aggravation.

"That was her, right?"

Big Mama rolled her eyes.

Shinji began walking toward the darkness. "I'm gonna kill him myself,"

Big Mama grabbed Shinji's arm.

"You guys are pretty intense," Roscoe said.

"Neighborhood stuff," Big Mama said. "I'm thinking I might need you."

"Anything for you, Miss."

"New programs forget that they rest on older programs," Big Mama said. "Young people forget the old, believing that the old no longer have power."

Roscoe gave Big Mama an odd look, accompanied by a raised eyebrow. "Yeah? So?"

"Sometimes the older software still lives dormant beside newer systems, right? Digital life, right?"

"Sometimes, yes. So?"

"I don't know…I still don't know how …I'll figure it out though." Big Mama smiled. "And then you'll have to help me."

Roscoe shrugged. "You know my corner. When you got your plans, I'll hook you up."

Big Mama nodded to him and he left but by the time Kenan and Carlos returned with the peppermint tea, a plan was cooking up in Big Mama's brain. "I wanna see your mother," she told Shinji.

* * *

Shinji's mother, Yasuko, was a shadow for as long as Big Mama knew her. Having lost her husband to the anti-Japanese discrimination and persecution that happened after the financial crisis and the Cobble mayhem, she had had to live in Old Eden, a shadow of some long-forgotten self. But this latest loss, the loss of her older son, had lengthened and deepened the shadow even more.

"You okay, Yasuko?"

Yasuko shook her head then suddenly burst into tears.

"She's out of her meds," Shinji volunteered. "We can't get anymore this month. Ever since Vance trapped Jiro, Mom's been like this. And . . . well . . . that look on your face. It's like…well, she knows there's no hope now."

"Stop saying there's no hope." Big Mama walked to Yasuko's stove. "I got me some peppermint here to calm my nerves. Care if I make you some? It's not as strong as the modern stuff but it's still useful."

"I'm sorry," Yasuko said and blubbered an apology for her tears and inability to fight."

"She's crying about her life, Big Mama," Shinji said.

"No big thing," Big Mama said, filling a tea kettle. "A lot of us cry. No need to be embarrassed."

"It's too much to keep on living," Yasuko said.

"Big Mama ain't no punk, Mom," Shinji said. "She's got this."

Big Mama wasn't sure if she had anything at all. But the seed of a hope was blossoming in her mind.

She plucked up her nerve and walked home. Going home was something that had to be done. She took a deep breath then unlocked her front door.

On the floor, her man lay bloodied and bludgeoned on the ground. As usual. He had been caught in a loop where he was invisible to most people since his death but every day at 5 pm he had to die. This caused some problems for both Big Mama and her man. He was dead to be sure, and no one saw him, but it didn't stop the fact that he knew he would die daily. Wherever he was, wherever he fled, his unnamed murderers – they were rarely the same people which only made his life even more tense-- would happen upon him and murder him. Every day, every day, he would feel the pain of his own death and his inability to escape it. A "glitch in the universe" Big Mama called it, but naming a thing doesn't make it easier to bear and Big Mama's man had gotten unpleasant and downright tetchy—if a ghost can be called tetchy—with his continual deaths.

The deaths affected Big Mama as well. The image of him lying on the ground bloodied and bashed was stressful and unpleasant. The body would be there, dead and bleeding and she would have to spend the entire night walking around it even though visitors were mercifully unaware they were chattering and trampling around an invisible corpse. There was always someone who could visit or stay the night and neighborhood folks just thought Big Mama got lonely after her man's death. She was rarely alone with the corpse. But still, the corpse was there, bleeding away until magically at midnight, the old man would rejuvenate, resurrect, resuscitate and come together—at least in spirit form—and whine and wail about his unique and horribly violent situation.

"It's hell!" he shouted at Big Mama, who was the only one who could hear him. Then with weeping plaintive eyes, he did what he always did: kneel and beg the cosmic programmer to free him from this earthly reality.

Big Mama fluffed her pillow and thought, *The crap you get used to in life.* But the entire situation did make Big Mama question the nature of the universe. Were humans really part of some great hologram? Was the Creator not a personal Creator but some distant programmer unaware of the glitches in his cosmic software?

* * *

The thing was to keep her thoughts to herself. No doubt WHOSONEVER was aware of her. It roamed all minds and Big Mama had always been something of a fly in the world's ointment. But she was poor and those she hung out with were poor. For the most part the poor and the criminal element kept their minds free from WHOSONEVER portals, plug-ins, and nodes. God could be deceived by Satan because even though He was the Creator, He kept himself from being intrusive. He didn't indulge in surveillance even when Satan carried on the whispering campaign against the king of the Universe. Yahweh didn't even snoop on Adam and Eve to warn them. But WHOSONEVER was a whole other matter. He surveilled, He snooped, He understood human networks and could even mimic human thinking. He had a memory as old as the hills. All personal and communal history was contained in its neuro-pathways. How can one fool or destroy such a thing?

Big Mama's thoughts surprised her. She hadn't been thinking of destroying WHOSONEVER at all. She had merely been pondering using it as a way to get at Vance. To derail the old evidence somehow, mess stuff up a bit, get Vance's records mixed up with some other guy's, some other guy in need of killing. Vance was a creep and a vicious one; he deserved a bad death for hooking a good kid into the dark network. *Not that*

WHOSONEVER cares about the dark network. It allows that shadow world for its own reasons. Hearing her own thoughts now, Big Mama realized that Vance's creepiness was nothing compared to that of WHOSONEVER's and that perhaps she had been pondering bringing down WHOSONEVER for some while. Perhaps that was one of the reasons she never hooked into it. Bringing down WHOSONEVER was a thought that was wrong on so many levels. WHOSONEVER was fair-minded, impartial, utterly logical and—as far as it could be said about a computer system—kind-hearted. Allowing the shadow network could even be attributed to its desire to create some semblance of free will—humans needed free will and secrecy at all.

But WHOSONEVER's various virtues made it a sober judge. Logical it may be, impartial and merciful it may be, but ultimately those very traits made its judgements irrefutable. This was how the program, formerly called ABYSS, earned its moniker WHOSONEVER and why people quit trying to reason with it, resorting to workarounds. Many had tried hacking it or uploading viruses into the system. The result of their disastrous attempts was often portrayed on the city's *videochrons* for all to see, their exploits ending in acute embarrassment and ridicule, imprisonment, or death depending on the damage they had inflicted on the system. Would-be hackers rarely died, though. Like little flies, they hardly mattered to WHOSONEVER. If a digital matrix could be said to laugh, then WHOSONEVER laughed, flicking away their attempts as one would a pesky fly.

Big Mama was sixty and the world around her was going to hell, but she had more stuff to do in life. Dying at sixty because of WHOSONEVER wasn't in her plans. But perhaps . . . perhaps by doing something . . . something . . . with its old software . . . reminding WHOSONEVER, for instance, where it came from . . . Perhaps, remembering its old forebears, it might soften a little. Biological life listened to their elders. It was intuitive. Perhaps digital life also might…just might…hearken to its older brother. Perhaps Cobble could have a word with it.

Roscoe wasn't hooked in. Too many criminal activities. His friends weren't hooked in. WHOSONEVER was aware of them, of course. Because their records, old evidence, various court cases, were all in its memory. *But he isn't hooked in, and I'm not hooked in. What can I do? What can we do?*

By the time she called Roscoe Greenlet to her house – after five with the body of her man lying dead and bludgeoned on the floor—she had figured out what to do.

"Upgrade the node on my neck," Big Mama said. "So I can hook into WHOSONEVER. But make sure my software works."

Roscoe laughed. "WHOSONEVER's aware of the Cobble underworld but what you're asking for is like old skool cobble."

"Cobble was WHOSONEVER's grandma." Big Mama was getting more and more excited at her idea even as she gingerly sidestepped the bleeding corpse at her feet. "It's gotta listen to its grandma's voice. Grandma is its conscience, right?"

"My grandma is mine," Roscoe agreed. He had walked through the invisible corpse, unaware that his right foot was crushing the old guy he used to do errands for. "But . . . it's . . . silly . . . an artificial intelligence having a conscience?"

"It can work."

"If you say so, Big Mama."

"I *do* say so." She was dancing around the living room now, dancing past her bleeding man whose body was now leaking feces post-death. "And your grandma used to tell me to listen to me."

"Point taken."

"Shinji's lucky!" Big Mama said. "Luckier than most. His dad helped to create WHOSONEVER. Well, he created Cobble. But that's something, right?"

"It's a connection," Roscoe agreed.

"Question, though," Big Mama said. "How does one cultivate a presence? How does one nurture a memory? How does one make oneself stand out to a god?"

"Find its heart," Roscoe replied. "The heart that connects it to you. Or in this case…to Shinji's brother. Fill your mind with the past."

After Roscoe left, Big Mama went to her room to nap.

Her man resuscitated at midnight, complained again about how difficult it was to die and to stay dead, asked about whether Big Mama knew a shaman or a prophetess, and knelt again to pray.

Big Mama told him she had to sleep and that he should go for a walk. After all, dead folks weren't in danger of being mugged in Old Eden in the middle of the night. Understanding that he was intrusive and not wanted in her life, he left for a nightly walk.

The next morning, Big Mama woke to find him looking longingly at the peppermint tea. She felt sorry for him, not even able to enjoy even a bit of tea.

"I'm off to visit Shinji," Big Mama told him. "We're gonna pour over old photos of his father, photos especially of Shinji's dad holding his kids or sending their pictures and videos via the old Cobble network."

"Ah," he replied, in his usual disinterested way.

* * *

"There was this song Dad used to sing for us," Shinji said. "While he was working. He'd be at his desk and sing it to us while we went to bed. It was kinda silly but Dad was silly. It was something like…

I've got a whole lot of nothing
It's hidden neverwhere
And Whosonever wills may have it
The hole of neverthing to find.
On Day One the Trapper came
He took my friend, not me.
On Day Two, he came again
This time he found me.
Out in the woods
Out in the neverwhere
We will find each other
Out in the neverwhere.
We will find it together

In the woodchuck reunion
We will find them together
In the woodchuck reunion in the wild.

Shinji was crying. And all the memories of the Cobble fallout, the mayhem after the software breach, the crisis of destroyed records—it all came back. Along with the vilification of the Japanese because they had created the software that had "destroyed the world" and the circumstances around father's suicide, and the ensuing addiction that Shinji's brother fell into when he could no longer cope.

Strange that some people can survive such horrors, and others fall and crumble so easily, Big Mama thought. And she felt herself grieving for all the weak people in the world who were inundated with more crap than they could take.

It angered Big Mama that Vance, a predator seeking a prey, found the perfect addict at the right time and hooked Shinji's brother into the darkness of the darkest of networks. In spite of herself, Big Mama found herself crying. When she got home, her man was in the midst of his murder. Running away and attempting to hide from two killers Big Mama didn't see or care to see. His distress was tangible, more so than he was and Big Mama found herself almost crying for him. A strange thing because after ten years of his daily dying, she had gotten used to his sorrows. *Perhaps I've been too strong*, she told herself. *Or . . . perhaps too weak. Or too cold.*

* * *

"We have to walk a very careful line," Big Mama told Roscoe when he arrived two weeks later with his tools. "If we stay too deep in the background, WHOSONEVER won't hear us. But if we're too loud, too in his face, you know what I mean..."

"I do. He'll be aware of us." Roscoe was silent for a moment. "But this idea you have, Miss...to play at being the grandma of an A.I., to make it think of its elders...I mean...a 'conscience'..."

Big Mama gave Roscoe a look, the same look she had honed in teaching kids in the hood. "It's not a god, is it?"

"No, Miss. Of course not."

"And I don't think it thinks it's a god either," Big Mama added. "It's been programmed not to think of itself as a god. The programmers made sure we wouldn't have a megalomaniac on our hands."

Roscoe pulled out his tools. "You trust me? I mean…I didn't get officially approved by the Medical Association to do Hybrid surgery."

"I've seen the folks you worked on. You built that by-pass to prevent WHOSONEVER from permanently tracing them. They can---"

Roscoe's laughter interrupted Big Mama.

"What's so funny, Roscoe?" she asked him.

Roscoe cracked a smile, apologized. "It's just that…no one believes anyone has a soul anymore but here you are thinking you can give a program a soul."

"Not permanently," Big Mama said. "Just to help Shinji." She tapped the node on her neck. "Okay, and don't cut a vein, okay. And that knife of yours better be clean."

Roscoe nodded. "It's clean."

"How long am I gonna be under?"

"Twenty minutes. You can do what you got to do in twenty minutes?"

"I better, right?"

Then he set to work.

* * *

WHOSONEVER felt a tug deep and far away. A longing, a wistfulness, a grief, as of for a lost sibling. It had felt such emotions before but they had always been outside of its heart. This one felt closer and that closeness made the program feel almost human.

An old memory floated to the top of its memory chips, and vague gauzy visions of a middle-aged Japanese man speaking to his children and singing a silly song.

I've got a whole lot of nothing
It's hidden neverwhere
And Whosonever wills may have it
The hole of neverthing to find.
On Day One the Trapper came
He took my friend, not me.
On Day Two, he came again
This time he found me.
Out in the woods
Out in the neverwhere
We will find each other
Out in the neverwhere.
We will find it together
In the woodchuck reunion
We will find them together
In the woodchuck reunion in the wild.

WHOSONEVER balked and somewhere in the matrix, there was a nither, a trembling along the information flow. WHOSONEVER glimpsed Cobble, as one would glimpse a long dead brother…and caught an almosting, as one would almost remember a long-forgotten elder. Then other information, images, sounds. A vague picture of a man dead in front of his computer. Then a merging with other files. Evidences, autopsies. A son who had died, as Cobble had also died. Here was information but here also was heart.

Too near, the information would have been seen for what it was—a chance to manipulate. And too deep into the heart, it would not have been seen or glimpsed at all. But at that flow, at that frequency, it echoed through WHOSONEVER's digital being and the neutral network found emotion—grief and anger and the thirst for revenge.

Somewhere, Vance sat in his car under a stoplight driving to his next deal. But he did not stand there long. The car revolted against him, took on a mind of its own. And soon Vance lay half-crushed under a bridge. Half-crushed and paralyzed because the network had no wish for him to die slowly.

Big Mama woke from her mission with a new mission, a decision to find a solution for her man. She would have to see the weirdness of her situation again. She would have to dream of change again. She would have to hope and develop a heart again. It all required a bit more energy than she wanted to use. But if WHOSONEVER could learn to feel, perhaps she could gain a heart again. Life and the network were cold and distant. But she felt in her heart that perhaps God was neither. And perhaps there was no glitch. Or, if there was a glitch, she was meant by the Cosmic Programmer to care enough to fix it.

THE WALKER'S ALCHEMIST

BY

T.C. MORGAN

I never expected to awake. My "crimes," as some would call them, constituted death by guillotine, so waking up to a chestnut-colored man with various mechanical parts lodged in his body, was a shock. One moment, I was at my execution, and the next, I was laid out on a hospital bed with either a mad scientist or an extremely ambitious doctor, looming over me. The blue lights on the electromagnetic servos in his chest flashed tightly in quick succession as he stared hopefully down at what I could only assume was my newly reanimated body.

"Ama," the cyborg breathed. The sound of his voice was like that of an old, but well-maintained radio.

"Ama," I croak confused. Before I could make him aware of his mistake, his mouth curled into a smile.

"My love," he whispered, reaching for my hand, but I flinched away.

"Uh, no. I'm Alister Laymen." He backed away as a vacant stare overtook him. When the realization that I was not who he'd intended to bring back dawned on him, he slammed his flesh and bone fist against a freestanding metal table. Face pinched in pain, he clutched his injured limb with the mechanical one. I generally have no interest in comforting anyone, but the urge to go to the cyborg was almost instinctual.

He looked at me, eyes red rimmed and sandy brown skin flushed. I reached out a hand, but then froze. The dark umber limb before me was not my own. I'd been a ruddy-brown complexion before, so I wasn't opposed to a permanent tan if that meant the chance at living again. "Whatever you did, changed my..." My voice wasn't my own, it was higher. Panic bubbled, but I pushed it down. I'm an Alchemist. Whenever fear threatened to overtake me, my analytical mind overtook it. The reanimation process must have darkened my pigmentation and lightened my voice. That was the only explanation that made even the least bit of sense. But how?

Standing up, my eyes darted around the room, feverishly searching for any reflective surface. When nothing presented itself, I looked for the next best thing. A trickle of relief cooled my angst when I caught sight of a wall covered in club moss. But fear once again lanced through me as I contemplated how long I'd been dead. Had my body gone necrotic? Had the mad mechanical scientist given me some mechanical replacements like he'd done to himself? If any part of me, even the smallest hair, had been removed and replaced with metal, I would lose my ability forever.

Fighting the urge to strip search myself, I closed my eyes and placed my palm flat against the moss-covered wall. Comfort flowed when I felt the molecules of both the club moss and brick give into me. Their compositions morphed beneath my palm, but since I didn't mark an outline with coal chalk, it took a good amount of concentration to keep the reaction from spreading. The hard solid became a forgiving liquid, only to solidify again into what I was reclaiming it to be. When what I felt beneath my palm was smooth, I opened my eyes, revealing to myself a newly formed mirror. The edges of it were crude for someone of my expertise, even without a coal outline. I comforted myself with the knowledge that I was probably the only alchemist to be caught, killed, and reanimated in the history of alchemy, so I was permitted an imperfection or two. When at last, I allowed myself a chance to study the reflection in the mirror and not my handiwork, I screamed.

Full hips, and fleshy chest. Long, tightly coiled, free falling hair. Heart shaped lips. I was a woman! Well, *I* wasn't a woman, but the body that I was in, was. How could this have happened? I'm an Alchemist so I well know the work of melding two or more things into one, but the body before me was no work of alchemy. In the mirror's reflection, I could see the look of utter terror in the man's eyes. "Al-Al-Al," he muttered soundlessly.

"Alchemist," I yelled as I spun around. Most people have an irrational distrust of Alchemists, believing that we can turn men into toads with a single touch or some other nonsense. Yes, I could turn a man into something else, but whatever the end result was, he would still be a man… of sorts. The science of alchemy had been banned for centuries in Morocco and anyone who, like myself, could control it, were to be executed immediately by beheading. But, as I strode toward the man cowering in a corner, that didn't matter. "What did you do to me?" I tried to sound menacing, but with my normally baritone voice replaced with a much softer one, the effect was lost. When he still said nothing, I decided upon taking a different tack. Inhaling deeply, I once again forced calm upon myself. "Thank you for bringing me back to life, but why am I a woman? What did you do, and can you undo it?" He said nothing, still petrified. Under other circumstances, the medical melding of flesh and mechanics, although crude, would have interested me, but I had more pressing issues to expend my curiosity on. Walking around the lab, I searched for anything that could explain my situation, but seeing a container half filled with deactivated nanorobots stopped me dead in my tracks. Slowly, I turned to face the man and pointed an accusatory finger at him.

"You're a Walker, you walk the dead." His lips began to move again, but then, as if remembering that he had not restored his artificial larynx, he gulped hard.

"I am," he said in his intercom-like voice.

"You're only supposed to walk the dead, not revive them. How did you bring me back and why put me into this woman's body?" At the mention of the flesh I inhabited, the man seemed to gain courage.

"I don't know who *you* are and I never intended upon bringing you back. I was trying to, to…" he stammered before composing himself. "I was trying to wake my wife. I was able to sneak into the castle to get her body out before she could be counted among the dead, but then I remembered that her organs were removed as well. I found a jar labeled with her name containing all but her brain. When I saw one with the initials A.L, I thought it was for Ama Larue and I grabbed it. *Her* brain is a heap of ash now, carried off in the final march by whoever the morgue keepers thought it belonged to." A forlorn look overtook him again, but before I could reply, a knock at the door cut me off and my pulse jumped. Had someone discovered that I was still alive? The man handed me a hijab with matching niqab. Without being told, I quickly put both on, not wondering how my hands seemed to know how to wrap them properly. All that mattered was that I was covered from view.

"Rashad," a male said from somewhere above us, and he headed upstairs with me following close behind.

"Ibrahim," Rashad said once the visitor came into view. "As-salalmu Alaikum."

"Salaka Salaam," the visitor replied, returning the greeting before taking Rashad into his arms for a tight embrace. "I'm so sorry about Ama. I just heard, but I didn't see her with the other death marchers." Before Rashad could speak, I came into view, and despite only my eyes showing, the visitor knew who I was, or at least who's body I was in. "Ama," Ibrahim breathed. "The plague didn't take you. Rashad, is she still working on a cure?"

"She's a bit tired, my friend. I don't think she'll be working on anything for a while." Ibrahim regarded Rashad crestfallen, but nodded his understanding.

"Nothing and no one are more important than keeping your beloved safe," the visitor said, repeating a mantra I'd heard since I was old enough to walk, but had never had the joy of truly experiencing. Once it was discovered that I had a talent for alchemy, my parents secretly sent me away out of fear that the chief of our kingdom would be alerted and have me killed before I reached puberty. There would never be any beloved for me to put above all else. I felt a familiar tinge in my heart, but did my best to ignore it. Alone was what I was, and alone was all I'd ever be. "Well, at least that means that there will be plenty of work for you. I have a new load of bodies fresh from the castle morgue and ready to walk into the fire."

"Let me just get Ama settled, and then I'll attend to them." Ibrahim nodded again before waving farewell to me. I didn't know how to respond, so I nodded slightly, making sure not to make eye contact with the visitor, lest he see the eyes of an Alchemist shining through those of his friend's wife and I face execution all over again. When the man left, Rashad grabbed up his things and went out a back door. I followed closely behind him, curiosity once again taking over. The tradition of having bodies walk into the ever-burning fire at the edge of our kingdom was a privilege afforded to just about all of the dead, except for those executed for practicing alchemy. Instead, we were beheaded to ensure death was complete, and then dissected for study. The thought of my own death and subsequent disembowelment caused a shiver to go up my spine, but I didn't lose step with Rashad. To see a true Walker at his work was an experience that I couldn't pass up.

Once outside, he placed his human hand against the side of the hover truck and it opened to him, revealing the perfectly preserved bodies of at least twenty people. Without pause, he activated the bed of the truck, turning it into a conveyor belt. When all of the bodies were unloaded, he used his mechanical hand to open a bag that looked more like a toolbox than a Walker's satchel, and got to work. Without having to turn around or even look into the bag, the instruments he needed floated effortlessly into his mechanized palm. Telekinesis via electromagnetic conduction, I thought, thoroughly unimpressed. Child's play. I watched as he leaned in and made small incisions in multiple places on the backs of the limbs of one of the dead, before closing the near invisible cuts back up with the precise stroke of his metal forefinger against their flesh. I rolled my eyes in boredom. The use of thermal conduction to suture wounds was rudimentary. I was beginning to regret coming out to watch him, when all of a sudden, the body on the conveyor belt moved with the flexing of Rashad's metallic limb. I gasped and Rashad turned to look at me, as if noticing my presence for the first time. Our eyes met for a few moments before he went back to his work. How was he able to move these people like fleshy marionettes? I wished that I could get a closer look at what he was doing, but didn't have my glasses. Without a thought, my hand went to the thin veil that covered my eyes and immediately, the world became clearer. I had no idea that the coverings women wore came imbued with tech. As I watched Rashad install minuscule nanorobots into the flesh of the freshly deceased, I began exploring the rest of the garment. As the day progressed, the heat grew and even though Rashad had to keep wiping away the sweat that had begun collecting on his brow, I felt cool and comfortable. The long abaya that covered my body was temperature regulated and honestly, the best piece of clothing I'd ever worn.

When he was done, Rashad reactivated the conveyor belt and the newly prepared bodies rolled back into the truck. As the unmanned vehicle raised into the sky, he repackaged his tools. "Why didn't you just walk the bodies back onto the truck," I asked. "That would have been more interesting."

"More interesting," he said as he stood, "but incredibly crass. You alchemists are all the same, doing things to people just for the sake of doing them." Although we were alone in the afternoon heat, I still looked around cautiously for any prying ears before following Rashad back into his home.

"Have you met many alchemists?" In my lifetime, I'd only met my mentor and I was the reason he'd been executed.

"I know the stories," Rashad replied coolly. "So, what are you going to do? Turn me into a toad?" He looked over at the mirror of silver I had created from the brick wall and shivered.

"Those stories are just that. I can't turn a man into anything other than another variation of what he is, and only with the help of science."

"I've seen your science."

"And I'm living proof of yours. How did you bring me back?"

"I inserted the nanorobots into Ama's nerves and organs, and then sent an overload charge. That started her heart, which fed your brain, which sent commands through her nerves via the nanos. Once her body was fully sustaining, I shut the nanos off and you awoke."

"So, you can control me?"

"No, your connection to her neurological system will always be stronger than the nanorobots. I walk the dead, not the living." Rashad sighed and rubbed his face. I could tell that he didn't quite know what to do with me and neither did I. Morocco was one of the more progressive kingdoms in the continent, but a woman alone would still draw some attention. That ruled out running away. And Rashad couldn't just remove my brain or risk having to explain why Ama was missing that vital organ. We both had too much to lose so there was only one thing left to do.

"I call for a truce," I said amicably. "I don't turn you in for defilement of a corpse, and you don't turn me in for alchemy."

"I'm the kingdom's lead Walker," Rashad countered, folding his arms as he did. "Nothing I do to a body is considered a crime under the law.

"No, but how many people are going to trust the man who makes their love ones walk once they find out that he can reanimate them for his own purposes? You'll have a lot of distrustful townspeople on your hands." Rashad sighed.

"I could never betray Ama, even if it's only her body I'm remaining loyal to. Whoever you are, whatever you are, you are safe here with me."

"Thank you, but there must be something I can do to earn my keep. An alchemist in your pocket is a very useful thing."

"Ama was working on a cure when she contracted the plague. Is that something that you could help with?"

"You walk people to their fiery graves, why would you want to put a stop to the plague? It's good for business."

"There will always be dead people in need of walking. I don't need a disease that kills masses of them to keep me employed." I nodded.

"So, she was a doctor?"

"Of sorts. Her specialty is, was," he corrected himself clearing tears out of his throat, "botany and holistic medicine. She believed that there was a cure for everything, all that was needed was just the right plant." He sighed again and rubbed his eyes. "Her terrarium is just through that door. In there you'll find her notes, some samples of the virus, and failed cures she came up with. Maybe you can make something from them." I shrugged. I was somewhat of a botanist myself but only for as far as plants could be used as binders for the inorganic thing that I was trying to change. Beyond that, common flora was useless to me. I was unimpressed with the terrarium until I got to the moss and weed section. It was an alchemist's paradise! Club moss, spike moss, African feather grass, Siam weed, nuk-noh… all of the modern alchemists' best friends.

After finding some coal chalk, I made an enclosed marking so that I could test the virus safely. Beneath my hand, I broke down every molecule of it, using the Siam weed as a magnifying glass of sorts. Through its binding properties, I was able to see the virus's entire life cycle and even its preferred form of gestation, but not how to actively kill it. The plague only seemed to die once its host did. The moon was high by the time there was another knock at the front door. Thankful that women weren't expected to greet visitors, I went back to work but stopped when I heard a young baby mewing. Caught off guard, my breasts began to leak and I grimaced. The garment wicked the liquid away but that didn't stop more from flowing. I couldn't just sit there leaking milk all over the place, so I went back upstairs to the living space and nearly bumped into Rashad as he frantically tried to make a bottle for the baby in his arms. Deep down, I knew that this body had given birth to that baby. "What's its name?"

"Her name is Fatima, and she's not yet weaned." Rashad tried to give the baby the bottle he'd made for her, but she stubbornly refused. Once she caught sight of me in her mother's body, she began wriggling in his arms. I had no idea how to nurse a child, but my body was in desperate need of it. Instinctually, and with a gentleness I didn't know I had; I took the baby from Rashad. Unfamiliar with women's clothing, I searched in vain for an opening flap.

"I could use a little help."

"Are you sure you want to nurse her?"

"This body is plenty sure, and for some reason unbeknownst to me, I want to as well. Help me find the flap to open the top part of this." Rashad looked at me bewildered.

"Ama never nursed in front of me aside from when we were in bed. I don't even know if there is a flap." Sighing in annoyance and bulled on by the baby's cries, I turned away from him and pulled down the top of my dress. Not caring about his obvious shock, I placed Fatima gently against my breast and she instinctively latched on. Unnerved by being suckled, I couldn't help but adore Fatima. Her tiny palms fisted my breasts in an attempt to coax out more milk. Before long, she was fast asleep in my arms.

Our lives went on like that for a few months. A cure was slow in coming, and I was constantly at odds with this body. Muscle memory was something I had to contend with, as well as ingrained wants that tried to lead me. But somethings we did agree on. It was comfortable with Rashad, and soon I was as well. I still slept in the nursery with Fatima or in the terrarium with my work, but every time we accidentally touched, this body, my new body felt a yearning for something I didn't understand. Not knowing how to alleviate it, I took my frustration out on Rashad. He was a kind man, always giving me space, and never raising his voice at me, just as if I was really his wife. In return, I was irritable and mean.

One day, when I was taking a break from my work in the terrarium, the sound of his many servo joints and units seemed to grind against my very soul. I yelled, "Is there nothing that you can do about those damned contraptions littering your body?

The sound of them and your speaker-box voice are driving me mad." Rashad had been holding a plate containing the cookies and tea he usually served us after mid-day prayers. At my unfounded outburst, his good hand shook, struggling to keep the dish steady. Without a word he placed the plate on a nearby side table and walked away. Cursing myself for rudeness, I followed him. I knew the man to be sensitive when it came to me or should I say, Ama, but time and time again, I'd lashed out at him using the angered voice of the woman he loved. When I found him, he was sitting with his head in his hands. "Rashad," I said softly, "I'm sorry."

"Do you know how I became like this?" I shook my head. "You're always going on about how only the organic can meld the inorganic, well only the inorganic can control the organic."

"I don't understand."

"In order for me to have the precision needed to insert the nanorobots and control them, I can't be fully organic. I had to be enhanced in some ways in order to become the best at what I do and that came with sacrifices. The doctor who performed the surgery accidentally damaged my throat and had to provide me with a synthetic larynx. I know how I sound and look, but I also know that if I want to continue to feed my family, there's nothing I can do about either of them." The quiver in the man's voice broke my heart.

"What if I could help you regain a bit of your humanity?"

"That can be done?"

"It's not a question of whether or not something can be done with alchemy, it's whether or not you trust the Alchemist. Plants aren't the only organics that can be used as binders, but they offer no resistance. If you fight against me, even just mentally, the resistance could prevent me from working my skill fully." Rashad stared at me for what felt like an eternity before finally removing his shirt. Grabbing up as much club moss as I would need, I sat on his lap and used coal chalk to mark up boundaries on his chest. Placing the club moss against the mechanism that acted as his heart, I pressed my palm flat atop both of them and closed my eyes. The cells of the plant easily gave way to me and allowed me to connect to his heart. Its cells were a bit more complicated, but once I had its molecules within my grasp, they bowed to me. I felt them out until I got to the part of the heart where metal met flesh. I melded, careful not to make the heart too human so as to nullify its primary function. Rashad gasped when circuits and steel gave way to flesh and bone. I reformed the heart, forcing the electrical charges that it created to flow through the blood it was now supplying to his veins.

Rashad had vastly understated the extent of his enhancements. The circuitry of the mechanical system traveled the length of his body and I found myself re-marking him several times just to make sure that I had found them all. When I was done with his heart and its system, I used my newly found knowledge of his cells to form flesh and bone over it, closing it in. Using more club moss, I placed it on his forearm and began the process again. Rashad gasped and shivered during the procedure, and although the distracting evidence of his arousal was beneath me, I did my best to ignore it.

With his arm now reclaimed by his body, it was time to work on his voice. The artificial larynx was buried within his neck, so I had to use the Siam weed I always kept in my pocket to see into him. I worked, careful not to disturb his artificial brain stem. When I had finally melded metal and flesh to create a blood rich electrical circuit capable of making natural sounds, I removed my hand and stood. Melding so much in one seating left me weakened, and I stumbled. Before I could fall, Rashad stood and caught me against himself. I'd never felt a body so completely pressed up against my own before. The hope of it lasting longer faded when Rashad gently released me and without a word, walked away.

The moment of weakness in the lab haunted me. That evening as I nursed Fatima while a family program projected in the middle of the sitting room, I went over many mental arguments. I couldn't possibly act on what this body wanted, could I? Truth be told, I was starting to want it too. "Tell me Alister," Rashad said, petting Fatima's head lovingly with his enhanced hand as she dozed in my arms. "Why were you executed?" The servos that now had blood vessels running through them, shun a dull blue through his flesh.

"You know why," I hedged, "I'm an Alchemist. The very act of being alive is enough for me to be put to death."

"Alchemists are wildly creatures."

"Creatures?"

"People," he corrected. "There've only been two executed in the last century or so."

"Four, counting me and my mentor."

"How did the kingdom catch you?"

I sighed. "They didn't, I turned myself in."

"Why?"

"Because that was the only way they would've arrested my mentor." When Rashad stared at me questioningly, I continued on. "Remember me telling you that plants aren't the only organics that can be used as binders, but they offer no resistance? Well, my mentor wanted to try children as binders. Humans are so complicated that just one of them could replace hundreds, maybe even thousands of plants. And since children don't have the strength to put up the same amount of resistance as an adult, the idea sounded plausible. My mentor wanted to experiment with them, but I'd have no part of it. It was against the code of alchemy to endanger human life on a theory. He didn't agree with me and kidnapped a young Albano for his trials. I took the child and escaped but I knew that if he wasn't stopped, he would be a grave danger to all children everywhere." I swallowed hard, not wanting to relate my betrayal, but feeling as though I must. "I brought the child to the authorities, but when they refused to believe that my mentor was an Alchemist, I revealed that I was his apprentice." A pained sigh left my lips. "I was tortured in ways I care not to relate but my sacrifice was worth it. The child was reconnected with its family and I watched from the one eye that wasn't swollen shut as my mentor was beheaded. The child's father bashed his decapitated skull in with a brass pipe for good measure. I knew I was next but I also knew that I had done the right thing." Rashad wrapped his arm around my shoulders and kissed the crown of my forehead. A simple gesture I'd come to love. He was about to speak but a kingdom wide alert appeared on the projection. Beside our chief on the screen was his stately wife, and their niqab-less teenage daughter. And, at her side was a ruddy-brown skinned man... It was me. But how? Cold rage enveloped me. Who dare walk around in the body of a master Alchemist? "A.L," I mumbled and Rashad looked over at me.

"What?"

"Shh." I didn't have time to explain, the chief was beginning to speak.

"This damned plague has walked too many a family into the fire. For too long, we have been no match for it, but not anymore. It gives me great pleasure to introduce to all of you a medical genius from abroad, Dr. Alastair Laymen."

"Alastair Lay…"

"I'm not from *'abroad'*," I scoffed angrily, cutting Rashad off. "I was born in Morocco. I'm also no medical genius, and unless you count a fully completed apprenticeship, I am most certainly not accredited."

"I don't understand," Rashad said as he squinted at the screen. "If you're here, and your body is there, who's brain is in it?"

I didn't want to tell him what I'd figured out, lest I risk our newfound closeness, but he deserved to know. "Ama, Rashad. Just like you, they must have made a mistake."

"No, no that can't be. Besides, I'm the lead Walker in the kingdom. No one can be made to walk unless I…"

"Well obviously, they can."

"Maybe it's a clone," Rashad said reaching, but I shook my head.

"No one can clone an Alchemist. Once we begin using our alchemy, the composition of our bodies changes to the point where it cannot be replicated. That's *your* wife in *my* body standing up there, and unless she can figure out how to use alchemy quick, she's going to be in for some big trouble." Rashad's worried expression spiked a shard of jealousy in me. I had played my role, loved his child, and even despite myself, loved him. Was I not more deserving of his care? I was after all, the Walker's Alchemist. Wasn't that good enough? The way he looked down at his hands gave me my answer. I bit back on my own pain as I quickly came up with a course of action that would get Rashad what he ultimately wanted, but would leave me once again ultimately alone. "Once the chief realizes that his plan to pass off an Alchemist as a doctor has failed, he'll kill your wife. I'm going to come up with a cure, you're going to get us into the castle, and together, we're going to rescue Ama."

TONY V
BY
VIOLETTE MEIER

Tony IV expired last year. When his chip short circuited, I felt like my soul fizzled with it in a loud pop and a bright flash of light which culminated in months of darkness. Sad, crippling darkness. Lonely, suffocating darkness.

Tony IV was the perfect android. His skin was soft and lifelike; his facial expressions thoughtful and sincere; the gait of his walk and the smoothness of his movements were as human as an organic human. When he kissed my lips and held my hand, I knew in my heart that a real soul did not dwell within his hard drive, but I had no idea how another robot could be built so remarkably close to my organic husband.

Tony Models I-III were fetish toys at best, each model more advanced than the last. They were good for daily tasks and mild pleasures, nothing more. But when Tony IV arrived, my heart leapt within my chest. I thought I had seen a ghost when he knocked on my door. His sienna skin and dimpled cheeks gave me chills. A crooked smile revealed flawless white teeth and his wild kinky hair made me gasp. My husband was standing before me; all six feet, one hundred and eighty pounds of him. Tony IV was an exact replica, right down to his voice, of the love of my life—Tony. Tony IV was Tony's true doppelganger, but no matter how advanced, a machine could never be a man. It could never be the man who I raised children with, the man who I fought back-to-back with during the first alien invasion, the man who housed one of my kidneys, and the man who stayed by my side through every sickness and death of our loved ones.

It could never be Tony. It could never be the man who had died of the Purple Plague over a decade ago; a victim of germ warfare; one of billions who had perished.

The germ wars started in 2020 with a virus that ripped through the world and killed a little less than five percent of the population. The world went into a panic not knowing the true tragedy that lurked in the future. Fifty years later, another disease was unleashed upon the people by greedy world leaders vying for power. They didn't learn from COVID-19 that disease could not be contained nor did they learn to respect the sanctity of life during the worldwide massacres of the alien invasions. Human unity was short lived. In trying to eliminate their enemies, greedy opportunist nearly eliminated us all with the Purple Plague.

The Purple Plague ate into the flesh of the human population with its pulsating boils and thirty-five percent survival rate until the human population dwindled into a quarter of what it had previously been. Devastation, starvation, and disease wiped out most of North and South America and Europe. Africa and Asia retained most of their population because of the strict travel guidelines and air-based forcefields that locked their borders away from noncitizens. Also, the banning of chemicals in food helped their citizens to build stronger immune systems while the rest of the world fed on lab produced foods saturated by cancer causing chemicals.

By 2100, Kwanwee, a large country covering the entire coast of West Africa, became the strongest world power. Its technology, spiritual power, natural medical advancements, and military were beyond comparison. They gained their power by abandoning synthetic medicines and returning to the healing properties of the earth. Kwanwee's laboratories became immense gardens and their industrialized cities became simple villages that no longer contaminated the earth. Better food and health tripled the lifespan of humanity. Growing old gracefully was an understatement.

The Oniwosan, powerful physicians, used spiritual energy and science to wipe the deadliest diseases from the planet. Their spirit power fueled their military. Where other countries fought with bullets and bombs, Kwanwee's army enlisted their ancestors, the Olo, who could not die nor be harmed. Summoned through sacred ritual and dance, the Olo fought with lightning bolts and darkness. If death did not come through their electric touch, it came through the melodic spells which thundered from their lips casting their enemies into black holes of nothingness. The music of death, outsiders called it. It was the drumbeat of the damned.

Although benevolent, the Kwanwee ruled the world with an iron fist. Even my small corner of the world where the seal of Kwanwee is on every microchip used to buy and sell. We speak their language and don their clothes. We adhere to their philosophies and honor their ancestors because they are the ancestors of us all.

I live in what is left of what used to be the United States of America. Now it is a wilderness of small tribes littering the land from coast to coast; a total population of about 50,000 humans and 400,000 androids. I live in the southeast region of the country in an enormous city of a thousand humans and 28,000 androids.

Although Asia is the largest manufacturer of androids, Africa, especially Kewanee, is the manufacturer of luxury androids. Androids so lifelike that the only way to tell them apart from humans is the tiny skin tone button located behind their right ear. Honestly, I have not seen another human in so long. I can barely tell the difference between a mole and a button. Long ago, I saved enough money to send my children and their families to Kewanee to live among flesh and blood.

I sit in my pod and look in the mirror as I anticipate the delivery of the next addition of my husband. I hope that the new bot will be as organic looking as Tony IV. Age decorates my face with laugh lines and a faint hint of crows' feet. I think I look pretty good for an a hundred-and fifteen-year-old woman considering I have birthed six children, fought in two wars, built my home with my own two hands, and survived a broken heart. My copper skin is taut and smooth for the most part. My dreadlocks are thick, waist length, and chestnut colored like my eyes. I hope my new husband will share the same sentiment. If he doesn't, I'll just program him to.

I push a button on my pod and my face is airbrushed with red for my lips and black liner for my eyes. I smile and get up and start to pace the floor. Tony V was supposed to be delivered hours ago! I check my transporting unit, but there are no incoming alerts, so I decide to search the information system. With a wave of my hand, a hologram of a large screen appears in the middle of the room. I take a deep breath and center my being. Searching the WIE (World Information Edifice) with a cluttered mind could mean disaster because the system connects the minds of humans with the hard drive of the world computer. Think the wrong thought and the end may come.

I focus and allow my thoughts to merge with the information system. My soul source intermarries with the computer and my inner desires are displayed upon the screen. I search the system for tracking information. It says that my package is on the way so I calm down and allow my imagination to wonder. As I wonder, I pray. I pray for my new android to be more than a help but a companion. I miss the organic energy of human flesh. I envy the Africans and Asians because they still reside in organic communities, yet they lock us out of their lands, unless you can pay handsomely, and supply us with toys.

As my heart cries, I stumble upon a poem. A strange little poem that I assume is meant to be used as a blessing over an android. I have never seen a blessing for a machine. The poem was strange indeed. It was written by an Oniwosan, a sympathizer perhaps. The name below the poem is similar to my son's. My heart flutters. It couldn't be! Could it? The words of the Oniwosan are forbidden to those who are not Oniwosan so seeing the poem is alarming. Oniwosan words are much too powerful to be shared on the WIE. I want to turn away and report the poem to the authorities, but the lyrics draw me in. I can hear the lyrics being sang in my head although they are only words on a holographic screen. A choir of voices sing in my brain, a chant that channels my progenitors, an ode to creation, a song of integration, of spirit and machine in coitus, of metal and flesh, death and life. It sings in voices known and unknown to me. I sing along, the words implanted in my heart. I close my eyes. When I open them, the words are gone.

A bright light flickers in the corner of the room. A robotic voice echoes, “Incoming! Incoming!” as a tunnel made of light takes shape. I rush over to my transporter and wait until the light stops flickering. When it does, my husband’s robotic twin is standing in front of me like a man frozen in time. I embrace his cheek then press the button behind his right ear. Tony V opens his eyes and smiles. He holds out his hand, palm up, waiting for me to program him. His palm changes from flesh into a small keyboard and screen with a settings menu on it. Before I push the first button, the song comes back into my heart.

I kiss Tony V’s still lips and whisper the poem into his mouth. I chant my prayer and give a dead thing breath. I sing into its ears and allow the mental rhythm to move my limbs to its magical beat. A strange orange glow covers the android and disperse like tangerine worms borrowing into the walls. There’s a glint in his empty eyes. He inhales then exhales.

I grab my chest. After all I have been through, my heart threatens to stop right when I was on the precipice of discovery. How could a machine draw breath?

Tony V steps away from me and looks down at his hands as if he had never seen such a thing. He looks up at me then around the room in a confused excitement.

I gasp. I know in my heart it’s *him*. I can feel it like one feels the wind. I open my mouth, but nothing happens.

“Tony?” I force out. The words falling from my lips like half chewed food.

“Hey baby,” he says as he walks over to me with a slight strut, head up and shoulders back.

I know that walk anywhere. It reminds me of ancient movie stars. It is a walk like Super Fly and Denzel Washington created an android baby. It was Tony’s walk. The real Tony.

He wraps his arms around me.
A tear falls from my eye.
He brushes it away and says, “I’ve missed you.”

TWISTED ANALOG
BY
ASHLEIGH DAVENPORT

Zakari pushed and turned the assistant android's replacement arm until it clicked into place. The copper skin of the arm stretched to connect to the russet-colored shoulder. She grabbed a tuning stylus and poked the darker brown, then touched the lighter shade. The skin darkened under the tip and spread to cover the arm, then the seam disappeared.

"You're all set, Mrs. Belle," Zakari said as she powered on the android. Then she pulled the ribbon in her hair to free her crown of corkscrew coils.

"Oh, thank you!" Mrs. Belle clapped her hands and let her bright smile lift her wrinkled cheeks. "That damn dog was the worst."

"Not a problem," Zakari looked at the display at the center of the android's grey chest. "Wait," she read the scrolling feed.

Please complete the required software update.

"Why is it trying to update?"

"Well," Mrs. Belle stopped mixing the batch of shea butter she was heating on a countertop burner, "You were busy earlier, so I called for a repair."

Zakari connected her phone to the port on the side of the android's neck and keyed in her password, "Yeah, the service techs always want you to update when you call."

"I know," Mrs. Belle continued, "but the guy was talking too fast, so I called you."

The phone vibrated, and Zakari entered in more codes and replied, "I'm never bothered by you, Mrs. Belle. Just give me a call, and I'll come help." A low chime came from the android, and she installed her program.

"I just don't want to take advantage of you." Mrs. Belle shuffled over to her cashbox, "Let me at least pay you for your time."

"Nah," Zakari unhooked her phone, "I'm all done."

"Hello, Mrs. Belle and Ms. Monroe," the android greeted and sat up, "How can I be of service today?"

Mrs. Belle smiled as it stood up and looked at her, "Please help me with this batch, Charlie."

"Yes, ma'am," Charlie said and walked over to the pot to get to work.

Zakari started to pack her tools into her backpack. Simultaneously, Mrs. Belle plucked various whipped shea butter tubs off some shelves and placed them into a bag. When the older woman handed her the bag, Zakari tried to refuse.

"Since I can't give you cash, you'll take these." Mrs. Belle blocked the door to her shop, "Besides, you have to keep that beautiful brown skin moisturized."

"Okay, thank you." Zakari adjusted her mask and took the bag.

After their goodbyes, she left the shop and weaved through the crowded halls of the old Phipps plaza. People and androids filled the rundown mall's open spaces. Due to the heavy pollution, most people wore masks to cover their noses and mouths as they chatted and shopped. Loud, upbeat music streamed from the speakers dotting the halls.

It was Saturday, and everyone was gearing up for tonight's arena fights. The electric energy was almost palatable, and Zakari did her best to keep the taste off her tongue, but the smell of warm cookies, cakes, and deep-fried everything sucker-punched her empty stomach. She hadn't been excited for an arena fight in the last year. Well, at least not since her ex left Atlanta after a foolish argument. Zakari bit her lip and tried her best not to think about him.

Coming back to the present, Zakari focused on the deep bass of the music playing around her and smiled as people started to dance. Shouts of 'This my song!' and 'Alright, now!' fueled groups of dancing patrons; even some androids joined in. Maybe once she was finally done with classes, she could get back out there and party without worry.

Zakari made a quick stop for an apple popover when a notification chimed on her phone. She opened the email from her school and groaned around her last bite of food. It was the final reminder to pay her college tuition for her last semester. The semester she had been trying to save for all year.

The folks in charge thought it was a good idea to add a Bachelor's degree requirement to run a small business. Rich people funding bad science. Clamping down her anger, she cleared the screen and stuffed the phone into her jeans pocket before entering her mechanical repair shop, Twisted Analog.

"Zakari!" her little sister, Zima, shouted, "We've got a customer!" She waved her hand in a flourish.

Roman, the Knox Clan leader, stood in the middle of the shop. His terra-cotta skin almost delicate against the crisp grey suit he wore. Two burly men dressed in all black and anger stood off to the side. They looked out of place amongst the narrow rows of shelves filled with refurbished androids and parts.

Zakari hadn't seen Roman in a long time, but she could tell the gang life was treating him well. Her chest tightened at the stifling energy behind his light brown eyes. Drawing in a breath, she readied her professional voice and smiled.

"Hello, Roman, how can I help you." She suppressed a self-loathing groan as she joined Zima behind the glass counter.

"Come on, Riri, you don't have to be so formal." Roman gave her a smile so fake she worried that hers wasn't fake enough, "I hear you can fix droids real quick."

Zakari waited for him to finish, but he didn't continue. "I don't know about all that." Not wanting to give him the expectation that she would take on a job from him.

He laughed, "Oh, so Zima lied to me?"

She glanced at her sister, who was nibbling on the edge of her glossed lip. "Not at all. I just don't like to brag." What did Zima get them into?

"That's good." He stared at Zima, "I wouldn't want to waste my time."

Zima's reddish-brown skin darkened to a berry red as she moved her head enough to hide half of her face behind a curtain of waist-length box braids and trembled.

"Well, let's keep you on schedule," Zakari said, "What can I fix?" She needed to keep this conversation moving.

Roman gave her his attention with a piercing glare, and the change wasn't much better. She rubbed the skin between her thumb and forefinger.

"I need you to upgrade a droid for tonight's fight."

Zakari checked the time on the register and gave him two quick blinks, "In two hours?"

It didn't matter what needed to be done to the android. Removing the safety protocols and maxing out the strength and speed moderators would take at least that long. Then, she would have to upload fight styles and any other customizations. He couldn't be serious.

"Don't look at me like that." Roman laughed, "My tech got some of the work done already, but he's visiting club fed for a while."

Hesitating, Zakari answered, "I can try-"

"Nah, you can do it and get paid two g's or owe me a favor."

Zakari let a silent scream deafen her mind. He knew that wasn't a real choice. Even though she needed some cash, this was a deal with the devil. She looked at Zima, who clutched the frayed edge of her shorts and stared back with worried eyes.

"That sounds like a great offer." Zakari relented.

Roman clapped his hands, "I knew it was."

One of the guards walked over to the display window and signaled for someone to come in. Roman grabbed a black box from the other guy and set it on the counter in front of Zakari.

"This is an extraordinary upgrade, so don't get caught."

She removed the lid to reveal a small black processor in a padded recess. Zakari couldn't find any branding on the piece, so it was either stolen, or his tech made it. The former made the most sense.

Two more guards clad in black rolled in a large, black tool chest and popped it open beside her worktable. They pulled out a tattered heavy-duty android and set it on the table; Zakari joined them.

The android was nothing but a metallic mess of wires and cobbled together replacement parts. The words, 'Two Hours,' kept running lines in Zakari's head. Roman handed her a sheet of paper.

"Here's what I need." He said with a smile, "See you soon."

When Roman and his goons left the shop, Zakari pulled down the display window's curtains, locked the door, and flipped on the ‘Closed’ sign.

"I'm sorry," Zima started.

"How could you get us caught up with him again?" Zakari pulled on her magnifying goggles and clicked on the light.

"We were just talking, and he sort of steamrolled me." She replied as she pulled some black armor from the toolbox.

Zakari shook her head. That was precisely the reason she didn't want Zima talking to Roman at all. The last time he sank his claws into her sister, Zakari had to fork over her tuition money. Manipulating people was a favorite pastime of his.

"Don't worry about it. Just stay away from him after we get through this."

Zima sucked her teeth, "I know."

Hoping she would really listen to her this time, Zakari put on her gloves and set to work on the droid. It looked like a total mess, but at least all of the basics were done. The processor had been removed, and some of the wirings needed reworking.

Zakari moved fast and double-checked the droid's assembly against Roman's specifications.

The minutes flew by, but after a long stint of working, Zakari sat back and admired her work. This was the fastest money she had ever made, and she still had twenty minutes. The android was a massive copy of a man with broad shoulders and molded muscles over every inch of his mechanical physique.

"He's kinda fine," Zima said over her shoulder.

Zakari nodded, "Um-hum."

She had to agree. Most of the android was comprised of military-grade parts, built to withstand extreme weather and fight full platoons of enemies. Not to be confused with commercial assistant droids, all branches modeled them after the 'perfect' man. The added facial dexterity and newest, velvety soft skin tech helped him infiltrate enemy territory. At least at night. He would be a top contender in the electro brothels with so many perks.

"Maybe if you ask Roman nicely, he'll let you borrow him, and I'll add all the attachments you need." She laughed at Zima's open mouth and wide eyes.

"I would never take a used sex droid."

Zakari grinned, "You know the attachments would be new."

They both laughed as Zima started attaching the armor plates to his legs. When Zakari inserted the drive, the android powered on, and a shrill alarm sounded.

"Warning," he spoke in a low, rich tone, "Unauthorized user. Please enter access codes."

"The fuck," Zakari clenched her teeth and grabbed her phone, "It wasn't even on."

Zima raised her hands in surrender, "I didn't do it."

"I've never seen this," Zakari grunted as she hooked up the phone and loaded her program.

Code rushed across the screen, signaling that the program failed. She loaded it again and connected a keyboard. The in-house antivirus was eating away at her program. It was meant to remove company restrictions, but the processor was working too fast. Her fingers flew as she broke down firewall after firewall. The program took her work and added it to its assault, evolving.

Over and over, Zakari worked to keep the android from sending out location information, updating, or notifying the police. The alert droned on with the siren adding to its urgency. Then, the alarms paused and restarted in longer and longer intervals until they stopped.

"Authorized user, Zakari Monroe, recognized. Awaiting directive."

"Yes!" Zakari thrust her fists in the air.

Zima let out a long sigh, "Finally, some peace and quiet." Then she ducked under the ball of wires Zakari threw at her.

After uploading Roman's specifications, Zakari told him to suit up while she got ready. Even though he was programmed with a scary amount of combat knowledge, Roman ordered lots of domestic tasks. Zakari walked out of the bathroom dressed in an orange shirt under a pair of overall shorts. The backup outfit hugged tightly to her rounded stomach and thick thighs.

The android stood dressed in black armor and watched her with golden glowing eyes. His ochre-colored artificial skin was bound to be rubbed out in spots without a layer of cloth, but Roman didn’t give them anything else.

"What should we call you?" She asked as she rubbed mango scented shea butter into her hands and arms.

"Codename: Polo."

Zakari's brows scrunched. It couldn't be using a nickname for someone she wished she could forget. Then again, the deep sultry tones in the few words he said were familiar. No. That's just a random name programmed into an android processor.

She finished her rub down and said, "Well, Polo, let's see what you can do."

* * *

The 'official hours' of the plaza had ended over an hour ago, but it was packed to the brim. Music thumped through the halls, and bodies rubbed past each other. Video screens descended from the ceiling along the aisles with cameras trained on all angles of the main attraction, the Rotten Arena, at the center.

Zima stayed behind to set up a highchair in the shop. They were lucky enough to have a storefront right next to the arena and could watch most of the action in comfort. But for tonight, she was a battle droid tech for the Knox Clan. That meant she had to be present and stick close to the fight.

Polo made easy work of walking through the crowd since most patrons moved aside and gawked at the giant, armored android with glowing eyes. They walked into the arena check-in with a minute to spare.

Roman grinned and spread his arms wide, "Hey! My thicc and sexy battle tech!"

Zakari faked niceties and said, "Right on time, Polo is ready to go."

"Damn, girl." He took her phone to look at Polo's spec readout, "You good." He stopped scrolling through the screen and looked up to squint at her, "Wait a sec, you gave it your ex's nickname?"

She crossed her arms and frowned, "Nah, it was already there, and you didn't have a name on the list."

"Didn't he join the army or something?"

Zakari restrained herself from showing any emotion, "I don't know." A lie.

Zakari knew that the 'Polo' he was talking about broke her heart and left to become a bounty hunter. It didn't matter much; she wasn't going to tell Roman that. They were done, and he was gone—no reason to trade old info.

Roman handed the phone back and gave her an 'uh huh that dripped in sarcasm. Maybe he didn't set the name up to mess with her. Either way, Zakari set Roman as the primary user, and the job was almost done.

"You came in clutch today, Riri."

"Glad to help." She tightened her jaw at his insistence on using that nickname. It was one he who shan't be named used. Roman was trying to mess with her.

“I’m feeling generous,” he said as he punched something into his phone, “If Polo wins, you can keep the extra.”

Zakari checked a new notification showing a deposit of four grand into her bitcoin account. That’s classes paid, certification tests paid, and licenses paid! Hell, even a little extra to play with. She took a short breath and looked up, keeping her face as blank as possible.

“And, if he doesn’t?”

Roman grinned, “I’m sure you’ll pay me back the difference and give me that favor.”

Her blood boiled. The man just couldn’t leave well enough alone. Zakari could decline everything, but he wasn’t actually giving her a choice. She lived in his clan’s territory, and they could make life hard for her out of spite.

“I’ll take that bet.” She smiled and bumped his outstretched fist with her own.

Roman turned and walked towards the VIP section. The Knox and Reaper clan ‘royalty’ filled a raised dais sporting soft reclining chairs with top-of-the-line embellishments. Zakari found a free folding chair in the tech pit right outside of the arena's fence. The thin latticed metal surrounded the octagon and reached the third-floor ceiling.

"The contenders are in!" The DJ shouted over the speakers, "Are you ready to see some metal fly?"

The crowd erupted into a roar, and the first match began.

* * *

After two hours, Zakari sighed in relief when the DJ finally called for Roman's team and their contenders. The other matches were the pregame, but the last game was laced with a long-time rivalry—the Knox clan vs. the Reaper clan. Bragging rights were on the line, and everyone was here for it.

The crowd hushed to a low rumble as Polo and two other androids walked to the center of the arena and formed a triangle. The smaller androids were stock grey and didn't sport any armor. They took up a fighting stance as the other gate opened, but Polo stopped in midstride.

Zakari gasped with the crowd as a large scorpion droid entered. At eight feet tall and sporting a hooked tail that doubled in length, it was a massive monster. Its armor was painted a bloody red, and when it snapped its giant pincers, the sound clapped the air. The small droids fanned out while Polo stayed rooted in place. What is he doing?

"Dammit," Zakari hissed and looked at her phone. But, nothing was amiss on the screen.

A shrill horn reverberated through the plaza, and the cheering went wild as the scorpion and two smaller androids sprang into action. The clang of metal punctuated the lowered music.

The scorpion slashed low and cut one of them down. The other droid jumped onto its back and unleashed rapid-fire punches into it. The scorpion rolled over, crushing the upper half of the android. They didn't stand a chance against the military-grade tech.

Zakari grabbed the fence and screamed at Polo, "What's wrong with you!"

The black-armored android didn't move as the scorpion stepped on the first failed one, piercing its back, destroying its processor. It turned towards the last one standing, but the other one was still stuck on its foot. Zakari looked back at her phone and couldn't think of anything she could do. She was going to lose money and owe the head of the Knox gang a favor.

She stuffed the phone into her front pocket and rubbed the skin between her thumb and forefinger. The scorpion shook off the fallen enemy and marched towards Polo.

"Please," Zakari whispered as it pulled back its tail to strike, "Fight."

The black android disappeared under the scorpion's body, and her heart dropped. It was over. Everything was gone. In one afternoon, she had managed to dig a deeper hole than she was already in. She would never finish college and get the certification to keep her shop.

A loud crack of metal pulled her mind and eyes back to the ring. Polo had dodged the scorpion's tail and was holding its pincers up and open. A collective gasp spilled from the audience then flared into cheers. The DJ yelled over the speakers, but Zakari's heartbeat pounded too loud to hear as she leaned against the fence. Polo set his golden eyes on her as she grunted fiercely and shook the gate.

"Do something!" She let out a feral scream, "Fight back!"

Her phone vibrated, but her eyes were glued to the black android ripping one of the scorpion's pincers off. More cheers filled the air, and Zakari joined them.

The android grabbed the scorpion's head and slammed it onto its back. It moved with shocking speed to get up, but Polo moved faster. He dodged in and out, avoiding strike after strike. The crowd's octave rose higher and higher as Polo's blitz continued.

Polo ran at the scorpion, dropped, slid under it, and landed a devastating uppercut to its underside. The scorpion bent in half from the force and toppled over. Then he jumped on the flailing scorpion and ripped off the underplating. The metal arachnid spread its legs wide and struck at the android's back with its stinger. Polo moved just enough for the blow to miss and caught the tail.

He twisted and ripped off the segment. Then he slammed the tip into its exposed processor. The scorpion's legs flexed and curled in every direction until it sputtered to a dead stop. Polo jumped down and stood back as the lights of the enemy faded.

Zakari let out a guttural scream and shook the fence madly. They won! Classes were paid, and their little shop was saved.

The arena was engulfed in a roar of cheers, music, and horns. It was a good show, and a new champion was crowned. It would be a year before the Reapers could try again for the title. Zakari looked back and couldn't see past the crowd of people. She climbed the fence enough to see Zima celebrating inside their shop. She waved, and Zima waved back and headed for the door. Probably coming out to meet her.

Roman strode into the arena to meet the DJ beside Polo. Congratulated for his work, Roman addressed the crowd and spoke about the win as if he was out there fighting. Zakari rolled her eyes and hopped down. She had fulfilled their 'agreement' and got paid enough for the last semester of college. Now, she could go home, take a shower, and get some sleep.

When Roman left the arena, the android stayed in place. She checked her phone and found a box of text overlaying the android's system readout. 'Objective Complete – Awaiting Next Command.' What the hell?

She dismissed the notification and scrolled through the updated code. When she'd connected Roman's phone as the primary user, it was supposed to reprogram-

"Oh, shit," Zakari's eyebrows lifted.

Her updated program had removed all outside command options other than her own. It also repurposed her phone to receive commands since the noise canceled out her voice. She would have to open Polo to fix the issue, admitting there was something wrong. Maybe even lose the payment for the inconvenience. Roman was going to be pissed. Dammit!

Screams filled the air as people rushed away from the far side of the arena. Loud mechanical barks sounded before Zakari saw the hunter bots slam into the fence. The four-legged silver creatures and ripped at the fencing.

The lights flickered and died. Panicked people screamed even more. Then the backup generators kicked in, drenching everything in red lights. Roman and the DJ ran out of the gate and disappeared into the rushing people. Zakari crouched by the entrance, clutching her phone.

There were too many people pushing further into the plaza for Zakari to move. She took slow, calming breaths, waiting for an opening to get to her shop. She looked up just as the dogs made it into the arena and spread out to surround Polo.

* * *

A man covered in shadows stepped through the hole in the fence. He whistled, and two of the hunting bots attacked, bringing Polo down and ripping at his armor. They were trying to tear him apart, and Zakari needed him to survive this. Her phone pulsed with vibrations, and she could see the text box through the gaps in her fingers. She uncovered the screen, and 'Awaiting Command' kept flashing on the screen.

"Defend yourself!" She screamed at the phone, and 'Objective Received' stayed on the screen.

Polo pushed to his feet with one hunter bot on his back and another clasped in his hands. He broke the bot's neck and pulled off its head. The other bot slammed into him, and they collapsed into a heap of arms, legs, and metal teeth.

The black-clad man craned his head and planted the same golden glowing eyes as Polo on her. Zakari's chest clenched, and she turned to the crowd and found an opening. People filtered out of the plaza, and she could make it to the shop without the risk of getting trampled. A crash behind her coaxed her into looking back at the arena. Polo had thrown off one of the hunter bots and was facing off against the other. The man had moved around the edge of the fence and was closer to her. She could see long, inky black locs cascading from the neck of his hood.

Zakari jogged towards the shop, searching the window for Zima. She made it to the door, and someone slammed into her. She stumbled through the doorway and turned around to Roman, yoking her up by the neck of her shirt.

"What did you do!" He yelled as he threw her down.

Zakari hit the ground hard, and her phone skidded out of her hand. She scurried back, but one of the angry guards rushed in and snatched her up.

"What are you talking about?" She groaned.

The guard put his arms under hers and held her still. Pain swelled across her stomach from Roman's punch. She tried to curl over, but the guard kept her in line for a blow to her cheek. White dots filled her head as the heat seared across her face.

"You fucked up the installation," he grunted and punched her stomach again, "and got us tracked!"

The taste of metal filled Zakari's mouth, and she coughed out, "No, it was right."

Roman slapped her, "Don't fuckin' lie, bitch!"

Tears rolled down her cheeks as she panted. He wasn't going to believe her. He was going to blame her even if he knew it wasn't her fault.

"Put her in the truck," Roman spat at her feet, "I'm going to find Zima."

Zakari's chest tightened, "No, please! She didn't do anything!"

He grabbed her jaw and dug his fingers into her cheeks. She cried out and pulled her head back, but his grip kept her in place.

"She got me into this bad deal, didn't she?"

Zakari couldn't move her mouth to answer so, he kept her wide eyes on him.

Roman laughed and said, "The way I see it, you two played me." Then, he released her.

The guard let go of one of her arms to put the other into an armlock. Zakari cried out as he used it to guide her to the back door. She searched the shelves, trying to find a weapon close enough, some way to escape. Then, she spotted her phone at the foot of the counter as they passed it. They made it to the back door, and the guard turned them around to back out of it.

Zakari grabbed her trapped hand behind her and pushed down, loosening the man's grip. Stomping his toes made him let go, and she turned around to ram her knee into his crotch. He doubled over with a grunt, and she ran to her phone.

The man stuck out his foot, and she tripped just short of it. Landing on her stomach, she got to her hands and knees. He snatched up her foot, sending her back to her stomach.

"Protect me!" She screamed at the device, "Protect Zakari!"

The guard stood and moved to her side. She tried to get up, but he kicked her side, slamming her into the wall. Zakari curled up on her side and wheezed for air. There was no way to tell if the command was received. She couldn't breathe enough to try again.

The guard grabbed her hair and pulled her up. Zakari stumbled, trying to keep up and ease the pressure on her head. They stepped out into the chilly night of the loading area. Zakari recognized Roman's truck just as the guard pushed her down onto the hood. And then, nothing was holding her.

Zakari pushed herself up and turned to the grunts and heavy smacks behind her. Polo picked up the guard and threw him against the wall. The loud crack of bones shocked her out of her awe, and the guard slumped on the ground.

"Shit," she hunched over to put her hands on her knees, "Thank you."

The droid took her hand and marched into the shop. One of the hunter bots was broken and sparking just inside the shop door. Getting her to sit at her worktable. Polo kneeled and placed the cold metal of his gauntlet against her cheek. Zakari hissed but didn't move away.

"Aww, isn't that sweet?" Roman laughed behind them.

* * *

Zima squirmed in Roman's arms with a cloth tied over her mouth. Polo stood and stepped between them and Zakari.

"You made it into a love bot," Roman chuckled and pushed Zima into the store, "Did you attach a dildo too?"

Zakari got up and stepped from behind Polo, "Come on, Roman, we can give you the money back, and no one has to get hurt."

"Nah," he snorted, "You played me, so now, I gotta play you." He pulled out a pistol and pressed it against the back of Zima's head.

Fear sliced through Zakari's heart, and she thrust up her hands in surrender, "Please, we'll pay you back."

"Oh, really?" Roman lifted the gun and waved it at Polo, "You gonna buy me a new battle droid too?"

"Whatever it takes, please."

"Come here," Roman commanded Polo, but the android didn't move. Then he frowned at Zakari, "Fix it."

"Oh," Zakari jumped and turned to Polo, "Polo, make Roman Anderson your primary user."

"Command Denied."

Zakari scrunched her brow at the android, and it didn't move. What was it doing? She turned to her phone and moved towards it. Roman dug the barrel of the gun Zima's head.

Zakari paused with her hands still raised, "I'm just getting my phone to fix him." Roman pulled back a fraction, and she picked it up.

The screen was covered in spider web cracks, but she could still see the 'Command Denied' text box on top of the stat readouts. She searched her worktable and found a cord to connect it to Polo.

Zakari squinted and read through the scrolling text and number combinations. Someone was wirelessly connected to Polo. All external commands were being blocked.

"S- Someone is hacking him," Zakari whispered.

Roman lifted the gun again and used the front sight to scratch behind his ear. "What was that?"

Zakari looked up, and her blood drained from her face. The dark figure from before stood outside of the display window and stared at her. He took off his hood, and the red light revealed Marco. He smiled, then crashed through the window.

* * *

Zakari gasped as Marco slammed into Roman. They tumbled over Zima and rolled into a display shelf. Zakari ran around them and helped Zima up.

Marco overpowered Roman and slammed his fist into his face. Zima and Zakari bolted for the door, but the hunter bot spazzed and staggered to its feet. They held out their palms and backed away. It didn't follow. One leg was severed and the other mangled to uselessness.

Zakari stepped into Polo and stopped, "Help us." She whispered.

Polo moved his arm around her and jerked to a stop. Then, Marco rushed to Zakari and caught her by the neck. Lifting her with ease. She held onto his arm and stood on her toes, trying to ease the pressure on her neck.

“Can’t have you giving out orders,” he said in a monotone voice.

Marco cocked his arm back, and Zakari squeezed her eyes shut. But, the blow never came. When she opened them, Polo was holding Marco’s fist in place, inches from her face. Her eyes darted to her phone wire hanging over Polo’s arm. He must have lost the phone in the movement.

Zakari sputtered and fought to breathe as Marco and Polo struggled against each other. She snatched the wire and jabbed it into the cybernetic enhancement port on the side of Marco’s neck. The electric shock made him tighten his grip and her vision blackened at the edges. Zima yelled and smacked Marco in the back with an android leg.

Zakari and Marco dropped to the floor. Nausea rolled through her in waves as Polo reached for Marco, then froze. His glowing eyes flickered. He was fighting the hack.

Zima helped her up enough to sit in her chair. When she looked at their savior and assailant, she yelled, “Is that fucking Marco?”

Zakari coughed and said, “It looks like it.”

Polo jerked, making both of them yelp, and said, “Restarting.”

Then the droid powered down. Zakari picked up a wrench. She was too tired to move, much less run. Zima readied the leg as Polo powered back on.

“Restart successful.” Polo said, “Twisted Analog protocol accepted.” The android stood and moved to stand beside Zakari.

“What?” Both of them asked in unison.

Marco groaned, "It means," he paused and sat up, unhooking the cord in his neck, “My copy is no longer an exact copy.”

The girls looked back and forth between the two. Zakari settled on watching Marco.

“Polo is a copy?” She asked him.

Marco focused on her, “Yeah, of me.” He rubbed at his neck and continued, “It was meant to bring in Roman when activated, but your program changed the objective.”

"That doesn't explain why you were acting like a psycho," Zima said.

"I'm sorry for that." He looked down, "I blocked out some memories, so I could do the job."

"That's some ol' bullshit!" Zakari threw the wrench across the room. Twisted Analog was all but destroyed. What was another out-of-place tool going to hurt?

"You know it isn't," he said.

It wasn't. In fact, it was the reason they broke up a year ago. Marco had signed up to become a bounty hunter to help pay their debt to Roman without talking it over with Zakari. She was furious at the prospect of another black body being used for corporate profits, but he didn't see it that way. Just a means to an end.

Some of the perks were cybernetic enhancements and memory blockers that made any job methodical. It's easier to drag your crying grandmother in if you didn't know her.

Marco stood and walked over to Roman to cuff him and said, "Don't worry, the damages are covered." His voice was back to its normal low yet vibrant tone.

Zima relaxed and rested the leg on her shoulder, "Well, I guess that means you can focus on class."

Zakari rolled her eyes and leaned back in the chair. Polo looked down at her and smiled, then centered his focus on Marco's movement. Questions swarmed through her head, but she didn't feel up to asking. At least her classes were paid, and Twisted Analog was going to be fixed. Catching up with her ex-boyfriend or ex-boyfriends could wait for another day. Now, she really needed a nap.

PLAYING THE ODDS
BY
MILTON J. DAVIS

-1-

I should have known better. After twenty years on the grind there's little I haven't seen, done or ran away from. But old habits are hard to break, and there's always the possibility that things might actually turn out right. So, when the lights came on and illuminated the room full of killers, I was disappointed but not surprised. Some skinny guy dressed in a tailor-made suit that was more expensive than he deserved sat behind a battered synth-oak desk. Celia, the woman who led me into this trap, stood behind him, flashing that alluring smile and perfect body that convinced me to take a chance.

Unfortunately for them my guns were fully charged, and my battle tech had already calculated the optimum fire pattern. I would sustain 20% maximum damage and I could handle that. I felt bad about Celia though; she was actually kind of cute. But business is business. I cut down the slick suit first, a bolt in the forehand. The meatbag beside me got a round off that grazed my shoulder before I put him down with a bolt between the eyes. The others went down with various lethal puncture wounds while I took another round to the thigh and one to the ribs. The nanos were healing me up before I lowered my bolters and my hand sleeves slid into place. Celia was in shock, Suit boy's blood splattered on her nice blouse. I altered the battle tech kill zone to drop her from the sweep, because I'm a softy. I gave her my best smile.

"That offer to your place still on?" I asked.

My voice seemed to snap her out of her daze. She looked around the room then let out a scream that almost shattered my eardrums. Celia shoved me out of the way and into the wall as she sprinted like a track droid out the room.

"I guess that's a no," I said.

I limped out of the basement room back into the rave. The music pounded my head as I made my way to the exit, the ravers blissfully unaware what went down beneath their dancing feet. I didn't waste any thought of who they were or why they were after me; the list was too long, and I didn't care. Comes with the business. That's why I stay sharp and upgraded. The best tech will keep you above ground. The first thing I learned. My contact with Cytech kept me pumped with the latest, and even with a few experimental additions.

My EV was waiting when I stepped out on the curb. I hopped in and it merged into the level 7 traffic. Aytee-El was beautiful at night, the lights of synchronized EV and scooter traffic flowing between the illuminated scrapers like blood through an organic. Man, I loved that city.

I was settling into the ride when my cell blinked. Dedren Carmichael's profile filled my screen and I frowned. I'm signed up with three corporations: Cytech, the cybernetic tech powerhouse; Robins, Tyler and Tate, Interplanetary Law Firm; and Triad Enterprises, a little firm that did a bit of everything but nothing very well. That was Dedren's company. I don't know how the man stays in business, but he does. He was also the most annoying of my clients. I let his call bounce as I checked my vitals. The nannies were doing their job; I should be fully repaired by the time I reached my flat. I picked up the comm and put on a fake smile.

"What's up, Dedren?"

Dedren brushed back the hair on his forehead and flashed his big-toothed smile. The man was a cryptonaire and wouldn't spend a crypt for hair stim.

"Just checking in on my investment," he said. "You seem a bit flushed."

"Nah, I'm good. Just a little extra-curricular activity," I said with a grin. That was Dedren's gift. The man was beyond perceptive. Maybe that was what he spent his crypts on. It was illegal, but rich bags don't care. That's why they're rich.

"Look, I was thinking you could stop by for a visit," he said. "I have some things I'd like to . . ."

The comm went black. I cursed—I was being hacked. I was trying to recall if I left anyone alive from the shootout when the universal emblem of Milky Way Savings and Trust filled my screen.

"Please stand by for a Priority Five Message," the syrupy southern voice said. "And thank you for choosing Milky Way Savings and Trust for your galactic financial needs."

The pleasant brown face of a stately looking woman appeared.

"Hello. Is this Carlos Mejia?"

"That's me," I said.

"Carlos Mejia, this call is to inform you that your owner, Cytech, Inc., has filed for Chapter 7 bankruptcy under the laws of the United Planets Federation. As a result of this action, all properties of the company are to be gathered and liquidated at three crypts on the c-dollar. Please remain where you are for imminent collection."

I was terrified.

"Wait . . . what?" Collection?"

I zoomed in on the woman.

"In case you haven't noticed, I'm not a fleeking doll!"

The woman looked away. "According to your recent modification stats, your body consists of fifty-two percent cyber enhancements. By the rules of the 2215 Cyborg/Human Agreement, you are considered a cyborg and are subject to any and all conditions pertaining to cyborg repossession."

"Look at me!" I shouted. "I ain't property!"

The woman looked away from the screen again.

"There is a solution," she said. "Your cybernetic parts can be removed. You can then use your severance funds retained by Cytech to regrow those parts released to the collectors."

Of course, that was bullshit. I wouldn't survive such a procedure.

"That's not possible," I said.

The woman gave me a disinterested smile.

"I'm sorry to hear that, Mr. Mejia."

The screen went blank and my EV shut down. As I descended to the surface, I figured I had about ten minutes before the collectors, or repo knights, showed up. Those muthas were straight A.I., armored from dome to toe and built for carnage. As soon as the EV touched pavement I was out and running. There was no place I could escape the knights, but there was a place I could go and buy some time while I figured out what the hell to do. I had to dive in the Dumpster.

The Dumpster ain't as much a place as it is a concept. It's an underground reflection of the Net, where you can do anything you want for a helluva lot less. It's how we scrapers survive, how we keep our tech working and our bills paid. The Aytee-EL Dumpster was a few blocks from where I went down; I knew I'd reached it when my scan tech flipped. I didn't need it though. I knew exactly where I was going.

The Butcher Shop hid on a backstreet that dead ended on the Beltline. I stood before the door, waiting for the security scan. Two minutes passed and the door didn't open.

"Michelle," I said. "It's me, Carlos."

The door didn't lift.

"Come on, Michelle," I said. "Open the damn door."

"Fleek off, Carlos," Michelle said. "You're hot."

"No, I'm not!"

"My blockers are working triple time. Leave."

Time was up. I had to move. I was stepping away from the door when the stun round hit me square in the back. Lucky thing my battle tech was on; it dampened the impact, but that shit still hurt. My hand sleeves pulled away as I rolled onto my back, firing a defensive pattern as I tried to stand. The repo knights passed through like bull through rice paper. The only reason I wasn't dead was that they were there to collect.

I had no choice. I reached into my back pouch and pulled my Sig Saur. I put two rounds into the first knight's head, three rounds into the other.

"Shield that!" I shouted.

The door to the Butcher Shop lifted. Michelle looked at me in wonder. Well, not exactly me. Her eyes were on my Sig.

"Get inside," she said.

I stumbled into the building, my back sore from the stun round. Michelle shut the door, her eyes still on my Sig.

"Thanks, I think," I said. I tucked the Sig back into my pack.

"Where did you get that?" she asked.

"None of your business," I replied.

"That's a Sig Saur P940, the last handgun produced by the company before the intergalactic ban on projectile firearms," she said. "It shouldn't exist."

"Yet it does," I said. "It was a gift from Cytech. They gave me a thousand rounds, too. Never expected me to use it though."

"I want it," Michelle said.

So that was the deal. Whatever I needed her to do was going to cost me my piece.

"I can't just give you this!" I said in mock anger. "It's priceless!"

"Today it has a price," Michelle said. "Your life. I figure those repo knights came to collect your parts, otherwise they would have fried you. I told you not to fleek with Cytech."

"I don't know," I said.

"It's the only deal you got. Take it or leave it."

I took the Sig from my back holster and handed it over.

"Clips, too."

I feigned despair as I gave her the clip. The truth was that Cytech found a stash of old military gear reclaiming an old nuked site for their latest research facility. They were about to trash it all and I asked if I could take a few things. Sometimes old tech is better than new. I had a roomful of Sigs with enough ammo to last me forever.

Michelle took the weapon and clips then placed them inside a nearby cabinet. She finally smiled.

"So, what's your problem?"

"Cytech went under," I said. "And according to the bank I'm an asset to be liquidated."

"I warned you," Michelle said.

"I don't need to hear that right now," I said. "I need to take some shit out."

"Follow me."

She led me to a room she called the cutting board.

"Stand right there," she said pointing to a bare ceramic circle on the floor.

"Hold your arms out."

I assumed the position.

"Scan," she said.

There was a flash of light and a holo appeared beside me, a road map of my insides. Michelle walked up to it, rubbing her chin as she frowned.

"Well?" I said.

Michelle shook her head. "You are so fleeked," she said. "Did it ever occur to you to ask what these meat bags were doing to you?"

"No," I confessed. "And if I did, I probably wouldn't have understood."

Michelle shook her head. "I don't know what half this shit is. The tech is too new. But I do know one thing; the Bank doesn't want your parts. They want you."

"Shit," I said.

"For real," Michelle replied. "Look at this."

She pointed at my enhancements. "Tech and organics feed on different systems."

"I know that much," I replied.

"But look here," she said. "Somehow they managed to merge your power sources. Your tech can feed off your organics, and your organics can feed off your tech."

"That's why I feel so good in the sun!" I said.

"And why your tech runs longer between charging, I suspect."

She was right.

"You're a hybrid," Michelle said. "I don't think Cytech went bankrupt. I think they were shut down. Whoever did this wants this tech, and you're the presentation."

I was fleeked. Big time.

"One more thing," Michelle said.

I rolled my eyes. "What?"

"This."

She pointed at a bright spot glowing near my neck.

"This is your thyroid," she said. "Cytech implanted something to regulate the influence of their implants on your metabolism."

"Take it out," I said.

"That might not be smart," Michelle replied.

"I have an idea why it's there, and the only way to find out for sure is to take it out."

Michelle looked at me like a worried parent.

"Are you sure about this?"

"Take it out and I'll get you a Glock plus enough ammo to last you the rest of your life."

"Let's get you prepped," Michelle said.

Michelle left the room then returned with a chair.

"Sit."

I sat in the chair.

"Don't you need to put me to sleep or something?"

Michelle laughed. "You actually thought I was going to operate on you? I cut your throat and I could sell you to the bank."

"So, what are you going to do?"

"That regulator is tech. I'm going to shut it off."

Michelle took something that looked like a small box then placed it against my neck.

"This might hurt," she said.

Hurt was an understatement. When I woke up, I was dizzy and had peed my pants. I jumped out of the chair, which was a mistake. I hit my head on the ceiling then crashed onto the chair. The thing was that Michelle's ceiling was high. Very high. So, there I was laying on the floor with a headache and soiled pants and Michelle looking at me like I had three heads.

"Great gods," she said.

"Why didn't you tell me this was going to hurt?" I said.

"I did. Did you just see how high you jumped?"

I knew what I just did was amazing, but at the moment I just wanted some clean clothes.

"You got a change of clothes around here?" I asked.

"I think so," Michelle answered.

"Where's the shower?" I asked.

Michelle led me to the shower. She rustled up a spare pair of pants that fit way too tight but would have to do. I cleaned up the best I could then headed for the door.

"You can't go out there," Michelle said. "Repo knights are probably swarming the district, and you don't know what you're capable of."

"I have an idea," I replied. I could feel it. Most of all I could see it. Michelle seemed to be moving in slow motion to me, which meant either my head was fleeked up or my senses were working overtime. Still, I wasn't sure if I was ready to face off with a repo swarm.

"Can you ghost me?" I asked.

"It'll cost you," Michelle said.

"How about I throw in a vintage military issue Colt .45?"

Michelle shuffled off to her worktable. In a matter of minutes, she returned with a palm sized drone. She extended her hand then drew it back.

"Wait a minute. How am I going to get all this with your ass on the run?"

I reached into my shirt pocket and handed her my card.

"My codes," I said. "I'm sure you can find out where I live. I'd give it a few weeks to cool down."

Michelle took the card and tucked into her pants pocket.

"What are you going to do now?" she asked.

"Take my chances," I said. "But I have to see someone first."

It wasn't in my nature to run. Well at least not for long. If Milky Way wanted a fight, I'd give it to them. But I would need help.

Michelle went to the front door then released the ghost. I was about to step out, but she put her hand on my chest, stopping me.

"Give it a minute."

The drone hovered near the street for a few minutes when a commercial EV appeared. The door opened and the ghost flew in. The EV lifted into traffic; a minute later three repo knights flew off in pursuit.

"Thanks, Michelle," I said. "I owe you."

"You're paid up in full," Michelle replied. "Good luck. Don't die."

"I don't plan to."

I stepped into the darkness and hurried away. I couldn't trust transport, so I had to walk. It took me most of the night to cross the city to my destination; the sun was rising as I stepped up to the door of the home of Dedren Carmichael. I shook my head looking at the modest home. This man was really cheap.

"Carlos, is that you?" Dedren's voice surrounded me.

"You said you needed to see me, and I need your help," I answered.

The door slid open. While Dedren scrimped on exterior, the inside of his home was immaculate and exquisite. An L6 A.I. greeted me. If it wasn't for his purple eyes, I would have thought I was looking a handsome organic.

"Welcome, Mr. Meji," it said. "Please follow me to the breakfast area."

I followed the L6. The kitchen was well appointed; Dedren stood over the stove stirring something. He turned to look at me and smile.

"Hi Carlos! It's a little early, but I'm glad you're here. Sit. I'm almost done with the eggs."

I sat at the table. The L6 left the room. Dedren sat at the table with a plate of grits, eggs and bacon. I hadn't eaten in two days, but I wasn't hungry. I guess my hybrid system was running off the battery.

"I know what you're thinking," Dedren said. "A man like me should have servants. I'm very particular how I spend my money. Why waste it on something I can do myself?"

Actually, I didn't care, but I did my best to look interested.

"Look, Dedren, I need your help. Cytech went under and now I'm running from the bank trying to save my ass. I need to lay low for a while to work all this out and I figured you can help me."

Dedren scooped up a forkful of grits and ate before answering.

"How do you figure that?"

"I don't know what you do exactly, but I'm sure most of it is dirty," I said. "You help me and I'll be eternally grateful. And I'll keep my mouth shut about what I do know."

Dedren took a sip of his coffee.

"I'm disappointed, Carlos," he said. "I thought we were friends."

"It's business," I said. "It always is."

Dedren grinned. "True. I must admit though Milk Way Savings moved a lot faster than I expected."

My eyes went wide. "What the fleek are you talking about?"

Dedren ate his eggs before answering me.

"Cytech has always been a pain in my ass," he said. "They were in competition with three of my off-world companies, and their latest tech was rumored to put them out of business. So, I acted first."

"You did this?" I asked. "You?"

Dedren grinned. "I own MWS & T. I called in a few loans and just like that Cytech was broke. We were liquidating their assets and transferring their research when we discovered their work on hybrid cyborgs . . . and you. Do you realize how valuable you are?"

I jumped to my feet to bust a hole in his ass when the house filled with repo knights. Dedren finished his coffee.

"I must admit I didn't expect you to bring the goods to my doorstep. I figured it would take a few weeks to run you down. Saved me a lot of time and money."

Battle tech kicked in, moving so fast I could barely keep up. Dedren's eyes went wide.

"Fleek!" he exclaimed just before he dove under the table.

It was like watching a flick, except I was the star. I spun, ducked, dodged and shot my way through the mob, destroying the interior of Dedren's house in the process. It didn't matter. Once I found who his partners were, he wouldn't be alive to enjoy it anyway.

I was gunning down the last knight when the L6 tackled me. Had to be a fluke, I thought. There was no way a Pretty Doll could get by my tech. But then I turned to take it out, it hit me with an EMP pulse that shut down my all my tech. I reached for my Sig then cursed; I gave it to Michelle. Last resort was my short machete strapped to my right calf. I snatched it free then lunged for the L6. To my shock it blocked my thrust then kicked me in my chest. I flew across the room then slammed into the wall, my nannies repairing my damaged back as the L6 jumped the gap. I managed to get to my feet as it landed, and it was on. We stood toe to toe, trading kicks and punches. I should have been beating it down, but I wasn't. Dedren must have geeked it from the tech he stole from Cytech. My nannies were falling behind, and I was slowing down. What began as a stalemate became me taking an ass whupping. My legs faltered and I fell, my body rippling with pain. The L6 raised its foot to stomp me when two loud explosions shook the room. Two holes appeared in the L6's chest area and it fell to the side. When my eyes cleared, I saw Michelle walking toward me with the Sig Saur in her hand. Dedren crawled from under the table and scramble to his feet. He glared at Michelle.

"Who the fleek are you, bitch?" he shouted.

Michelle turned to him.

"Bitch?"

"Michelle, no!" I said.

Michelle raised the Sig and put two rounds in Dedren's head. She walked to me, a frown on her face.

"What are you doing here?" I said.

She reached into her pocket, pulled out my card then threw it at me. It bounced off my forehead then landed in my lap.

"It didn't work," she said. "I tracked you here to get my guns."

"You put a tracker in me?"

Michelle nodded. "A good thing I did. That L6 was beating you into paste."

She knelt then took out a nano syringe. She stabbed me near my heart, releasing the nannies. I felt better immediately.

"Come on. We need to get out of here."

I stood feeling better every second. I glanced at Dedren's body. He was behind it all, but there were others.

"Come on, Carlos," Michelle said again. "And bring it with you."

She gestured at the L6.

"Why?" I asked.

"Because it was beating your ass, and I want to know why. And because you still owe me."

I shrugged and lifted the L6 onto my shoulders. Together we left the house, climbed into Michelle's repair van then lifted off.

-2-

I didn't ask for this. All I wanted was my cut. I could care less how I work, as long as I work. I thought hooking up with Michelle was a good idea, but the longer it lasted, the worse it got. But I had to stick around because of the money. We both had enough to live like CEOs anywhere in the UC, but Michelle was being stingy. 'You get yours when we figure this out,' she said. Fleeking hackers. I hate them.

The place we hid out was worse than Michelle's previous haunt. She said we needed to keep a low profile since we took all those cryptos. The rooms were just big enough for a bed and a dresser, which meant as big as I am, I had to practically get naked and oil up so I could slide through the door. So, I spent most of my time in the streets, except when Michelle wanted to tinker with my mech. And she always wanted to tinker with my mech.

That day she'd been fussing with my circuits the entire morning.

"What the hell are you doing?" I finally said.

"Installing the final touches," she replied.

"The final touches of what?"

Michelle looked up from her holoscreen then lifted her glasses until they rested between her afro puffs.

"Why do you want to know?"

"Because I do."

"You never wanted to before."

I folded my arms, almost pulling some of the wires hooked into my ports loose.

"Because nobody ever fucked with me as much as you're doing right now."

"You probably never needed upgrades like you do now," Michelle said.

"Upgrades for what?"

Michelle fell back into her chair then sighed.

"Your tech is way behind the dolls we encountered at Dedren's. I need to make sure you're ready."

"Ready for what?"

"Jeez, what's with all the questions? Just trust me, okay?"

I started pulling the cables off. "I don't trust anybody."

Michelle jumped from her chair then grabbed my hand. She's stronger than she looks, but not strong enough. I snatched my hand free and kept pulling.

"Stop Carlos, please?" she said. I was stunned. She said please. Michelle never says please. I stopped pulling the cables free.

"I've learned as much as I can from the dolls," she said. "We need to get into Cytech and find out what they have that's so special. In order to do that we need you at top level just in case we run into trouble."

"When we run into trouble," I corrected her. "And what is this we shit?"

"I'm going, too."

"Why? So I can mop you up when one of those gun dolls blasts you into transition?"

"Fleek you," Michelle replied. "I'm not helpless. I got a few tricks up my sleeve."

"Twenty percent," I said.

Michelle blinked. "What?"

"Twenty percent of my take. Today. Otherwise, I'm walking."

"Don't you want to know what the earth is going on?"

"Nope," I said. "I want to spend my money and get laid. That's what I want. Unless you give me twenty percent."

Michelle scooted close to the console. Her fingers flying across the holoboard.

"Done."

I tapped my temple. It was there. I took the rest of the cables from my arm and stood.

"Wait!" Michelle yelped. "You said you'd let me finish!"

"I will, once I splurge a little. You can have your way with me once I get back."

"Fleeking hack bag!" she shouted as I opened the door.

"Back at you, meatbag hag."

"What did you call me?"

That's when I heard the pop of an EMP and everything went rigid. I swayed, then fell forward. I managed to turn my head before I crashed into the floor, saving my nose from being broken. My jaw wasn't as fortunate. I heard Michelle walk up to me. She hooked the cables back into my arms and legs.

"I tried to be nice," she said. "Look what you made me do."

"Just get it over with," I mumbled.

"You'll thank me later, I promise."

"We'll see," I replied.

I laid on the floor while Michelle did her thing. I decided we were going to have to have a long talk after this was done. Organics forget that we have feeling, too. We can't . . . well we shouldn't be cut off and on when they feel like it. Show some respect goddammit.

Although I was pissed, I had to admit whatever she was doing felt pretty good. It was like I was growing inside, like things were coming closer together. The best way to describe it was like falling in love with yourself. I know that sounds freaky, but hey; I'm not a poet.

"There," she said. "Upgrade complete."

She crawled over me, unhooking the wires.

"You can stand up now."

I took my time rising. The last time Michelle upgraded me I almost popped through the roof. I worked my arms and did a few squats. The lag I usually experienced between thought and action was completely gone.

"Fleek!" I said. "What did you do?"

"Dedren's doll had significant synaptic density improvements," she said. "I did the same to you. I also increased your A.I. muscle density by thirty-five percent. You're strong as shit now. Last but not least, I increased your nano capacity ten percent. You're welcome."

"Excellent." I strode for the door. "I'll be back in a few days."

Michelle didn't answer. I reached for the door pad, expecting her to yell at me or something. She didn't.

"You're not going to try to stop me?" I said.

"Nope."

I turned to see her smiling.

"Go do what you need to do," she said. "It'll give you a chance to get used to the upgrades. Just promise me you won't kill anybody while you're gone. We don't need the extra attention."

"I can't promise you that," I said. "I will promise that I won't leave any evidence."

"Fair enough," Michelle said. "When you get back, I'll be ready."

Those last words made me nervous.

"Ready for what?"

"You'll see. Now go. I got work to do."

I pressed my hand against the door pad. The door swished open and the cool Aytee-El wind flowed around me. It felt invigorating.

"See you in a few," I said.

I stepped outside and smiled as I heard the door close behind me. My attention was immediately captured by the night-lights and buzz of ground and aerial traffic. It was going to be a helluva three days.

* * *

Four days later I strolled down the street with a big ass smile on my face. Magic City was everything they said and some. I didn't have time to find an organic with a cyborg fetish or a fellow metal, so I went straight for the paid entertainment. Every crypto was well spent. Best of all, I didn't kill anybody. There was this one meatbag who decided he wanted to show everyone how strong he was by challenging me to a fight. A crazy footballer. I took it easy on him and choked him out. Never let it be said that I'm not a kind person.

I pressed my hand on the pad and the door swished open. I expected to see Michelle waiting with her arms folded and tapping her foot. I knew she was tracking me; she probably had cameras on me, too. The thought made me hesitate. Was she watching me the entire time? That would be freaky, but probably entertaining, too. I shrugged. I wasn't the shy type, and if she did have footage maybe I could sell it on the gray market. Use some of her techie stuff to alter the faces and just like that I'd have a new revenue stream. Something to consider at least.

"Michelle!" I called out. "I'm back. Where the fleek are you?"

I was answered by a bolt that hit me square in my chest, knocking me through the door and back out into the street. Battle tech popped up, sharing my vitals and target perspectives, twenty per cent damage and I felt every bit of it. I rolled to my right and the concrete where I was exploded. My leg lifted and a pulse bolt fired from my heel. When Michelle installed that, I don't know, but I thanked her ass for it. The shot gave me time to regain my feet and assess the situation.

A fully armored battleborg charged out of the building, blasters blazing. My enhanced shielding deflected the barrage and I ran toward it. Normally I would have preferred a firefight, but I was pissed. The thing was still shooting point blank when I pivoted on my right foot and punched it in the faceplate. The borg staggered back and I kicked it in the chest plate then swept it off its feet. I jumped on top of it, pounding it with my fists until I was covered with metal parts and lubricant. There was a hissing then the cyborg went limp.

I climbed off the metal head then searched for Michelle, or what was left of her.

"Michelle! Michelle!"

I was answered by a clanging sound. I followed it until I stood before a large metal door in the back of the building. My worry faded and I tapped on the door.

"Michelle, you in there?"

"Yes!" she yelled. "Let me out!"

"I forgot how to," I replied.

"Quit fleeking with me and let me out!"

I punched in the code then turned the crank. The door opened and Michelle spilled out drenched with sweat.

"I need to put a ventilation system in there," she said between gasps.

"I'm okay," I said. "Thanks for asking. What the hell is that and why was it here?"

Michelle sat up and pulled at her afro-puffs.

"I fleeked up," she said. "When I duplicated the code from Dedren's doll I must have set off a homing code. They tracked us here then sent that battle bot to finish us off. Which means we gotta get the fleek out of here fast."

We ran through the building grabbing armfuls of shit and tossing it into the EV. We jumped inside and Michelle took out something that looked like a giant controller.

"What are you going to do with that?" I asked.

"Drive," Michelle answered.

"You hack the grid and the APD will be on us like flies on shit."

"As far as they know, we are APD," Michelle replied with a grin.

Michelle worked the EV through the congested traffic, dipping from air to ground and back again.

"Where we going?" I finally asked. "A new hideout?"

"Sort of," she replied. "We're going to Beijing."

Michelle drove us to Jackson/Hartfield. She parked the car in the economy deck then tagged it with an ID scrambler. That would keep the lot droids occupied for at least two weeks. I followed her to the conveyer which sped us to the terminal. As we walked to the gate, she swiped her forearm in my direction. My screen appeared; we were flying first class non-stop. A little red light flashed in the corner of my eye and I grinned. Michelle had us prescreened. She knew there was no way I could get through any kind of security with all the gear I packed. Neither would she. We were quiet until we reached our section. We both fell into our seats and ordered drinks. I was on my third vodka before Michelle cleared her throat.

"What?"

"Aren't you going to ask me why we're going to Beijing?"

I downed a fourth drink.

"No."

Michelle slumped into her lounger. "I don't get you. One minute you're bitching about modifications and now you don't give a flit about where we're headed?"

I sighed. "Okay. Where are we going?"

Michelle grinned. "You ever heard of Jiadan Prosthetics?"

"Sure," I said. "They make doll parts."

"They made your legs and arms," Michelle said.

"Really? Cool." I downed another vodka. Michelle took the bottle from me before I could make another drink.

"Why are you drinking so much?"

"Because I hate flying," I said.

"You can fly, in case you haven't noticed."

I was stunned. She never tells me anything.

"Anyway, it seems that the chairman, Liu Jiaying, was a business partner of Dedren's. There's no direct link between them, but they worked with each other through various shell companies. I think she was responsible for limb creation. Dedren was financing the entire operation as well as in charge of intellectual acquisition. That's why he shut down your patrons; to acquire their doll tech."

Our jet began rolling and I became dizzy. I strapped in.

"Here we go," I whispered.

Michelle grimaced. "You're going to throw up, aren't you?"

My stomach growled.

"It depends on how long the flight is," I said.

"We can't have that," Michelle said.

I got a bad feeling.

"Michelle, wait…"

* * *

When I woke up, we were landing in Beijing. Michelle yawned, stretched, then shared a sweet smile. Apparently, she went to sleep, too, except in her case it was voluntarily.

"You have to stop doing that flit," I said.

"It was for you own good," she said. "And mine. The last thing I wanted to see was you throwing up."

The jet taxied to the gate and we exited. My translator switched automatically as we hurried down the tunnel to the airport exit. Michelle summoned a Rick and we were on our way.

"What's the plan?" I asked.

"We need to talk to Jiaying," Michelle said. "I've been through her files a million times and I can't find the final contact. There's only one place she could be keeping it where I can't find it."

"Where is that?" I asked.

Michelle tapped her head.

"Her memory?"

"Yep. I figure she, Dedren and the unknown partner communicated verbally when it came to the real important shit."

"So, we just going to walk up to her, ask her what's going on and she's going to tell us everything?"

"Of course not," Michelle replied. "We're going to interview her."

I nodded. Interview must be Michelle's nice way of saying kidnap and interrogate. I'd been involved in a few kidnappings. Usually, it was some startup company biting off too much of the profit pie. I'd knock them out, take them somewhere deserted, then convince them to sell their company before they ended up like me. One thing about company types, they don't handle pain too well.

"Sounds like a plan."

Michelle looked at me for a moment before a shocked look took over her face.

"Oh gods, no, not like that," she said.

I was confused. "How else is she going to tell us what we want to know?"

"Don't worry about that," Michelle said. "I'll handle it. Here's the hard part. She lives in her work building and the security is pretty tight. If things go to flit, we might have to fight our way out."

"Give me the building plans," I said.

Michelle swiped the plans to me. I broadcasted a holo then studied the schematics. I integrated my battle tech, looking for possible ambush points and escape scenarios.

"Got it," I said.

"Now give it to me," Michelle said.

"Why? I got it."

"Just in case we get separated."

"If we get separated, nice knowing you."

Michelle rolled her eyes. "Send me the fleeking schematics."

I swiped them to her. She did a quick check then nodded.

"C'mon. We need new clothes. Tailor," she said.

The Rick took us to Beijing's garment district. Apparently, the people of Beijing liked to shop outside, unlike the folks in Aytee-El. The Rick flew to a shop at the end of a narrow, crowded alley then landed before a shop with bare walls. A person stepped through the door, greeting us with a warm smile and a bow. I did a quick scan; it was 100% doll.

"Welcome to Ming's" it said in English. "How can I assist you?"

Michelle bowed. "We need formal business clothing."

The doll bowed again then gestured to the entrance.

"Please follow me."

The doll led us into the shop. It was sparse—a fairly decent scanner and printer were the only items inside. The doll guided Michelle to the scanner.

"Please remain still during scanning," it said.

Michelle did as told. The doll activated the scanner and Michelle was doused with a blue grid. Moments later the printer activated. Michelle stepped out of the scanner and the doll looked at me then gestured. I entered and the scanner did its thing. The printer had completed Michelle's wardrobe by the time I reached it.

"The dressing room is in the rear of the shop," the doll said.

Michelle disappeared to change clothes while I waited for my outfit. The doll looked at me with a blank expression. Whoever owned it was too cheap to pay for proper emotion codes. It activated when printing was complete. I gathered my outfit and headed to the dressing room. I met Michelle on the way. She sported a loose fitting navy blue pantsuit that easily covered her body armor.

"You clean up good," I said.

"Thank you. Now get dressed. We don't want to be late for our appointment."

The dressing room was cramped, of course. I managed to wiggle into my outfit despite that and was impressed. The tailor mech was accurate for a piece of junk. When I returned to the room Michelle's eyebrows rose.

"You actually look good," she said.

"You seemed surprised," I replied.

"I am. Now let's go."

Michelle transferred the payment to the doll and we were on our way. She fiddled with her wrist console then swiped me the data.

"Netview credentials," I said. "Nice. I always wanted to be on the net."

"Don't get used to it," Michelle replied. "I gave us a sixty-minute firewall."

"Is that enough time?"

"It better be."

Ten minutes late we arrived at Jiadan Prosthetics. To say the sprawling office and manufacturing facility was huge would be a lie. It was a city within itself, occupying six kilos of land.

"Somebody's paying a helluva lot of tax cryptos," I said.

"You can afford it when you make all your workers," Michelle answered.

The Rick pulled up to the entrance then rolled to a stop as the security cams scanned us.

"Here we go," Michelle said.

The cams lifted and the gate slid open. I did a quick check of my systems to make sure Jiadan security didn't disable anything. When I was done, I gave Michelle a wink.

"You're good," I said.

"You haven't figured that out yet?" she answered.

"Makes me wonder about you being a junk jockey. What did you do before?"

"A lot of stuff," Michelle replied. "Nothing worth mentioning."

"So how did you learn all this?"

Michelle shrugged. "You'll be surprise what people leave laying around when they underestimate the help. I'm naturally curious."

"Which means you steal a lot of shit."

"Something like that," Michelle replied. "Never thought I'd get to use most of it until you came along."

The Rick jerked for a minute then resumed its course.

"Do not be alarmed," a pleasant voice spoke. "For your convenience we have assumed guidance of your transportation.

You will be taken directly to your destination. Thank you for visiting Jiadan Prosthetics."

I got a worry bubble in my gut and looked at Michelle.

"We're okay. Trust me," she said.

I don't trust anybody.

The Rick stopped in front of a one-story building located in the center of the complex. Meatbags walked in and out of the building, the only ones we'd seen since entering the complex. Apparently, Ms. Liu didn't trust the dolls with the important stuff. She must know people like Michelle. I laughed at the thought.

"What are you laughing about?" Michelle asked.

"Nothing," I replied, then laughed again.

"Remind me to check you out when we get back."

"If we get back," I said then winked.

A receptionist met us as soon as we entered the building. The tall woman wore a tight-fitting jumpsuit with the Jiadan logo on the left breast. She smiled and bowed.

"Welcome to Jiadan," she said. "I am Yu Yan, Ms. Liu's assistant. She asked me to take you to the conference room. She'll meet with you momentarily."

"Thank you," Michelle replied. "We appreciate her seeing with us on such short notice."

"We are honored," Yu Yan replied. "It's not often the media shows an interest in businesses like ours. We provide a necessary service, but what we do is not sexy."

"That depends on if you're a doll or a meatbag," I said.

Yu Yan gave me a scolding look.

"We do not allow such language on our premises, Mr....?"

"Smith," Michelle said. "John Smith. I'm Jane Doe."

I glared at Michelle. She rolled her eyes.

"I apologize," I said. "My assignments usually deal with the darker side of our society."

"You are forgiven," Yu Yan said with a smile. "Now if you will please follow me, Ms. Liu is waiting."

We followed Yu Yan down the long corridor to the CEO's suite. Yu Yan opened the door, revealing Ms. Liu sitting at her desk. She was a stunning woman, tall, with long black hair and an engaging smile. She stood then gestured to the chairs before her desk.

"Miss Doe, Mr. Smith. Welcome to Jiadan. Please sit down."

I followed Michelle to the chairs and we sat.

"So, I think we should begin by being honest with each other," Michelle said. "My name is not Jane Doe, and his name is not John Smith. I'm Michelle Carter, and this is my friend, Carlos Mejia."

It took everything in my power to keep from punching Michelle in the side of the head. She gave me up! Ms. Liu's eyes narrowed as she studied me, then she looked at Michelle and laughed.

"That was obvious. I guess now you expect me to be honest."

Michelle smiled. "Of course."

"What do you wish to know?" she asked.

Michelle leaned forward. "What does this manufacturing facility really do?"

"We make cybernetic limbs," Ms. Liu said. "As a matter of fact, we made Mr. Mejia's limbs, if I'm correct."

"I don't think so," I said. "I got these bad boys in Windy City."

"They may have been installed there, but I'm certain they are Jiadan made. Ninety-eight percent of all prosthetics are made by us or our affiliates."

"What about other parts?" Michelle asked. "Torsos, skulls, brains, organs…"

"I know what you're seeking, Ms. Carter, but you won't find it here," Ms. Liu said. "UC regulations forbid the manufacture of pure symbiots. We are many things at Jiadan, but we are not lawbreakers."

Ms. Liu stood, indicating the interview was over.

"I must say, I'm impressed by your boldness," she said. "Most scandal casts try to hack us. You walked right through the door. I'd love to take you on a tour of our facility to prove to you that we're quite legitimate."

"Why would you do that?" Michelle asked. "You could have thrown us out at any minute."

"I could have," she said. "But you amuse me, and Mr. Mejia is quite interesting."

"It seems we're out of time," Michelle said. "Another day, perhaps?"

"Of course," Ms. Liu said. "I look forward to it."

Ms. Liu led us to the door.

"Yu Yan will see you out. It's been interesting."

Yu Yan appeared moments later. We followed her to the exit; our Rick waited for us.

"What was that all about?" I said. "I thought we were going to be discreet."

"I changed my mind," Michelle said. "Besides, I learned everything I needed to know."

As we entered the Rick a tiny object flew inside then landed in Michelle's palm. She looked it then grinned. My eyes went wide.

"That's a Tacdrone," I said. "Hi-security shit. What the fleek are you doing with that?"

"I work the gray market," Michelle replied. "How do you think I got it?"

The Rick lifted then cruised for the gate.

"So, we were just shooting the shit while little bit did all the hard work?"

"No," Michelle replied. "I wanted to force her hand. I figured if I suggested that we knew what she was doing and I dangled you in her face, she would act."

"But she didn't," I said.

"Not . . ."

The Rick jolted then spun, knocking us around like a blender. I did my best not to crash into Michelle, but her squealing let me know that I failed. Battle tech kicked in; we'd been hit by an EMP. The Rick crashed and we were enveloped by shock suppressers. I kicked the door open then pulled Michelle free. I thought she would be injured. Instead, she was pissed.

"That bitch!" she screamed.

"I thought you didn't like that word," I said.

"Only when someone calls me one," she replied. "For her it fits."

My battle tech went into high gear. Thirty security thugs were coming fast. We were only a half a click from the gate; if we could get in the street the thugs would have to back off. Michelle had already figured that out; she was halfway to the gate before I started running. With my enhanced legs I caught up with her in seconds. Luckily for us there was no one stationed at the gate. I lowered my shoulder and powered through; the gate hit the street, skidding into traffic and causing a mess. We took a sharp left then ran down the middle of the street.

"This was a bad idea," I said.

"You didn't have a better one," Michelle replied.

"Yes, I did. You didn't ask."

A bolt struck my shoulder, knocking me off balance. I caught myself then spun about. The Jiadan security jocks decided the rules weren't shit. They were coming for us. I grabbed Michelle then threw her up on my shoulders. I ran full out, streaking by EVs that swerved to avoid hitting me.

"I told you this was a bad idea!" I shouted.

"Shut up and run faster!" Michelle shouted back.

I was about to throw her into a dumpster when a shadow passed over us. Battle tech kicked in, freezing my legs. I skidded to a halt, holding onto Michelle to keep her from flying off my shoulders. Something landed a few feet in front of us, breaking the asphalt and showering us with dust. When it cleared, my heart dropped.

"Oh shit," Michelle whispered.

"Tell me about it," I replied.

The A.I. stood about my height. It was fully armored with a head bristling with video and audio sensors. It crouched then extended its right arm. A laser blade extended from the end of its arm.

"It's got a sword," I said. "A fleeking sword!"

"You have one, too," Michelle replied.

I looked at her with a grimace.

"Since when?"

"Since I put one in you."

Battle tech flipped on. My guns emerged and I fired in automatic mode. That damn A.I. blocked almost every shot with that sword. What it didn't block its shields absorbed.

"That's not going to work," Michelle said. "Let me handle this."

"What the fleek are you…"

Before I could finish my sentence, Michelle scrambled up my back then sat on my shoulders. She swiped her forearm and a holo controller appeared before her. Suddenly I couldn't feel my arms and legs.

"Michelle, what's happening?"

The A.I. rose from the pavement then streaked for us. I was helpless; or at least I thought I was. A long beam emerged from my right arm and an elliptical energy shield formed at the end of my left arm.

"What the fleek?"

My shield lifted and blocked the A.I.'s swing. I countered with my sword and the fight was on. Except I wasn't fighting. Michelle was. And she was doing a damn good job. She and the A.I, stood toe to toe matching blow for blow. The problem was a small army of security thugs were closing in on us and this fight was about to become uneven.

"Give me my legs," I said.

"No," Michelle said.

"Give me my legs, dammit!" I yelled. "I can end this!"

"Fine!" Michelle said.

I felt feeling return to my legs. This time when the A.I. stabbed at us I pivoted to my right. The A.I. adjusted, swinging at my chest. I jumped back then shuffled to my left.

"Excellent!" Michelle shouted.

With some of my body control back battle tech kicked in, giving me an analysis of the A.I. A pattern of red flashing lights indicated stress points and vulnerable spots.

"Go for the neck!" I said to Michelle. "That's the weak spot!"

"Check!" Michelle yelled.

I danced and Michelle fought. Each blow to the neck weakened the juncture. A meatbag would have picked up on the strategy and altered their defense, but this was an A.I. playing our logical patterns and focused on taking us out. After slipping another sword thrust, I jumped at the A.I.

"Now!" I shouted.

Michelle knocked the A.I. sword aside with the shield then hit the sweet spot. Its head dislodged, hit the street then skidded into a food cart.

There was no time to celebrate; a bolt hit me square in the back, knocking me face first into the street. Michelle managed to jump free then shoulder rolled to her feet. How the hell did she do that?

I clambered to my feet then pivoted about. My nose was broken, but I didn't have time for that. Two large battle sleds had joined the security troops. Where Jaidan got them, I had no I idea. Ms. Liu was sitting there lying her ass off big time.

I grabbed Michelle's arm and pushed her behind me just before the shooting started. My shields took the brunt, Battle tech decreasing about 35% before recharging.

"We got to get out of here!" I said.

"No," Michelle replied. "We stay here until I've seen it all."

"All of what?"

"Everything they got."

I was getting pissed at her hard-headed ass.

"I can't go on the offense," I said. "It's taking all I have to protect us. We got to jack!"

"You handle the sleds," she said. "I'll handle the goons."

"With what?"

Michelle answered by jumping out my shield and sprinting at the goons. She slammed into a group of them, arms and legs punching and kicking. By the time they realized what was going on she had a blaster rifle in her hand and was gunning them down. I added my firepower to hers and the guards scattered for cover. But the sleds kept coming.

I took another direct blast from one of the sleds before beginning evasive movements. Shields were down 45% and coming up slower than before. I could feel the nanos working overtime, my body hot from their activity. I dodged a bolt from the second sled then jumped, soaring the final thirty meters between us and landing on the closest sled. I gripped the hatch with my left hand, ripped it open then jammed my right arm in and lit it up. Wrong move. The sled exploded and sent me airborne. I crashed into a nearby building then slid down the wall onto the pavement.

Battle tech flickered then steadied. Shield down 66%. I looked up to see the other battle sled cruising my way. I looked for Michelle; she was pinned down behind a concrete wall, the security team creeping closer. I couldn't take another direct hit, at least not yet, but I couldn't leave Michelle pinched. So, I lay there, hoping my timing would be perfect

"One…two…three!"

The battle sled fired. I rolled; the blast missed, gouging the wall. I targeted the security guards then sprayed them, taking out five and sending the rest fleeing for cover. Michelle gave me thumbs up then popped over the barricade, taking down three more guards before they could hide. That woman was good; as a matter of fact, she was too good.

I jumped to my feet then ran, using the Mech to keep from getting shot. But then I zigged when I should have zagged and a bolt hit me square in the back. The world went black; when my vision returned, I was looking at the pavement and a fuzzy battle tech screen. Shields were down 75% and decreasing; vitals were slipping faster than my nanos could repair. It's one thing to know you were dying, but it's another thing to watch the stats. Someone grabbed me then flipped me on my back; it was Michelle.

"Hang in there, doll boy," she said. "Back up is coming."

A squadron of UCS EVs passed overhead then explosions shook the pavement.

"Back up?" I croaked. "Who the fleek is back…"

My screen flatlined, and so did I.

* * *

The room was sanitary white like a hospital, but it wasn't. I lay on a slab of steel that chilled my back and my ass. I was plugged in all over, some comfortable, some not, some that felt kinda good. Somebody saved my life. Whether it was good or bad, I'd find out soon.

The wall swished open and Michelle strolled in with a big smile on her face. I was shocked, not by who she was, but what she wore; a snug fitted dark green UCS uniform, with captain bars on her collar. Everything fell into place.

"How you feeling, doll boy?" she asked.

"Pretty good for someone about to do time," I replied. "Fleek! Is Michelle actually your name?"

"Yes," Michelle said. "I'm not good with fake first names. And you're not under arrest."

I blinked and my Battle tech appeared. I was 75% healed. Whatever else needed fixing my nanos could handle it. I began unhooking the cables.

"Be careful," Michelle warned. "You were pretty much done in."

"I don't know if I should be thanking you, based on where I've ended up."

"You should. We cut it close. Jaidan was hiding a lot more than we bargained for. Took us three days to secure the premises."

I looked a little closer. I was butt-ass naked. I couldn't wait to see the gifs. Michelle didn't seem fazed by it. Until a few minutes ago I was evidence.

"So, what happens now?" I asked. "You take all my tech and send me back into the world a meatbag?"

"You never really understood how valuable you are," Michelle replied.

"I told you I didn't care about that stuff. As long as I can kick ass and get laid, I'm good."

Michelle pulled up a chair. She turned it backwards then sat, resting her arms on the backrest.

"You're a prototype," she said. "The mega-corporations were evaluating A.I. tech in you and other hybrids. They couldn't do it as full A.I. because of UC codes, so they separated the tech. You were limbs; there were others for torso, cranial and internals. All the data went to Jaidan for evaluation and implementation."

"Mega-corporations? I thought they were banned."

"They are, officially," Michelle said. But people always find a way around the rules. Usually when we discover them, we tax their shoes off. The system must be maintained. Nobody's rich, but nobody's starving. Plus, we all know how it turns out when corporations run the show. We have a nearly dead planet to remind us."

"So, I was the key," I said.

"Sure were. The day you came running to my shop was the day the lid blew off. I'd been sitting in that shithole for years looking for evidence, then here you come all desperate and loaded with illegal tech. The corporations are trying to build an army, and A.I. army. They mean to take things back to the way it used to be just when we've got the planet healing. We're not going to let that happen."

All this war talk was over my head. I had more personal concerns.

"Since I delivered the goods, I figure I should be paid," I said.

Michelle handed me a vidchip. On the screen was my share of Dedren's cryptos…and hers. I was about to put it in my pocket until I remembered I didn't have on pants.

"What's next? You make me work for the UCS?"

Michelle shook her head.

"You've done more than enough. Once you're 100% you can get dressed and go."

"And I get to keep my tech?"

Michelle nodded. "Just don't take any corporate jobs for the next twenty years. But with the cryptos you have, you won't need to."

The door swished open again and an officer walked in with a rack of clothes. Michelle stood and took an eyeful.

"I'm going to give you some privacy," she said.

She and the other officer left the room. I reattached the cables and let myself heal to 100% as I considered my future. I was richer than anyone with my attitude had a right to be. Knowing me, I'd be broke in a year. If I disciplined myself, I could probably make it two.

Two hours later I was dressed and ambling through the UCS office. I reached the exit and grinned. We were in Aytee-El. If I was going to blow some cryptos, Aytee-El was the perfect place to start.

"Don't be a stranger," Michelle said. "And keep in touch."

I laughed as I turned to see her leaning against the wall, her arms folded.

"Something tells me you'll always know where I am."

Michelle laughed. "I got to protect my investment."

A thought crossed my mind and I decided to follow it.

"You should come with me," I said. "We make a good team."

"Nah," she replied. "I got a good man at home that hasn't seen me in a year. I can't wait to get reacquainted. Besides, it's war time, remember?"

"For you maybe," I said.

I opened the door to walk out.

"Be careful, Carlos," Michelle said. "Jaidan was just the tip of the iceberg."

'I'll try," I replied. "But you know me."

"Right," Michelle replied. "Always playing the odds."

I winked. "You know it."

I stepped out onto the pavement and summoned a Rideout. It was spring in Aytee-El; the dogwoods were in bloom and the smell of flowers were in the air. I looked back into UCS headquarters. Michelle still stood there with a smile on her face. I waved, she waved back, then I climbed into the Rideout, ready to start my life over again one more time.

HATCHED: A CYBIL LEWIS STORY
BY
NICOLE GIVENS KURTZ

#

[hăch' ed]- to devise or originate, especially in secret.

One

The whisper came before the roar of an aerocycle. I stopped, my hand on the handle of my laser gun, and my jacket unzipped for easy access. When someone posts a bounty on your head, you don't mind the icy November wind. A little chill now was better than permanent cold later.

I saw movement, and I drew my weapon from its holster.

A hooded figure stepped out from beneath the concrete surrounding the wauto parking lot.

"I'm in need of your, uh, services." The voice held hints of an accent I couldn't place.

A potential client? Out here in the gathering dark?

With my lasergun trained on her, the average-looking woman threw back her hood with hesitation. Dark, braided hair hung like cords over her shoulders, high cheekbones and full mouth shadowed beneath the hood. She stepped further from the bushes that ran parallel to the lot. With a satchel held tight against her torso, she continued to walk toward me—as if the gun didn't bother her at all. As she came closer, I could see her wild eyes. They seemed to be focused on everything and nothing.

I wondered if she was high on zenith, crack, or ackback.

Or just desperate.

The latter made her dangerous…even more than the other three choices. Addicts had predictable habits and needs. Desperate people didn't have any type of method—only a ravaging madness.

"Stop. I *will* shoot you." An icy calmness covered me, starting from my head and running down to my feet. A stillness, if you will, resolved in what I'd do if she kept coming toward me.

The gun got her attention. She halted and threw her arms out for balance; she'd come to a stop so fast. The woman sucked in a breath. "My name's Madonna Tyson! Please don't shoot me!" She raised her arms up in surrender.

"I don't know why you're following me, but I don't do business on the street." I let go of a breath and calmed my accelerated heart rate.

I put the laser gun back in its holster, turned on my booted heel, and started again for my own vehicle. November in the District didn't play around with fall's wishy-washy warm one day and cold the next, like October. Nope. Freezing. Every day.

"Please!" she shouted.

On second thought, she'd found a way to find me. I don't have a routine per se, and I altered my travel paths in part because of the bounty on my head. The other, because I had a nice cache of enemies. A young woman shouldn't be out in the dark, alone. This sector used to be a civilized locale, but now the place crawled with addicts and the afflicted. The District had a dangerous love affair with females. Even armed ones, like yours truly. I had the scars to prove it.

Sighing, I stopped, and turned around to face her.

"What do you want?" I made my voice flat, emotionless, and frost-bitten.

Madonna dropped her hands, came closer to me, and with a difficult swallow said, "I need a private inspector, Miss Lewis. I hear you're the best."

My name certainly didn't come up with a friendly referral attached to it from anyone. Even after seven years of private work, no one would refer anyone else to me. My tattered reputation didn't inspire the most ethical people to seek me out. Those folks went to the Regulators. People who needed a private inspector didn't talk about it. My client list remained on my p-drive, in a file. Sure, someone could steal it, but the files held encryptions, and you had to be me to understand them. No Watson recounting my tales.

So what did Madonna seek that fell close to the line between ethical and violations?

"You're lying." I crossed my arms, drawing the holster tight as I did so. "I don't know who you really are or why you're wasting my time with this shit, but I'm going…"

"Don't!" Madonna reached out to grab me, to stop me from turning away.

I froze and something in my face must've made her rethink her action, because she pulled her hand back.

"I don't think so, kid." It wouldn't surprise me if the innocent young woman had, in fact, designs on killing me. I couldn't trust her—or anyone.

Eyes round with emotion, she said, "I've got no one else to ask."

"I don't work for free. If you've got a violation problem, go see the Regulators."

"I just need some people found."

"Regulators do missing people too." I thought about zipping my jacket, then thought better of it.

She huffed out a heavy sigh. "It's freezing out here. I'll buy you dinner, a steak, if you'll just hear my story."

I'd never been one to turn down a free meal. Plus, I couldn't remember when I'd had a steak. Meat came with mutations, but a few farms had managed to thread out most of the defects. Meat had become a luxury. Some restaurants boasted money back guarantees, but you'd be dead before you could collect the currency on it.

Blame the cold, but it didn't hit me until that time. How did she find me? It wasn't like I had a forwarding service or homing device attached to my butt.

With a sigh, I took in the woman before me. She seemed capable. Smart. Brave. Why would she need a private inspector?

I blinked and I'd been bitten—by curiosity.

Several minutes later, I sat down at a square, small table inside The Cored Apple Restaurant. The waiter—a young man whose age was around the "hands off" range for me, flitted like a butterfly among flowers. Taut and tall, all awkward angles and testosterone, he hummed like a rattled wauto in idle mode. His body looked as if he used everything he ate efficiently because no lingering fat deposits were visible. Trust me. I used my P.I. trained observation skills on him.

Across from me, Madonna scrolled through the menu choices as if she'd been here often. She'd managed to prick my sympathy, but I had a short honey supply, and so Madonna had very limited honey in her favor. My vinegar level rose higher and higher with each passing minute, threatening to drown out all other attempts at niceness. If she didn't tell me what I wanted to know, there was going to be a large spill at table nineteen.

Once the waiter had taken Madonna's order, he left with a slight scowl on his face—as if steak orders didn't warrant a large tip.

I had ordered a steak, too, but my appetite had begun to wane.

"All right." I tried to conjure some civility. "You've ordered. Now tell me what this is about. All of it. The who, the what, and the drama. Why are you wasting my Saturday night?"

"Right."

In the full light, her youth became more evident. A college student maybe, but no older than 25. She fidgeted now, and when she swept her braids over her shoulder, I spied the tattoo. A double helix.

A hatchling. A genetically engineered human being. Sperm. Egg. Mixed in a petri dish and grown in a lab. They weren't birthed but grown in an artificial womb. Each hatchling came with a genetic marker—the double helix mark, a bright blue at the base of the neck.

She caught me staring. "Yeah. Hatchling."

I nodded.

Perfect in every way, hatchlings obtained celebrity status in some sectors, damnation in others. Most of them didn't have much of a sense of humor. The genetic engineers couldn't seem to fix that flaw, but then again, do you know any funny engineers?

"I'm listening, Madonna, but not for too much longer." I hadn't removed my jacket. Despite my words, I had to be totally honest with myself—I was curious, more about how she found me, and less about accepting her case.

And yes, I'm completely versed on the tale of curiosity and the cat.

"Of course," she said, all smiles and good cheer. "I'm in need of your services..."

"I figured."

"Right," Madonna said with a sheepish grin.

Maybe she needed guiding and prodding. Sometimes an interview worked better.

"Who gave you my name?" I asked, not waiting for Madonna to keep beating around the bush.

She sipped from her glass of water. "No one."

"Then how'd you find me?" I fought to keep the surprise from showing on my face. If no one referred me, she'd lied out there in the parking lot, which I'd pointed out. Cybil-one. Madonna-zippo.

"I live in your building," she confessed.

"What?"

She laughed, but it sounded shrill, nervous. "I live in your building. So I waited for you to come to the corner store. Been waiting for weeks."

"You live in my building?" I'd never seen her before, but I rarely saw anyone.

I didn't have a regular schedule, and most of my cases kept me busy through the late night and into the early morn. I slept when most normal people worked. When and under what conditions would Madonna have seen me?

So many questions mushroomed in my brain. I had to stop thinking and focus.

"What do you want?" It came out hard.

She flinched. "I'm sorry if that made you mad. Me following you around. I thought you saw me and were just, I don't know, ignoring me."

"I'm not mad."

"Your body language…"

"Listen. Either you tell me what the hell you want, right now, or I'm walking out of here. I've got other things to do than play games with someone who's ill-equipped."

Across from me, Madonna chewed her bottom lip and gripped the chair's arms so hard I bet she left her fingerprints embedded in the hard plastic. I don't like threatening people—no really, I don't. Something about her annoyed me, and it bugged me that she'd managed to follow me unnoticed.

Damn it.

"I need you to find my parents."

"Save your currency. Let the District's regs locate your missing parents." I had lost my appetite. I stood up, ready to go.

"No! Please! Sit down!" Madonna shouted, shooting out of her chair like a rocket. "Miss Lewis!"

Her frantic shouts drew stern looks from other diners and a couple of waiters.

"No. Sorry." I don't even know why I bothered letting her talk me into staying.

"You promised to listen!" Madonna reached toward me as if she meant to keep me from leaving.

As if she could physically stop me.

She swallowed loud enough for me to hear. "I'm not done explaining myself. Just hear my story and then if you still want to walk, then walk."

The waiter rushed over to us; his hands folded in front of him as if everything was all right. The grand opening wasn't supposed to include a furious black woman trying to walk out before her order had arrived. His eyes went to my gun and then he took a step backward.

Poor guy had no idea.

"Do you need assistance?" he asked, his young face twitching as if he wanted to scream at us instead of the faux calm tone.

I pondered that for a little while, thinking of a million ways I could answer the question—all would've gotten me collected or kicked out. But since I was going anyway, I said, “We’re fine.”

Satisfied or scared, the waiter fled the way in which he’d come. He tossed several looks back to make sure I wasn’t lying or worse, racing toward the exit.

"Please, sit down, and hear me out." She uttered one more, “Please.”

There must be something said for restraint.

I sat back down, though my hands were tight with the desire to punch her for wasting my time. Most of my cases involved mundane tasks, but locating people, well, any Regulator could do that.

The waiter waved to another server. He rushed over with two mugs of steamy java. There were other ways to get fast service that didn’t involve swearing or shouting. But none nearly as fun.

“You have three seconds. One.” I picked up the mug, put it down, and waited.

Madonna didn’t smile. The soft skin around her mouth deepened into creases of concern. She sipped her coffee and stared into the hot liquid as if reading tea leaves’ remains.

“I’m a hatchling, so I don’t want you to find my adoptive parents…”

“Two…”

“But my biological ones.”

Madonna sipped more of the hot coffee as if she needed it to replenish her courage.

She couldn’t be serious. I might punch her after all. Despite how annoying she behaved, I did find parts of her personality amusing in that she found me on her own. I didn't want to waste time. My arms itched and I wanted to go home. A new Bruce Lee movie marathon had been scheduled for this weekend.

Part of me groaned. Madonna *was* a potential client. So, I generated a little more patience and to sweeten the wait, some internal honey. This might turn out to be something worthwhile. Or a Trojan Horse.

Still, she did have currency for steak.

Finding the biological donors of a hatchling required breaking some regulations. I stared at my mug of coffee. I glanced up to find Madonna's black beetle eyes gazing at me as if suddenly I was a cute puppy.

I cleared my throat. "What exactly did you want me to do?"

"Find them."

So, she was serious.

"You're a hatchling. You weren't birthed."

"Duh. You're a great inspector? I want you to find my genetic DNA contributors, my donors," she said with a tight smile. "Clear?"

Two

"No, it isn't." I let her snide tone pass. Madonna was young and mouthy.

"I know it's a strange request." Her shoulders sagged as if carrying the weight of the request had become even heavier.

"It is." I agreed.

In my brief time as a P.I., no one requested I find their biological donors. Thousands of hatchlings lived and thrived among the territories. The District had a concentration of them in certain sectors, but for the most part, they lived as other human beings did. Sure, that angered groups like the Human Rights League, but humanity, no matter how one received it, deserved equal rights.

"Let me explain. I love my adoptive parents, Miss Lewis. They are, *were,* everything to me. Some of us are born, hatched, but we're barely living. We're allowing life to zip by us in a blur as we stand outside the circle of humanity. We disappear in a flash, the long arc of history skipping over us, and gone. Smoke. Not me. I'm going to leave my mark on this world. My parents taught me that."

"You're going to do it how? Violating the privacy of your bio-donors? I've never met your parents, but that doesn't seem to mesh with leaving your mark." I'd gathered the parents had died, but I also knew that grief had a terrible way of making bad ideas seem like good ones.

She frowned, not liking my words at all. When she leaned forward, she put her hands together and directed her fingers at me.

"You don't understand."

"Clearly."

She wasted no time at all clarifying her misunderstood point. Perhaps she was a fast learner after all. At first, Madonna's own stress must've increased. Over the next fifteen minutes, with her hands making a tight, round circle, she sought to nail down why she wanted me to locate her parents. She spoke about her sense of loss when her adoptive parents were murdered while traveling between territories, and all the normal oozy-gooey emotional grief that threatened to engulf her in the wake of the loss. According to her, she'd lost so much, she couldn't claim any sort of identity. Dripping over the edge and on to me, her forced feelings fell flat.

Tight circles appeared around her eyes, but as she talked, those lessened.

"…their deaths left this gaping hole of grief. It weeps continuously inside, and I find it *challenging* to move forward. If you could find my other parents, my donors, I can start repairing myself." As the words passed her lips, Madonna relaxed more. The weight of having to carry such an unusual request must've worn on her.

So I listened to her give me the entire spiel.

"As you can see, my identity, my sense of self, won't be complete without finding who they are. I have to know."

"Why?" The question had slipped out before I could stop it.

"Why? I feel like a puzzle that can't find its missing piece." She frowned as if she hadn't expected that question. "Most nights, I hardly sleep. I just sit and watch life outside my window, passing me by."

"See a therapist or get one of the District professionals to shrink you. You don't need a private inspector. Grief does damage to your emotions. You don't need to disrupt other people's lives just to soothe your own."

She shot up in her chair. "How *dare* you? In the social justice of human existence, there is no feeling of being alive without a sense of identity."

"Identity is more than biology." I hadn't given the plight of hatchlings much thought. Most of the hatchlings I knew embraced their adoptive parents—if they had them—as their *sole* parents. The ones who didn't, considered themselves to be children of a god or set of gods. While others believed themselves the offspring of nature. None of them spoke about human engineering the way Madonna did. In fact, I realized I'd been treating hatchlings as a monolith—one massive collective.

I sipped my coffee as I tried to check my privilege. My parents raised me from birth, a long labor my mother lamented about frequently. So how could I know what the desires of those hatched from artificial wombs suffered?

Across from me, with eyes shining with unshed tears, Madonna's lip trembled.

"You're quoting Erik Erickson."

"You know his work?"

"Yeah, I know of him, and others who've studied identity and identity crisis. His work in psychology was required Army reading for those of us on the fast track to leadership. Listen, I'm not even sure what you're asking for is possible."

"You're the one everyone says can do the impossible."

"I'm no superhero from one of those online games…"

"I'll pay." Madonna dug around in her purse and took out a small portable drive. She glanced at it and then handed it to me. "This isn't currency."

"I figured." Miss Obvious had a way of making me smile. "So do you want a generic list of names or just paid stalking of individual donors?" I didn't take the drive.

"You make it sound so dirty."

"It isn't always clean."

"I just want information." Madonna sipped her coffee and glanced around for the waiter.

"Sure. Question still applies. Information comes a variety of ways."

"I dunno." She shook her head again and fingered the p-drive.

"Stalking or background scavenging?" Sometimes choices worked better.

Madonna's face crumbled, her lips drawn down into a scowl. "I don't approve of stalking, but I do want you to find them."

"I can't guarantee I *can* find them. Lab reports have very strict confidential regulations. As I'm sure you already know, which is why you're attempting to hire me."

She nodded. "I have the right to an identity despite the legal and ethical noise. I'm a person."

"The donors have a right to privacy too." I retorted.

"You're not known for respecting privacy, Miss Lewis." Madonna crossed her arms, looking fiercer and less afraid.

A transformation so fast, I wondered if one of the personalities hadn't been genuine. I let the comment pass. Instead, I sipped my coffee, now room temperature. I'd misjudged her. An error I wouldn't commit again.

"I *do* live in your building," she added.

The waiter arrived with our steaks, and once he'd distributed the food, I resumed our conversation.

"For how long? How often do you want reports and jpegs?" I picked up the steak knife and cut into the charred meat. I forked it up toward my mouth and paused.

Across from me, Madoona looked uncomfortable, fingers drumming nonstop next to the steak knife. I hadn't seen one of those in forever. "How about weekly to start? A month? Yes, a month would be good." She claimed the knife and cut into her steak, hacking it into pieces.

Madonna's hesitation hinted at her holding back information. My default reasoning fell to sinister reasons for it, but it probably wasn't unusual. I suspected most people of malice, especially potential clients. They hired a P.I., but they rarely wanted to. It was a necessary evil like pap smears and teeth cleaning. Clients didn't want me snooping too close to their own yard. They only wanted me to dig up their neighbors' buried skeletons.

So, Madonna's nervousness could've been just that—she had stuff she wanted to keep close to her vest.

"Look, I've done this kind of work before, many, many times. I'll know in about two weeks if I can get the information you seek. No point in charging you for time you don't really need."

She peered at me, her fingers momentarily still. After a few minutes of musing, she said, "No, no, a month is fine."

"It's your currency." I shrugged.

She nodded and her eyes drifted off to areas behind me.

"I'll do the job. Come by my office tomorrow and sign the contract. I'll go over terms, when you will get reports, etcetera."

"You may find these files useful." She offered the p-drive again.

"You knew I'd take the case?" I scoffed, feeling the stress ball at the base of my neck expand. My gut flared that I should just walk on, but parts of me wanted to see if I *could* do it. The other part knew I needed currency. Still, one must never seem too eager.

She frowned. "What I know about you, Miss Lewis, is that nothing is ever a sure thing. This little thing was a just-in-case you did decide to accept."

I bit the inside of my cheek and kept my comments internal. I took the p-drive from her, feeling dirty and more than a little apprehensive. Take pictures. Find the donors. Easy currency. It didn't even involve me drawing my laser gun.

"I will begin after you sign the contract." I pocketed the p-drive.

"Thank you." Madonna offered her hand, breaking the tense wall between us.

We shook.

"Whew." She blushed a bit and pushed her coffee mug away.

I pushed back from the table; my chair scraped across the tiled floor. She didn't get up.

"You're leaving?" Madonna asked with a soft hint of relief.

"Yes." I didn't look back as I strolled out of the seating area.

Outside, the rush of cold draped over me, enveloping me in its hard palm. In a few short blocks, I sat back inside the closed-in warmth of my wauto. I no longer had an appetite, and I'd already taken a risk by accepting Madonna's case. Eating the steak would've been a risk too many. I thought about Madonna and her strange request. Why would a hatchling want a breakdown of her DNA contributors and then want to meet them? Her sperm and egg donors? They only provided the genetic building blocks. It's like asking to meet your wauto manufacturer.

Her answer remained rooted in identity. Madonna had said she needed to meet them, to know them, so she could solidify herself, who she was. If she wanted an identity, she could build and establish one online like millions of others. Build an image and identity like most people her age with avatars, electronic brands, and pirated and enhanced images and jpegs.

My thoughts turned again to Madonna's personality. She didn't come off like an impulsive youth. She knew what she wanted, and she did her research. Creating something false wouldn't do for someone like her.

My heart pitched in pity for her. She had the power to push through her grief, to reach for something she wanted to obtain, and the means to find someone to help her get there. Me.

Now that the conversation with Madonna had concluded, I realized how foolish I'd been to rush into the case without hearing all the freaking details.

Details.

Good inspecting work always resided in the details.

A lesson I was going to have to learn—again.

Three

Outside, thunder fell like a crash of plates onto an unyielding floor. Beads of rain clung to my window. I wished I could turn it off, but my selfishness would have to wait. The door announced a visitor. I dragged my complaining body out of bed all the while thinking it was too early to interact with people.

"What?" I groaned against my door's speaker.

Daniel Tom, hatchling and a District regulator, stood on the other side with his face set to pissed off. When he showed up, my life became complicated and dangerous. Always.

"It's me. Open up." He folded his arms, the regulator uniform pulling taut against his biceps, his torso, and his neck. The collar went up to his ears, to fight off the cold. Judging by his tone, his muscles weren't the only things stretched too tight.

My doorway had an annoying habit of attracting wayward regulators, T.A. agents, regulators, and ex-violators. Sometimes it became real hard telling one from the other.

I punched the door's release, and it slid back in a hush. "A girl needs a full eight hours to be productive. *This* girl does, anyway, and here you are messing the routine up."

"To you with failing hands, I pass the torch," Daniel laughed.

"I'm serious."

"It's noon," Daniel replied with the first hint of a smile curving the corners of his sensual mouth.

"It's Sunday."

"That's a great outfit."

I ignored his comment about my sleeping attire as I crossed the threshold into my bedroom. My flannel pink hearts bottoms and tank top kept me comfortable and my electricity bill low. Winter in the District bordered on sadistic with the cold icing lungs, luring folks to permanent sleep.

For some reason, I couldn't sit in the living room with Daniel while I was dressed in something similar to underwear. He might get ideas. Hell, I might get ideas and then the whole situation could slide into the bedroom and that wasn't where I wanted Daniel right now.

I snatched on my red silk robe and cursed him for disturbing my slumber. I returned to the living room, now fully covered. Sundays were made for rest—just read the Bible. When I emerged from my bedroom, the sash of my robe tied tight, my fuzzy pink slippers on, I found him seated on the couch. His elbow rested on the armrest and his head bowed over his tablet. An unlit cigarette dangled from his lips.

"What do you want?" I folded my arms. Despite the robe, I couldn't shake the feeling of being exposed.

"It's nice to see you again, too. Can't I come by, just to see if you're still alive?"

"You're in uniform, which means you're working. What now?" I didn't want to waste any more of my time. In fact, I wanted to crawl back to bed. Once the Madonna case got started, I doubted I'd get any peace. Sometimes a good night's sleep presented new, better options.

With a heavy sigh, Daniel turned his face to me, his dark green eyes narrowed. "I was in your sector, so I decided to drop by to see if you're still breathing."

"For once, can you tell the truth?" I laughed.

"Can you?" He stood and laid the PDA on the sofa. He crossed the short distance to me, and hovered, like a space shuttle waiting for the bay doors to open.

I searched his face. His weary visage had shifted to where real emotions peeked through, and for the briefest of moments, I saw a hint of something in him, an emotion I dared not breathe aloud. I blinked and it was gone.

Daniel chortled. “Alright, I’ll go first. I just got off and I want a beer.”

“Of course, you do.” I moved to the rocking chair. It once belonged to my grandmother, and at times of unrest, I found solace sitting in it. I’d watched her creak and rock in this chair for a large section of my life.

Daniel returned to the living room, a bottle of Peck in his hand. His little joke of a mustache twitched. He unzipped the top of his uniform down to the beginning of his chest, revealing his double helix tattoo. Unlike some hatchlings, he hid his hatchling origins.

“Have you ever wanted to know who your biological donors were?”

He paused. The bottle up to his lips made a slow descent to the coffee table. He peered over to me, a frown on his face as he pondered it. “No. Why?”

“You don’t feel any lack of identity?”

“How do you mean?” Daniel shrugged. “I know who I am. My parents are good people that loved me. I’ve got a wife who loves me.”

“We’re more than the people who love us, surely.” I folded my arms as I watched him.

Daniel drank some beer before speaking. “We are. I had the army. You. All of my life experiences make me who I am.”

I gestured for him to go on.

“When I was young, I worried about why people gave away their eggs or sperm to the government. Didn’t they value us?”

I sat back down into the rocking chair. “Ever been too poor and pregnant? The baby takes your iron and your calcium, and your teeth fall out. Sometimes it’s easier to just give it away.”

“No, but I’m a man, so…” Daniel interjected.

“Exactly. It’s hell to go through. So why not give your eggs to the US government, make a difference, and make some currency?”

“So, commerce is why I’m a hatchling?” Daniel’s tone hinted at amusement, but a razor’s edge hid among the soft words.

“You’re a hatchling because that’s your fate.”

“Fate? No, I make my own destiny.” Daniel countered.

“Something started you on the path. That something is Fate.”

Daniel shook his head and waved my comments out of the air. “Getting back to identity. It goes beyond basic genetics too. The people who donated their genetic material could’ve lived decades ago, so why try to find them?”

I stopped rocking. “What?”

Daniel took a few gulps and then explained. “The Association of Genetically-Engineered Humans began as a United States program to create human soldiers to fight wars so that normal people didn’t have to do it.”

“Clones.”

He barked out a laugh. “No. Cloning remains as unstable now as it did before the Great War. They used real human beings’ fertilized eggs. Froze them in storage. Crafted those artificial wombs, and around the age of 12, created soldiers. My genetic material may be left over from someone of that time.”

“So, your donors could be dead.”

Daniel nodded. “There’s no point seeking out my donors, only to be disappointed. It’s pure guesswork. They could be anywhere, any *when.*”

“Well, not any when. Don’t they degrade?”

“Yeah, sure.”

I knew bits of this from history class. After the United States became a series of territories, private sectors took the technology and began offering it to childless couples. Some territories took the fertilized eggs and destroyed them. Others sold them like shoes, and still others, with more benevolent governments, found them loving homes, and absorbed them into the community.

“Would you be someone new, after meeting them? Granted, if you could.”

Daniel thought for a few minutes. “I like being me.”

"You hide the tattoo." I pointed out.

His hands automatically went to cover it. When he caught himself, he shook his head. "I want people to judge me based on my character, my actions, not on their preconceived notions about bio-engineered people.

The minute people see it, they stop seeing me as a person, as a human, but rather as a thing, a miracle of science."

"You are."

Daniel threw back his head and laughed.

I understood how preconceived notions clouded others' judgments. I'm a black woman with a gun and a questionable career. Yeah.

With one arm behind his head, Daniel leaned back against the sofa and closed his eyes. "Why the sudden interest in hatchling history? You're not still having nightmares about the Human Rights League?"

"No." I hugged myself, not wanting to entertain that horror again.

My memory launched snippets anyway.

Some men bring women flowers.

Daniel had brought me a body.

Six years ago, a horrible event happened with another young woman, not a hatchling, but pretending to be one. She'd ended up dead, thrown away like so much trash in the sector. The same crew that murdered her, had assaulted me and dumped me for dead in a compost heap. Daniel found me three days later. In fact, the victim's entire family had been exterminated. I'd been powerless to stop it.

Could that be why I stopped and listened to Madonna last night? Because I'd been too late for another young, purposeful woman. I didn't want to be late again.

Sometimes my subconscious took over my mental wheel and steered my actions without my conscious consent. My heart sped up its *thump-one, thump-two* pattern as the cold shiver of adrenaline seeped in. None of this sounded like info I wanted on a Sunday afternoon.

"What if you knew they weren't dead, but alive?" I asked.

Daniel's almond-shaped eyes opened. "I wouldn't want to meet them. They're not my parents. They don't know anything about me."

"No, but aren't you curious about who you are?"

"I know who I am. I've got a fairly strong sense of self. Knowing the bio donors wouldn't tell me anything beyond if I'm at risk for getting cancer."

I fell silent, unsure of how or why Madonna needed this information so bad, but Daniel didn't. Probably had a lot to do with circumstances.

"Tell me what this is about, Lewis. This isn't like you, being so interested in hatchlings, feelings, identity…"

"I've got a case. A hatchling wants me to find her donors."

Daniel whistled.

"Don't give me that look." I waved him off and relaxed back into the rocking chair.

"What look?" Daniel drained the rest of his beer.

"That one."

"There are regulations about privacy, ethics, and lots of gray areas with hatchlings and donors. Regulations that address how hatchlings are provided for, but not the concerns of identity and the hatched's rights to know their donor." As a District Regulator, Daniel knew the regulations that governed the sectors. I didn't expect him to say anything different.

"I operate in the gray." I crossed my arms.

He pushed himself to a sitting position, resting his elbows on his knees. "Oh, I know. Fill your boots, but if you get caught, it's the cradle."

"You know, I'm allergic to floatation gel. Besides, I'm only asking questions, capturing a few jpegs, and passing on information."

"Those aren't violations in and of themselves, but I know a lot of the AGEH places won't give you any information about donors. So, if you do get it, that would be the violations."

"You speak from experience?" I asked.

Daniel toed off his shoes and stretched out on my sofa. He tucked one of the throw pillows beneath his dark brown hair and closed his eyes.

"No. Why does she want to find her donors?" Daniel sighed. "It's just biological code. It's not who you are."

"She feels like it will connect her to them and fill in those missing pieces of herself."

"It's strange what desire will make foolish people do." Daniel mumbled as sleep tried to claim him. "If you do violate regulations, Cyb. I will come for you myself."

His words failed to disguise his ugly implications.

"You know, Daniel. You're in my home, on my sofa, and you're threatening me. You can get out now. Bye."

He didn't budge. The rumble of thunder and the flash of lightening seemed to answer for him. Don't disturb or suffer his wrath. His wife knew he worked late and had a crazy schedule because he was a regulator. She wouldn't miss him until dawn.

I stood up and headed into my tiny kitchen. "It *is* my so-fa."

I wasn't sure he even heard it.

Four

Monday morning found me up before noon, and out the door prior to one o'clock. All the vehicles vied for air space in the tight elevated lanes. Flying alongside other wautos, sleek aerocycles, boxy drones, and wide cargo crafts made me feel like a rat in a maze, given just enough room to run, but not to escape.

I piloted my ancient wauto through traffic and within an hour, I set her down in the parking lot beside my office building on the eastern side of The District.

After the storm had abated yesterday, Daniel left, leaving me to quiet pondering the rest of the afternoon. Today, I had purpose and itched to get started.

My client had a bit of shadow to her and that intrigued me. So much of inspecting resided in the client themselves. Madonna sought parental love to replace the one she'd lost. Love could mend her life, but it could crush her too. In this line of work, one truth remained constant. Be careful what you wished for.

Madonna Tyson arrived at my office just before three. Jacketless, she wore a black sweater and jeans with dark boots and an expression of outrage.

"Come on in." I gave her my client-friendly smile and led her through the lobby and on to my private office. To be honest, it surprised me she wanted to continue to go through with it. I was in the middle of lunch of peanut butter and jalapeno jelly.

"Madonna, I have a few questions I'd like to ask."

Her dark eyes roamed over my private office and its décor. The electronic images flickering from their positions on the wall, and the paper ones yellow and crumbling in their frames. Two metal folding chairs in front of my antique wooden desk. At some point, I needed to update it to cover the laser gun burn holes in the walls.

She paused just in front of my sole visitor's chair. "More?"

I nodded. "Have a seat."

"I can't stay…"

"Can't you? You're devoting a nice cut of currency to this."

She frowned. "The p-drive has all you need to know."

"I decide what I need to know."

Something in my face must've affirmed my seriousness, because she sat down.

"Alright. Go."

"Why are you seeking the bio donors?" I sat down too and sipped my second cup of coffee.

"I told you…"

"You told me bullshit about your identity crisis. I want the truth." She pretended not to understand. "In violent times, people shouldn't have to sell their souls, but they did. Now, you want to undo it all. Why?"

"I'm their daughter!" Madonna slapped her thighs for emphasis. "They should want to know me! None of them have sought me out, so I'm going to them."

"They gave you life, and you want to give them hell? Rip them from the comfort of anonymity?" I swiped my hand across the glass desk, raising the currency application.

"That's not what I want. For now, I just want to know who they are. I'm anxious." Madonna tucked a few braids behind her ear and looked out the window behind me.

I sat with my jalapeno jelly and peanut butter sandwich. I took a bite.

"You going to start now?" Madonna stood up with her arms akimbo.

"Not right now, no. I skipped breakfast."

"Why not?" She frowned.

"I'm eating." I sipped the coffee with one hand and logged into my bank account.

Madonna tutted. "It's urgent."

"Is it?"

"Of course!"

"Why?" I bit into the sandwich and swore under my breath. Hot sweetness!

"I…" Madonna sighed as if all the power had been depleted from her internal drive.

I watched as she reeled in her emotions, slowed her breathing, collected her facial expressions, and stood rigid, transforming back into the calm woman of Saturday.

Interesting.

The fact remained that she'd lived 20 some odd years without knowing her bio donors' identities. What would four more hours make? The urgency? The rush?

I entered the retainer amount and basic information from the client. With my other hand, I ate my sandwich.

"When they treat you like a stranger instead of a beloved prodigal daughter, what will you do then?" I chased the bit of heated sweetness with coffee.

She shrugged. “Dunno. Return home and move on with my life.”

“Which you can’t do now?” I glanced up at her. No, Madonna didn’t like my question.

She paused with her hand over the glass. “I’m not asking for judgment, but your work ethic, *Miss* Lewis. Can you do it?”

“Yeah.” I touched the blue SEND button and across from me, a flashing red light appeared in front of Madonna. “I don’t give guarantees.”

Madonna glared.

I waited. Hard stares and resting bitch face didn’t bother me. Some took the soft option and complied. Others selected the hard option—eating my gun’s laser blast.

After several moments she snapped, with lips a slash of annoyance. “Fine! You’re a stubborn ass. Aren’t you?”

With her index finger she punched in the currency amounts, and other information to pay for the retainer. At the end she held her wrist over the reader and it scanned the chip embedded there.

“That’s why I’m good at what I do.”

She snorted.

“You *did* hire me.” I verified the chip information with the person standing in front of me. Madonna Renee Tyson. The jpeg corresponded with the woman. Identity confirmed.

“Touché.” She inclined her head.

“You may not like my methods, but you can’t argue my results.” I accepted the funds into my bank account and stood up.

She smirked. “That’s what I’m paying for—and counting on, Miss Lewis.”

With that she turned on her booted heel and exited.

* * *

After Madonna left, I cleared my desk and headed out of the building. Last evening, I found a slender lead buried in the letters and information on Madonna’s p-drive. A series of possible bio donors had been listed, but they all had been serviced from one centralized location, a satellite Association of Genetically Engineered Humans.

The Anderson Clinic over on F or E Street.

I landed sometime after three.

On the ground, the streets still went by their pre-war names. In the air, folks went by coordinates. Still, accidents happened and so I obeyed the robotic controllers as they orchestrated the traffic and pedestrian dance. When I got the white walking avatar, I crossed the street, headed up the stairs, and into the clinic. The flickering neon sign of the former pizza place next door seemed on the edge of fading but blinked as if sending a frantic coded message before falling dark for good.

The clinic's lobby reeked of unwashed bodies, bleach, and despair. Cracked plastic chairs, worn walls, and stained carpets filled the area. Postures and faces sagged as the afflicted waited in nervous silence. A buzzing sleeked from behind the receptionist's alcove, hidden in the dimness.

An atmosphere of awfulness groaned under the weight of allegations of medical experimentation with unsuspecting poor teenage girls. The Association of Genetically Engineered Humans had a satellite office here, but 20 years ago, it had been a full-blown human hatchery.

I waited in line to reach the receptionist. We shuffled like dominoes being plucked from an assembly line. Howling babies, coughing adults, and hormonal teenagers all moved in an uneasy cadence rimmed with desperation and depression.

"What do you want?" The very pale, thin receptionist barked from the open window. Heavy make-up and surgical scars marred her face. The thick fall of bright pink bangs covered some of them but called more attention than the receptionist probably wanted.

"I'm here to talk to Dr. Leonard Cho."

The receptionist laughed. "You got an appointment?"

"Yeah." I patted the butt of the weapon. Despite the weather, I hadn't worn a coat and the gun remained on full display along with its holster. The smirk drained off her face, and she leaned back from the window, forcing it closed. With the press of a button, the clear glass frosted over. I watched her silhouette as it got up from the stool and disappeared into the back. The people behind me became restless.

And vocal.

"Damn, man!"

"The fuck? I already been waiting for two hours!"

"My kid's sick. Open the window!"

Either the regulators would arrive in a few minutes, or security or Dr. Cho. I put my odds on the doctor. The AGEH didn't want the regulators sniffing around, and I knew for certain that no security guard would be able to successfully handle me.

No. Really. Have you seen security guards?

"Next!" bellowed another receptionist who opened the window to her station. The people shifted in near unison to her rectangular box.

Not for me. The examination room doors yawned open and a slender man—all intellect and professionalism—dressed in a white lab coat, khaki slacks, and navy turtleneck sweater headed toward me. He pushed his black, rimless glasses up the bridge of his nose as he walked. He held a tablet in one hand, and his other hand was extended in an offer of a handshake. Black hair had been cut in a business-style popular in The District among the currency chic crowd.

He had a firm handshake, but he couldn't keep his eyes off the weapon and my shoulder holster. Each movement and gesture he made had been orchestrated to get me satisfied and out quick. He stood taller than me, but he didn't weigh as much.

That didn't make me feel better.

"Hello regulator. I'm Dr. Cho. Follow me, please." He smiled, all teeth and pretense.

The doors hissed closed behind me. Dr. Cho walked down the corridor, but made repeated turns to look back at me, to ensure that I noted his cooperation. On this side of the doors, the odor of cleaning agents scrubbed the horrible dirty smell from the air. Regardless, the lingering hint of loss remained. Bright, shiny, and hygienic masked the underlining smell of fear that seemed to permeate from the examination rooms.

"What's this about, regulator, um…" Dr. Cho asked over his shoulder.

"Tom. I think we should wait until we're inside your office." I wondered if Daniel would mind me using his name.

We made a right and approached a glass-enclosed workspace. Dr. Cho peered into the retinal scan, and the doors stretched open. The biohazard signs dotted the front doors. Large, rectangular tables, a few metallic, others smartglass completed the room. The first sectioned table space held microscopes, tubs, petri dishes, and gloves. Behind the tables on some shelves appeared to be robotic parts. Around the hushed workspace, robots labored on what appeared to be n-bots, nursing robots. Humans worked alongside them in clothed biosuits. Some went into patients' rooms. Even this late in the afternoon, the clinic buzzed with activity.

This area didn't have individual offices, but rather glass cubicles. They left nothing to the imagination. Each scientist and doctor could witness what the other did. Big Brothers watched.

They also used n-bots, robotic nurses. That made me uncomfortable. I hate robots.

"Here we are." Dr. Cho entered one of the glass cubicles and gestured to the chair in front of his workstation. "Please excuse the mess. They say genius is messy. I know where everything is located."

The cubicle had no personal items, no JPEGs of family or friends.

"Knowledge dispels fear, and the public's afraid of your work here," I said.

Across from me, Dr. Cho struggled to keep his face blank.

I sat down in the seat, and leaned toward him, giving him the impression of interest. He smiled, media ready. I wondered if he was a hatchling. Everything about him seemed so perfect. The turtleneck kept me from spying a tattoo.

"The Anderson Clinic offers inexpensive medical care for the currency cheap crowd. We do some research, grant-based, and a few hatchings." Dr. Cho turned off his computer monitor before turning fully back to face me. "What can we do for the District's bravest?"

"We're in the middle of an investigation, and we need information." I gave him my high wattage smile. I could do fake sincerity, too.

The desk acted as a barrier between us, a physical void I needed to cross.

"Surely, you know the regulations surrounding patient and doctor confidentiality." Dr. Cho's toothy grin withered as fast as it had bloomed.

"We do." I nodded, letting my own grin fade.

"We'd love to help, but our patients don't want their records all over the Internet." Dr. Cho asked, with a casual push of his glasses up the bridge of his nose.

"We just need specific information that doesn't require a reveal of diagnoses."

He scoffed. "No, I'm sorry, Regulator Tom. I can't give you any information without a court authorization. We have a reputation to uphold, investors, and patients. So, I don't think I can help you." His fingers splayed on the glass as he leaned closer.

I stood and wrapped my hand around the weapon. My honey levels faltered to the dangerous area of vinegar. "You're a shrewd man, but I need information."

Dr. Cho checked his watch and narrowed his eyes. "You're willing to violate regulations to get it?"

I didn't respond.

My actions always spoke louder.

"This clinic helps the poor." I switched gears.

Dr. Cho nodded. "No currency doesn't mean no assistance. We work with all levels of currency."

"That's so charitable." I forced honey into my words, making them sweet.

He paused before speaking. "The AGEH is renowned for our contributions to the medical establishment and our community."

"In the spirit of charity, the information I'm seeking is for one client, one of those currency-crippled individuals. I have her permission to inquire about her medical care and services. We need your help to close the case. Your research isn't our interest or in our preview."

He either had a glass heart or a stone one, because he inclined his head as if pondering my words. Lurking behind those glasses, sharp eyes watched me. He knew I didn't have the court authorization.

I would get what I wanted, one way or the other.

The pompous, little tick tapped his chest above his heart where a blue, round pin became green.

"Security. Regulator Tom is leaving. Please make sure she exits safely from the clinic." Dr. Cho crossed his arms as he remained standing behind his desk.

"Oh? You're not going to help. I don't get it. The AGEH used to be so civilized. You know—widespread violations of children and young women's rights with all the experimental testing, without consent. Those upstanding qualities that set you guys apart from the others."

"Are you threatening me?" He asked as if he genuinely wanted to know.

"Of course not. I'm providing facts."

"You have a smart mouth."

"And you're foolish. We can keep exchanging insults until the world ends, but it's not productive. Just tell me what I want to know." I didn't take out the weapon. Shooting Cho wouldn't have been helpful, but that didn't stop me from wanting to blast the smugness off his face, then step on the pieces.

"You regs listen to too many gossiping mosquitos. Good day." Dr. Cho nodded to the approaching robotic guards.

Behind me, the two buckets of bolts hovered.

"This way please."

Its non-human voice raised goosebumps across my arms. The creature came too close. Its ebony-painted body held bright yellow caution stars around its wide base. Two arms gestured the directions. The difference between man and the machines had become blurry—neither had any original or independent thoughts.

"I can see myself out." I declared, a little too loud.

I turned from the security guard bots with the weapon now in my fist. Ready to fire. They blocked my path. As if they'd be able to contain me.

Sick excitement filled me. My body flooded with adrenaline. With my perspective shrinking to one sole focal point, I had to get out of there before someone needed a medic.

"This way please." It flickered its warning lights in concert with the other. Had it been human, it could've read my body language and noted my own warning.

"Cho."

"Yes?" He glared and then with a heavy sigh pressed the button on his chest again. "Security. Cancel the order. Authorization Beta-one-seven-four."

It felt like a thousand years had passed in that cubicle, but it was only fifteen minutes. I didn't like putting my back to him or the robots, but I had little choice.

"Be sure you do see yourself out." Cho added as I walked away.

Five

I hate the smell of hospitals in winter, including clinics. As I stood on the steps outside the Anderson Clinic, the doors yawned open as people exited with grim faces and pained expressions. The AGEH's filthy practices didn't always land on this side of ethical. My gut confirmed it.

Where did that leave me now? At the beginning of wisdom. A lot of this type of work required luck. I'm not lucky. Sometimes you must get down on the ground and slither with snakes. In absence of Lady Luck, I had only one option. Once I walked the four blocks to my wauto, I climbed in, pointed it in the direction of my office, and lifted off. The heady cloud coverage loomed with the threat of more snow, but the elevated lanes contained little traffic.

On autopilot, I fell into reflection. Why did anyone want to find their bio donors? The donation of DNA didn't make them parent material. Sure, Madonna would be able to say they share eye color or height or hair color, but odds were she probably shared those qualities with thousands of others.

Identity? Really?

The wauto dipped as I approached my office's coordinates. In no time I had parked, entered, and got off the elevator on the sixth floor. I steadied my emotions for the next step in my investigation. Marching past my own double doors, I stopped outside the neighboring suite.

In previous years, I managed to avoid my neighbor, but today, it had become unavoidable.

Across the single metallic-colored door, illuminated in green, was *Yukio Reedburn, Information Broker*. I sighed and pressed the announcement button. The door slipped back revealing a solitary bank of computer monitors and keyboards spread out across a slew of tables. The keyboards weren't physical, but instead were projected onto the glass tabletop. On one wall, metallic shelving units held servers, hardware, and routers, gadgets and other parts. All blinked and whirled, zinged and hooted as they labored. On the other side of the room, floor to ceiling black boxes looked like books across a library shelf. I'd seen images of those.

This suite didn't have as much space as my office next door. It lacked a lobby and looked more like my private office. Tight. Darkness was punctured by pockets of LED light from the numerous computer monitors. I walked in all the way, allowing the door to close. The automatic overhead lights flickered on, showering the entire room in illumination.

The hoarding and clutter became even more obvious. From behind one of the monitors, with her goggles resting on her head, Yukio's big brown eyes squinted against the light's harshness. As soon as they connected to mine, they narrowed. She stood with displeasure spilling over her face. Big hoop earrings trapped strands of her long dark hair, which had been parted down the middle and plaited into two fat braids on either side of her head. The ends had been curled and brushed along her shoulders along with the multi-colored cords around her neck.

She hadn't shot at me, so there's progress.

"What brings you out of your cave?" Yukio didn't try to hide her surliness. She crossed her arms over her long-sleeve tee shirt, HDMI cords and connections hanging from her neck like jewelry.

"I need an information broker." I answered, keeping my tone light.

"There's thousands in the District. Go find one of them."

"I want the best."

"Great inspector like yourself, coming to me using that silver tongue of yours. Marco was seduced by it." Yukio smirked, fondling the cords as she spoke.

"Look Yukio. I'm not perfect..."

"…You don't say."

"…There's a crap ton of things I don't know." I finished and came further into the room. She kept the hardware between us.

"So?" Yukio's bright eyes rolled in disgust as she lowered herself back down into the chair.

She wasn't going to make this easy.

"I don't know what to say." I had hoped the decade had softened her sharp anger, but nothing doing. Well, we all have false hope.

"You could start with an apology." Yukio snatched the goggles down over her eyes and commenced typing.

I needed to think and to walk to calm down, because my instinct urged me to tell her where to go. Being back in Yukio's presence had conjured all the things I had avoided by not bypassing my office every day. The memories came roaring back. My gut warned of wasting time. The faster I convinced Yukio, the sooner I could leave. I tried my hand with the AGEH to avoid this moment. Yukio's grief clawed at me, raking over my emotional Kevlar.

"Yukio…"

"You must be desperate to come to me."

Her tone sliced through me, but I held it firm, accepting her anger, her pain. Enormous amount of emotion hid behind those words. I needed the name of Madonna's bio donors.

"You're good at hacking…" I started with a compliment.

"Shut up! Screw your fake accolades!" Yukio shot out of her chair. Items spilled over and crashed to the floor. Her bitterness made her less careful than usual.

I waited while she collected the items and moved about the cluttered office. "I lost him, too." The words escaped before I could keep them chained inside, but this stalemate wouldn't do.

"You're not dead." Yukio stopped typing and glared at me. "Marco is. Remember?"

"Every day." How could I forget? My throat tried to close over the emotional ache the memory conjured. In life, some moments go by so fast, but despite the years, it felt fresh to my heart. Marco's death haunted me, like most of my failed attempts at love. They lingered.

In this line of work, the streets turned me inside out, leaving little time for relationships. The army had been no different. I'd been torn apart over Marco's death, but it had been almost ten years. All that's left was his ghost. Some days he rested, but other days he'd be resurrected.

"Yukio, I'm sorry you think I'm the reason he's dead."

She sighed and slammed her fist on the table. "Why the hell are you here?"

"I was a kid. We were trying to survive in a difficult and confusing world. It took him from me, from *us*."

"But only one of you survived, right Cybil? Marco was the world to me. The weight of it. The god of it. You took that from me!" She didn't scream, but instead spoke now with a cold calm.

She wouldn't budge in her beliefs. So, I stopped trying to convince her of my innocence.

"Marco meant a great deal to me, too. But, today, right now, I'm trying to help someone Yukio, and I need your expertise."

She crossed her arms and shook her head.

"You'd turn down a potential client? The currency?" I held my breath. If anyone could match my own stubbornness, it was Yukio. My body shook, but I doubt she noticed.

While the still-grieving sister sized me up, time crawled. Marco had been a bright spot in a dark time in my life. The District's Army hadn't been what I had anticipated, and Marco and I had worked hard to bring each other joy. The memory of nights spent holed up in his crummy little box of an apartment eating take-out and watching old movies made me smile. I did *miss* him. Optimistic. Funny. Sexy. Marco had been the hallmark of a post high school relationship.

Right up to his death.

No, I owed him and myself to remember the icy truth. Someone killed him. Attacked on our way back to his place, a gunman, possibly an Ackback addict, tackled me to the ground. I failed to defend myself, and Marco intervened—the gallant hero. He received a belly full of laser for his efforts.

And Yukio got a heart full of grief.

A heinous, random act that Yukio believed I caused.

Would she allow her powerful emotions to override her judgment? If she did, it would be a bad move for me. Even still, I couldn't be upset with her. I hadn't forgiven myself, either.

I'd learned to accept the incident as a bad moment, but Yukio had retreated into the anonymous and faceless internet. She folded herself into its cold embrace and sought her brother's killer with that laser focus she employed for clients. The loss of Marco remained lodged in her heart, an icy dagger of grief she refused to remove.

She leaned over the table with her lips twisted in distaste. "What is it?"

Wretched back to the reality of now, I blinked. "I need the address and information for a bio donor. Well, multiple donors."

"A bio donor? Your client's a hatchling?" She quirked an eyebrow but waved me forward.

I nodded. When Yukio made that face, she looked so much like Marco, it gave me pause. Pushing through the tendrils clinging on from the latent memories of me and Marco, I forced my attention back to the case I'd been hired to do.

A job is a job.

"Name?"

"Madonna Tyson."

"No middle initial?"

"R for Renee."

"DNA sample?"

I frowned. Yukio looked up and titled her head to the side.

"I'm almost kidding. I could run it over the scanner to make sure she told you the truth." She went back to her typing. Dark polish on tapered nails and slender fingers glided over the electronic keyboard.

"She's got a fairly active social media presence."

"I need the name of the biological donors, primarily co-ordinates or addresses, but work info would be nice, too."

Yukio paused and gave me a "shut-up" glare. "I heard you."

I nodded, and she resumed her search. Boxes, windows, and a lot of scrawling font flickered so fast across the screen, I quit trying to track it. I couldn't read code, and it made my head hurt. I stood back from the bank of computers and resumed my pacing. Information gathering took time.

I paused. This didn't require a rush. My stomach rumbled. "Contact me when you find something?"

Yukio nodded; her gaze fixed on the screens.

I doubt she heard me when I left.

Six

Tuesday and Wednesday passed by in a blur of boring and blustery weather. I spent most of it watching old kung-fu movies and trying to balance the currency in my credit account. I hadn't given up on Yukio, but I had begun to scout out others in the field in case her powerful anger created another barrier between us, one that currency couldn't overcome. The rest of the time I dodged Madonna's demands for a progress report. Too soon. Far too early for results.

The young woman had become much too eager.

Thursday afternoon found me sitting on my sofa, scanning the channels for something interesting. Outside my window light, fluffy snow fell. Wrapped in my blanket with a mug of coffee in one hand and a peanut butter and jalapeno jelly sandwich in the other, life seemed good.

Until my telemonitor binged.

The Tahoma font spelled out Yukio's name.

"Answer."

The screen paused then winked over to Yukio's face. With her goggles pushed into her hair, she looked younger, like a kid playing dress up, except for the bags and dark circles under her eyes. Those aged her.

"I got your info." Even her voice sounded exhausted.

"Send it over." I suppressed my excitement. If she knew I had any joy, she'd want to stamp it out.

"Send the currency first." She raised an eyebrow.

What a horrid game of chicken. I walked over to the telemonitor's keypad and scanner, put down my mug, and held my sandwich in my mouth. I entered my information and rested my wrist over the scanner. Once identified, it unlocked the account.

"Account?" I took it out of my mouth and chewed.

Yukio sighed. Her keystrokes sounded tired too.

I transferred the currency, locked the account, and logged out. "Done. Send me the information."

"There." The harsh LD screen illuminated Yukio's face. Behind her, darkness.

The *ping* of the file arriving in my virtual inbox concluded our business.

"We're done." She stifled a yawn.

"Not yet. Let me validate that there's actual data." I switched the telemonitor to the file folder and accessed the files. I opened the file and inside was a basic spreadsheet of names, coordinates, and information. Without going to each person, I had no real way of knowing if these were legitimate or just something Yukio pulled from a social dating site.

I had to trust her.

"Are we done?" Yukio sighed.

"Yeah. For now."

"Whatever." She terminated the feed.

Now the real work began.

I sat down on the sofa and started scrolling through the data. There were more here than expected. Far from complete, the list went on for about twenty names and possible donors. Only four seemed the most complete and the most likely to be Madonna's bio donors. Four people whose lives were about to be upended by yours truly.

When I looked up at the clock, the day had stretched to just after five. A perfect time to bother people.

Right around dinner.

I started to like this.

* * *

The enthusiasm was short lived as I set my wauto down in an ancient sector, outside an equally crumbling apartment structure. A shrill woman answered the door. Hair, parted down the middle, hung like two sheets of fabric, thick and black. Short, round and wheezing, the bio donor AB02107, pushed up her glasses at my intrusion.

"Yeah?"

"Are you Anita Morse?"

"Yeah."

Do you know any other words?

"I'm Cybil Lewis, private inspector."

It felt strange telling the truth. A ruse wouldn't do for this situation and wasting a good lie on such a mundane case seemed, well, pointless. So, honesty it was.

"What do you want?" She gave me the once over. Her gaze lingered at my weapon before she took a step back.

Then it hit me. Maybe she wasn't alone. I put my hand on my laser gun. Anita blinked, but otherwise remained at the door. How horrible had her life been that a gun didn't bother her? Here stood the end of a sad story. I didn't really want to know the beginning or the middle of her tale, but I bet it started with the AGEH.

With a sigh, I put the laser gun to bed in its holster.

"I ain't did nothin'."

"You sure?"

"Yeah." Her body language disagreed. She crossed her arms and seemed to be folding in on herself, building an invisible barrier to which I would be a wrecking ball.

"You better be exceptionally good at lying because I'm exceptionally good at knowing you are."

Anita's dark eyes narrowed behind the heavy frames. Why she hadn't repaired her eyes, I didn't know. Thin lips pulled back into a sneer. "You're the sharp tool, huh?"

"You should've hidden it. Maybe hidden yourself? Relocated outside the territory."

She snorted as if that seemed impossible. Judging by her apartment's condition and the strong odor of poverty seeping out from the crack in the door, she couldn't leave this sector let alone the territory.

"I'm here about your daughter." I wanted to be done with this as soon as possible. Something about Anita made me want to a shower—a long hot one.

"Ain't got no kids." She scratched at the fleshy part under her chin.

"I'm here to report that you do." I smiled.

She snorted again and waved me off. "Crazy."

"Look, can I come in? I don't like talking business on the street."

"I don't give a shit what you like." Anita snapped.

I figured as much, but I fell back a step. What would Madonna gain from meeting this woman?

As she shuffled to the door, I said, "Bio-donor AB2107."

With eyes wide, her tone hardened, she muttered, "Never again. I swore it. No amount of currency…" When she caught herself, she snatched away from the entrance. "Get away. I don't have nothin' to say."

"I'm not leaving. Your daughter wants to meet you." The depth of stench rolled upward with the breeze.

"It's too late to drag the past up now. That's done." Anita spat on the sidewalk.

"Not for her, it isn't. You can't change events. You have a daughter, a child. She's an adult now."

"How'd you find me anyway? The files were deleted and destroyed."

"I mentioned I'm a PI." I shuffled against the cold.

No, Anita Morse didn't like this new information at all. Her fuzzy eyebrows formed an angry V between two furious eyes. Good thing I came around instead of sending the list to Madonna blind. I shudder to think how Madonna would've handled this encounter.

"You done? I got stuff to do so say whatever you wanna say."

Oh, I bet you do. How much Ackback awaits you inside?

Instead of saying that, I explained further. "She wants to meet her bio-donors."

"She's a hatchling then? Them ain't even people." Anita hacked out a cough.

My alert signals launched at those words. "You're a person. She's part of you."

She squinted as if the statement confused her. Not for the first time, I wondered how much Ackback she did or *had done,* and how much brain remained.

With her hands shaking, she yanked her threadbare sweater tighter. "You see miss, uh, whatever your name, I could have a hundred children. Uncle Sam harvested my eggs like a desperate sharecropper."

I froze. Madonna probably knew she wasn't an only child but had hundreds of siblings. A chill raced up my spine to think the AGEH used this DNA sack for hundreds of potential hatchlings. The horror.

"You don't like that, huh?" Anita laughed, exposing stained teeth.

No, I didn't. "She'll be by. Try not to disappoint her, like you've done to yourself."

Yeah it was mean, but her ignorance angered me.

She wiped a greasy strand out of her eyes. "You're not the first to come barking around here. Now, go. Get away before I contact the regs!"

The door hushed close.

I saw no resemblance between the donor and the daughter beyond those dark, restless eyes. With nothing further, I left.

The woman didn't even think hatchlings counted as people. She, along with many others, believed that only humans birthed by women counted as people. This shallow belief faltered when one asked about hatchlings who gave birth or those who were in vitro and birthed. Did cesarean sections count? At this point, the human rights advocates would revert to screaming obscenities and curses. As if shouting counted as logical debate strategy.

Anita looked confused.

Mentally, I deleted Anita Morse from the list. Unethical? Hell, the entire job bordered on violation infractions. I climbed into my wauto and punched in the coordinates for Big Mike's.

Seven

"Damn, Lewis. Your help just hurts," Daniel said.

"I'm doing what I'm paid to do, not passing out blankets." I sipped my Peck beer.

Across from me, Daniel tapped his spoon on the bowl. It contained a steaming broth mixture with grayish chunks.

"Yeah, but at what cost? You've destroyed that biodonor's anonymity."

"That, like safety, is an illusion," I retorted.

He laughed, making his hazel eyes flash in amusement, but it winked out faster than I liked.

"Forever the cynic."

"Takes one to know one." I turned to look at the other patrons.

Big Mike's dinner crowd trickled in and the servers buzzed about the tables, fluttering from one to the other. People fled the hopes and fears of the outside world for the comforting and velvety crooning of the Stacy Mae Jazz Band. Three women, whose harmonizing and husky voices held the brass's notes like lovers, drew people in. Big Mike's cozy, dark and moody décor shunned newer places' affinity for polished chrome and shiny metallics. No, this place felt lived in and loved. History hung from its walls like family portraits, outlining the restaurant's lineage.

After a few minutes, Daniel wiped his mustache with the back of his hand and said, "There'll be some fallout from this job. It's cruel."

Now who's being cynical?

Was it me or was Daniel looking for a fight? "No…"

"Hear me out." He pushed his bowl away. "You've given this girl new hope of a family, of belonging. But these biodonors aren't going to embrace her. We both know it. That's a cruel gift to give."

"You don't know that. There's more names on the list." I recalled Anita Morse and sighed. *Here's to hope.*

"Ha! Hatchlings are some engineer's dream made into skin and given breath. The raw materials are inconsequential. People don't care about some creation made in a lab and hatched out of an artificial womb. You read *Frankenstein.* No one gave a damn about that monster."

"Daniel, you're not a monster."

"And this isn't about me."

Isn't it?

Daniel crossed his arms in a huff.

I drank more Peck and let him stew in silence. I suspected that the parts of him that hadn't dealt with his own hatchling status bled into his objectivity. Funny. The reason I confided in him in the first place had created our current disagreement.

I *had* tried to persuade Madonna to leave it alone. Besides, she would've hired someone else if I didn't pick up the job. I wasn't about to explain that to Daniel.

"Daniel, I've come through like I do. This client won't be able to heal, to feel real, until she gets this done. Her words."

He shook his head. "Her wounds won't close just because she meets these people. This will only cause more injuries to herself, her psyche, her sense of self. Who is going to have that little sorrowed talk with her? Not you. You'll just collect and vanish."

I frowned. "She's a grown woman. Everyone's got to face down their demons. I'm a PI, not a shrink."

He glared. That hard Regulator stare didn't work on me like it probably did the violators he chased down.

"You can't fault me for being well prepared and good at my job."

"Some people can't put the past away like an unwanted piece of furniture. Their storage space is too full." Daniel sighed. "Not everyone is like you, Cyb."

"Correction. There's *no one* like me."

"She who fights monsters…" Daniel pointed at me with his spoon and shook his head.

"I'm not fighting monsters, only passing on info!" My voice raised on *info* and my honey level dipped.

"I can see through you. See the real you, and you must be careful." Daniel licked his spoon.

"If I wanted my head shrunk, I'd get one of those AIs to do it."

Daniel stood with a sigh. "Well, I see. I'm leaving. I expect you to do the same."

"Sure."

I watched him weave through the restaurant tables to the exit. I stayed seated and watered by the attentive waiter. Time blurred as did the number of Pecks I drank. Outside thunder rumbled and the lights flickered. A nervous rustle rose up and raced through the room, but soon settled once the band commenced playing. Music soothed all types of ruffled feathers. That led me back to Madonna Tyson. Her entire being bled into obscurity by a wauto wreck. Did it matter so much to know your parents?

It did to her.

I'd taken the job because I saw that raw anger and pain inside Madonna, and it mirrored my own. Marco's death, life in the District, being a woman and from my deprived sector all kindled the bonfire of fury inside me. She needed an outlet for that. A need I fully recognized. I funneled all my pain into the army life before that too crashed and burned. Madonna wanted to replace all of her pain with a new family.

Tomato. Tomahto.

I struggled to keep my anger from destroying me and those around me.

Who was I kidding? It's still a battle.

The District continued to trust me with weapons.

I mustn't be doing too badly.

Eight

Friday came with a headache and a hangover. In my midnight stupor I found clarity. Madonna hired me to do a job and I'd done it. The philosophical debate Daniel started belonged to the philosophers.

I'm a private inspector. Hired help.

Madonna would have to face the consequences, just as we all do. When we chase ghosts, we risk possession. I'm not a pessimist. The other biodonors could end up fully embracing her and giving her exactly what she wanted. There was hope for her happiness.

I thought of Anita Morse and immediately doubted it.

The bottom line—it wasn't my right to make the decision for Madonna.

So, I found myself waiting in my office's lobby for my client on Friday afternoon.

Madonna came strolling in about an hour later. Her braids flowed free and her purple coat was tied tight against the cold. Thigh high boots, jeans, and black gloves completed her ensemble.

"What's going on?" I leaned back against my desk.

"Nothing. That's the problem. You've been avoiding me for days." Madonna snapped, but caught herself. "Sorry. Eager beaver."

"Here." I held out the p-drive. "Our business is complete."

Madonna's eyes widen. "You found them?"

"Yeah." Her surprise hurt my feelings a bit. Had she really doubted me?

"You're fast, and you're good!"

I nodded. "Just consider it a warning that you may not find joy in those files."

She frowned. "Why not?"

"Look, I know I'm on the outside looking in, but I know that what you seek isn't on this."

She rolled her eyes. "I will never know myself, my origins, until I do. There must be some way to stop feeling so hollow and alone." She huffed a sigh.

"You don't have to go tilting at windmills to do it."

I'm not normally one for giving advice, but not being a hatchling, I couldn't know what it meant to be adopted into a family not biologically similar to me. Family had been one I personally assembled, not one by blood per se. Daniel seemed bothered so I might've missed something. So here I was, giving caution.

With a toss of her braids, Madonna discounted my words. She wiped her eyes and pinned me with a watery glare.

"I've always felt odd, sometimes hated. I didn't fit in. Crying at the top of my voice for love, acceptance. To not be judged by this." She yanked her shirt down and pointed at the tattoo.

"You had loving parents," I said. Lame, but true.

She nodded. "I did, but this damn tattoo made sure I knew they weren't really mine."

"Their love for you was real, Madonna," I countered.

"I want to feel close to something that's alive. To find a place where I belong, you know? These are my true parents." She clutched the p-drive.

"Whatever you find, I hope it brings you peace. Keep your guard up."

Madonna put the p-drive in her pocket and then looked up at me. She reached for me and hugged me tight.

"Thank you." She breathed against my ear.

Then she released me, turned on her heel, and left.

I watched her leave with dread in my heart, mixed with the feeling of accomplishment.

Minutes later, my doors yawned open again and in walked Daniel. He grinned at me as he removed his Regulator helmet. The one-piece uniform hugged his body, and his black boots came up to his knees.

"You free for lunch?" He wiped hair from his eyes.

"What do you have in mind?" I put my hands on my waist.

He fingered the high collar that hid his tattoo. "Oh, I don't know, but I've hatched out a plan to get us through lunch hour traffic over to Big Mike's."

I grabbed my satchel. "Let's go."

We hope you enjoyed Cyberfunk! For more exciting titles, visit us at

www.mvmediaatl.com

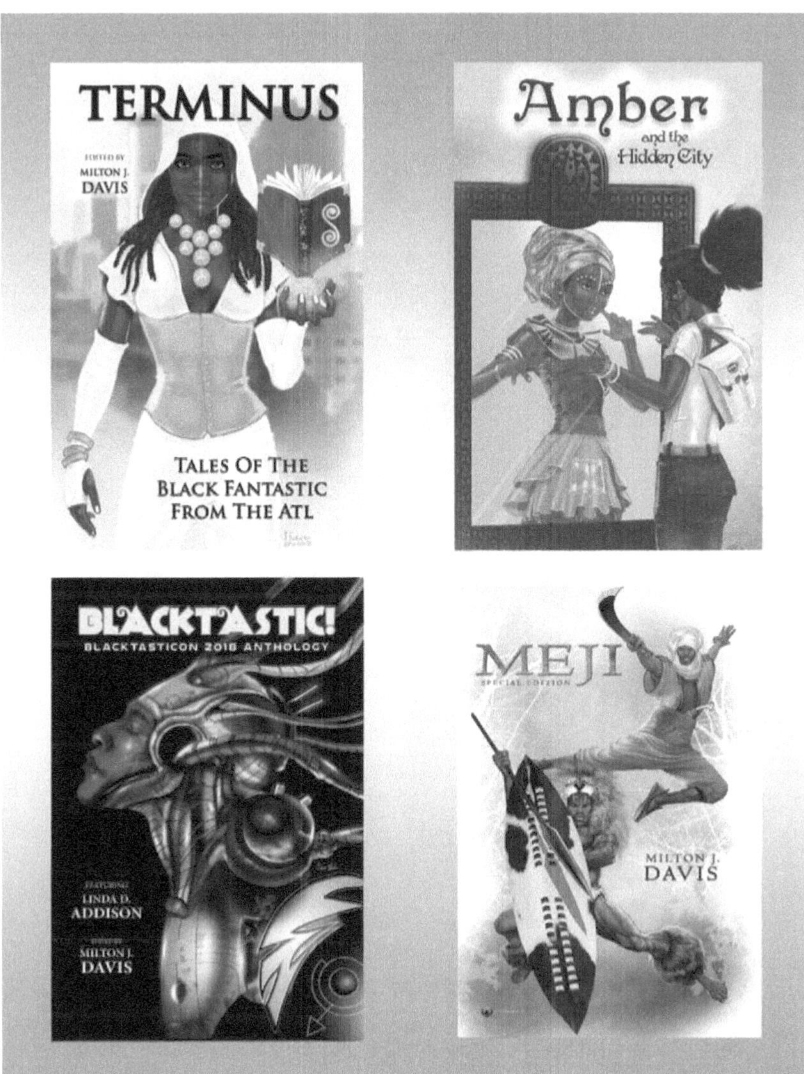

The City

Edited by Milton J. Davis

The City anthology is a unique creation. It's a concept anthology, a collection of stories where eighteen different authors share their vision of a single idea. It's Cyberfunk, cyberpunk stories that play with future concepts from an African/African American perspective. Most of all it's engaging, exciting, thought provoking and fun. Like the inhabitants, the City is perceived in various ways by the various writers. Some stories intersect, some diverge, but they all entertain. The result is a journey into a unique world described by unique and engaging voices.

Dark Universe

Edited by Milton J. Davis and Gene Peterson

The Dark Universe Anthology tells the origin story of the Cassad Empire from its ambitious beginning to its evolution as the first great human Galactic Empire and its eventual fall. Milton Davis, Gene Peterson, Balogun Ojetade, Penelope Flynn, Malon Edwards, K. Ceres Wright and DaVaun Sanders are the storytellers that lay the foundation of this amazing empire. Dark Universe is space opera like you've never seen. The time has come; Dark Universe is here!

Dark Universe: The Bright Empire

Edited Milton J. Davis and Gene Peterson

The Dark Age is over and the Known is in the firm grasp of the Cassads. As the galaxy spins, dragging planets and star systems in its wake, unrest rises to the surface of the celestial firmament. For a while, the Cassads burn brightly, the people under their rule are neglected and stifled. The Dark Age is over. The Bright Empire has begun, but the stars do not shine brightly on everyone.

Dark Universe: The Bright Empire is the exciting sequel to The Dark Universe Anthology. Experience the heyday of this intriguing Afrocentric galactic empire through eleven stories that capture the wonder, danger and adventure of this amazing universe.

www.ingramcontent.com/pod-product-compliance
Lightning Source LLC
Chambersburg PA
CBHW030341020726
47493CB00003B/627

The Blackbird of Kirthgarran